Fra

WINNERS AND LOSERS COLLECTION

including

Jessica Quits the Squad

The Pom-Pom Wars

'V' for Victory

BANTAM BOOKS
NEW YORK • TORONTO • LONDON • SYDNEY • AUCKLAND

"I read about them in *Cheerleading* magazine," Jessica said with pride. "At first I thought they might be too complicated, but you guys didn't have any problem with them."

"That's because you're such a great teacher," Robin said, smiling.

"Here's to Jessica!" Maria Santelli raised her glass of soda, and all the cheerleaders did the same.

Just as they were about to click their glasses together, Jessica's attention was diverted by a stunning blond girl walking into the Dairi Burger. She apparently wasn't the only one to notice her, as a hush had fallen over the entire room.

"Who's that?" Jessica asked, annoyed that this stranger had interrupted Maria's toast honoring her.

"I don't know, but the guys look like their tongues are about to fall out of their mouths," Lila Fowler teased. "They're practically salivating over her."

Lila, who was Jessica's best friend and at times her biggest rival, had a knack for saying the exact thing that would make Jessica's blood boil. This was one of those times. *Why can't she just keep her mouth shut?* Jessica wondered.

"She's certainly creating a big stir," Helen Bradley said as everyone watched the girl make her way over to the take-out counter. "You'd think the entire football team had been hit over the head with a hammer."

"I don't see what all the fuss is about." Jessica scrutinized the girl who was stealing her thunder. "She looks pretty plain, if you ask me."

"If that's plain, then in my next life I want to be plain," Jean West said, taking a bite of her sundae. "Check out that body. You probably don't catch her eating sundaes."

"Hey, Winston, put your eyes back in their sockets," Maria said to her boyfriend, Winston Egbert, the class clown, who was sitting on a stool next to the girls' booth.

"Oh, sorry," Winston said with an impish grin. "I was just trying to read what was on her T-shirt."

"Yeah, right," Maria said, shaking her head. "You know, a gorgeous girl walks into the room, and relatively intelligent males are reduced to cavemen in one second."

"Rick Hunter looks like he's about to fall off his stool," Amy Sutton said.

Jessica hardly heard her, though.

"A diet Coke with lemon, please," she heard the girl say, flipping her hair. Then the newcomer gave a dazzling smile to the kid behind the counter. "And I'd like that with a straw."

"Oh, please," Jessica said to her friends, rolling

her eyes. "A diet Coke with lemon, please," she mimicked, hair flip and all. "And I'd like that with a straw. Gimme a break."

"That's probably how she stays so thin," Jean said as she watched the girl walk toward the door sipping her soda.

Everyone in the restaurant seemed to hold their breath as they watched her walk out the door.

"Whoa, mama!" Bruce Patman yelped as the door swung shut behind her.

"Major babe!" Rick Hunter exclaimed.

Jessica, more annoyed than ever, watched as the girl got into a brand-new white convertible Mazda Miata with "Cheerleader" plates and revved the engine before she pulled out.

I hope I never lay eyes on that girl again, Jessica thought as she pushed away her hot-fudge sundae.

"So who's psyched for the victory barbecue at the beach?" Jessica asked, loudly enough for the whole restaurant to hear. "We have plenty to celebrate!"

"I am! I am!" different voices echoed around the room. "Party on!"

"I've got a great tape I just made of all my favorite dance songs in case anyone gets the urge to boogie down," Jessica said as she moved her arms around in the air and snapped her fingers.

"What are you doing, Jessica?" Lila asked. "Are you losing it?"

"I'm booth dancing!" Jessica announced. "It's the latest thing; in fact, it's so late that I just invented it this minute!"

Jessica was pleased to see that everyone was laughing at her joke, and once again she was the center of attention. *Back where I belong!* she thought with a smile.

Will I ever have another boyfriend? Jessica wondered as she sat alone on a blanket at the barbecue, watching the sun set over the ocean. The excitement about the game had died down, and now everyone had paired off. Maria Santelli was sitting with Winston Egbert. Elizabeth and her boyfriend, Todd Wilkins, were laughing and kissing a few yards away, and Amy Sutton and Barry Rork were strolling along the shore, holding hands. She felt as if she were the only person in the world who wasn't part of a couple.

Jessica had never had a hard time getting a boyfriend in the past. In fact, she almost always had *someone*. Her heart had been broken recently, however, and she didn't know if it would ever be whole again.

Jeremy Randall had been older and gorgeous, and she'd fallen madly in love with him the first second she'd laid eyes on him. In fact, they'd met on this exact beach. It had all seemed so magical. She'd been hit on the head with a Frisbee, and the next minute a hunky blond fantasy man with the most inviting smile she'd ever seen was looking down at her, asking her if she was all right.

But the man of her dreams had turned out to be a nightmare. Not only had he planned to hit her on the head with the Frisbee so he could get to know her, but Jessica found out that he'd only been using her to swindle a fortune out of another woman, the Wakefields' houseguest, Sue Gibbons. The thing that had hurt the most, though, was accepting the fact that all the love he'd claimed to feel for Jessica was only an act. *How will I ever be able to trust another guy again?* Jessica thought, watching the sky turn a deep red as the sun slowly slipped behind the water.

Jessica swallowed hard to make the lump in her throat go away, and she hugged her knees to her chest.

"What's a beautiful girl like you doing sitting alone watching the sunset?" Ken Matthews asked Jessica as he sat down next to her, his shoulder brushing against hers.

Jessica had been so lost in her thoughts that she practically jumped up from the blanket at the sound of Ken's voice. She pushed a strand of hair out of her face and looked into Ken's eyes. *He's really handsome,* Jessica thought, feeling a slight flutter in her stomach in spite of herself. She had known Ken forever, but as she looked at him now with the glow of the sunset on his face and his shiny blond hair, it was as if she were seeing him for the first time.

Ken had been an especially good friend to her when she'd been going through the hard time with Jeremy. He had encouraged her to go out with the whole Sweet Valley gang one night—something she hadn't done since she'd met Jeremy—and one day at school, when she was feeling particularly low, he'd surprised her with a perfect white rose.

He'd even invited her to the Mistletoe Madness dance, but she hadn't been able to go, as that was the night she and Elizabeth and Sue Gibbons were laying the trap to catch Jeremy. When it was all over, and Jeremy had been arrested for fraud, it was all everybody at school was talking about. After all, Jessica had been *engaged* to him, and now he was in prison. But despite all the gossip, Ken had stayed by her side as a supportive friend.

Now she wanted to tell him how much she'd appreciated his friendship during that difficult time.

"I just wanted to say . . ." Jessica began.

"You know, I've been meaning to . . ." Ken said at the same time.

They both laughed awkwardly, and Jessica, feeling herself blushing, turned away.

"Let's go for a swim," Ken said, pulling Jessica up by the hand. "I'll race you to the water."

Jessica, relieved to have the tension broken, jumped up and pulled off her yellow halter sundress, revealing the new white bikini she was wearing. They ran together into the waves laughing and splashing, and Jessica couldn't remember the last time she'd felt so happy.

"That was one of the most beautiful sunsets I've ever seen," Todd said to Elizabeth as he pulled her closer to him. They were huddled together on a blanket, and the sky was almost completely dark. "I could sit like this forever, just feeling you next to me, watching the water. Are you as happy as I am?"

"Huh? Oh, yeah," Elizabeth said, distracted. She was barely listening to a word Todd was saying. Her attention was focused on the couple frolicking in the waves.

"Do you want to go to a movie tomorrow night with Maria and Winston?" Todd asked, stroking Elizabeth's long blond hair.

"Hmmm," Elizabeth muttered.

"Earth to Elizabeth!" Todd teased as he waved

his hand in front of her face. "What planet are you visiting?"

"Sorry?" Elizabeth asked, turning her gaze toward him for the first time.

"The question is, what are you *thinking* about?" Todd said. "I feel like you're a million miles away."

"Oh, I'm not thinking about anything in particular," Elizabeth lied. The truth was that Elizabeth was thinking about the sick feeling she was having in her stomach. She looked back at the water where she could still see her sister and Ken laughing and splashing each other in the fading twilight.

"So do you want to go to the movies tomorrow with Maria and Winston?" Todd asked again. "If you'd rather do something just the two of us, that would be great too." Todd kissed her left cheek. "You know I'm always happy to be alone with you."

"A movie sounds great," Elizabeth said, trying to force her attention back to Todd. "Whatever you want to do is fine with me."

As hard as she tried, Elizabeth couldn't push that sick feeling away. And she couldn't keep herself from watching Jessica and Ken in the distance.

"That felt great!" Ken said as he and Jessica emerged from the water. They were standing close together, shivering from the water. The air was getting chillier now that it was completely dark.

Jessica looked up at Ken, whose face was glowing in the moonlight. "It sure did," Jessica said, squeezing the water out of her hair. "Whew! That last wave almost knocked the breath out of me."

"Jessica," Ken started in a serious tone as he gently put one hand on her hip and then took it away. "I wanted to tell you that I . . . I think you're really terrific."

Jessica's heart raced, and it wasn't just from the waves and the cold. She was totally charmed by Ken's awkwardness and sincerity. It was so unlike Jeremy, who was always so smooth and in control.

She suddenly realized that they were in total darkness and no one sitting on the beach could see them. She stepped toward him. Their faces were so close together, they were almost touching. Ken took Jessica's face in his hands and held it tenderly as he looked deeply into her eyes. She could feel his whole body tremble as he moved even closer to her and kissed her on the lips.

"What's going on?" Elizabeth asked Todd. She had been lying on her back looking for constellations, trying to distract herself from thoughts of Ken and Jessica cavorting in the waves, when suddenly there was a commotion on the beach. People were laughing and cheering.

"It's just Bruce showing off the spotlights on his father's new Jeep," Todd said, lifting himself up on one elbow. Bruce usually cruised around in his own black Porsche, but his father had just gotten a new Jeep Cherokee that Bruce had driven down to the beach.

There were more cheers and catcalls, and Todd and Elizabeth stood up to see what all the excitement was about. The Jeep's spotlights, which were incredibly powerful, were shining on a couple deeply engrossed in a kiss.

"Isn't that your sister with Ken?" Todd asked Elizabeth.

"It couldn't be," Elizabeth said, hearing her own voice shaking.

"Take another look," Todd said, laughing. "It looks like there's a new couple on the horizon."

Elizabeth squinted. *It can't be,* she thought in desperation. Laughing and splashing in the waves was one thing, but *kissing*? Jessica and Ken?

Everyone on the beach started clapping for the couple. Everyone except Elizabeth.

"Slow down, Jess!" Elizabeth said as she braced her hand against the glove compartment of the twins' Jeep on Monday morning. "You're going to have an accident if you don't stop driving like a lunatic."

"Stop worrying so much. It's bad for your health," Jessica said as she whirled around a corner. "You know I'm an expert driver."

"Since when have you been in such a hurry to get to school?" Usually Elizabeth had to force her sister to get out of bed, but that morning Jessica was the first one up. "What are you so excited about? Algebra class?"

"Yeah, right." Jessica laughed. "You know I live for algebra." She stopped at a red light and reapplied her matte pink lipstick in the rearview mirror.

"So what *is* the big rush for?"

"I'm just anxious to get to school because I know everyone's going to still be buzzing about the awesome job we cheerleaders did on Friday, thanks to me; of course," Jessica said excitedly, flooring the gas pedal when the light turned green. "And second of all, I'm looking forward to seeing Ken."

Elizabeth looked out the window at the houses and trees that were whizzing past, so Jessica wouldn't be able to see the pained expression on her face. She wished she could tell her sister what she was feeling, but that was impossible. She couldn't tell her, because Jessica didn't know that she had had a fling with Ken when Todd had moved to Vermont for a brief period earlier that year. Nobody in the entire world knew except Elizabeth and Ken.

Todd and Ken were best friends, and when Todd was away, he had asked Ken to keep an eye on Elizabeth. They had spent a lot of time together, and at first they were just good friends. After all, they had known each other forever. They could talk for hours on end about anything, and they had so much in common.

But eventually they realized that their feelings for each other were more than just friendly. Elizabeth had tried to push away her romantic feelings, out of loyalty to Todd, but soon she was overcome by her attraction to Ken. When he had finally kissed her, she hadn't been able to resist him, and they dated on the sly for a couple of weeks.

Finally, though, they had decided to end the relationship before anyone—namely, Todd—got hurt. The guilt they had felt over deceiving him was destroying them both, and they knew it couldn't go on. When Todd had come back to Sweet Valley, their relationship had already been over for a long time, and she and Ken had gone back to the way they had always been, just friends. They promised each other never to tell anyone about what had happened while Todd was gone. But because they'd broken off the relationship so quickly—before it had had a chance to cool down naturally—it hadn't really come to a natural end, and now Elizabeth was worried. *Maybe I still have feelings for Ken,* Elizabeth thought as she looked over at her sister's radiant face.

Elizabeth knew better than anyone how horrible it had been for Jessica when Jeremy had turned out to be nothing more than a callous criminal, and she wanted to be happy about her sister's new romantic interest—but why did it have to be Ken? The idea of the two of them together drove Elizabeth crazy. *Maybe that kiss they shared on the beach was a fluke,* Elizabeth hoped. *Maybe it will all blow over. . . .*

Where is everyone? Jessica wondered as she stood by her locker later that morning. She had been taking her time hanging out in the hallway before going to her first class, wanting to give people a chance to shower her with praise about Friday's game. Normally, her friends swarmed around her on Mondays before first period, eager to talk about the weekend, but nobody seemed to be around. *That's strange,* she thought as she brushed her hair before the little mirror that hung on the inside of her locker door.

That morning when she'd gotten dressed, she'd been thinking of Ken and had wanted to look her very best for him. She'd decided on her favorite—faded blue jeans and her blue-and-gold gauzy blouse that looked as if it were from the sixties. For a minute she had wondered if it was her style, but then she'd decided that since she'd seen blouses like it in all the fashion magazines, it was just right. Besides, blue was a great color on her, and she knew she looked beautiful.

She couldn't wait to see Ken again after they'd kissed on Friday night. All weekend she'd played that moment in the moonlight over and over in her head. Just when she'd been about to give up on romance and guys, she mused, Ken had come along with his gorgeous smile and had swept her away.

Just then she heard a buzz of voices down the hallway. She looked toward the commotion and caught a glimpse of Ken at the end of the hall. He was standing in a big crowd of people who were swarming around someone or something. At that moment Lila spotted Jessica and, breaking free from the crowd, met her at her locker. "Did you see her yet?"

"Did I see who yet?" Jessica asked, flipping her hair over her head and then letting it fall back into place to give it more volume. Now that she'd spotted Ken, she wanted to look as good as possible.

"Heather Mallone," Lila said, pointing down the hall to the crowd of people. "That girl at the Dairi Burger on Friday who caused such a big hoopla with the guys."

"What about her?" Jessica said, slamming her locker door. She knew she wasn't going to like whatever Lila was about to tell her, and she already felt the great mood she'd been in that morning start to fade away.

"Well, that's her down there," Lila said. "She just moved to Sweet Valley, and she's a student here now. You should see the way the guys are flirting their heads off with her."

"And that's headline news?" Jessica said, trying to sound casual.

"Well," Lila said. "I have a feeling she's going to be pretty popular, judging from the reaction she's getting after being here just a few minutes."

"Whoop-dee-doo," Jessica said, twirling her finger in the air. "Let's call the local television station and tell them the big scoop—a new girl has arrived in Sweet Valley. I mean, who cares?"

"I do. She seems like someone we might want to know. She seems like our type. Oh, and by the way," Lila added casually, looking closely at Jessica, "I think I heard her saying something about being a big deal on her old cheerleading squad."

Jessica knew her best friend well enough to know that Lila was just trying to get a rise out of her.

"As I said in the Dairi Burger," Jessica replied, doing her best to smile, "I don't see what the fuss is about. 'Big deal' is a relative term, and besides, she's probably got some major personality flaw."

"How can you possibly know that?" Lila asked as she adjusted the tight purple minidress she was wearing. "You haven't even met her yet. I think I just might detect a note of jealousy."

"Be real," Jessica said, rolling her eyes. "I can tell things about people from just looking at them." *And major personality flaw or not, I can tell that I don't like anything about this girl*, Jessica thought, mad that for the second time in a row this Heather Mallone had stolen her thunder.

"Here she comes," Lila said.

Jessica turned to watch Heather and a sea of people walk down the hall toward her. She scanned the crowd for Ken, but he wasn't there. Her heart sank for a moment, and then her gaze landed on

Heather, who was beaming at her with what Jessica knew was a phony smile.

"Lila, you know Heather, right?" Annie asked.

"Well, we just met a little while ago in the parking lot," Lila said, extending her hand to meet Heather's. "But we weren't properly introduced. I'm Lila Fowler."

"Hi, I'm Heather Mallone. Thanks again for letting me have that parking space."

"No problem," Lila said. "That's a great car you have, by the way. It's totally cool."

Jessica couldn't believe how Lila was kissing up to her. And she let her have her parking space?

"Thanks," Heather said. "I'd be happy to take you riding in it sometime. I'm still unfamiliar with Sweet Valley, and I could use a good tour guide."

"That would be great," Lila said.

I'll be your tour guide, Jessica thought, *I'll show you the way right out of town.*

"This is Jessica Wakefield," Lila said, pushing Jessica forward.

"Hi, Jessica," Heather said, smiling that same syrupy smile as she extended her hand to Jessica. "What an adorable little blouse you're wearing. It's so, uh . . . retro."

"Retro?" Jessica repeated, not knowing exactly what Heather meant, but pretty sure it wasn't a compliment. *I knew I wasn't going to like this person,* Jessica thought as she scrutinized the girl standing in front of her.

Heather had long blond hair that was wavy and curly and hung in layers around her face. She had big blue eyes and a dainty little nose, and as much as Jessica hated to admit it to herself—she *was* beautiful. She was wearing skintight designer blue jeans that showed off a muscular but thin figure, and a white silk blouse that looked tailored and elegant. She had on expensive-looking black loafers with no socks. And her jewelry, which consisted of gold earrings, a gold bracelet, and a gold choker, were from a line Jessica recognized from one of the most exclusive jewelry catalogs she'd seen at Lila's house.

Jessica suddenly knew what Lila had meant when she'd said that Heather was "our type." *She really meant that Heather was her type, as in super-rich!* Lila herself was the richest girl in Sweet Valley. Although Jessica loved to hang out in the sprawling mansion where she lived with her parents, she couldn't help being jealous of all her money and her ability to buy whatever she wanted whenever she wanted it.

"Yeah, you know, 'retro,' like from the sixties," Heather explained authoritatively. "That look is very trendy these days."

Jessica looked at Lila, then at Annie in disbelief. She was waiting for them to acknowledge the fact that Heather was insulting her, but nobody else seemed to notice. *Not only is she a fake, but she's condescending and rude,* Jessica thought.

"Excuse me, but I have to get to class," Jessica said as she turned and stormed off. In just a few minutes Jessica's mood had taken a nosedive, and it was all because of one person: Heather Mallone. *The less I see of that girl, the better,* Jessica thought as she walked down the hall, leaving behind Heather and her group of adoring fans.

"Can you believe what a phony that new girl is?" Jessica asked her group of friends at the lunch table later that day. "I couldn't believe how rude she was to me this morning."

"Oh, please, Jessica," Lila said. "She was perfectly nice. In fact, I think I'm going to like her a lot."

Jessica's mouth dropped open incredulously. "She totally trashed my blouse this morning in front of everyone. You were standing right there when she did it."

"I think you're being paranoid," Lila said as she poured two packets of sugar into her iced tea. "She was complimenting you."

"Excuse me, but since when is 'trendy' considered a compliment?" Jessica asked. She couldn't believe that her best friend didn't even see how awful Heather was.

"Hey, guys," Annie said brightly as she set down her tray at the table. "Look who's joining us for lunch."

Jessica looked up from her plate of fettuccine Alfredo and almost dropped her fork. Heather plopped herself down at their table and sat directly across from Jessica. She had that same fake smile plastered on her face that she'd had that morning. *My lunch is ruined,* Jessica thought.

"So how do you like Sweet Valley High so far?" Amy asked. "Are you finding your way around OK?"

"It's fabulous," Heather said. "Everyone's so nice and friendly here."

"Especially the guys," Annie said, giggling. "You should see the way every male in this school has offered to show Heather around. She already had five guys ask her out for this weekend."

Jessica's dislike for Heather was mounting with every minute.

"I have to say, though, that the guys seem pretty immature here," Heather said.

This is just too much, Jessica thought. *Now she's insulting the guys in our school!* Jessica looked around the table to see if anyone else was bothered by Heather's rude comment, but nobody even seemed to notice.

"You're right about that," Lila agreed. "They're totally unsophisticated. Look at that table over there by the window. Every single day those guys are over there playing paper football. Talk about childish."

Jessica looked over at Aaron Dallas, Ronnie Edwards, and the other guys Lila was referring to. They did look pretty ridiculous the way they were so engrossed in their game, making a lot of silly cheering noises over a little piece of paper being flicked from one end of the table to the other. Still, they were Sweet Valley guys, and she suddenly felt very loyal to them.

Everyone burst out laughing at Lila's observation, except Jessica. *How can Lila agree with her like that?* she wondered. *What a traitor. She's just agreeing with Heather because she thinks she's cool, and rich.*

"That pasta you're eating is loaded with fat," Heather said, pointing to Jessica's plate.

"So?" Jessica said, looking up from her lunch defensively.

"Fat clogs up your arteries and causes heart attacks. I've completely eliminated fat from my diet. If I ate like that, I'd never be able to fit into my jeans."

"Well, I can understand that, judging from the kind of jeans you like to wear," Jessica said, trying to make her voice light.

"What do you mean?" Heather asked.

"Oh, I just mean that you obviously like to wear

your jeans really, really tight," Jessica said. "I'm surprised you can even walk in them. How long does it take you to put them on in the morning? I'd imagine you'd have to have a crew of people pulling them up for you."

Jessica looked around the table expecting to see her friends giggle in agreement, but everyone just stared at Jessica as if she had leprosy or something.

Heather smiled at Jessica, ignoring her comments. "I just don't know any girls my age who eat food like that anymore. Everyone I know watches their weight."

She looked at Heather's plate, which was full of carrot and celery sticks and some tuna without a trace of mayonnaise. "Well, I guess I'm just one of those lucky people who don't have to worry about their weight," Jessica said, wrapping a huge helping of fettuccine around her fork. "I don't believe in depriving myself of anything."

"You do have a great figure, Heather," Maria gushed. "You look like you exercise a lot."

"I guess you could say I'm pretty athletic," Heather said as she chomped on a carrot stick. "I jog five miles every morning before school, and I play a lot of squash and tennis. Oh, and I'm an avid skier."

"Really? Where do you go?" Lila asked.

"Aspen, naturally, and every Christmas my family goes to Gstaad," Heather said, as if everyone knew where she was talking about.

"I love Gstaad," Lila said, "especially the boutiques there."

"Shtad?" Jessica asked. "It sounds like some kind of sausage or something."

Lila and Heather looked at each other and laughed.

"It's a very exclusive ski resort in Switzerland," Heather explained as if she were talking to a child.

"Don't you remember when my dad and I went there a few years ago?" Lila asked, sipping from her iced tea. "I'm sure I sent you a postcard."

"Gee, I guess I forgot. I'll have to go home and dust off my collection of postcards from Lila's travels," Jessica said sarcastically, furious that Lila was siding with Heather.

"Well, I can't imagine doing as much exercise as you do, Heather," Amy said. "You must be exhausted at the end of every day."

"It helps keep me in shape for cheerleading," Heather said before chomping on a carrot stick.

"Heather was just telling me that the cheerleading squad at her old school were the state champions of Nevada for seven years," Annie gushed. "And she was the captain!"

"Wow, that's great," Maria said. "You must be a really wonderful cheerleader."

"I understand that you're one of the captains of the squad here," Heather said to Jessica. "What kind of stuff are you into?"

"Well, I make up most of the cheers myself, but sometimes I use *Cheerleading* magazine for inspiration," Jessica said, proud that she had the vision as a captain to keep up with the latest moves. "You should have seen us on Friday. We were awesome." Jessica waited for her friends to agree with her, but nobody did. They were all too focused on Heather.

"*Cheerleading* magazine?" Heather laughed. "That's so *dated*. If I were you, Jessica, I wouldn't waste my money on a subscription. Don't you watch VTV? Hip-hop's the latest thing in cheerleading," Heather said knowingly.

"I guess our cheers would seem pretty boring to you," Robin said. "They're not that exciting, nothing like VTV."

Not that exciting! Jessica was mortified. She had worked on those cheers for weeks, and now her very own cocaptain was putting them down in front of this awful, show-off Heather! Just when she thought she wasn't going to be able to take it anymore, Jessica saw that Ken was walking toward their table.

"Who's that? I noticed him this morning. He's one of the cutest guys I've seen all day," Heather said, sitting up and running ran her fingers through her hair.

"That's Ken Matthews," Lila said, looking warily at Jessica. "He's the quarterback of the football team, and he threw the winning pass on Friday."

If he's coming over here to talk to Heather I'm going to have to throw my fettuccine in her face, Jessica thought as she watched Ken's gaze closely to see if he was checking Heather out. To her delight he didn't even glance at Heather. Instead, he walked right over to Jessica and leaned down to her from behind her chair.

"Hey, Jessica, do you want to come over and sit with me?" Ken asked timidly but sweetly.

"I'd love to eat lunch with you, Ken," Jessica said loudly as she stood up and picked up her tray.

To Jessica's dismay Heather and Jessica's friends barely even noticed that Jessica was leaving the table with Ken. Heather was going on about how great her cheerleaders were at her old school.

They're too busy falling all over Heather to notice me, Jessica thought as she followed Ken to his table.

"I really had a good time on Friday night," Ken said to Jessica, putting his tray down at an empty table. "I hope that you weren't too embarrassed when everyone saw us kissing like that."

"I had a great time too," Jessica said. "And I wasn't embarrassed at all."

Jessica looked back over at her table of friends and was pleased to see that finally she was getting some attention. They were all obviously talking about her and Ken, because they kept looking in Jessica's direction. Most important, Heather was watching them with particular interest.

Ken looked down at his plate and moved his fettucine around nervously. Finally, after what seemed like an eternity of silence, Ken spoke.

"Jessica, I was wondering if you'd consider going out with me on Friday night," he said, avoiding eye contact with her. "I mean, if you don't want to, that's fine too. I just thought it might be fun, you know, to do something together."

Jessica was thrilled beyond belief. "I'd love to!"

"You would?" Ken asked incredulously, looking into her eyes for the first time since they'd sat down. "Well, then it's a date."

Chapter 3

Elizabeth was going over "Personal Profiles," the column she wrote for *The Oracle*, on Monday afternoon. Todd was sitting across from her in the newspaper office waiting for her to finish, and she was getting slightly annoyed by his constant talking and joking around. Usually she welcomed his playful moods, but today he was getting on her nerves.

"Aren't you ready yet?" Todd asked impatiently as he threw the tenth piece of crumpled paper into the wastebasket. Each time he threw one in successfully, he clapped his hands and said, "Two points!"

"I'm just trying to get this column finished," Elizabeth said. *And I'm having a hard time doing it because of that annoying game you keep playing with yourself*, she wanted to say.

"You've gone over that column a hundred times."

"I just keep trying to think of something else to put in it to give it a little more life. This has got to be the most boring column I've ever written," Elizabeth complained. "The profile of a new chess-team member is not my idea of juicy."

"I have something that will spice up your column," Todd said with a big smile. "The profile of two people starting a new romance."

"Really?" Elizabeth looked up from her notebook. "Who is it? I'm desperate for anything."

"I'll give you a hint—they're both really popular . . ." Todd said.

"Are you going to tell me, or do I have to guess?" Elizabeth said, unable to mask her impatience.

"You have to guess," Todd said playfully. "One of them is a cheerleader, and one of them is a football player, and they're both really good-looking."

"That could be a lot of people," Elizabeth said, afraid of what—or who—Todd was getting at.

"You're not very good at guessing games," Todd said. "It's Jessica and Ken!"

Even though Elizabeth had known that's who Todd had been talking about, her heart sank. Careful not to let Todd see her disappointment, she asked simply, "What makes you think they're a couple? One little kiss doesn't constitute a relationship."

"But a date for this coming Friday does," Todd said.

"How do you know they're going on a date?" Elizabeth asked, trying to sound nonchalant.

"Ken just told me he asked your sister out during lunch today," Todd said, flipping a pencil in the air. "He's really excited about it. It seems like he's into Jessica in a big way."

Todd's words cut like a knife through Elizabeth's heart. "They've been friends forever," she said. "Maybe he just asked her out as a friend." Elizabeth was desperately trying to convince herself that it wasn't anything more than just a simple, friendly date.

"I guess it's like that movie we saw together about those people who were friends for years, then suddenly they realized they were in love," Todd said. "I think it's great. As you know, I've never been the biggest fan of your sister's, but I think she could be good for Ken. And I'm happy for him. It's great to see him so excited about somebody. They'd make a great couple. Don't you think?"

"Oh, yeah, they'd be perfect together," Elizabeth lied.

Todd leaned across the table. "Just like we are," he said before he kissed Elizabeth tenderly on the mouth.

Elizabeth closed her eyes and kissed Todd

back. But instead of kissing Todd with all her heart, she was remembering her kisses with Ken. Horrified, she opened her eyes. *I'm kissing Todd and thinking of Ken! I'm a terrible person!*

The cheerleaders were stretching on the far end of the football field when Jessica arrived at practice that afternoon. Jessica was excited to start teaching a new cheer she'd worked on all weekend. She quickly read it over and couldn't wait to share it with the girls.

She dropped her notebook onto the ground, feeling proud of the great new words, and ran in front of the waiting squad.

"OK, girls," Jessica said loudly. "You all did a fantastic job on Friday, and I'm not the only one who thinks so. The crowds loved us and we were better than ever. We can't rest on laurels, though, so I want you to pay close attention to the new routine I'm about to show you."

When Jessica had finished talking, she realized that most of the girls were looking at something behind her. She turned around and saw Heather standing with her hands on her hips and a smirk on her face.

"May I help you?" Jessica asked, unable to keep the annoyance out of her voice.

"Yeah, as a matter of fact you can," Heather

said. "I want to try out for the squad."

Over my dead body, Jessica wanted to say. But instead she cleared her throat and said sweetly, "Well, then, you can come back in the spring and try out with the other seventy-five or so girls who want to be on our squad. Why don't you run along home now and practice, and come back next season?"

Jessica turned back toward the girls and raised her arms to start the first cheer.

"Wait, Jessica!" Robin shouted. "I asked Heather to come to practice. I thought that we could really benefit from her expertise, so I invited her to try out. I know it's not really the usual time of year that we audition new people, but I thought we could make an exception since she was the captain of a champion team at her old school."

Jessica could hardly believe her ears. Now she had no choice. Robin was her cocaptain, and if Jessica made a big stink about Heather trying out, everyone would think she was jealous. "Fine, Heather can try out," Jessica said. *But she's going to wish she never came to practice today after I'm through with her.* "I want you to do a triple herky, a back flip, a Y-leap combination, a no-hands cartwheel, and a landing jump in the splits. Oh, and you'll need to do that in under three minutes."

"No problem," Heather said nonchalantly. "Do you have a watch to time me with?"

"Yes, I do," Jessica said. "On your mark—get set—go!"

Jessica sat down with the other girls and, much to her dismay, watched Heather complete the routine in two minutes. Not only did she do everything Jessica said, but she added complicated, funky dance steps between each move. When she finished, she gave Jessica one of her sickeningly sweet smiles. Jessica had never seen anyone do such a complicated routine with such expertise and grace, and her head was starting to pound.

Everyone stood up to applaud and cheer, and Jessica was desperate. "Sorry, but that was over three minutes," she lied. "OK, we've wasted enough time, girls. Let's get down to business."

"Jessica, that was two minutes," Robin protested. "I timed it with my new stopwatch."

"It must not be working," Jessica said dismissively.

"My watch said two minutes, too," said Annie.

"So did mine," Helen said.

"Well, I guess I'll have to get my watch fixed." Jessica was flustered, and she felt her face turning red. She looked at Heather, who was as cool as a cucumber. She wasn't even sweating or breathing heavily after that strenuous routine.

"So I think that does it," Robin said. "It looks like we have a new member on the squad."

"Not so fast," Jessica said over the cheers coming from the girls. "We have to take a vote on it."

"Judging from the reaction of the entire squad, I would say that Heather's a shoo-in," Robin said, "and I think it's a waste of time to even take a vote on it. Everyone seems to love her."

"We still have to vote. And we need to do it in private." She turned to Heather and gave her back one of her syrupy smiles. "So maybe you could leave now."

"Sure thing," Heather said, smiling back and turning on her heel.

"'Bye, Heather!" the girls chanted as if she were God's gift to cheerleading.

"See ya later," Heather said sweetly, looking over her shoulder. "Have a good practice!"

Heather walked off the field and into the parking lot, where she got into her covertible and drove off.

Have a good practice! Jessica didn't think she'd ever disliked anyone as much as she disliked Heather Mallone. And if she had anything to do about it, Heather would never be on her cheering squad.

"She was awesome," Amy gushed. "She made it all look so effortless."

"And she made a normal routine look like a fun dance," Robin said. "She really jazzed up our usual moves."

"I don't think we even need to vote," Jeannie said. "We obviously all loved her."

"We have to take a vote," Jessica said, wondering how she was going to manage keeping Heather off the squad. "It's standard procedure."

"OK, all those in favor of Heather joining our squad, raise their right hand," Robin said.

Everyone raised their hand except Jessica. *Think of something, think of something,* she told herself.

"That settles it," Robin said. "Sorry, Jessica, but majority rules."

"No, in this case we have to discuss it further," Jessica said. "Just because she's a good cheerleader doesn't mean she's right for our squad."

"What are you talking about?" Robin asked. "Isn't that what we care about? Someone who can do all the routines?"

"We have to think about the personality and character of everyone on our team," Jessica said. "Everyone in this school looks up to us. We have a reputation to live up to. We can't let just anyone on our team just because they can do a cartwheel."

"Jessica, you have to admit she did a lot more

than just a cartwheel out there," Robin said. "If there were an Olympics category for cheerleading, she'd have a gold medal."

"And besides that, think about how much we could all learn from her," Annie said. "She could really liven things up a bit. Not that we're not fabulous already, but we could be even better."

"I just think it's important not to be too hasty about this decision," Jessica said, grasping at straws.

"So what do you propose?" Robin asked.

"As cocaptain, I'm going to come up with a series of tests that she has to pass before we can accept her on the squad," Jessica said.

"What kind of tests?" Jeannie asked. "Cheerleading tests? Written tests?"

"Tests that demonstrate her strength of character," Jessica said. "I'm going to think about them tonight when I go home, and we can start the testing process tomorrow."

"It seems sort of silly after her performance today," Robin said.

"Well, I *am* the cocaptain, so I guess you'll all just have to go along with what I say," Jessica said, jumping up from the circle. *And I'm going to have to come up with tests that she'll never be able to pass! I don't care if she has to walk across a bed of nails—she's not going to be on this squad!*

• • •

Elizabeth sat on her bed before dinner that night trying to concentrate on the book she was reading for American-history class about the labor movement in the thirties. She kept reading the same paragraph over and over again. All she could think about was the kiss she'd shared with Todd earlier that day. *What does it mean if I'm kissing Todd and thinking of Ken?* she worried. *I must still have feelings for Ken!*

She loved Todd, but she couldn't stop thinking about Ken. Was it possible to love two people at the same time?

"Hey, Liz, I have the best news," Jessica said as she came flying through the door.

"Does the word 'knock' mean anything to you?" Elizabeth was startled out of her thoughts, suddenly afraid that her sister would be able to read her mind. "I *was* trying to study."

"Grouchy, grouchy, grouchy," Jessica teased as she plopped down onto Elizabeth's bed. "It's been medically proved that too much studying is bad for your health." Jessica grabbed Elizabeth's book and flung it onto the floor.

"Now you made me lose my place," Elizabeth said, picking up her book.

"So guess who I have a date with on Friday night?" Jessica asked, grinning ear to ear.

"Ken Matthews," Elizabeth said unexcitedly.

"How do you know?"

"Todd told me today. I guess Ken told him."

"Isn't it fantastic? He's the greatest, cutest guy, and he's always been such a good friend."

"Yeah, it's great," Elizabeth forced herself to say.

"You don't seem too excited for me," Jessica said.

"I just think you should take it slowly," Elizabeth said, hating herself for putting a damper on Jessica's happiness. "It wasn't so long ago that you had your heart broken by Jeremy, don't forget."

"How could I ever forget what he did to me?" Jessica asked, looking melancholy for a moment and then perking right up again. "That's exactly why I'm so happy about Ken. I thought I'd never be interested in another guy ever again after Jeremy."

"All I'm saying is be careful," Elizabeth cautioned.

"Ken is nothing like Jeremy," Jessica swooned. "He's so natural and unpretentious, and I can tell he really likes me."

"How can you be so sure?" Elizabeth asked, hating herself for making her sister doubt Ken's feelings for her, but not being able to stop.

"I can tell from the way he kissed me on

Friday," Jessica said. "He was so tender but passionate at the same time. I felt his whole body trembling when he was standing next to me. Our attraction to each other was overwhelming."

As Jessica described her kiss with Ken, Elizabeth remembered her own secret kisses with him. Her entire body felt heavy with sadness and longing for something magical in the past. Magical yet fleeting, she thought.

"Kissing can be deceiving," Elizabeth said in spite of herself. "Just because two people like to kiss each other doesn't mean they should be together in a relationship."

"But before we ever even kissed, he acted like such a loyal friend to me when most of my supposed friends were just gossiping about me. I feel like he knows me in a way Jeremy never even began to know me. I've never felt this way about a guy before. It's like the perfect combination—friendship and romance."

"I wish I had a dollar for every time you've said you never felt that way about a guy before," Elizabeth said. "I'd be a millionaire. You've fallen in love more times than I can even remember."

"But this time is different," Jessica said. "I really feel like we were meant to be together. I think this could develop into a really serious relationship."

"I think you should still date around," Elizabeth said, though she could hardly believe she was saying it. "It's never a good idea to go from one relationship to another without checking out the other fish in the sea for a while."

Jessica laughed. "That's really funny, coming from you," Jessica said. "I've never seen you date around."

Yeah, well, you'd be surprised, Elizabeth thought, but then continued, "You're totally on the rebound. It's easy to think you're falling for someone new after being hurt the way you were. In a week or two you'll probably just want to be friends with Ken."

"I promise you you're wrong," Jessica said. "And I wish you'd be a little happier for me. I'm going to go get ready for dinner. Mom said it's almost ready."

Elizabeth felt like a rotten sister. She knew how important it was for Jessica to be with somebody new. *Maybe* I'm *in love with Ken,* Elizabeth thought. *Why else would I be trying to take away my sister's happiness?*

Chapter 4

Elizabeth hesitated by the door of Mr. Collins's office on Tuesday morning, trying to decide whether or not to knock. Mr. Collins was the faculty adviser to *The Oracle*, and Elizabeth had gone to him on many occasions to ask his advice. She needed to talk to someone more than ever, and she didn't want to talk to her best friend Enid Rollins or any of her other friends about it, because she was afraid of what they'd think of her.

When she'd woken up that morning, she'd felt an overwhelming sense of doom. Her first thought of the day had been about Jessica and Ken and the date they were going to have on Friday. She felt so alone in her feelings of guilt and jealousy. The two people she felt the closest to in the world—Jessica and Todd—were the two people she couldn't talk to about her problem, because it was about them.

Maybe it's a bad idea to talk to Mr. Collins about it, Elizabeth decided as she turned to walk away.

Just as Elizabeth took two steps away from his office, Mr. Collins opened his door and peeked into the hallway.

"Good morning, Ms. Wakefield," Mr. Collins said happily. "What brings you here so early? Problems with this week's issue of *The Oracle*?"

"Well, I do have a problem, but it has nothing to do with journalism," Elizabeth said. "Actually, it's a problem, umm . . . a friend of mine is having. I can come back another time, though, if you're busy."

"You know I'm never too busy to talk to you," Mr. Collins said as he led Elizabeth into his office. "What's on your mind?"

"Do you mind if we shut the door?" Elizabeth asked. She didn't want to run the risk of someone walking by and overhearing her. It was hard to keep anything a secret at Sweet Valley High—especially the kind of thing Elizabeth was about to tell Mr. Collins.

"This sounds serious," Mr. Collins said as he stood back up to close the door, looking concerned. "What kind of problem is your friend having?"

"It's a relationship problem," Elizabeth started awkwardly. "A few months ago my friend's boyfriend was out of town for a few months. Well, while he was gone, she had a sort-of fling with his best friend."

"I see," Mr. Collins said thoughtfully. "And did your friend tell her boyfriend about it when he came back to town?"

"No, she didn't tell anyone about it," Elizabeth said, feeling those guilty emotions creep back. "The problem now is that somebody else, someone who's really, really close to my friend, is starting a relationship with this same guy."

"And this is making your friend feel jealous," Mr. Collins said.

"Exactly!" Elizabeth said. It was amazing to her that Mr. Collins was always able to understand a situation without her having to explain it. He was wiser than almost anyone Elizabeth knew. "She didn't realize she still had feelings for this person until he started dating someone else."

"It sounds like things between your friend and this person she was secretly seeing never really got resolved," Mr. Collins said.

"You're right," Elizabeth said. "Before my friend's boyfriend came back to town, she'd stopped seeing the other guy. They both agreed that it wasn't right to keep seeing each other. But since things ended, they never really had another conversation about everything that had happened between them. My friend felt so guilty about betraying her boyfriend that she tried to push it all away—pretend like it never happened."

"But seeing him with someone else makes that difficult," Mr. Collins said, reading her mind again.

"Yes, it's unbearable," Elizabeth said, and then quickly added, "for my friend. It's unbearable for my friend."

"Obviously your friend hasn't resolved her feelings for this other person. Until she does, she's going to be miserable."

"I know you're right, but it's going to be hard for her," Elizabeth said sadly. *Everything he's saying makes sense, but I'm afraid I'm just going to have to swallow my feelings,* Elizabeth thought. "Thanks, Mr. Collins. I guess I should get going now."

"Are you sure that's all? I don't think I was much of a help," Mr. Collins said.

"No, you were a great help, as always," Elizabeth said. *But how am I supposed to resolve my feelings when I'm going out with Todd?*

"Heather, before I tell you what the first test is," Jessica said, "I just want to let you know that I totally understand if you want to back out of this whole cheerleading idea. I mean, it's going to be pretty strenuous, so you might want to just forget about it."

"I wouldn't dream of it," Heather said. "I can't wait to start the first test."

The girls were sitting with some of the cheerleaders and Lila at lunch on Tuesday, and the cafeteria seemed louder than usual. Jessica had intentionally chosen a big juicy hamburger and a large order of french fries from the lunch counter to show Heather she wasn't about to start counting fat grams just because she did.

Jessica took a big bite of her burger and put it back down on her plate. "OK, the first test is designed to see if you have the kind of self-confidence that's required to be on our squad. In order to measure your confidence level, you'll have to sit with the chess team during lunch for two days in a row."

"That's cruel and unusual punishment," Lila said. "They're the biggest nerds in the entire school."

"I don't know if even cheerleading is worth going through that humiliation," Robin said.

"Yeah, how is that a test of her self-confidence?" Annie asked. "I don't get it."

"Most people wouldn't be caught dead sitting with those guys," Jessica pointed out. "But if a person's really secure with herself, she won't care who she's seen sitting with. Also, it's important that as a cheerleader, she's able to get along with all kinds of people."

"When was the last time you sat with the chess team?" Lila teased. "I haven't exactly seen you being all buddy-buddy with Sean Lowry."

Jessica glared at her friend. "Maybe I have friends you don't know about."

"I don't think sitting with the chess team should be too difficult," Heather said, not skipping a beat.

"You could run the risk of damaging your reputation early on," Jessica warned. "After all, you're new in school. You don't want everyone to think you're a geek."

"I'm secure enough with myself that I don't care who I'm seen eating lunch with," Heather said as she stood up from the table and picked up her tray. "In fact, at my school in Nevada I got along with everyone. I'm going to start my test right now. I'll see you guys later."

Jessica watched aghast as Heather swaggered across the room and sat down with the startled chess team—smiling all the way.

"What's Heather wearing?" Lila asked Jessica on Wednesday morning. "She looks like a construction worker or something!"

Jessica stood calmly at her locker and looked down the hallway where Heather was obviously the laughingstock of the school. A group was formed around her, and Jessica was sure people were making fun of her clothes. *Good. My plan seems to be working perfectly,* Jessica thought triumphantly.

She had called Heather the night before and told her she had to wear whatever Jessica brought in for her the next morning. She'd rummaged through the garage and found a pair of purple-and-green-striped overalls her father had worn in a play when he was in college. She brought the overalls and a big orange cowboy hat to school and told Heather she had to put them on and wear them all day.

"It's one of the cheerleading tests I came up with," Jessica said proudly.

"You mean *you're* responsible for the way Heather looks today?" Lila asked incredulously.

"Yes, I take full responsibility. It's her second test."

"And what exactly are you testing? Her bad taste?" Lila looked back over at Heather and shook her head.

"It's a test of her depth."

"What's that supposed to mean?" Lila asked cynically.

"She seems like someone who's totally superficial, the way she's so obsessed with her looks and everything," Jessica explained. "I wanted to see if there was more to her than just her concern about her appearance."

"As if *you're* not interested in your own looks?" Lila asked, laughing. "I never knew that was one of the criteria for being on the squad."

"Well, I guess you wouldn't know because you're *not* on the squad," Jessica quipped.

"I can't believe she went along with it," Lila said. "How did you ever get her to do it?"

"She's desperate to cheer, but I'm sure that within the hour she'll be changing back into her usual clothes," Jessica said with an impish grin. "I must admit that this is one of my more clever schemes."

"It is pretty harsh," Lila said, readjusting the headband that was holding back her long brown hair. "I'm glad I'm not trying to be a cheerleader. She looks like a clown."

"Let's go hear some of the mean things people are saying to her," Jessica said, grabbing the books she needed for her first class.

Jessica and Lila walked down the hall together, and Jessica was pleased to see everyone laughing. What didn't please her was seeing that Heather was laughing as well.

"You really look cool," Bruce Patman was saying to Heather. "You're really pulling off that grunge look that's so in style these days."

"It's true," Amy agreed. "The models are wearing that stuff in all the fashion magazines I've seen recently."

"Yeah, you're on the cutting edge," Rick Hunter said. "Most girls would be too afraid to wear stuff like that. I think it's a sign of confidence that you're wearing whatever you feel like wearing."

"I agree," Sean Lowry, a member of the chess team, said. "You look really terrific."

"Thanks, Sean," Heather said, as if he were a close friend. "Oh, and that was fun last night when we worked on our math homework together."

She's hanging out with the chess team now? Jessica thought in total shock.

"How did you ever come up with this great outfit?" Annie asked.

"I have Jessica to thank," Heather said, turning to Jessica and smiling brightly in her direction.

"Don't thank me yet," Jessica said to Heather. "It's only the morning. It might get harder going around like that all day long."

"I doubt it," Heather said, walking off with Bruce. "Toodles!"

I'd like to "toodle" you, Jessica thought as she watched Heather swagger down the hall. *I have to think of another test before tomorrow, when we're supposed to vote again. But this time I'll make sure it'll be something she'll never pass.*

It was Thursday morning, and Jessica had arrived early at school. She was waiting for the students to file into the classroom for homeroom. The third and last test for Heather was about to happen, and Jessica couldn't wait to see Heather fail.

She'd called Heather the night before and told her that she had to get up in front of the entire homeroom and sing the national anthem. Even though Heather had said that would be no problem, Jessica was sure she'd back out at the last minute. After all, she'd clearly make a total fool of herself.

"Hey, Jessica, this is the first time I've seen you here so early," Annie said, sitting down next to Jessica.

"I didn't want to miss the special event," Jessica said excitedly.

"What special event?" Maria asked. "Are we getting a half day for some reason? Are they going to announce it in homeroom?"

"That would be awesome," Lila said. "There's nothing I'd rather do than close my eyes and lie on the beach all afternoon."

"You can hold on to your beach towel, because

we're not getting a half day," Jessica said.

"So what's the big event?" Maria asked. "Don't tell me you're excited to hear the roll call."

"It's a surprise," Jessica said secretively.

"Give us a hint," Lila said.

"OK, Heather's about to do her last cheerleading test," Jessica said. "And you're about to see her fail it before your very eyes."

"Excuse me, everyone! Can I have your attention?" Heather was standing at the front of the classroom. "This morning I'd like to start off homeroom with something a little special."

She sure looks calm and collected for someone who's about to make a total fool of herself, Jessica thought.

Heather opened her mouth, and out came the sounds of a professional singer. All of the students sat perfectly quiet and still as Heather filled the room with her beautiful voice. She did a funky version of the national anthem, and some students were even clapping their hands and snapping their fingers.

How is this possible? Jessica thought. She was furious. Jessica's tests kept backfiring and making Heather an even bigger star.

When Heather finished her song, the classroom went wild. People were jumping up from their seats to congratulate Heather on her performance.

"You sound like a professional singer," Amy gushed.

"You could really go far with your talent," Winston said.

"Well, I've actually had a few offers from different record companies to record a CD," Heather said. "My manager wanted me to pursue a career in music, but my parents want me to finish high school first."

"What exactly were you testing, Jessica?" Maria asked. "We never had a musical tryout as far as I can remember."

"I was trying to see, umm . . . I was trying to see if Heather had the ability to perform in public," Jessica said. "After all, that's what we do as cheerleaders."

"Could you sing another song?" Annie pleaded. "This is the best homeroom we've had all year."

"Sure," Heather said. "I'll sing one I wrote. I even brought my guitar along."

Jessica slid down in her seat in total misery as Heather started to sing a slow, bluesy song. Not only was Heather a great singer, but she was a fantastic guitar player as well. Jessica just couldn't believe that she was responsible for getting more attention for Heather. She had been so sure that Heather would fail her final test. *It's just not fair,*

Jessica thought. *Not only will Heather make it on the squad, she'll be more popular than ever because of me!*

"Well, Heather passed all of your tests, Jessica," Robin said at the beginning of cheerleading practice on Thursday afternoon. "I guess she might as well start practicing with us. I'll go call her over here."

"We haven't taken a vote yet," Jessica said.

"The last time we took a vote, everyone except you was in favor of her joining the team," Robin pointed out. "I'm sure nobody's changed their mind since Monday."

"And those tests you put her through were pretty rigorous," Jean said.

"Yeah, I'm glad I didn't have to do any of those things when I was trying to be a cheerleader," Amy agreed.

"They were just standard tests of confidence, depth, and performance," Jessica explained.

"Well, she passed them, so that's the end of the discussion," Robin snapped uncharacteristically. Clearly she was losing patience with her cocaptain. "Let's get on with it."

Jessica looked up at the bleachers where Heather was waiting. *That girl has some nerve,* Jessica thought.

"A lot can happen in a couple of days," Jessica

said, desperately trying to keep the inevitable from happening. "People might have gotten to know Heather a little bit better. Maybe they see her for what she really is."

"What's that supposed to mean?" Robin asked. "Are you saying there's something we should know about Heather?"

"As a matter of fact, I am saying that," Jessica said. "From what I've seen, she's a fake. She pretends to be really sweet, but the truth is she's not a nice person at all."

"I have to disagree with you," Annie said. "I've spent a lot of time with her since she started school here—a lot more than you have—and I think she's really great. She's nice and funny and totally cool. Just perfect for our squad."

"I agree," Amy said. "Yesterday Heather told me that she started a tutoring program at her old school. She got students to go to the poor areas around her community and help kids with their homework."

"She really sounds like a great role model," Annie said. "I think she could be a positive force for all of us."

"If she joins the sqaud, our standards will really drop," Jessica said forebodingly. "We just haven't known her long enough to see if she's really cheerleading material. People can appear one way on the outside, but the more you get to know them, you see that they were just putting on an act."

"I just don't understand why you have such a thing about Heather," Robin said. "I think you're really being weird about this. What has she done to you that's made you dislike her so much?"

Jessica couldn't really put it into words, and she didn't like Robin calling her weird. In fact, she thought Robin was being unusually testy.

"I was wondering the same thing," Amy said. "Nobody else except you seems to have a problem with her."

Jessica was being put on the spot. She couldn't explain that there was a certain way Heather smiled at her that made her cringe or a smugness about her that rubbed Jessica the wrong way. It was just something she felt so deeply, but it was frustrating not to be able to articulate it. It was more than the fact that Heather kept taking attention away from Jessica.

"It's hard to say exactly what it is," Jessica said. "It's just an attitude that she has that I know would be wrong for our squad. You just have to trust me on this. I'm a good judge of character."

"But she passed all the tests you came up with to test her character," Sandy Bacon said. "They were pretty tough, too. I don't think any of us would have come to school dressed the way she was yesterday. Most of us are too vain."

"It turned out to be a big success for her," Jessica said. "Everyone told her how in style she was."

"But she didn't know it would work out that way for her, and she wore those hideous-looking overalls anyway," Jeannie said.

Jessica felt as if she were being pushed into a corner. *No matter what I say, they're still determined to have her on this squad,* Jessica thought. "I really feel strongly about this, and I think if somebody has such a passionate feeling about something, everyone else has to go along with it."

"That's ridiculous," Robin protested. "That's like saying that if you want something and we don't, we all have to do what you say. If you said we should all jump off the roof of the gymnasium, would we have to do that too?"

"I'm not saying that at all," Jessica said. All of Jessica's points seemed to be getting twisted around, and she wasn't any closer to making her case than when she started.

"Don't forget how opposed you were to Annie joining the squad," Robin said. "Now she's one of the best cheerleaders we have."

Jessica looked at Annie and felt a guilty pang. When Annie first tried to be a cheerleader, Jessica had fought it tooth and nail. She told everyone that Annie was the wrong kind of girl for their squad because she had a reputation for being fast with the guys. Jessica had done everything in her power to keep Annie off the squad, and Annie had ended up trying to kill herself. She had swallowed a bottle of pills and was rushed to the hospital just in time to save her life. *It's really unfair of Robin to bring that up,* Jessica thought. *She knows how bad I feel about what I did. This is different. Heather really is a mean person. Why am I the only person who seems to realize that?*

"This is a totally different situation, and you know it," Jessica protested. She was starting to feel as if everyone was ganging up on her.

"Why don't you just admit that you're jealous of Heather?" Amy blurted out as she stretched over and touched her toes. "It's not a federal offense to be jealous. It happens to everyone. I just think in this case you should put your jealousy aside for the moment and think about what's best for the team."

"First of all, I'm not jealous of Heather, and second of all, I *am* thinking about what's best for the team," Jessica cried. "I can guarantee that voting for Heather to be on our squad will be the biggest mistake you'll ever make."

"Speaking of voting," Robin started, "that's exactly what we're going to do. We've wasted enough time on this discussion as it is. All those in favor of letting Heather on the squad, raise their right hand."

Jessica closed her eyes. She knew that her arguments for keeping Heather off the squad hadn't worked the way she'd hoped they would. She couldn't bear to see everyone raising her hand again.

All the other cheerleaders started clapping and cheering as Jessica opened her eyes. Heather stood up on the bleachers as if she were a movie star and walked slowly down to the field.

"Way to go, Heather!" Robin shouted.

"Congratulations!" Amy added.

"Welcome to the team," Annie said.

"Let's start practice," Jessica commanded, refusing to look Heather in the eye. "We're going to start out with the 'Be Aggressive' cheer." Jessica stood facing the girls, who were in a line. She spread her legs, extended her arms to the side, and started the cheer. "Be aggressive! Be aggressive! B-E-A-G-G-R-E-S-S-I-V-E—"

"Excuse me," Heather yelled, jumping in front of Jessica. "If you don't mind, I have a suggestion that might really make this old, tired cheer a little more hip."

"As a matter of fact, Heather," Jessica said

evenly, trying with all her might not to lose her temper, "I *do* mind! Maybe when I'm finished—"

"Jessica, as the cocaptain," Robin said, stepping out of the line toward Jessica and Heather, "I *would* like to see a new version of this cheer. Even you have to admit that this one is incredibly boring."

"You never said anything about its being boring in the past," Jessica pointed out. *How could she embarrass me like this in front of Heather?* Jessica wondered as she felt her whole body shaking with anger.

"It never occurred to me that there might be a more interesting way of doing it," Robin said.

Jessica watched in horror as Heather proceeded to do the same cheer over again but with a funky rap beat instead. The girls went nuts, and Jessica wanted to punch Heather in the stomach.

"It's like a whole new cheer," Robin enthused. "That was about a hundred times more exciting than the way we do it."

"Do you think you could show us how to do that?" Amy asked.

"Sure, no problem," Heather said. "Just imagine that you're dancing and singing instead of cheering."

"But we're supposed to be cheering," Jessica

said, putting her hands on her hips. "That's why we're called *cheer*leaders."

"Jessica, it wouldn't hurt to change our cheer just a little bit," Robin said. "And besides, look at all the girls. They obviously wouldn't mind learning Heather's version."

Jessica knew Robin was right. She looked at the faces of the girls, beaming with admiration for Heather. Jessica reluctantly and angrily stepped to the side and allowed Heather to teach them the cheer *her* way. *I can't stand that girl, and if I have anything to do about it—she won't be on this squad for long!* she vowed to herself.

Chapter 5

Elizabeth felt a chill and pulled her jean jacket around her tightly. She watched the foam crash against the sand and felt the cool water sneak up between her uncovered toes. She'd driven to the beach after school on Thursday to try to clear her head. When she looked out at the enormity of the ocean, her problems always felt smaller and less overwhelming.

She was trying desperately to keep everything in perspective. *I'm sure about my feelings for Todd, and I know I want to be with him,* she told herself as she threw a shell into the water and watched it splash. *I would be miserable if anything caused us to break up.* But as she kept walking, Ken's face continued to creep into her thoughts as it had for the last week.

All day she kept going over her talk with Mr. Collins. How was she supposed to resolve her feelings for Ken if she didn't spend any time with him? She wished that her older brother, Steven, were home from college. He'd be a good person to talk to because he knew her so well and he was good at giving advice.

Elizabeth knew that spending time with Ken now that Jessica was seeing him would be impossible. She kept going back and forth about whether or not to tell Jessica what had happened between her and Ken. *Maybe she will stop seeing him until I figure out my true feelings for him,* Elizabeth thought hopefully. The more she thought about that, though, the more she knew it was absurd. *Knowing my sister, that would probably make her even more determined to see Ken.*

Elizabeth broke into a run along the water's edge. She wanted to run away from everything. Away from the guilt and the jealousy. She felt the sea air burning against her cheeks, and she felt freer and lighter than she had in days.

She saw a figure of someone sitting on the beach, but she couldn't tell who it was from a distance. As she got closer, she realized it was Robin Wilson. *She must have just come from cheerleading practice,* Elizabeth thought as she got closer.

Thinking of cheerleading reminded her of Jessica, and all her problems came flooding back to her.

"What brings you out here?" Elizabeth asked, plopping down on the sand next to Robin. "You look a little glum."

"I'm more than a little glum," Robin said sadly. "I tried to act like everything was normal at practice. As soon as it was over, I jumped in my car and headed for the beach. I can think better here for some reason."

"So can I," Elizabeth said. "It always helps me put things in perspective." Both girls stared out at the horizon over the water. They had never been particularly close friends, but Elizabeth always liked Robin a lot, and in some ways she was happy to be sitting with someone who didn't know her so well. "I can't imagine not living near the ocean. I need it for my sanity."

"That's exactly what I was just thinking," Robin said. "I'm really going to miss this beach—not to mention my friends, the cheering squad, Sweet Valley High, and everything else."

"What are you talking about?" Elizabeth asked, turning to face Robin. "Are you going away somewhere?"

"Yes," Robin said, sighing heavily. "My dad just got a job transfer to Denver, Colorado, and we have to move as soon as possible. I haven't told anyone else yet. I guess I thought if I told anyone, it would make it real."

"You poor thing," Elizabeth said, but really she couldn't help thinking that she would love to be moving away herself. Then she wouldn't have to decide what to do about Ken and Todd and Jessica.

Robin wiped away a tear. "I love it here. I can't stand the idea of having to make all new friends at a different school."

"Maybe if you look at it as an exciting new adventure . . ." Elizabeth said, trying to comfort her. "It's great to have new experiences in life. If you want to know the truth, I'm actually a little envious of you. What I'd give to just move away . . ."

Robin looked at her, surprised. "You? But you always seem so happy. Is something bothering you?"

"Let's just say I have a lot on my mind these days," Elizabeth said, and anxious to change the subject, she stood up and brushed the sand off her sweater and blue jeans. "Come on, I want you to tell me all about Denver on our walk back to the parking lot."

"Can you turn down the CD player? I'm having a hard time concentrating on my English essay," Elizabeth said. She and Jessica were sprawled out in the family room on Thursday night, doing their homework.

"Elizabeth, I'm a little worried about you. It seems like you've been burying your nose in your work a little more than usual lately," Jessica said. "There's more to life than homework, you know."

It was true. Elizabeth had been spending more time on her studies lately—it was the only thing that helped keep her mind off Ken. She was immersing herself in her schoolwork, hoping the whole situation would just go away. But of course it hadn't, and in the meantime she couldn't remember the last time she had just let loose and enjoyed herself. "This happens to be an interesting essay, actually," Elizabeth said for Jessica's benefit. "It's about Zelda Fitzgerald."

"Zelda! Who would ever name their daughter Zelda?" Jessica asked as she walked back from turning down the music.

"She was the wife of the writer F. Scott Fitzgerald," Elizabeth explained patiently. "She was a writer herself, and she lived a really exciting but tragic life."

"Well, I'm living a tragic life right now thanks to the arrival in Sweet Valley of Heather Mallone," Jessica groaned as she flopped down onto the couch. "She's making my life absolutely miserable."

"What has she done to you?" Elizabeth asked, eager to hear about anything that didn't have to do with Jessica's growing romance with Ken.

"Everyone except me voted for her to be on the squad this afternoon," Jessica said.

"What's so bad about that? I've heard she's a really good cheerleader."

"I don't care how good a cheerleader she is," Jessica said. "The point is that she's a horrible, awful person, and I know she's going to be the worst thing that ever happened to our squad. Nobody except me seems to see her truly evil personality."

"Why don't you try looking at the positive side?" Elizabeth suggested.

"And what positive side could there possibly be?" Jessica asked skeptically.

"She obviously has a lot of cheerleading experience," Elizabeth started. "You could probably learn a lot from her. Maybe she'll even improve the squad. After all, her old squad won their state championship, right? Even I know enough about cheerleading to realize that that means she must be a pretty good cheerleader."

"First of all, you really *don't* know anything about cheerleading, although I do appreciate your trying to help. Second of all, if I hear one more time that her squad won state, I'm going to scream."

"I'm just saying she could be a positive influence," Elizabeth said gently.

"As long as I'm one of the captains, she will have no influence on my squad whatsoever," Jessica said.

"If you go into practice every day thinking that you have to fight her, it will be counterproductive for everyone," Elizabeth warned. "I have a great idea—and before you completely reject it—just consider it for a minute. What if you make Heather a cocaptain? That way you'll be working together for the same purpose instead of in conflict with each other."

Jessica laughed. "You're really weird, Liz. I already *have* a cocaptain, as you very well know."

"But Robin's moving to Denver," Elizabeth blurted out, then quickly covered her mouth when she realized what she'd said.

"What are you talking about?" Jessica was sitting straight up on the couch. "You hardly ever even see Robin. How would you know something like that?"

"I'm really sorry I blurted it out like that," Elizabeth said. "I ran into her this afternoon after your practice, and she told me her dad got a new job. It sounds like they're leaving pretty soon."

"Great, now my horrible day is even worse," Jessica said. "Not only am I losing one of my good friends, I'm losing the cocaptain of the squad. Now that I think of it, Robin wasn't really acting like herself today at practice. And she was so adamant about Heather's being on the squad. I guess that's because she was thinking there'd be a new slot left to fill when she leaves."

"So maybe you *will* consider letting Heather be your cocaptain," Elizabeth said.

"I can promise you that Heather Mallone will be my cocaptain just as soon as it snows in Sweet Valley in August," Jessica said. Both girls laughed at her joke.

"My life really is a tragedy like that woman you're writing about," Jessica continued. "But at least I have one thing to be happy about."

"What's that?" Elizabeth asked.

"My date tomorrow night with Ken," Jessica said dreamily. "I wish I could just go to sleep and wake up tomorrow night. I can't wait!"

And once again Elizabeth felt as if someone had knocked the breath out of her.

"I just can't believe you're leaving," Amy said. "I'm going to miss you so much."

"It's too sad to even think about," Annie said. "Let's just not think about it."

It was Friday at lunch, and Robin had just announced she was moving. Everyone at the table was teary-eyed. Jessica hated that Heather was sitting at their table at such a sad and personal time. After all, Heather was really still a stranger.

"I could see if my parents would let you come and live with us," Lila said excitedly. "There's obviously more than enough room, and it would be a total blast."

"You're really nice to offer that, but I seriously doubt my parents would go for it," Robin said, forcing a weak smile.

"Do you think you'll come back and visit us?" Helen asked.

"My parents promised me that they'd let me come back and visit all the time," Robin said. "Denver's not so far from Sweet Valley. Maybe you guys could come and visit me for a ski trip sometime."

"That would be awesome," Jeannie said.

"I'm really going to miss you guys," Robin said. "And I'm especially going to miss being on the cheerleading squad. I feel like I'm letting you all down."

"I don't want you to worry about that," Jessica said. "I'm fully prepared to be the only captain when you leave. It won't be the same without you, but I'm going to keep the squad together."

"Don't you think that will be hard to just have

one captain?" Heather asked. "I mean, a good squad really needs two captains."

"Hi, Heather!" said Charles Stewart, one of the nerdiest guys on the chess team, as he passed by the table.

"Oh, hey, Chuck!" Heather waved and flashed one of her toothy smiles.

"Excuse me," Jessica said, annoyed by the reminder that all her tests for Heather had backfired, making her more popular than ever. "I believe we were in the middle of a conversation about cheerleading."

"Oh, right. I was saying that it's next to impossible to have one captain for a squad," Heather said.

"And I was about to say that I'm perfectly capable of leading the squad by myself," Jessica said defensively. Even though she was definitely going to miss Robin, part of Jessica was secretly starting to get excited by the idea of being the only captain.

"Being the only captain of a squad is an enormous responsibility, especially if you're interested in taking your squad on to competitions," Heather said.

"I have an idea!" Amy was beaming with excitement. "Since Heather has so much experience, why don't we make her the new cocaptain!"

Jessica was fuming. *Over my dead body!* she wanted to shout. But before she could say anything, Helen had started talking.

"All those in favor of Heather being the new cocaptain, raise their right hand," Helen said.

Everyone on the squad raised her right hand except Jessica, who was practically in shock. She couldn't believe that she was really going to be leading the squad with Heather. The thought was too incredible to take in.

"It looks like we have a new cocaptain," Annie said. "I hope we'll measure up to your standards."

"Oh, I'm sure you will," Heather said. "I am absolutely thrilled by the honor."

"I feel better now that I know the squad will be left in the capable hands of Jessica and Heather," Robin said.

"I'm really looking forward to working with you, Jessica," Heather said in that fake voice of hers.

Jessica was so upset she couldn't even speak. She looked across the table at Heather, who was beaming at Jessica with a sickening smile. Now the one thing that Jessica loved more than anything—cheerleading—was ruined because of Heather Mallone.

"Is *that* what you're wearing on your date?" Elizabeth asked Jessica later that night as she opened the door of the bathroom that connected their two bedrooms. "That looks like a nightie."

Elizabeth was referring to the white sundress Jessica was wearing that came way above her knee and was cut low in front. It was very sexy—too sexy, in Elizabeth's opinion—and it showed off Jessica's perfectly tan, fit body. The thought of Ken seeing her sister in that dress was enough to make Elizabeth want to lock Jessica in the house.

"You've seen me wear this dress about a zillion times before, and you've never said anything about it," Jessica said as she flipped her head over to brush the underside of her hair.

"I just don't think it's appropriate for tonight," Elizabeth said, trying to sound sincere.

"I can't think of a more appropriate time to wear it than tonight," Jessica said. "I'm going on my first real date with a gorgeous guy who happens to be the quarterback of the football team and who I'm absolutely crazy about. If this isn't the right occasion to wear this dress, then I don't know what is."

But you can't wear that dress tonight, because I might still be interested in Ken, Elizabeth wanted to say. "Well, maybe you should wear a jacket over it."

Elizabeth left the bathroom, then came right

back carrying her pink oversize knit sweater. "Here, this would look great over it. It could get chilly tonight."

"Liz, are you a total moron? I'm going on a date, not on a picnic with a kindergarten class."

"Well, you don't have to wear this sweater, but you should wear something over that dress," Elizabeth said. "You don't want to look too—"

"Too what?" Jessica asked, putting on bright-red lipstick. "Too sexy? Sexy is *exactly* what I want to look like."

"But Ken's not that kind of guy," Elizabeth said.

"Not what kind of guy?" Jessica laughed. "Not the kind of guy who likes pretty girls?"

"I know he's Todd's best friend and everything, but he's a pretty boring guy," Elizabeth lied. "He'll probably think a sexy dress is a total turnoff. Ken's a real snore, Jessica. I only tolerate him because of Todd."

"If Ken's a snore, then Todd's a coma," Jessica teased.

"No, really," Elizabeth continued, ignoring her sister's slight to Todd. "Ken's actually very serious, and I'd imagine that he'd prefer a girl who was a little more bookish—less flashy."

"You're way off base, Liz. And no offense, but I do believe I'm the expert when it comes to guys."

"I just think you need to go slowly," Elizabeth said, grasping at straws.

"The greatest thing about Ken is that I really feel like he's a friend of mine," Jessica said, making a pouting face in the mirror to see if her makeup looked OK. "I mean, I feel like I can talk to him about anything. I can't wait to tell him about what happened today with the cheerleading squad. He's so supportive and understanding. I know he'll totally be on my side when I tell him how horrible that Heather is."

He is a good person to talk to, Elizabeth thought as she remembered all the hours she and Ken had stayed up talking about life and literature and love and everything else under the sun.

"So how do I look?" Jessica asked as she turned to face her sister.

"Beautiful," Elizabeth said morosely. "Just beautiful."

Elizabeth's heart sank as she walked out of the bathroom, swallowing back the tears.

Chapter 6

"I'll get it," Elizabeth yelled as she bounded down the stairs to open the door for Todd. They were going to the movies, and she was anxious to get out of the house and get her mind off Jessica's date.

When she opened the door, her heart stopped. Instead of looking at Todd, she was looking at Ken. For some reason she had thought Jessica was meeting Ken somewhere else. It never occurred to her that he would come to their house. He looked as stunned to see Elizabeth as she was to see him.

"Hi, Elizabeth," Ken practically whispered as he looked down at his feet.

Elizabeth noticed that he was holding his hands behind his back. *He brought flowers,* she realized sadly. *He brought flowers for my sister and not for me.*

"Hi, Ken," Elizabeth said. She felt as if she were talking with marbles in her mouth. Until recently they'd been able to talk to each other normally, but tonight she could barely say two words to him.

They just stood there silently, both afraid to be the first one to speak. Ken continued to avoid eye contact with Elizabeth. *Look at me,* Elizabeth wanted to say. *Talk to me about what happened between us. Tell me what your feelings are toward me. Tell me that you're not really interested in Jessica.*

"Hi, Ken!" Jessica said excitedly as she practically leaped down the stairs. She threw her arms around Ken's neck and gave him a kiss on the cheek. "Boy, am I glad to see *you*. You're not going to believe what happened to me today."

Elizabeth kept standing there and watched Ken as his face turned bright red. *He's embarrassed by this situation because he remembers what happened between us,* Elizabeth thought. That made her feel better somehow. At least he remembered their secret past.

"We should get going," Ken said timidly.

"Are those flowers for me?" Jessica asked as she grabbed the flowers from behind Ken's back. "That was so sweet of you."

Jessica handed the flowers to Elizabeth. "Liz,

we're in a hurry. Could you be a doll and put these flowers in water for me?"

Before Elizabeth could answer, Ken and Jessica were in Ken's car, and she was standing there holding a beautiful bouquet of roses that wasn't meant for her. Elizabeth watched as they drove away, leaving her alone in her misery.

"You look great tonight," Todd said to Elizabeth as he nuzzled up to her neck. They were sitting in the Sweet Valley movie theater before the previews had started. "And you smell wonderful, as usual."

He is so sweet, Elizabeth thought. She had thrown on a denim shirt and blue jeans and pulled the front part of her hair back in a barrette, and here he was acting as if she were dressed for the prom. Elizabeth felt a familiar twinge of guilt. *He's so good to me and he loves me so much. How can I even think about another guy?*

As hard as she tried to concentrate on Todd and to stop thinking about Jessica and Ken, she couldn't help wondering where they were right at that moment and what they were doing. She kept having an image of Jessica in that skimpy white dress, and she wondered if Ken thought she looked sexy. *Of course he does,* Elizabeth thought. *But it doesn't matter anyway, because you're sitting right here with your wonderful boyfriend who adores you*, she told herself.

"All week I look forward to Friday night so I can be with you without worrying about getting up early for school the next day," Todd said. "You're what gets me through the week."

Elizabeth gave Todd a big kiss on the lips.

"What was that for?" Todd asked, obviously pleased by Elizabeth's show of affection.

"Because I love you," Elizabeth said. She leaned her head on his shoulder, and for one moment her jealous thoughts were almost gone.

Todd pointed toward the front of the theater. "Look who's here."

Elizabeth looked in the direction where Todd was pointing. She couldn't believe it. Ken and Jessica were sitting down just five rows in front of them.

"Ken was really excited about their date," Todd said. "That's all he was talking about this afternoon. I even went to the florist with him. He spent about twenty minutes choosing the right flowers to bring your sister."

"The movie's about to start," Elizabeth said. She couldn't say anything else. She couldn't even pretend to be excited about Jessica and Ken and their stupid date.

The lights went down and the movie started.

Elizabeth wasn't watching the movie. She couldn't take her eyes off her sister and Ken. She watched as Ken put his arm around the back of Jessica's chair. *Stop looking at them,* she told herself. She just couldn't stop torturing herself. Jessica turned toward Ken in that flirtatious smile Elizabeth knew too well, and whispered something to him. Ken leaned down and gave Jessica a little kiss on the lips.

Elizabeth felt as if a knife were going through her heart. She kept remembering times that she and Ken had gone to movies together. They had sat in the back together and whispered like that to each other, and he had kissed her sweetly when nobody was watching. *How can he do the same things with her?* Even though Elizabeth knew she had no right to be mad at Ken—she was with Todd, after all—she was furious. She felt betrayed.

Does he like Jessica more than he liked me? Does he like kissing her more? Does he think she's sexier than me? Does he like talking to her better? Elizabeth kept thinking the same thoughts over and over again, and throughout the movie her gaze never left the happy couple sitting just five rows in front of her.

"I loved that movie," Jessica enthused. She was sitting at a booth at Casey's Ice Cream Parlor with

Ken, Todd, and Elizabeth. They'd all run into each other in front of the movie theater, and Todd had suggested that they get some ice cream together. So far it had been a great evening. She and Ken had whispered and giggled and held hands during the entire movie.

"I thought that the acting was great," Todd said. "But the plot didn't really hold up. I mean, how realistic is it that that woman would have married the same man in a second life?"

"I think the point is that it's a *movie*," Jessica teased. "It's not real life. Now I see why you and Elizabeth get along so well—you're both as serious and practical as the other one."

"How did you like it, Ken?" Todd asked.

"Oh, I liked it a lot," Ken said. "And I really liked all the scenes that took place in the first life of the characters."

"Me too," Jessica said, moving closer to Ken in the booth. She thought Ken seemed a little distracted, but she decided it was probably just because he was still a little nervous. They *were* on their first date, after all. "Those costumes they were wearing in that ball scene were gorgeous."

"What about you, Elizabeth? What was your favorite scene?" Todd asked.

Elizabeth looked up from her sundae as if she'd been in another galaxy. She'd been acting totally spaced out ever since they'd sat down in the booth. "I'm not sure."

"What planet are you on?" Jessica asked her sister. "You seem really out of it."

"I'm just thinking about the movie," Elizabeth said weakly. "I liked it a lot, but I can't decide which scene was my favorite."

"Hey, kids!" a female voice said from behind Jessica.

Jessica looked up from her banana split and saw Heather looking down at her. She was standing by their booth, surrounded by about four or five guys who were practically drooling all over her.

"How are you, Jessica?" Heather asked in her supersweet voice. "That's a serious banana split you're eating. I can't imagine what the fat count for that would be."

Jessica remembered how rude Heather had been that first day about the fettuccine she was eating. It had been all Jessica could do not to pick up her plate and throw it into Heather's face, but tonight she was having such a good time with Ken that not even Heather could bother her.

"Would you like a bite? It's delicious," Jessica said, delicately taking a bite of whipped cream, vanilla ice cream, and butterscotch sauce.

"No, thanks, but I would like a bite of Ken's

hot-fudge sundae," Heather said, smiling flirtatiously at Ken.

Jessica looked at Ken, who was smiling back at Heather. She watched in horror as Heather leaned over their table and opened her mouth while Ken fed her a bite of his sundae.

"Thanks, that was yummy," Heather said, licking her lips. "It's amazing that you're able to stay in such great shape and eat sweets like that, Ken."

"I'll just have to jog an extra mile or two tomorrow," Ken said.

"Are you a jogger?" Heather asked.

"Yeah, I jog every day," Ken said.

"So do I," Heather said, as if it were the most interesting thing in the world. "I've been looking for someone to jog with. Maybe we could start jogging together. Why don't you give me a call?"

"Sure thing," Ken said.

Jessica's blood was boiling. *The nerve of that awful girl flirting with my date right in front of me,* Jessica thought as she watched Heather slink away. *She's got another thing coming if she thinks she can make a move on my guy!*

Jessica looked at Elizabeth, who looked as upset about Heather's little flirtation as she was. *That's a loyal sister,* Jessica thought lovingly. *She's protective of me and my date. I'm lucky to have her on my side.*

• • •

"I wouldn't worry about Heather," Ken said. He and Jessica were sitting in his car in front of the Wakefields' house after they'd left Casey's. Jessica had just finished telling him about how Heather was going to be the new cocaptain. "You're a fantastic cheerleading captain, and there's no way she could possibly compete with you."

"Do you really think so?"

"Absolutely," Ken said, looking deeply into Jessica's eyes.

"She *is* really pretty," Jessica said, trying to see what Ken's reaction would be. She was still a little jealous about the way Heather had been flirting with him at the Dairi Burger.

"*You're* the one who's really pretty, and in fact, you're looking exceptionally beautiful tonight," Ken said as he took a strand of Jessica's hair in his fingers and twirled it around. "You really take my breath away."

"So you don't think you'll be calling her like she asked you to?" Jessica asked, trying to sound as if it were an innocent question.

"No way," Ken said. "Why would I ever want to call her? I'd rather call you *any*day."

"I had a great time with you tonight," Jessica said.

"So did I."

"I'm glad to hear that. I was worried there for a minute. You were almost as quiet as my sister was at Casey's."

"I guess I just wanted to be alone with you," Ken said.

Jessica was dying for him to kiss her. At Casey's she couldn't wait to get away from her sister and Todd so she could be alone with Ken. *I can tell he really likes me, and I know he would never hurt me the way Jeremy did,* she thought as he leaned toward her. *He's too nice a guy to do that. Elizabeth was wrong to warn me about going slowly with my feelings.*

"I feel really comfortable with you, Ken," Jessica said. "And I've been wanting to tell you how much your friendship meant to me when I was going through that hard time recently."

"I hope you think of me as more than just a friend," Ken said.

"I think that's pretty obvious," Jessica said. She put her face close to his and closed her eyes. Ken kissed her so tenderly that Jessica felt as if she never wanted the kiss to end.

"Excuse me, but I believe this dress has J-E-S-S-I-C-A written all over it," Jessica said as she walked out of the fitting room at Bibi's. "This is exactly what I want to wear to Amy's going-away party for Robin tonight."

"You're not seriously thinking of buying a new dress just for one party, are you?" Elizabeth asked. "That's pretty indulgent, if you ask me."

It was Saturday afternoon, and the twins were spending the day at the mall. Elizabeth had been in a bad mood all day. Last night had been a nightmare. It was pure torture sitting with Ken and Jessica on their date. She could tell that Ken was as uncomfortable as she was. He wouldn't look at her the entire time they were sitting in the booth at Casey's. And it was torture to watch her sister flirting with Ken right in front of her.

She didn't want to spend the day with her sister, but Jessica had insisted she go to the mall with her. Every time Jessica would start talking about Ken, Elizabeth tried to change the subject.

"First of all, it's not like I'm only going to wear it tonight and never again," Jessica said as she posed in front of the mirror to see what it looked like from all different angles. "And besides, I'm really buying it to look good for Ken tonight."

"It makes you look fat," Elizabeth blurted out.

Jessica looked mortified. "Are you saying I've gained weight?" She scrutinized herself in the mirror. "I have been eating a lot of banana splits at the Dairi Burger and Casey's recently."

"No, I just think that dress isn't very flattering on you," Elizabeth said. The truth was that the dress looked fabulous on Jessica—a little too fabulous. She didn't want Jessica to look so good for Ken. It was totally out of character for Elizabeth to lie to her sister like that, but she couldn't help it.

"That dress fits you like a glove," the salesgirl said as she passed Jessica.

"Really?" Jessica asked excitedly. "My sister thinks it makes me look fat. What do you think?"

"I think your sister needs glasses," the salesgirl said. "You're as skinny as a rail."

"That settles it," Jessica said. "I'm going to take it."

"I didn't realize Ken was taking you to the party," Elizabeth said as she followed Jessica into the changing room. "Did he actually call and invite you to go together?" Elizabeth was pretty sure he hadn't called, but she couldn't resist placing a little doubt in Jessica's mind.

"No, he didn't," Jessica said. "But I know he'll be at the party, and I'm sure we'll be there as a couple."

"Hmmm," Elizabeth said, trying to sound doubtful.

"What?" Jessica asked, obviously worried.

"It's nothing," Elizabeth said, making a face that implied the exact opposite.

"Come on, Liz," Jessica pleaded. "Tell me what's wrong."

"I just think it's odd that Ken wouldn't have invited you as his date to the party," Elizabeth said. "I mean, the party is for one of your best friends, and if you're really starting to be a couple, I don't know why he wouldn't want to take you out in public."

Jessica scrunched up her face as if she were concentrating on a really difficult math problem. "I never thought of that. I know he really likes me a lot, though, so I don't think I have anything to worry about."

"You're probably right," Elizabeth said. "But I'd be careful if I were you. Heather Mallone sure looks like she's trying to get her claws in him."

"Why do you say that?"

"Well, she was falling all over him at Casey's last night," Elizabeth said, hating herself for making her sister worry. "She seems like someone who usually gets what she wants. She certainly succeeded in becoming your cocaptain."

"I'm not afraid of her. I can handle Heather," Jessica declared as she walked out of the dressing room with the dress in hand. "Ken even said to me that he didn't think she was pretty."

"I guess he *would* tell you that," Elizabeth said. "I mean, he wouldn't come right out and tell you if he liked her, I guess. Did you ever think he might just have said that because he knew that's what you'd want to hear?"

"I suppose so," Jessica said, handing the dress to the salesgirl at the counter. "Liz, why are you trying to make me paranoid about Ken?"

"I just don't want you to get hurt," Elizabeth said.

"I appreciate your concern, but I can take care of myself," Jessica said. "Don't worry about me. I'll be fine."

That's what I'm worried about, Elizabeth thought. *Things with Ken might be a little too good.*

Chapter 7

"Attention, everybody! I want to make a speech! It is my party, after all," Robin shouted above the noise. It was Saturday night, and Amy was throwing a good-bye party for Robin in her backyard. Some people were standing on the patio around the pool drinking exotic nonalcoholic drinks, and others were dancing on the lawn.

Jessica was really sad about Robin leaving, but she was just a little bit thrilled to have an occasion to get dressed up and see Ken again. She'd thought about him all day long, and it was almost too good to be true that she was seeing him two nights in a row. She was enormously pleased with the peach linen minidress she'd bought that day. When she'd tried it on, she'd known it was a "must buy," in spite of Elizabeth's trying to discourage her.

Jessica was so sure about Ken's feelings for her that she didn't even mind that he hadn't come by to pick her up for the party. After all, it was a last-minute party, since Robin had announced she was leaving only the day before. All of the doubts Elizabeth had expressed to her at the mall didn't worry Jessica. She knew her sister was overprotective of her. She'd always been that way. When Jessica had first started seeing Jeremy, Elizabeth had practically physically prevented her from going out with him. Unfortunately, in that case Elizabeth's fears had been justified, but it was an entirely different situation with Ken. She decided not to be annoyed by her sister's warnings. She knew Elizabeth was behaving that way only out of love and concern. Luckily, she knew she had nothing to worry about as far as Ken was concerned.

Jessica turned to look at Robin, who was giving her speech, but she was also trying to strike a sexy pose for Ken, who was standing on the other side of the pool.

"I am going to miss all of you so much," Robin was saying as she obviously tried to fight back the tears. "I can't imagine what my life will be like without all of you in it. One thing I'm really going to miss is the pleasure I get from being a cheerleader here. But I'm pleased to officially announce that Heather Mallone will be my replacement as the cocaptain of the cheerleading squad. I know she and Jessica will lead the squad in their continued support of the Gladiators, the best football team in California!"

People cheered and applauded, and a couple of guys shouted, "Babearama!" and "What a dish!"

Jessica had managed to forget about Heather and cheerleading for the time being and resented this ugly reminder.

"Hey, Jessica, how was your date last night?" Lila asked Jessica as she bounded up next to her. "I want a full report."

"Let's just say it was a night I'll never forget," Jessica said, sighing heavily. She was happy to have her thoughts taken away from Heather for the moment. "Ken's the greatest guy in the world. I can't believe I've known him all these years but I'm just now realizing how terrific he is."

"It looks like you're not the only person who thinks so," Lila said. "Check out the action by the refreshment table."

Jessica turned around and, to her horror, saw Heather talking to Ken! They were standing by the table, which was at the edge of the pool, and Heather was laughing loudly and gesticulating wildly.

"That girl is seriously out to ruin my life,"

Jessica fumed. "It's bad enough that she's moving in on my cheerleading domain. Now she has to go after my guy."

"Well, I'm sure that if Ken is as great as you say he is, you'll have nothing to worry about," Lila said. "Although Heather *is* dressed rather seductively. I guess he'd have to be superhuman to resist her charms."

Jessica scrutinized Heather from across the pool. She was wearing high heels, a supertight pink miniskirt, and a white halter top, and her long blond hair was curlier and fuller than ever.

"First of all, Ken has already told me that he's not the least bit interested in Heather," Jessica said. "And I think Heather is wearing about the tackiest outfit I've ever seen."

"But you have to admit she's got an awesome body," Lila said. "I mean, I'd kill for legs like that."

Jessica glared at Lila. "I think Ken is smart enough to see past a good pair of legs," she said, trying to sound calm.

"I kind of like her," Lila said. "Do you really think she's that bad?"

"I knew she was bad news since the first moment I laid eyes on her," Jessica said. "I can't stand that girl."

"So I guess you're really excited about being a cocaptain with her," Lila said sarcastically.

"I *hate* the idea of being a cocaptain with her," Jessica said, feeling her face turn red. "I've put too much work in the squad to let some *interloper* take it away from me."

Heather and Ken were still talking to each other, and it was more than Jessica could take. Her dislike for Heather was stronger than ever, but she had a sudden feeling of power. *I'm not going to let her destroy what I've worked so hard to create,* Jessica thought. *I'm going to show her who's in charge, and I'm going to start right now.*

Jessica walked over to Ken and Heather, ready to do battle. "What a cute little bitty skirt you're wearing," Jessica said, smiling.

"Thanks," Heather said, posing with one hip out by the side of the pool. "I just bought it at the mall today. It was hard to find anything halfway decent there. This was the only thing that wasn't totally hideous."

"I know what you mean," Jessica lied, flashing Heather a bright smile. "Come on, Ken, why don't we dance?"

"Great idea," Ken said.

Jessica slid her arm through Ken's and as she did she "accidentally" bumped into Heather. Heather, teetering on her high heels, tried to regain her balance—she even reached out for Jessica so she wouldn't fall. But Jessica artfully stepped away, leaving Heather to fall into the pool with an unceremonious splash.

"Oh, Heather, I'm so sorry!" Jessica said when Heather surfaced, her long blond curls a sodden mess and mascara dripping down her face. "I'm so clumsy sometimes. And you were wearing your brand-new skirt. Oh, and Heather, a word to the wise: always were waterproof mascara to pool parties."

And with that Jessica walked away, hand in hand with Ken, enormously pleased with herself. *Now she'll know who she's doing business with,* Jessica thought triumphantly.

"Those two really look like they're getting serious," Todd said to Elizabeth as they slow-danced at the party for Robin. "If they stand any closer together, they'll have to be surgically removed."

Elizabeth didn't need to have it pointed out to her that her sister and Ken were extremely cozy on the dance floor. She'd barely taken her eyes from them since they'd started dancing. "Can we not talk about Jessica and Ken?" Elizabeth asked.

"Sure, but I thought you'd be happy about the two of them being together," Todd said. "It's pretty neat that my best friend and your twin sister are a couple. We could have a lot of fun together double-dating and stuff. As you know, I'm not crazy about Jessica, but with you and Ken there, it could be cool."

"I *am* excited about their being together, but I just want to concentrate on you and me," Elizabeth said, putting her head against Todd's chest. The more Todd talked about Ken and Jessica, the guiltier Elizabeth felt. But Elizabeth didn't know which feeling was stronger—her guilt or her jealousy.

Elizabeth looked at her sister, whose face was right up against Ken's. They were speaking to each other in an extremely intimate way, and Elizabeth was dying to know what they were talking about. They were so wrapped up in each other that they barely even moved to the music.

Elizabeth couldn't stand it any longer. She started to move Todd gently in Jessica and Ken's direction. When the two couples were right next to each other, Elizabeth saw that her sister and Ken were about to kiss.

"Why don't we change partners?" Elizabeth suggested suddenly. She ignored the irritated look Jessica shot her way.

"That's a great idea," Todd said. "Hey, Ken, can I cut in?"

Suddenly Elizabeth was standing in front of Ken, and she felt her heart pumping ten times its normal rate.

"How've you been, Liz?" Ken asked awkwardly. He was still avoiding Elizabeth's gaze, just as he'd done the night before when he'd come to pick up Jessica for their date.

"Fine," Elizabeth murmured. Now that she'd arranged to dance with Ken, she was unable even to speak to him.

What's wrong with me? She felt her palms get sweaty as Ken put one hand on her waist and another on her shoulder. They started to sway slowly to the music, when Elizabeth felt as if she was going to be sick. *This is too weird,* she realized. It was almost harder for her to be close to Ken like that in front of everyone, unable to talk about their shared secret, than it was to see him at a distance.

"I'm sorry, Ken, but I have to go." Before Ken had a chance to respond, Elizabeth ran into the house and headed for the bathroom, where she wiped away the tear that had fallen down her cheek.

"I love that dress you're wearing," Ken said to Jessica after most people had left Amy's party. They were sitting close together on the edge of the pool, dangling their feet in the water. Only a few couples, Robin's close friends and their dates, were left, and the only light came from inside the pool. "It's a great color on you."

"Thanks, I've had it forever," Jessica lied. She certainly wasn't going to tell Ken she'd bought it just for him. They'd had only one real date so far, and she didn't want to scare him away.

"This was a great party," Ken said. "I love dancing with you. You're a terrific dancer."

"I do like to dance," Jessica said. "I felt terrible about Heather falling in the pool like that. I guess I was just a little overeager to get to the dance floor."

"She seemed pretty upset," Ken said. "She went home right after that."

"Well," Jessica said, "I just hope she realizes it was an accident and doesn't think I did it on purpose."

"Why would she think that?" Ken asked.

"I don't think she likes me very much," Jessica said in her most innocent voice. "She's a little competitive with me."

"That's understandable," Ken said. "You *are* really popular and pretty. I'm sure a lot of girls are jealous of you."

"You really say the sweetest things," Jessica said.

"I just call it like I see it," Ken said, kissing Jessica on the cheek.

"Speaking of saying things, what did you say to my sister tonight?" Jessica asked.

Jessica noticed that Ken's whole body seemed to tense up, and he moved away from Jessica a few inches. "Nothing," he said abruptly and defensively. "I didn't say anything to her. Why do you ask?"

"I'm not suggesting that you said anything mean to her," Jessica said, confused by his reaction. "It's just that she ran off while she was dancing with you. She looked upset about something. I just thought you might know what she was upset about."

"I have no idea," Ken said. "Maybe you should ask her."

Ken's whole demeanor was suddenly different. He seemed nervous and upset, and Jessica couldn't figure out what she'd said that had got him so agitated.

"Maybe she and Todd were having a fight or something," Jessica said. "Whatever it is, I'm sure it's not very interesting. I love my sister, but she *is* pretty boring."

Ken was staring off in the distance, and he seemed miles away. "I wouldn't know," Ken said quietly.

"She's been kind of weird lately," Jessica said.

"How do you mean?" Ken asked.

"She keeps warning me about you," Jessica said.

"Warning you how? What did she say about me?" Ken's attention was focused back on Jessica, and he seemed intensely interested all of a sudden.

Maybe he's just worried that I'm going to stop liking him, Jessica reasoned. *He doesn't want Elizabeth to say anything negative about him that would turn me away from him.*

"She's just protective of me," Jessica said. "She didn't say anything bad about you, don't worry. Elizabeth would warn me about *anyone* I was dating right now. She doesn't want to see me get hurt again like I was by Jeremy."

"Oh, well, she doesn't have anything to worry about," Ken said, putting his arm around Jessica and breathing a sigh of relief. "I should get you home. It's after midnight, and we don't want your sister worrying about you."

Jessica knew she should have Ken take her home, because for some reason she felt unusually tired, and her shoulders had that aching feeling she got whenever she was about to get sick. She knew she ought to get some sleep, because getting sick now was the last thing she needed, but she couldn't bear to leave Ken.

Let her worry, Jessica thought as Ken kissed

her on the lips. Jessica was in heaven. She never wanted their kiss to end.

"I can't believe you're leaving tomorrow morning," Annie said as tears streamed down her face. "This all feels so sudden."

"I know, I feel like my whole life is changing overnight," Robin said between little sobs. "I don't want to say good-bye, though. Let's just all say we'll see each other later—kind of pretend like this isn't happening."

Robin was saying good night to her girlfriends after the party while their dates waited outside in their cars.

"Just think of all the good stuff you have to look forward to," Jessica said.

"Like what?" Robin asked, sniffing.

"Like all the boys to have crushes on, and all the new stores to discover," Jessica said.

"But I'm going to miss my friends like crazy," Robin said.

"You'll make new friends instantly," Amy said.

"They won't be like you guys," Robin said. "They'll never be as much fun."

"We love you, Robin," Annie said as everyone gave Robin a big group hug.

"I love you guys," Robin said, and the tears really started to flow. "Let's always stay in touch."

Jessica was glad Heather wasn't there to spoil

that moment. *Good thing I sent her running home in those wet clothes,* she thought. *Otherwise, I'm sure she'd be here faking her own tears.*

"We'll always be here for you," Jeannie said. "You can come back for big parties and proms. We'll just pretend like you're going on a long vacation."

Jessica wished she *could* pretend. *Then Heather wouldn't be my cocaptain, and my life as I know it wouldn't be ruined!* she thought.

Elizabeth was lying on a lounge chair by the Wakefields' pool on Sunday afternoon while Jessica worked on her cheers nearby. It was a beautiful afternoon, and Elizabeth was determined to stay in a good mood. She'd jumped out of bed that morning telling herself that she just had to forget about Ken. Whatever happened between him and Jessica was beyond her control. Besides, she already had a terrific boyfriend whom she loved.

She'd given herself the opportunity to be close to Ken the night before, and she'd blown it. *Maybe I don't like Ken as much as I thought,* Elizabeth decided as she closed her eyes and enjoyed feeling the sun against her skin.

"I'm coming up with the best cheers I've ever done," Jessica said, startling Elizabeth out of her thoughts. "They're going to blow Heather out of the water. I've decided that I'm not going to let her get me down."

"That's great," Elizabeth said. Because Elizabeth had been feeling guilty about the jealous feelings she'd been having toward her sister, she was glad that things were going better for her in terms of her cheerleading. "That sounds like the Jessica Wakefield we all know and love."

"I'm working on a cheer that has a salsa influence," Jessica said. "Here—watch."

Elizabeth watched as Jessica showed her her new routine. Elizabeth was about as bored by cheerleading as a person could be, but she feigned interest for Jessica's sake. She knew how important cheerleading was to her. Sometimes Elizabeth worried that it was a little *too* important.

"Bravo," Elizabeth said, clapping her hands. "That was great."

"Could you tell that it had a salsa influence?" Jessica asked. "I tried to add a few dance steps and rhythms that I saw in that movie I rented about salsa dancing."

"I definitely see the salsa influence," Elizabeth lied. She couldn't tell the difference between one silly cheer and the next, but she didn't need to tell Jessica that. "I'm glad you're not letting Heather bother you anymore."

"I think one reason I'm not letting Heather get to me is because of Ken," Jessica said.

Please don't talk about Ken, Elizabeth wanted to say to her sister. She'd been trying so hard to put him out of her mind.

"What does Ken have to do with Heather?" Elizabeth asked, not sure that she really wanted to know the answer.

"He's just so incredible," Jessica said, bending down to stretch. "On Friday night we had a long talk about Heather and cheerleading, and he really made me feel confident about my cheerleading abilities. He also made me realize that Heather is really nothing special."

"What did he say exactly?"

"He just said that he didn't think Heather was all that pretty," Jessica said. "In fact, he said she was boring looking."

Elizabeth felt relieved—not because of Jessica's interest in Ken, but because of her own. She had been a little jealous on Friday night when Heather was flirting with him at Casey's. *But I shouldn't feel relieved,* she told herself. *I shouldn't feel anything at all. I just decided I don't care about him anymore.*

"So it sounds like you and Ken are good friends," Elizabeth said, trying to sound cool. "I mean, it sounds like maybe you're *just* friends."

"We *are* friends," Jessica said, getting that annoying, dreamy look in her eye she'd been getting every time she mentioned Ken lately. "But the really wonderful thing is that we're also *more* than just friends. In fact, I think we're getting pretty serious."

"One date is not exactly serious," Elizabeth said. She knew she was bursting Jessica's bubble, but she couldn't help it.

"That was just the beginning. Last night, when we were slow-dancing—and I mean *slow*-dancing—Ken asked me out again for this coming Friday," Jessica said as she leaped into a cartwheel.

"What are you going to do?" Elizabeth knew that she should stop asking questions for her own good, but she couldn't.

"He wouldn't say," Jessica said, coming back up into a standing position. "He just said he wanted to do something extra special. I can't wait. I wish it was tomorrow. I don't know how I'll get through the entire week!"

"Jess, I really think you need to watch out," Elizabeth warned. "I mean, I'm really happy that he asked you out again, but I just think you should be careful."

"Ken is so wonderful," Jessica said. "Of all people he's the last person who would ever hurt anyone. I'm surprised you would doubt that. He *is* Todd's best friend, after all."

"I know that, but sometimes you never really

know about a person," Elizabeth said. "You had no idea that Jeremy was going to turn out to be the kind of jerk that he is. Sometimes appearances are deceiving."

"But it's not like I just met Ken," Jessica said. "I've known him since kindergarten, and so have you, for that matter. I thought you'd be really happy for me."

"I *am* happy for you," Elizabeth lied. "I just think you should take it slowly, that's all. Also, I just don't see how you and Ken could ever work as a couple."

"Why is that?"

"You just seem so different from each other," Elizabeth said. "I mean, you're a lot more fun than he is. He's a pretty serious guy."

"Haven't you ever heard the expression 'Opposites attract'?" Jessica asked. "Besides, look at you and me."

"What about us?"

"Well, we're both totally different and we get along—most of the time," Jessica said.

"Just watch out," Elizabeth said. "It might seem great now, but anything could happen."

"I really wish you'd stop raining on my parade," Jessica said, picking up her pom-poms. "All I want is a little excitement about the fact that I've found a new guy that I really like. Instead all I'm getting is negative warnings."

Jessica walked back into the house, and once again Elizabeth felt terrible about how she'd discouraged Jessica from being with Ken. She was still so confused about her own feelings for him. One minute she thought she was over him, but then, as soon as Jessica started talking about him, she realized that maybe she wasn't. *How am I ever going to know how I really feel about Ken?* she asked herself. *Would I even be thinking about him at all if Jessica weren't seeing him?*

"We gotta fight—fight—with all our might. We gotta dance—dance—and take a chance. We gotta win—win—and do a spin," Jessica wrote on Sunday night after dinner. She'd been sitting at the kitchen table, writing down words to the new cheer she'd just made up while her mother finished the dishes. She put her hand on her throat and felt that her glands were a little swollen. Every time she swallowed, it hurt, but she had too much on her mind to think about being sick.

She looked up from her notebook and drifted into a daydream about leading her squad to the state championship. The daydream didn't end there, however. Not only did her squad become the state champions, they went on to the nationals and became the champions of the entire country.

The best part of the daydream was that Heather

was disqualified from the squad because none of the judges liked her. When Jessica was being photographed and interviewed by dozens of journalists, Ken came running up to proclaim his love.

Jessica looked over to the crowd and saw the stricken Heather, sobbing her eyes out. . . .

"Jessica, honey," Mrs. Wakefield said. "Are you OK?"

"Yes, I'm fine," Jessica said, quickly snapping out of her daydream. "Why do you ask?"

"You've been coughing," Mrs. Wakefield said. "Maybe you're coming down with something."

"I'm as fit as a fiddle," Jessica said.

"Well, let's make sure you stay that way." Mrs. Wakefield put a vitamin-C tablet and a glass of water in front of Jessica on the table. "I want you to start taking vitamin C every four hours to make sure you don't get really sick."

"Mom, I'm not getting sick," Jessica groaned.

"Jessica . . ." Mrs. Wakefield warned.

"OK, OK," she said, gulping down the pill. *I guess the more vitamins, the better. After all, I need all my strength to lead us to the nationals! Sometimes dreams do come true!*

Chapter 8

"What's going on here?" Jessica asked Heather on Monday afternoon, her hands on her hips. "Practice isn't supposed to start for another ten minutes!"

"Oh, I thought I told Annie to tell you," Heather said, widening her eyes in an effort to look innocent.

"Tell me what?" Jessica fumed.

"I called practice for three thirty instead of four today," Heather said, smiling. "I thought we could use the extra half hour. The more time we spend practicing, the better we'll be. In fact, we should start practice earlier from now on."

"You're a *co*captain," Jessica said, shaking from head to toe. "It's not your job to make big decisions like that without consulting me first."

"I'm really sorry you weren't told about the change," Heather said. "I'll make sure it doesn't happen again. I was sure I told Annie to tell you, but I must have been mistaken."

"Jessica, look at these great pins Heather gave us," Helen said excitedly as she ran up to Jessica holding out a little pin in the shape of a cheerleading megaphone. "She gave one to each of us."

Jessica looked down at the miniature pin and wanted to rip it off Helen's shirt and throw it at Heather.

"Aren't they adorable?" Annie asked, beaming at Heather.

"What's the occasion?" Jessica asked, trying to remain calm.

"I just wanted to give the girls a little something to celebrate our new working relationship," Heather said. "Here's yours."

Jessica took the pin from Heather's palm and clasped it in her own. She walked away a few feet, and when nobody was looking, she threw it onto the ground and stomped it into the dirt with her sneaker. *That's what I think of your adorable little pin.*

"OK, I've worked out a really exciting new cheer that I think you're all going to love," Jessica said, trying to swallow her anger about Heather's starting practice without her and trying to buy the team's affection. "I want you all to watch closely while—"

Jessica turned around to face the girls and stopped in her tracks. They were all in some kind of formation, with Heather leading them.

"Jessica, look at this new cheer Heather was just in the middle of teaching us," Jeannie said. "I know you're going to love it."

"But I was just about to teach a new cheer," Jessica said. "I worked on it all weekend!"

"You go ahead and teach your little cheer," Heather said, moving to the side.

"But we were just in the middle of learning your cheer, Heather," Maria said. "It was just getting to the really fun part."

"Yeah, I want to know what comes next," Helen said. "I was really starting to feel like I was dancing instead of cheering."

"Jessica wants to teach her cheer," Heather said. "Maybe we can work on this one another time."

Jessica looked over at the girls, who had whiny, disappointed expressions on their faces.

"Please, Jessica," Jeannie pleaded. "Can't we just finish learning Heather's cheer? I promise you're going to love it."

"That's fine," Jessica said between clenched teeth. "Let's do Heather's cheer."

Jessica reluctantly moved into line with the rest of the squad. Even though she'd decided that she was going to show Heather who was in charge, she didn't want to make a big fuss about doing Heather's cheer instead of her own. After all, she didn't want Heather to have the satisfaction of thinking she was jealous of her.

Heather proceeded to teach her extremely complicated cheer, which was full of difficult steps.

"You all have to concentrate," Heather commanded them with a booming voice.

She sounds like a drill sergeant in the Marine Corps, Jessica thought. *Probably the girls will start hating her and change their minds about having her as their captain. Maybe I should just let her keep it up like this. Eventually, they'll be voting to kick her out of Sweet Valley and back to where she came from.*

"Sandy, you're moving around like a cow," Heather scolded. "Pretend like you're dancing. Try to have a little more fun with it. You really look ridiculous."

Jessica looked over at poor Sandy, who was huffing and puffing. Her face was bright red, and sweat was pouring down her face. Jessica got more and more excited as she realized that Heather would soon fall out of favor with the squad.

"Come on, Maria," Heather shouted. "You're not getting it. Watch me."

Heather did her stupid cheer and made it look totally effortless. *Of course it's easy for her. She's the one who made it up*, Jessica thought.

"Maria, put some effort into it," Heather scolded. "You really have to work harder than that. This isn't going to cut it on a national level."

"I'm trying, Heather," Maria said, practically in tears.

"I want to see you girls sweat," Heather said. "There's no way our football team will win if you get out on the field with that kind of low energy."

And there's no way you're going to win "most favored captain" if you keep yelling at everyone like that, Jessica thought gleefully.

"That was a great dinner," Elizabeth said to Todd. "Your mom's such a good cook."

It was Tuesday night, and Elizabeth and Todd were sitting in the Wilkinses' den on the couch. Their schoolbooks were next to them, but they hadn't cracked them open yet.

"Mom's the best cook in Sweet Valley," Todd said proudly, pulling Elizabeth closer to him. "They love it when you come over. I think Mom and Dad love you almost as much as I do, if that's possible."

"I love them too," Elizabeth said. "Your dad's hysterical. I know where you got your sense of humor."

"Yeah, he's a pretty crazy guy," Todd said, moving even closer to Elizabeth. "And you're making *me* crazy right now." Todd started to kiss Elizabeth passionately on the lips.

"Hey, I thought we were supposed to be studying," Elizabeth said, wriggling away.

"I'm studying you," Todd said, whispering in her ear.

Elizabeth wiped her ear with her hand. The sweeter Todd was being, the more he was bothering her. The last thing she felt like doing was fooling around.

"Come on, I have a lot of homework to do." Elizabeth slid away from Todd on the couch and opened up her American-history book.

"You've been more studious than usual lately," Todd said, sliding back toward her. "I mean, I know you're a serious student and everything, but usually you still have time to have fun."

"I guess I just have more work these days," Elizabeth said quickly. "Work that I have to do *now*."

"OK, I'll try to control myself, but it's not going to be easy," Todd said, opening his calculus book. "You're irresistible tonight. I love what you're wearing."

Elizabeth looked down to see what was so special about what she was wearing. She had on a pair of blue jeans and a pink cotton T-shirt. Her hair was pulled back in a white headband, and she wasn't wearing makeup. *He certainly is easy to please,* she thought, somehow annoyed by the fact.

They both read their books for about five minutes; then Todd closed his book and grabbed Elizabeth's.

"What do you think you're doing?" Elizabeth asked.

"Taking a study break," Todd said, kissing her neck.

Elizabeth closed her eyes and let Todd continue to kiss her. It felt good at first, but suddenly, before she knew it, she had replaced Todd in her mind's eye with Ken.

"What's wrong?" Todd asked.

"I thought you said we were going to study," Elizabeth said angrily. "I came over here because I thought I'd get some work done, but you're making that impossible." Elizabeth hated the way her voice sounded. Todd looked like a wounded puppy dog. *Why am I being so mean to him?*

"I thought you came over to see me and have dinner with my parents," Todd said sadly. "I'm sorry you're not having a good time. Are you mad at me about something? I mean, besides trying to kiss you?"

Elizabeth was consumed with guilt. But instead of being nicer to Todd because of her guilt, she just seemed to get meaner and meaner. She was mad at herself, but she was taking it out on poor Todd, who had no idea what was going on.

"I'm not mad at you about anything," Elizabeth said, hating herself. "I think I should just go home." Before Todd could say anything, Elizabeth was on her way out the door. *I'm going to destroy this relationship if I keep acting like this*, Elizabeth thought. *How much more will Todd be able to take of my weird behavior?*

What are those two talking about? Jessica wondered as she walked up the front steps of school on Wednesday morning and saw Lila standing with Heather.

"Thanks for last night," Lila was saying to Heather. "That was a blast."

"I'm so glad you guys came," Heather said. "We'll have to do it again soon."

"Good morning, Jessica," Heather said cheerfully. "You're looking really pretty today."

And you're acting as fake and two-faced as ever, Jessica felt like saying.

Jessica noticed that Lila suddenly looked uncomfortable. She blushed slightly and started twirling a strand of her long brown hair with her finger.

"Hi, Jessica," Lila muttered. "I didn't see you come up the stairs."

"Are you ready for the big game this afternoon?" Heather asked Jessica.

"As ready as ever," Jessica said energetically. *And ready to show you that you can't push around Jessica Wakefield*, she thought.

"I'll see you guys later," Heather said as she hurried into the school.

Jessica turned to look at Lila, who was avoiding eye contact with her. "What were you two talking about?" Jessica asked suspiciously.

"I forgot," Lila said nervously. "I'm sure it was nothing interesting. We need to go inside. We're going to be late for homeroom."

"I don't care if we miss homeroom all together," Jessica said. "You were saying something to Heather about last night. You said whatever it was was a blast."

"Oh, right," Lila said, obviously pretending as if she were just then remembering what they'd been talking about. "A couple of us went over to Heather's last night for dinner," she said quickly.

For a minute Jessica thought she must have heard Lila incorrectly. It couldn't be possible that her best friend went to Heather's house. Could it? "Can you be a little more specific? Who went there and why?"

"Annie, Amy, and a couple of guys and I went

over to her house," Lila said. "She had a little dinner party. Sort of a 'get acquainted' thing."

"What guys?" Jessica asked.

"Barry, Bruce, Rick, and Ken," Lila almost whispered the last name.

"Ken Matthews?" Jessica asked in disbelief. "What did you guys do? How could you go there? Why didn't she invite me?"

"Calm down," Lila said. "It was really nothing. We just ate dinner out by her pool. Apparently, at her old school she and her friends used to give dinner parties all the time. She wanted to do that here. And as for your not being invited, she talked to me about that."

"I'm dying to know what she had to say," Jessica fumed.

"She said she would have loved to have invited you, but she had the feeling you didn't really like her," Lila explained.

"Gee, I wonder how she got that idea," Jessica asked sarcastically.

"I'm sorry you didn't come. You would have had a good time. Her house is amazing. It's almost as big as mine, and she has a tennis court like I do."

"Well, I'm sure she's really sorry I wasn't there," Jessica said, getting more agitated by the minute.

"She was," Lila insisted. "She's upset that you

don't like her. She even asked me if I would put in a good word for her because she'd like to be your friend."

"That'll be the day," Jessica said. "How could you go to her party? You're supposed to be my best friend and you know I don't like Heather. You could have shown some loyalty."

"Just because you don't like somebody doesn't mean I can't like them," Lila said. "You and I are still best buddies, but we don't have to have all the same friends."

"You honestly like Heather?" Jessica asked.

"Yes, I do," Lila said. "And I think you'd like her too if you'd just give her a chance. She's really cool. She made a fabulous dinner, and she really created a cool ambience, with candles and everything. She's very sophisticated."

"Excuse me while I throw up," Jessica said. It was truly amazing to her that even her best friend was being seduced by the fake charms of her enemy. "So tell me what Ken was like last night."

"There's not much to tell," Lila said.

"Come on, how did he act with Heather? Were they flirting? Did they sit next to each other at dinner?"

"They did sit next to each other, but it didn't look like anything was really going on between them," Lila said. "They were just being friendly."

"How friendly?" Jessica asked.

"You're starting to sound paranoid," Lila said. "You have nothing to worry about. He asked *you* out for Friday night, not Heather. Now, can we please go to homeroom? We're already five minutes late."

Jessica walked into the school feeling lousy. *It's not enough that Heather has to try to steal my squad—now she's trying to steal my new boyfriend and my best friend!*

"Sweet success!" Heather yelled at the top of her lungs, leading the cheerleaders in her victory cheer. Then she jumped on top of the pyramid the cheerleaders had made, and the crowd went wild. It was Wednesday afternoon, and the Gladiators had just beaten Whitman in an overtime game.

Every time Jessica had started to lead a cheer, Heather had practically jumped in front of her and started off on one of her own. And what made it worse was that she'd choreographed practically every cheer so that it featured her. At the end of the cheers Heather would finish it off with a splashy flip or running splits.

The worst part was that the fans seemed to love Heather and her routines. Jessica didn't think she'd ever heard them respond to the cheering squad so enthusiastically. She was in a terrible mood.

"That was amazing," Lila said to the girls after the game.

"Your squad has never been so good," Winston Egbert exclaimed. "I thought the bleachers were going to collapse—the fans were going wild!"

Yes, we have been this good, Jessica wanted to say. *We were ten times this good two Fridays ago before anyone even knew who Heather Mallone was!*

Even though Heather had once again stolen the spotlight, Jessica took some comfort in the fact that she was still cocaptain and their squad was getting a lot of attention. Jessica would at least get some of the credit for their strong performance.

Jessica saw a handsome reporter from the local newspaper coming toward her with a notebook and pen. "I understand you're the captain of the cheerleading squad," he said to Jessica. "I was wondering if you could answer a few questions about the new cheers you were doing out there today. You were certainly a crowd pleaser."

"Actually, I'm the person who made up all those cheers," Heather said, jumping right in front of Jessica.

"And what's your name?" the reporter asked eagerly.

"Heather Mallone. I'm one of the cocaptains. I'm new to Sweet Valley."

Jessica was so livid she couldn't even speak. She just stood there with her mouth open.

"How long have you been here?" the reporter asked.

"Just a little over a week," Heather said in that annoying, flirtatious voice Jessica had heard before.

"What a great story," the reporter said. "In just one week you've come to town and turned this squad around. I have to go to a lot of football and basketball games for my job, and I must say, I've never seen better cheerleaders."

"Why, thank you," Heather gushed. "It's going to take a while to really get these girls into shape, but we're off to a good start. Rome wasn't built in a day, after all."

Rome wasn't built in a day! Jessica repeated in her head. That was about the dumbest thing she'd ever heard. How dare Heather put down the squad like that to a reporter? This was the last straw. *From now on it's back to the Jessica Wakefield way of doing things,* Jessica decided as she stormed off the field.

Chapter 9

"That's really turned into a nasty cough," Mrs. Wakefield said to Jessica on Thursday morning at breakfast. "And you don't look well at all."

"I'm fine," Jessica said, though the truth was that she was feeling lousy. Her throat was so sore, she couldn't bear even to swallow her orange juice. "I'm probably just coughing from yelling so much at the game yesterday."

"Your squad did a great job," Elizabeth said. "As you know, I don't usually pay much attention to cheerleading, but I did notice that the crowds were more enthusiastic than usual at yesterday's game. You must be really proud."

"Don't you go jumping on the Heather bandwagon along with everyone else," Jessica said. "I'll really be in trouble if my own sister sides with her."

"What are you talking about?" Elizabeth asked.

"Let's just say that yesterday was the Heather Mallone show," Jessica said. "She took all the credit for the work the squad's been doing all year. She's only been in Sweet Valley for a little over one week."

"Jessica, your cheeks are all flushed!" Mrs. Wakefield said. "I think you're running a temperature."

"Don't worry, Mom," Jessica insisted. "I just turn red whenever I talk about Heather."

Mrs. Wakefield felt Jessica's forehead with the back of her hand and shook her head. "You're burning up. I don't even need a thermometer to tell me that you're running a temperature."

"It's just hot in here," Jessica said, even though she was feeling chilled, the way she always did when she had a fever.

"No, it isn't," Mr. Wakefield said, looking over the top of his newspaper. "It's actually a little cool in here."

"You have a fever, and you're staying home from school today," Mrs. Wakefield said.

"Jessica, you're usually thrilled to stay home from school," Elizabeth pointed out. "You can watch your silly soap operas all day."

"I can't stay home from school today," Jessica protested. "It's out of the question."

"I'm sorry, but this isn't open for discussion,"

Mrs. Wakefield said. "There's no way you're going to school today, and that's that. Elizabeth, honey, could you pass me the marmalade, please?"

"You don't understand," Jessica pleaded. "I can't let that horrible Heather person lead practice this afternoon without me. She's trying to take over the squad, and she's about to succeed."

"You do look pretty rotten, Jessica," Elizabeth said. "And I heard you coughing for most of the night last night."

"But I feel perfectly fine," Jessica said, annoyed with her sister. "It's not fair."

"You can watch TV all day long," Mrs. Wakefield said. "And I'll even make you a nice fruit salad before I go to work."

"And I'll bring you home a hot-fudge sundae from the Dairi Burger on my way home from school," Elizabeth offered.

"I guess I don't have any say in this," Jessica said.

"You're right. You don't," Mr. Wakefield said.

"Feel better," Elizabeth said, leaping up from the table. "I'll see you later."

"Thanks for nothing," Jessica yelled after her. "You've succeeded in helping to ruin my day!"

Elizabeth sat on the bleachers on Thursday afternoon watching football practice. She was not a football fan, and she should have been in the *Oracle* office working on an article, but there was something she had to do that was more important.

Number seventy-five. That was Ken's number. Even though he was wearing a helmet, Elizabeth couldn't keep her eyes off him. His great personality was evident even at a distance. He was making the other players laugh, and when one of the guys fumbled the ball, Ken put his arm around him, reassuring him that it was OK.

She felt bad about helping to convince her mother that Jessica should stay home from school that day, but she knew it would give her a chance to talk to Ken without Jessica's getting in the way. *If Jessica's still sick tomorrow, she won't be able to go on her second date with Ken,* she thought hopefully. It was awful to wish for her sister's ill health, but she just couldn't help it.

Elizabeth didn't even know what she was going to say to Ken. Maybe if she just spent some time alone with him, she'd be able to tell what her true feelings were. She also wanted to find out what his feelings were for her.

Just watching him during the practice made her remember how much she used to like him. But was it just the memory of their time together that she was holding on to? If Todd had never come back from Vermont and they'd continued to see each other, would things have ended naturally? Would they still be together now? Would Ken be interested in Jessica?

Maybe I should just leave now, Elizabeth thought as practice ended. *No,* she thought resolutely, *I have to settle this once and for all.*

When practice was over, Elizabeth walked down to the field and waited for Ken to come by on his way to the locker room.

"Ken!"

Ken was undoing the hook of his helmet and taking it off when he turned around and saw Elizabeth. He looked surprised and startled. His face was all red from practicing, and his blond hair was matted down from the helmet, but he looked more handsome than ever.

"Elizabeth," he said under his breath. "What are you doing here? Todd's not here, if you're looking for him." Ken looked off into the distance, averting his eyes from Elizabeth.

Just hearing Todd's name made her feel guilty, and all the things she wanted to say to Ken escaped her. He looked more nervous to see Elizabeth than she was to see him. This was a bad idea, she thought, suddenly feeling very foolish.

"Do you know where he is?" Elizabeth asked. She knew she sounded cold and distant, but she couldn't help it.

"No. No idea," Ken muttered.

"OK, thanks," Elizabeth quickly said, then rushed off, feeling ridiculous.

"Elizabeth?" Ken yelled after her.

Elizabeth stopped and turned around. Her heart was pounding. *This is it*, she thought. *The moment I've been waiting for. He's going to tell me now that he's really not interested in Jessica but he's just trying to get to me, or that he's still in love with me but he can't hurt his best friend.*

"Yes?" Elizabeth asked, holding her breath.

"Uh, say hi to Jessica for me," he said awkwardly, almost as if that wasn't what he had intended to say. "Tell her I hope she feels better."

Ken's words stung her ears. "Sure thing," she practically whispered, and turned back around.

He doesn't care about me at all, she thought as she walked off the field. *He acted like nothing had ever happened between us. Like all the kissing and laughing and late-night talks never happened. So I have to forget him, too. That's exactly what I have to do—forget what we shared and just concentrate on Todd. As hard as it's going to be, I have to let him go.*

Chapter 10

It was Thursday afternoon, and Jessica was lying on the couch in the family room watching her favorite soap opera, *The Bold and the Beautiful.* She'd been watching television all day. She was feeling a little groggy and sleepy, and as much as she loved her soaps, she was starting to get bored.

She looked at the digital clock on the VCR and saw that cheerleading practice was probably over. What a relief. She hated thinking about Heather leading the girls without her. The big game was in only two days, and she was determined not to let Heather steal the show the way she had at the last game. *Heather's moment in the sun is over,* Jessica thought as the cordless phone that was right next to her on the couch started ringing.

"Hello," Jessica said into the receiver as she hit the mute button on the remote control. She heard someone crying on the other line, but she couldn't tell who it was or what they were saying. "Who is this?"

"Jessica, it's Maria," she said between small sobs.

"Maria? What's wrong? Are you hurt? Where are you?"

"I'm OK physically but . . ." Her voice trailed off.

"OK, take a deep breath and tell me what's going on," Jessica instructed her calmly.

After a long silence Maria finally spoke. "It's Heather."

Jessica bristled at the mention of the name. "What has she done *now*?"

"She kicked Sandy and me off the squad," Maria blurted out. "I feel so terrible. I love being a cheerleader. It's so embarrassing. I never want to show my face in school again. Nobody gets kicked off the cheering squad. I feel like a total loser."

"Slow down!" Jessica sat up straight and threw the remote control she was holding onto the floor. "Heather kicked you off the squad? Start from the beginning."

"Heather said we just weren't working hard enough and that we'd make everyone else look bad in the routines. She said that everyone had to be at the same level or else there was no point in having a cheering squad at all."

"But she can't do that!" Jessica felt her temperature going up a degree every second.

"She already did it," Maria cried.

"You and Sandy are great cheerleaders, and all the girls on the squad agree. I'm sure they must have put up a strong protest."

"That's the worst part," Maria said, sniffling. "They all stood by Heather's decision. I thought they were my friends, but I guess I was wrong."

"They *are* your friends," Jessica said. "It doesn't make sense. Why would they side with Heather against you guys? They barely even know her."

"Heather's convinced them that if they do everything she says, they'll make it to the nationals. She gave this whole speech about how when she saw our squad for the first time at the Big Mesa game, she didn't think we stood a chance of even making it to the state finals."

"But we were better than ever at the Big Mesa game," Jessica cried. *And that was the last time that I was really in control of the squad,* Jessica thought, remembering how happy she'd been after that game.

"She said that after Wednesday's game, she realized that we actually had some potential," Maria said.

"Of course she'd say that. That's when she was jumping in front of everyone and making it *her* squad," Jessica said bitterly.

"She said the squad had to make sacrifices if they wanted to get anywhere, and that if Sandy and I stayed on the squad, we'd hold them back."

"So she sacrificed you and Sandy! That girl has some nerve!"

"You don't think I'm a bad cheerleader, do you?" Maria asked, then started to cry even harder.

"Of course not," Jessica said. She was suddenly more awake and clearheaded than ever. "This is just another one of her ways to try to take control away from me. Don't worry, I'm not going to let her get away with this!"

"Who do you think you are?" Jessica yelled at Heather on Friday morning. Heather was standing at her locker, and Jessica slammed it shut.

"I don't understand the question," Heather said calmly. She smiled at Jessica as if her behavior were perfectly normal.

"I see through that fake sweetness act that everybody else is buying, so you can lose that stupid smile."

"I'm afraid I don't know what you're talking about," Heather said with an innocent expression on her face.

"You know exactly what I'm talking about," Jessica said. "You have no right to fire people from the squad without consulting me first. What you did yesterday was completely out of line, and you're not getting away with it."

"Oh, you mean letting Sandy and Maria go," Heather said, pushing a strand of curly hair behind her ear.

"Sandy and Maria were on the squad long before you arrived in Sweet Valley, and they're going to be on it long after you're gone," Jessica said. She hadn't let off steam like that in a long time, and it actually felt good. Speaking her mind—especially when someone had crossed her—was one of the things she did best.

"Relax, Jessica," Heather said smugly. "You're getting yourself way too worked up. You don't want to make yourself sick again."

"Don't tell me to relax," Jessica said. Jessica hated being told to relax, especially by someone she couldn't stand. "I would never have given approval for you to kick Maria and Sandy off the squad."

"Your loyalty is really sweet, but even *you* have to admit that those girls just aren't up to speed," Heather said. "They were really an embarrassment to the squad."

"That's the most ridiculous thing I've ever heard,"

Jessica fumed. "They're both fantastic cheerleaders, and besides, that's not even the point."

"What *is* the point?" Heather asked impatiently as if she were late for an important appointment.

"The point is that you can't do something like that on your own without talking to me about it first," Jessica said.

"Actually, you're wrong about that," Heather said. "According to the guidelines and regulations of the Sweet Valley cheerleading rule book, if one captain is gone, the other captain has the authority to make any decision she sees fit at the time."

Heather pulled out the book and opened it to the page she was referring to.

"I've never seen this before," Jessica said, reading the page. "And besides, I was only gone for one practice."

"Sorry, but it doesn't matter if you were gone for one day or one month," Heather said, shaking her head. "You weren't there when I made the decision, and it's too late for you to do anything about it."

"I'm sure none of the other girls are going to go along with this, and you're not going to have much of a squad if everyone quits," Jessica said.

"Go ahead and talk to the other girls on the squad. They all agree with me."

"You haven't heard the last of this," Jessica

said, throwing the rule book at Heather's feet. "You're going to be sorry you ever set foot in this school."

"I'll see you at practice, Jessica," Heather said, turning on her heel to walk away. "Oh, and try not to be late again. Toodles!"

OK, this is war! Jessica thought as she stood trembling with anger. *Those girls are coming back on our squad, and Heather is going to be history!* Jessica felt sure that if she just talked rationally to the rest of the squad, they'd all stand by her. *It's Wakefield against Mallone now!*

"That's really rotten about getting cut from the cheering squad," Winston said to Maria on Friday. They were eating lunch with Elizabeth and Todd, and the lunchroom was buzzing with excitement as everyone talked about their weekend plans.

"I still can't believe it," Maria said. "When I went to practice yesterday, that was the last thing I expected to happen."

"That Heather Mallone seems like trouble," Elizabeth had to admit. She hated to see her friend so upset even if it *was* about cheerleading. She knew how important it was to her—almost as important as it was to Jessica. "I know my sister really doesn't like her."

"Jessica's been great," Maria said. "She's as upset about all this as I am."

"With her on your side, I'm sure you'll be back on the squad in no time," Elizabeth consoled. "She almost always gets what she wants, and I know she wants you back on the squad."

"I hope you're right," Maria said, smiling weakly.

"Speaking of Jessica, I understand she and Ken have a big date tonight," Todd said. "Ken told me he'd planned something very romantic."

Elizabeth dropped her tuna sandwich onto her plate. *Don't get upset,* she told herself. *Remember, you decided to let Ken go.*

"They make a great couple," Winston said. "They really look like they go together."

And since I look just like Jessica, I guess we look like we go together as well, Elizabeth thought.

"Ken seems to be really nuts about Jessica," Todd said, putting his arm around Elizabeth. "I don't think I've ever seen him get so excited about a girl before."

Elizabeth couldn't help wondering if he'd been as excited about her as he was about Jessica. As much as she was trying not to get upset, those familiar jealous feelings were creeping up again. She had a flashback to the day before, when she'd tried to talk to Ken at the football field. He wouldn't look at her, and she felt as if she were talking to a complete stranger. Suddenly she was overcome with a heavy sadness, and she knew she wouldn't be able to sit through the rest of the meal.

"Excuse me, but I have to go do something," Elizabeth said, standing up from the table.

"Are you OK?" Todd asked. "Do you want me to come with you?"

"I'm fine," Elizabeth said. "I'll see you later."

Elizabeth rushed out of the lunchroom and out the front door of the school. She sat down on the grass and closed her eyes. It was impossible. As hard as she'd tried, she couldn't shake Ken out of her system.

"Jeannie, I'm using your brush," Jessica said as she flipped her head over and brushed it underneath. "I must have left mine in my locker."

It was Friday afternoon, and Jessica, Lila, and some of the girls from the cheerleading squad were in the school bathroom, primping between classes. Every Friday they usually convened in the bathroom at the same time. Since it was the start of the weekend, they made an extra effort to look their best. This was an especially big weekend, since the big football game was the next day and Lila was having a party that night after the game.

Jessica thought this was the perfect time to plead her case against Heather. She decided to do it calmly, presenting a rational argument in favor of keeping Maria and Sandy on the team rather than insulting Heather. She knew that the squad was totally blinded by Heather's charms, so she had to proceed cautiously. She had to wait for the right moment and bring it up in a subtle way.

"Who's got my new lipstick?" Helen asked.

"I have it," Annie said as she rubbed her lips together and studied them in the mirror. "I don't think it's my color, though."

"You're right," Lila said, pausing in the middle of applying mascara. "You look like Joan Crawford. Wipe it off and try mine. It's less harsh."

"Is it true that you're having a band at your party tomorrow night?" Amy asked Lila.

"Yeah, it's going to be great," Lila said. "They're a band from Los Angeles, and they just cut a new CD."

"I can't wait," Jeannie said.

"Are you excited about your date tonight with Ken?" Jeannie asked Jessica.

"I'm totally excited," Jessica said. Just thinking about it gave Jessica goose bumps and made her feel a little bit better after her ugly scene with Heather. "But I'm still upset about Heather's firing Maria and Sandy yesterday while I was gone."

"I guess she felt like she had to do it," Annie said. "She really seems to think we have a chance to go to the nationals. She just didn't think we'd make it with Sandy and Maria dragging us down."

"What do you all think?" Jessica asked. "I mean, Sandy and Maria are your friends. Do *you* think they're dragging down the team?"

"I don't know," Helen said sheepishly. "Maybe she's right."

"Heather seems to really know what she's doing," Jeannie said. "She's had a lot more experience in these things than I have, so I guess I trust her decision."

"But she's only been here a couple of weeks," Jessica said. "She doesn't know our school *or* our squad, and you don't know *her*. Most of you have known Maria and Sandy practically forever. How can you turn your backs on them?"

"Let's face it," Jeannie said. "We really want the chance to go to the nationals, and it seems like Heather will be able to take us there."

"Jeannie, who is your very best friend in the whole world?" Jessica asked, knowing very well what the answer was.

"Sandy's my best friend," Jeannie practically whispered.

"Exactly," Jessica said. "Sandy's your best

friend, yet you're willing to just forget about your friendship because of some person who just rode into town in a Mazda Miata telling you you can make it to the nationals."

"Jessica, I would think that you of all people would be excited to go to the nationals," Amy said, pulling her hair back in a headband. "After all, you've said in the past that going to the nationals would be a dream come true."

"It *would* be a dream come true if we did it the right way," Jessica said.

"You mean if we did it *your* way," Jeannie said.

"You guys are totally blinded by that girl's big promises," Jessica said. "She's fooled all of you. She's nothing but a self-centered, conniving troublemaker, but you can't see past all the flashy talk about the nationals and those stupid little pins she gave you." Jessica just couldn't keep the insults from flying out of her mouth. She'd tried it the other way, but it wasn't working. *Maybe tough talk is the only way to get through to these people,* Jessica thought.

"I happen to like Heather," Helen said.

"So do I," Jeannie said.

"Me too," Annie said.

"If I didn't know better, I'd say you were just jealous of Heather," Amy said.

"Jealous?" Jessica gasped. "Me, jealous of someone as two-faced and rude as Heather Mallone? I hope you're kidding. That's the second time you've said that to me, Amy, and I hope it's the last. Nothing could be further from the truth."

"I just think it would be really selfish of you to deny the rest of us a chance to follow our dream just because you have a personal problem with the one person who can help us," Amy said.

She's brainwashed them! Jessica thought, mortified. She felt as if some horrible conspiracy were going on that she couldn't stop. *How can all these girls be so mean to their friends? How can they buy into Heather's phoniness?*

"I'll see you guys at practice," Jessica said on her way out of the bathroom. "And I hope you'll think long and hard about what I've said here. Just imagine how you'd feel if you were Maria or Sandy. Think how it would be to have all your friends forget about you—and about all the hard work you'd put into cheering over the year." Jessica slammed the door behind her, feeling lonelier than she'd ever felt before.

Chapter 11

"Hey, Jessica, you look like you just found out you have six months to live," Lila said.

"That's exactly how I feel," Jessica groaned. She was sitting by herself under a tree on the front lawn of the school, holding her head in her hands. It was almost time for cheerleading practice, but Jessica didn't want to go. After that awful talk she'd had earlier in the day with the girls on the squad, she felt defeated.

Normally, she'd try to find her sister at a time like that, but Elizabeth had been acting so distant lately. Every time Jessica started to talk about Ken—the only thing that had been giving her any pleasure in the last couple of weeks—Elizabeth had to make some negative comment. She felt too far away from her to confide her feelings.

She didn't even feel like talking to Lila. After all, Lila seemed to be as big a fan of Heather's as everyone else was.

"If you don't mind, I think I want to be left alone," Jessica said, lying down on her back.

Lila, obviously choosing to ignore Jessica's wishes, sat down next to her and plucked a blade of grass, which she wrapped around her fingers. "You were great today with those girls. You really stood up for Maria and Sandy. And I want you to know that if I were on the squad, I'd be on your side."

Jessica looked at her friend and felt a flood of warm emotions. Even though Lila could be a real pain sometimes, she always came through when it really mattered. "Thanks, Lila. That really means a lot to me. I wish you *were* on the squad."

"And I agree with you about Heather," Lila said, lying down and looking up at the sky.

"You do? I thought you liked her," Jessica said. "Just the other day you were saying how cool and sophisticated you thought she was."

"Yeah, I guess I thought so at first," Lila said. "She can certainly be charming when she wants to be."

"What made you change your mind?"

"The more I've been watching her, the more I'm seeing her true personality," Lila said. "I think that it was really rotten of her to fire Maria and Sandy from the team. And I think the way she's been competing with you and turning the girls on the squad against you is the lowest."

"You have no idea how happy that makes me to hear you say that," Jessica said. "I've been feeling like I'm on a totally different planet from everyone else. Like I'm the only one that could see Heather for what she really is."

"You're not the only one," Lila said. "I think she's sneaky and selfish."

"Why can't anyone else see that?"

"People just see what they want to see when they think they can gain something," Lila said. "Those girls really want to go to the championships, and they honestly believe Heather can take them there. I know it's hard, but you can't really blame them for wanting that. It's just too bad they're turning their backs on you and their other friends."

"I guess you're right," Jessica said. "But it doesn't help. Heather's managed to turn the one thing I love more than almost anything into a nightmare."

Lila looked at her watch. "Shouldn't you be getting ready for practice?"

"I don't think I'm up to it," Jessica said glumly. "What's the point? Heather has them totally in her camp. I thought for sure that when she fired Maria and Sandy, they'd see Heather for what she really is. Obviously, I was wrong. I don't know what else I can say that I haven't already said."

"Excuse me, but what have you done with Jessica Wakefield?" Lila teased. "The Jessica I know would be marching onto that football field, demanding that Maria and Sandy be put back on the squad."

Jessica felt a sudden surge of energy. "You're right! I'm not going to sit here and let Heather destroy the lives of my squad members, and I'm not going to let her take my squad away from me! I've fought bigger battles than this one, and I'm not going to let Heather get me down!"

"Now, that's the Jessica I know," Lila said, sitting up.

Jessica jumped up on her feet. "I'm going to march onto that field like you said, and I'm going to give them an ultimatum—either Maria and Sandy are back on the squad, or I'm off it for good!"

"Three cheers for Jessica Wakefield!" Lila shouted as she stood up and did a cartwheel.

"Hey, not bad!" Jessica said. "Maybe you should be on the squad."

"I think you have enough problems as it is," Lila teased.

"Speaking of problems, Heather Mallone, hear I come!" Jessica ran as fast as she could to the locker room to get ready for practice.

Jessica was out of breath by the time she reached the far end of the football field. The girls were standing around talking and stretching before practice. Jessica was feeling stronger and more determined than ever after her talk with Lila, and she was ready to deliver her ultimatum to the squad. She looked around the field, but Heather was nowhere in sight.

My timing couldn't be more perfect, Jessica thought with excitement. *She'll be surprised when she shows up and finds out that the squad has stood by me.*

"Excuse me," Jessica yelled to the girls. "I need to talk to all of you about something really important. As you know, yesterday Heather—"

"Oh, hi, girls!" Heather shouted from behind Jessica. "Sorry I'm late. I was picking up these new uniforms."

Jessica turned around and saw Heather carrying two big cardboard boxes. As soon as Heather dropped the boxes onto the ground, all the girls crowded around them. They pulled out the new red-and-white uniforms, one by one.

Jessica looked at the uniforms as the girls

held them up for inspection. She was actually pleased. They were so hideous looking that Jessica was sure the other girls would hate them. The skirts were supershort with fringe around the bottom, and the shirts were skimpy little tank tops. *Fine. Maybe I won't even have to give an ultimatum,* Jessica thought. *They'll be so disgusted by Heather's uniforms that they won't want her to have anything to do with the squad.*

"These are *fabulous,*" Amy gushed.

"They don't even look like uniforms," Jeannie exclaimed. "I would wear this to a party."

"They're totally sexy," Annie said, holding one of the shirts up to her chest. "These will really get us some attention."

"Our other uniforms are so boring compared to these," Helen said.

Jessica couldn't believe what she was hearing. *How could anyone think those ugly things are fabulous? Has Heather brainwashed them so much that they now have her same tacky taste?*

"First of all, you and I never had a discussion about new uniforms," Jessica said to Heather. "And second of all, we can't afford these. Our budget is low as it is."

"They're a gift from me," Heather said, beaming. "I couldn't bear seeing these gorgeous girls wearing those drab, juvenile uniforms anymore.

They looked like children in those things."

"I chose those uniforms," Jessica said, clenching her fists tightly.

"Maybe Jessica's right," Heather said to the girls. "Why don't you put those back in the boxes? You should stick with Jessica's uniforms. After all, she was your captain before I came along."

"No way!" Amy protested. "We want these new ones. Don't we, girls?"

"Yes!" everybody shouted at the same time.

Jessica was once again humiliated by Heather. *She set me up*, Jessica thought. *She tried to make me look like the bad guy. Why can't anyone else see that?*

"Sorry, Jessica, but it looks like they want to go with my uniforms," Heather said. "I guess that's just the way the cookie crumbles."

Jessica was too angry to speak; she just glared at Heather with a hateful expression.

"Now I want everyone to sit around in a circle," Heather commanded.

Jessica stood to the side, refusing to sit down in Heather's stupid circle.

"Uniforms alone are not going to get us to the nationals," Heather said, pulling out a stack of papers from her knapsack. "It doesn't matter how great you look out there. If you're not in shape, you're not worth diddly."

"Jessica, could you pass these around?" Heather asked, handing Jessica the pile of papers.

"No, I couldn't pass them around," Jessica said curtly, taking one of the pages for herself. She was curious to see what else Heather was up to.

"That's fine," Heather said sweetly. "Who *would* like to pass these around?"

"I would," Amy volunteered.

Jessica looked down at the piece of paper in her hand. It contained a daily diet-and-exercise regime that looked like something designed for a labor camp.

"Oh, Jessica, I didn't consult you about this, but I'm sure you want the squad to go to the nationals as much as I do," Heather said, smiling sweetly at Jessica.

Jessica looked around the circle at the expectant faces waiting for her reaction. *I'm not going to let her set me up again*, Jessica decided. *She's turned them against me enough as it is.*

"That's just fine," Jessica said, smiling back at Heather with the same syrupy smile.

"Great. As you'll see on the handout, I've put together a program that everyone on the squad has to follow," Heather said. "It's going to seem hard at first, but you'll realize that it's worth it. Every girl on this squad is expected to jog three miles a day. This is something you're going to have to do on your own time. If it means waking up an hour earlier every day, then so be it."

They're going to be running right off this field and straight to the Dairi Burger by the time she's done with this stupid diet-and-exercise nonsense.

"In addition to jogging, you're all going to have to lift weights for an hour a day," Heather said. "There are weights in the gym, and I have a Nautilus machine at my house, which you're all free to use whenever you want."

"That's so generous of you," Jeannie said.

"Not at all," Heather said as if she were Mother Teresa. "I'm happy to do anything for this squad that I possibly can to help you get to the nationals."

Jessica, who was about ready to throw up, was trying as hard as she could to keep her mouth shut and let Heather dig her own grave. She couldn't believe that nobody had protested yet about the exercise, but she knew it was only a matter of time.

"At the beginning of every practice, we're going to start with seventy-five sit-ups, thirty push-ups, and fifty jumping jacks." Heather paused and looked around the circle. "I know I'm asking a lot, so if anyone wants to get off this bus now, this is the moment."

Jessica held her breath as she waited to hear the first person say she didn't want to do Heather's stupid exercises, but nobody said a word. *Wait until she gets to this diet plan,* Jessica thought, looking down at her paper. *That'll scare them.*

"OK, then, let's proceed to the diet portion of the regime," Heather said. "In order to achieve the perfect, healthy body, we have to combine exercise with diet. I want you to start thinking right now that fat is your enemy. You're all going on a strict no-fat diet. If I hear of anyone eating any fat, they're off the squad. That means you can only have skim milk in your coffee, and obviously milk shakes are out of the question. If you must eat pizza, ask to have it without cheese. I do it all the time."

Pizza without cheese? Jessica had never heard of anything so ridiculous. *They'll never go for this!*

"You can eat as many fruits, vegetables, and grains as you want," Heather said. "That's all I ever eat, and I never feel deprived."

"You do have a fantastic figure," Amy gushed. "I guess this plan really works. I'd kill for a body like yours."

Oh, great. Heather really needs people to tell her what a great body she has, as if her ego weren't already big enough, Jessica thought.

"I want you to keep in mind that this is not

about having a great body for vanity purposes," Heather said. "The idea is that your bodies will be stronger than ever and therefore able to do the different cheers and steps that will be required. The better the body, the better the cheerleader. You'll see that I've written down a typical day of eating. You can start with one half of a grapefruit for breakfast and a big glass of water. For lunch you can have any kind of vegetables that you want as long as you don't put anything on them. You can even eat rice with your vegetables as long as it's brown rice. For dinner you can have a salad, but you have to use lemon juice for your dressing. Oh, and in the afternoon you can have a piece of fruit or a carrot stick."

Jessica started laughing out loud in spite of herself.

"What's so funny, Jessica?" Heather asked. "Did we miss a joke?"

"I'm just laughing at this diet plan," Jessica said. "There's no way these people are going to go along with it. I mean, get real, pizza without cheese?" Jessica looked at all the girls, expecting them to smile at her in agreement, but they all just looked at her as if she were a complete stranger.

"Maybe this *is* too severe," Heather said. "Would you all like to just forget about this whole thing and go back to the way things were before I became a cocaptain? You probably won't even make it to the state finals, but maybe that's what you want. Obviously, that's what Jessica wants."

Nobody said a word, and Jessica was starting to feel as if she were getting a fever again, even though her mother had given her a clean bill of health that morning. *I will not be humiliated again,* she thought.

"Look, guys," Jessica started. "Cheerleading is supposed to be fun. This program Heather just got through explaining is more like something you'd do at a military boot camp. After two days of doing this diet-and-exercise thing, you're all going to hate cheerleading. You're never going to want to pick up another pom-pom again."

"I've been wanting to get in better shape for a long time," Helen said. "I think this sounds like the perfect way to do it."

"Me too," Amy agreed.

"I'd do anything if I could have a body like Heather's," Jeannie said. "She's totally sexy, and all the guys think so."

Jessica's blood was starting to boil. "But it's only cheerleading. This isn't supposed to be something that's like life or death. Is it really worth putting yourselves through all that misery?"

"We want to go to the nationals, Jessica," Annie said. "This sounds like the best way to get there."

"Even if it means starving yourselves and putting your bodies through absolute torture?" Jessica asked in disbelief.

"Let's take a vote," Heather said. "All those in favor of following my plan and going to the nationals, raise their right hand."

Everyone raised her hand except Jessica.

"That settles it," Heather said, jumping up. "OK, hit the decks. I want seventy-five sit-ups from every one of you, and I want to see you sweat!"

Jessica watched in total amazement as every girl started doing sit-ups. The worst part was that they all looked completely happy and ecstatic to be doing them! *So much for my ultimatum,* she thought glumly.

Chapter 12

"Jessica! You look beautiful!" Mrs. Wakefield exclaimed as Jessica entered the room on Friday night.

Elizabeth's heart sank. Her sister was looking more ravishing than ever in a pale-blue sleeveless dress that fell just above her ankles. It was sophisticated yet sexy, and it showed off her lanky figure. Her hair was perfectly blown dry so that every piece fell into place, and the makeup she was wearing finished off her polished look. Even though Elizabeth knew she could look just like that if she made the effort, she still felt incredibly jealous.

"Liz, don't you have to get ready for your date with Todd?" Jessica asked as she plopped down onto a chair. "I thought you were going on one of your nerdy literary dates."

"I'm already dressed for my date," Elizabeth snapped, feeling defensive about the jeans and old sweatshirt she'd thrown on. "Todd likes me just the way I am. I don't have to put on a bunch of makeup to get him to like me."

"Well, Ken likes me just the way I am too, but that doesn't mean I want to go dressed like a janitor on our date," Jessica teased. "I mean, really, you look terrible."

"Thanks for the compliment, sister dear," Elizabeth said curtly.

"What are you and Ken doing tonight?" Mrs. Wakefield asked.

"I don't know," Jessica said dreamily. "Ken said it was a surprise. He's planned something special for our second date. I can't wait. I need a fun night after the nightmare day I had."

"Nightmare at Sweet Valley High?" Mr. Wakefield joked.

"No, really," Jessica said. "Heather Mallone is ruining my life. I talked to the girls on the squad about Maria and Sandy being fired, and they didn't care. Heather has them eating out of her hand."

"I had lunch with Maria today, and she looked pretty upset," Elizabeth said. "Maybe you should ask her to join you on your date tonight."

Jessica burst out laughing. "Yeah, right. I'm really going to ask Maria to come on my date with

Ken. I hope you're joking, because if you're not, I think you need to have the Jell-O taken out of your brain. Besides, Maria has a boyfriend. I'm sure she's seeing Winston tonight."

"Winston had to, umm . . . go visit his grandparents," Elizabeth lied. "I know she'd like the company."

"Well, if you're so worried about her, why don't you ask her to join you and *your* date?" Jessica said. "After all, she's really more your friend than she is mine."

"But I know she really feels close to you," Elizabeth tried.

"Liz, give it a rest," Jessica said, shaking her head. "She's not going on my date. Period. Finito."

Even Elizabeth had to admit to herself that that was a pretty lame way to try to ruin Jessica's date, but she was desperate. She knew there had to be some way to keep her from going out with Ken.

"Mom, don't you think Jessica still looks a little pale?" Elizabeth asked. "Maybe you're not over your sickness, Jess."

"I feel great," Jessica said. "The only thing making me sick is Heather Mallone. She's a virus of the worst kind, and I'd love to find the cure to get rid of her."

"Are you sure you feel better?" Mrs. Wakefield asked with a worried expression. "You *were* running a fever yesterday."

"I thought you were supposed to wait a couple of days after having a fever before you did too much activity," Elizabeth said. She knew her mother well enough to know that if she thought one of her kids was sick, she'd do anything to make them better. *If I get her worried enough, Mom will forbid Jessica from going on her date,* Elizabeth thought.

"I promise you, I never felt better," Jessica insisted.

"You were coughing all last night," Elizabeth lied. "I could barely sleep from all the noise coming out of your room."

"I was?" Jessica asked. "I don't remember that at all."

"I guess you were just coughing in your sleep," Elizabeth said. "You probably still have whatever bug it was that you had yesterday. I doubt Ken will really want to be exposed to it."

"Do you have the chills or anything?" Mrs. Wakefield asked, looking more and more worried. "Do you feel feverish?"

"I don't have a fever!" Jessica yelled. "Here, feel my forehead." Jessica walked over to her mom and knelt in front of her.

"You don't feel warm," Mrs. Wakefield said, putting one hand on Jessica's forehead and the other on her own.

"There. That settles it," Jessica said. "Now you can all stop worrying about me."

"I don't know," Elizabeth said, shaking her head. "You still look sick to me."

"Liz! What's with you tonight? If I didn't know better, I'd say you didn't want me to go on this date tonight!"

"Why would you ever think anything as silly as that?" Elizabeth asked innocently. "I'm just worried about you."

"Well, don't worry about me," Jessica said. "I can take care of myself. Especially with the help of the handsome Ken Matthews."

"I just heard a car pull up," Mr. Wakefield said.

Jessica looked out the window. "It's Ken!"

Elizabeth felt a wave of jealousy and sadness flood over her.

"See you guys later! Don't wait up!" Jessica called out as she jumped up and flew through the front door.

Elizabeth was sitting next to Todd at the bookstore listening to one of her favorite writers read a short story, and she had no idea what the story was about. Normally, she would have been hanging on every word, but her thoughts were miles away.

She had one thing on her mind, and it wasn't literature. *Where are they right now?* Elizabeth wondered as her eyes stared blankly at the psychology bookshelf to her right. *What does "very romantic" mean? Todd said Ken planned something "very romantic" for their date. I'm afraid that doesn't mean bowling.*

She looked at Todd, who was absorbed by the reading. Their shared interest in books and writers was one of Elizabeth's favorite things about her relationship with Todd, but now it all seemed boring. *I'm sure Ken and Jessica are doing something a lot more romantic than this right now.*

"This is great, isn't it?" Todd whispered in her ear. "Let's buy a copy of her new book when she's done."

"Yeah, great," Elizabeth whispered back.

Her guilt was unbearable. Todd was so eager to please. The reading had been her idea, and he was there jumping right into it with enthusiasm, as he did everything. *He's a great guy. Why can't I just be happy with him and forget about Ken?*

Elizabeth turned her face toward the direction of the writer and tried to plaster an interested smile on her face, but it was taking all her effort. Every now and then Todd would smile at her to acknowledge something funny or well written, and Elizabeth smiled back, even though she had no idea what she was smiling about.

After what seemed like an eternity, the audience applauded the author, and Elizabeth realized the reading was over.

"So which story did you like the most?" Todd asked.

"What do you mean?" Elizabeth asked.

"She read three different stories. I was just wondering if you liked one more than the other."

Elizabeth was so out of it that she didn't even realize that the writer had read more than one story. "Hmmmm, well, it's hard to say which one I liked best. They were all so good."

"I know what you mean," Todd said. "I think I liked the one about the old women at the post office the most."

"Yeah, that was a great one," Elizabeth said. "Do you want to browse around awhile?" She was eager to stop a detailed conversation about the stories, since it would be obvious that she hadn't been listening. She certainly didn't want to have to explain *why* she hadn't been paying attention.

"So I wonder what Ken and Jessica are up to tonight," Elizabeth said as they walked slowly through the poetry section of the bookstore. She was trying to sound as nonchalant as possible.

"Ken was really secretive about it," Todd said, pulling out a volume of Robert Frost's poems. "All he said was that he'd planned something totally romantic."

Romantic. I'm starting to hate that word, Elizabeth thought as her curiosity grew stronger by the minute. "Do you think he just meant that they were going to a movie?"

"Like I said, he was vague on the details, but from the look on his face I would imagine they're doing something pretty special," Todd said as he flipped through the pages of the book he was holding.

"Did he say anything about his feelings for Jessica?" Elizabeth asked. She pulled out a book of Adrienne Rich's poetry and flipped through the pages in an attempt to seem casual.

"Liz, you're holding that book upside down," Todd said.

Elizabeth looked at the book and saw that in fact it *was* upside down. She quickly put it back on the shelf. "I guess I'm just still thinking about those wonderful stories Kate Staples just read."

"Yeah, you seem a little spacey," Todd said, kissing her on the cheek.

"So did he say anything to you about how he feels about my sister?" Elizabeth asked again. She hated pumping him for answers like that, but since he was Ken's best friend, he was the best source for finding out the information she wanted.

"Well, it seems like he really has the hots for her," Todd said.

"How can you tell? Did he actually say that?"

"Hey, why such a big interest in Ken and Jessica?"

Because I had a fling with him when you were in Vermont, and I can't stand that he's dating my sister, Elizabeth thought miserably to herself. "Just normal sisterly concern. I guess I'm just afraid of Jessica getting hurt again. You know how awful that whole thing with Jeremy was. I just want to make sure Ken has good intentions."

"Well, you don't have anything to worry about," Todd said, taking her in his arms and hugging her tightly. "And I think it's really touching that you're so worried about your sister."

Not as touching as you think, Elizabeth thought guiltily.

"You didn't answer my question," she asked as they stood at the counter while Todd bought a signed copy of the book of short stories.

"Which question? You asked fifty already," Todd teased.

"How can you tell he has the hots for Jessica? Did he tell you that?"

"He didn't really come out and say it in those exact words. He didn't have to—it was written all over his face. He gets this kind of look when he mentions her name."

"What kind of look?"

"Kind of gooey and embarrassed—I guess it's a guy thing. I probably look the same way when I'm talking about you."

Elizabeth and Todd walked outside hand in hand. "So do you want to go get some ice cream at Casey's?" Todd asked.

Elizabeth didn't think she could bear having to put up a cheerful front any longer. All she wanted to do was go home and wait up for her sister. "I think I might be coming down with the same thing Jessica had. Do you mind taking me home?"

"Sure, if that's what you want. Do you want to rent a video on the way to your house? We could watch it together."

"No, I really think I just want to go to sleep. I'm sure I'll feel better tomorrow."

"OK, close your eyes," Ken said to Jessica.

Ken and Jessica had driven up the coast to a beautiful secluded beach, and they were sitting on a blanket in the moonlight.

As soon as Jessica was in Ken's car, her problems of the day started to drift slowly away. They had chatted nonstop on the drive up the coast, and Jessica didn't think she'd ever dated anyone she felt so comfortable with. It was a whole new concept to her—dating someone who is also a friend.

"You can open them now."

Jessica opened her eyes. Ken had lit two little lanterns that were on the sand, and he'd packed a gourmet meal that was spread out on the blanket. There was pasta with pesto, French bread with Brie cheese, strawberries dipped in chocolate, a Caesar salad, and chocolate cheesecake. He'd also brought along a boom box, which was playing some cool jazz.

"This is incredible! Where did you get all this?"

"I went to that new gourmet deli earlier today and asked them to pack a romantic picnic for the beach," Ken said. "I wanted tonight to be special."

"It is special," Jessica said. "And you're really special, Ken." She leaned over and kissed Ken tenderly on the lips.

Ken filled two champagne glasses with sparkling apple cider and handed one to Jessica. "I'd like to propose a toast. To the beginning of a beautiful relationship."

"You're quoting Humphrey Bogart from *Casablanca*," Jessica said with excitement. "That's my favorite movie."

"That's *my* favorite movie," Ken said, laughing. "I've seen it about five times."

"I think you're the first guy I've met who loved that movie," Jessica said. "I'm starving—let's eat."

Ken smeared a huge chunk of Brie onto a piece of French bread and handed it to Jessica. "How's that for a start?"

"Perfect," Jessica said, taking a big bite. "This definitely is *not* on Heather's starvation diet. She'd probably be horrified if she saw me eating this. I read somewhere that Brie has more fat in it than any other cheese. I'm loving every last fat gram."

"Heather's diet-and-exercise plan sounds really ridiculous," Ken said, preparing a piece of bread and Brie for himself. "If she's not careful, she's going to have a squad of anorexic cheerleaders."

"You're right," Jessica said in a serious tone. Jessica looked out at the water that was lit up by the full moon and thought about Robin and her bout with anorexia. She had gotten so thin and weak that eventually she had to be hospitalized and fed intravenously. She felt a pang of sadness. *If only Robin were still here,* she thought. *All my problems with Heather would be nonexistent. Robin would still be my cocaptain, and Sandy and Maria would still be on the squad.*

"I still can't believe that people are going along with her," Ken said. "I give them about two days of dieting and exercising before they come running back to you, demanding that you be the sole captain. I would just wait it out and let them see for themselves how terrible Heather's plan is."

"Do you really think that will happen?" Jessica asked hopefully. "Heather has them so convinced that she knows what's best for them. Maybe she does."

"Jessica, you're a great captain, and I don't want you to think for a minute that Heather knows more about cheerleading than you do. Your squad was better than ever at that Big Mesa game two weeks ago."

"Even better than last Wednesday's game?"

"A thousand times better," Ken said. "And I'm really in a position to know, since I'm on the team. What you girls do out there on the field really affects how we play. We count on that energy and support, and it was so much stronger when you were in charge than when Heather was."

"Are you just saying that to make me feel better?" Jessica asked as she studied Ken's gorgeous face in the moonlight.

"If it makes you feel better, I'm glad, but that's not why I'm saying it," Ken said. "I honestly think that."

"You're the best," Jessica said.

Ken looked deeply into Jessica's eyes and took her face in his hands. "And you're beautiful, Jessica Wakefield. If I don't kiss you right now, I'm going to have to run into the water and drown myself."

"We can't have that," Jessica teased. "Your parents would never forgive me, not to mention the football team."

Jessica closed her eyes and Ken kissed her sweetly on the lips. She felt her heart pounding, and even though she didn't really want to, she pulled herself away from Ken's embrace before they went any further.

"I think we better eat," Jessica said. "And I want you to fill up my plate with high-fat food. This girl is *not* on a diet!"

Chapter 13

Why aren't they home yet? Elizabeth wondered as she looked at her digital clock. *If they went to a movie or dinner, they'd be back by now.* It was after midnight, and Elizabeth was waiting up for Jessica to get home from her date. As every minute passed, her agitation and jealousy grew. She kept having images of Ken and Jessica kissing each other, and it made her feel sick to her stomach. Even though it was crazy, Elizabeth was on the verge of jumping into the Jeep and finding them.

She was also feeling incredibly guilty about Todd. He had been so sweet when he thought Elizabeth was sick after the reading. He offered to take her to the drugstore to buy her some cold medicine. It was awful lying to him the way she'd been doing, but she thought that the truth would even be worse.

Ken and Todd were best friends. There was no way Todd would ever be able to forgive Elizabeth or Ken for what had happened between them. The worst part of all was that Elizabeth was afraid she was still in love with Ken.

Elizabeth reached under her bed and pulled out her secret box. It was an old cigar box she'd covered with different kinds of wrapping paper, and inside she kept little mementos that she didn't want anyone to see. There was a corsage of dried red sweetheart roses Todd had given her the first time they'd gone to a dance together. There were five poems no one had ever seen that she'd written after she was in a car accident and Jessica's boyfriend, Sam Woodruff, had been killed. There was a little heart necklace Todd had given her in the sixth grade, and wrapped in a lace handkerchief was a picture in a frame.

She slowly untied the handkerchief and looked at the picture. When Ken and Elizabeth had been together, they'd gone to the boardwalk and had their pictures taken inside a booth. Elizabeth had put them in a purple frame, and she hadn't looked at them for months.

There were four shots. In the first they were looking at each other and laughing. *I really was happy with him,* Elizabeth thought, smiling at the memory of that day. *And I know he was happy with me too.* The next three pictures made Elizabeth ache. In all of them they were kissing.

Elizabeth lay down on her pillow and closed her eyes, clutching the frame to her chest. *He's probably kissing Jessica right now. Is he thinking of me? Is he with her because she looks like me?*

She looked at the pictures again, and she tried to go back to that day in her mind. They'd driven to an amusement park on a boardwalk about an hour from Sweet Valley. They'd wanted to find a place where nobody they knew would see them.

Elizabeth remembered how they'd spent hours sitting at an outside café on the boardwalk and talked about everything from books, to music and religion. Elizabeth had felt so light and free that day. They'd been so comfortable together.

When the sun had started going down, they'd strolled along the boardwalk, hand in hand. Except for the occasional stolen kiss at the movies, it was the only time they'd been physically affectionate in public, and it felt great. They'd stopped to play a shooting game at one of the booths, and Ken had won a big pink teddy bear, which he'd given to Elizabeth. She didn't want to have to explain to anyone where she'd gotten the bear, so she'd given it to a little girl who'd been crying by the merry-go-round.

The pictures helped Elizabeth remember that they really had been together. They were the only reminder she had. The last few times she'd seen him, Ken had been so cold and distant—as if they'd never been anything except friends. *These pictures are proof,* Elizabeth thought. *Are they all I'm ever going to have? Will Ken and I ever talk about what happened between us? Will we ever rekindle our brief but magical relationship?*

Elizabeth looked at the clock again. Twelve thirty. *I'm not going to sleep until Jessica's in this house,* Elizabeth thought, sitting up on her bed, still clutching the picture frame.

The waiting was driving her crazy, so she decided to play some music. She put on a song that Ken and she had listened to in his car on the way to the beach the day they'd had the pictures made. Ken had said that that would always be their song. It was "Unforgettable" by Natalie Cole. She listened to the song and looked at the pictures, and she imagined kissing Ken. . . .

"Elizabeth! You're still up!" Jessica flew through the door, and Elizabeth quickly hid the picture underneath her pillow.

"I didn't even hear you come in," Elizabeth

said, looking startled. "Where have you been?"

"I've been having the most wonderful time of my entire life," Jessica said dreamily. "I feel like I'm floating on air."

Jessica plopped down next to Elizabeth on her bed and took a deep breath. It was torture having to say good night to Ken in his car. She felt as if she could have stayed there all night, kissing him on the lips and feeling his hands gently stroking her neck and hair.

"Pinch me," Jessica said, holding out her arm.

"What are you talking about?" Elizabeth asked. "Why would I pinch you?"

"Because I feel like I must be dreaming," Jessica sighed. "I didn't want the night to end. We would have stayed in his car, kissing good night for hours, if we both didn't have to get up early tomorrow for the big game."

"You're home really late as it is," Elizabeth said, sounding like a mother. "You're going to be exhausted tomorrow. You shouldn't have stayed out so long."

Jessica thought that was a strange reaction, but she was too elated to give it much thought. "Ken is the most wonderful guy in the whole world," she gushed. "You're not going to believe what he did tonight."

"What?" Elizabeth asked curtly.

"We drove up the coast to a deserted beach and had a gourmet picnic, which Ken planned himself. He brought lanterns and music, and we danced in the moonlight. He's so romantic."

"Sounds great," Elizabeth said unenthusiastically.

"What's with you?" Jessica asked. "You seem totally unexcited for me."

"What do you want me to do? Jump up and down? Throw a party?"

What's her problem? Jessica thought. *She probably had a fight with Todd or something.* "Forget about it," Jessica said. She was too happy to let Elizabeth spoil her euphoria. "Anyway, we sat on the beach, talking about everything. He made me feel a thousand times better about that stupid Heather and the whole cheerleading situation. He's such a great listener and he gives wonderful advice. I feel like the luckiest girl on earth."

"Uh-huh," Elizabeth muttered.

"So we're sitting there under the stars, and it's like a movie," Jessica said. "He even quoted *Casablanca*, which we both said was our favorite movie."

"That's *my* favorite movie," Elizabeth snapped.

"Well, it's mine too," Jessica said. "I didn't know there was some law that says only you can have

Casablanca as your favorite movie. I mean, what's the big deal?"

"Nothing," Elizabeth said.

"Well, anyway, we're starting to eat our beautiful dinner, and Ken starts kissing me so passionately—"

"That's enough, Jessica! What makes you think I want to hear every little detail of your stupid date?" Elizabeth barked.

Jessica was stunned. *Where is this coming from? She's acting like a total crazy person.* "Liz, I thought you'd be thrilled for me. I'm sitting here telling you how happy I am, and you're being downright mean to me."

Elizabeth stood up and her body was shaking. "You're just so selfish, Jessica Wakefield. You think the whole world revolves around you, and that I have nothing else to do or think about than listen to every word that Ken said to you. For all you know, Ken might be seeing somebody else. Don't forget how deceived you were by Jeremy not so long ago. Ken could turn out to be the same way, and it will be too late because you're going so fast with him."

"But Ken is nothing like Jeremy, and I can't believe you'd say something so cruel and nasty," Jessica said. Elizabeth's words were like swords through Jessica's heart. She'd just decided to open herself up to love again, and her own sister was telling her she'd probably get hurt.

"Don't expect me to be there to pick up the pieces of your broken heart again," Elizabeth said as she stormed out of the room, slamming the door behind her.

Jessica was on the verge of tears. Only moments before she'd been happier than she'd been in months, and now her sister had made her feel absolutely miserable. She was suddenly overcome with exhaustion. She'd been trying all night to fight the sickness she knew she still had, but her sister's words made her feel physically beaten up.

She fell back on Elizabeth's pillow and felt something hard. Reaching underneath the pillow, she pulled out the picture in its frame. She turned it over, and almost choked at the images of Ken and Elizabeth kissing. *What's this? This picture must have been taken this year,* Jessica realized as she recognized a shirt Elizabeth had bought several months earlier. *No wonder she's been acting so bizarre about Ken and me.*

She was having a hard time breathing. It didn't make sense. Ken and Todd were best friends. Elizabeth didn't even seem like Ken's type. A tear rolled down Jessica's cheek. *I knew Ken was too good to be true,* she thought sadly as she remembered kissing him only moments before.

I have to find out what happened between them, Jessica decided as she put the picture back under the pillow. *But I can't do it until after the game tomorrow. I need to put this out of my mind as much as possible and concentrate on Heather Mallone. But I'm going to get to the bottom of this no matter what it takes!*

Jessica walked onto the football field before the big game against Claremont High with the determination to take back her squad. She refused to let her discovery the night before of the pictures of Ken and Jessica get her down. When she'd looked in the mirror before leaving the house, she'd said out loud, "You're Jessica Wakefield, and you're not going to let anything or anyone keep you from getting what you want. You never have in the past, and you're not going to start now."

Excited crowds filled the bleachers. It was a beautiful sunny day, and there wasn't a cloud in the sky. Jessica stood in front of the cheerleading squad with her pom-poms on her hips and gave a pep talk to the girls. Everyone was wearing the new skimpy uniforms Heather had given them, and reluctantly, Jessica was wearing hers as well. The new uniforms were creating a stir in the stands from the male fans, but Jessica tried to ignore it.

"Every one of you is a great cheerleader, and we have a fabulous football team out there, so let's show the other team what Sweet Valley High is made of," Jessica said enthusiastically. "I want you to yell louder and jump higher than you ever have before. A football team is as good as the people cheering for them!"

Jessica noticed that Heather was being unusually quiet. *Good, maybe she finally realized that I'm really the one in charge and she should just leave everything to me,* Jessica thought as she positioned herself to lead the first cheer.

She raised her pom-poms in the air and was ready to start the cheer that they always did right before the game when Heather jumped in front of her.

"Ready, girls?" Heather shouted. "One, two, three, go!"

Jessica watched in horror as they started doing a cheer that she'd never seen before. She stood to the side feeling like a total fool. The cheer was too complicated just to jump in and follow the steps. They were doing some kind of fancy dance and reciting the words as if it were a rap song. The people in the stands were snapping their fingers and clapping along, and the cheerleaders looked as if they were having a blast. At the end of the cheer the crowd was on their feet applauding and whistling wildly. *This is the last straw,* Jessica thought angrily.

"Well, Heather," she said to her cocaptain. "You finally got what you set out to do. You've been trying your best to take over my squad, and you finally did it. These girls have demonstrated that they feel no loyalty to me at all, and they've allowed you to come in and brainwash them. You'll all be happy to know that I *quit*!" Jessica threw down her pom-poms and stormed off the field.

Chapter 14

Jessica was sitting in a booth at the Dairi Burger pushing her hot-fudge sundae around on the dish with her spoon. After she'd stormed off the field that afternoon, she'd gone straight home and up to her room for a good cry. Ken had come by the house and practically dragged her out to get ice cream.

He was trying his best to cheer her up, but it wasn't working. Not only was she upset about quitting the squad, but she was still confused and devastated by the pictures she'd found the night before of him and Elizabeth. *Coming here was a big mistake,* she thought as she felt a lump in her throat. She didn't want to go out with Ken in the first place, but he'd been so forceful, and she didn't want to have to tell him about finding the pictures. She just wasn't up to it.

"I think quitting the squad was the best thing you could have done," Ken said. "I'm really proud of you."

"You are?" Jessica asked, looking up from her sundae dish. Even though Jessica was upset about the pictures, she still appreciated Ken's support. After all, she'd been talking to him more than anyone else about the whole cheerleading fiasco. *Just put the pictures out of your head for now*, she told herself.

"Absolutely. There was no way you could have continued on the squad like that," Ken said, popping a big spoonful of whipped cream into his mouth. "You would have gone completely crazy. Some people are born to be natural leaders, and you're one of those people. You don't need someone like Heather Mallone telling you what to do."

Ken's words were sweet, but they didn't make Jessica feel any better. "I still can't believe they chose Heather over me," Jessica said, eating a big bite of hot fudge and vanilla ice cream. "I mean, what does she have that I don't?"

"Nothing at all," Ken said. "She's a total loser, and I'm amazed that people can't see that. She's totally fake. I can tell that just from the way she talks to me."

"She's been pretty flirtatious with you from what I can see," Jessica said. Jessica wasn't even jealous of Ken and Heather. Her own sister was the only person she had to worry about in terms of Ken. As much as she tried to put it out of her mind, the image of them kissing each other kept creeping back. *How could he have kissed her?* she wondered as she studied Ken's face. *Did he think of Elizabeth when he was kissing me last night? Is he using me to get to Elizabeth?* She had to believe that he'd been sincere with her. More than anything else they were good friends. Ken couldn't have been pretending to be her friend . . . could he?

"And she's the worst kind of firtatious," Ken said. "She's not at all natural like you are. And you're about ten times prettier than she is."

"Thanks," Jessica said glumly. Normally, hearing that would have made Jessica happy, but even that didn't seem to matter anymore.

"Let's go to Lila's pool party and celebrate winning the game with everyone," Ken said. "It'll be fun. I think it would cheer you up."

"You go ahead," Jessica said. "I just want to go home and be by myself." The last thing Jessica felt like doing was going to celebrate the football game. She couldn't stand the idea of facing everybody after she'd quit the squad like that. *Thank goodness tomorrow's Sunday,* Jessica thought. *I wish I never had to go back to Sweet Valley High.*

Robin's lucky—she gets to start over at a brand-new school.

"Come on, Jessica," Ken urged as they walked out of the Dairi Burger. "You have nothing to be ashamed of. I think you should hold your head high and show the world that you're stronger than ever."

"Can you just take me home?" Jessica asked, getting into Ken's car.

"Are you sure that's what you want?"

"I'm sure," Jessica said as she fought back the tears. The reality was sinking in. *I quit the cheerleading squad,* she thought in horror. *What am I if not a cheerleader?*

"Have you talked to your sister since the game?" Lila asked Elizabeth, who was standing next to Lila's pool with Todd, Enid, Winston, and Maria. "I tried calling her to make sure she was coming here tonight, but there was no answer."

"I didn't have a chance to speak to her yet," Elizabeth said. *And I'm probably the last person she wants to see right now,* she thought sadly. She hadn't talked to her sister since the night before, when Elizabeth had said those awful things about Ken. She was at the football game earlier that day and had seen Jessica quit the squad. She felt terrible for her twin. She knew how much cheerleading meant to Jessica, and she knew her sister must be feeling awful.

"I'm so glad she did that," Maria said. "Heather is a horrible person, and she just totally stole the control of the squad out from under Jessica. She's better off not having anything to do with those girls, since they didn't show her any kind of loyalty."

"I agree," Lila said. "Look at the way Heather's flirting with the entire football team in the pool. I didn't even invite her to my party, but there she is."

"She was making me sick the way she acted like a movie star after the game," Maria said. "She kept bouncing from one interviewer to another, taking all the credit for the team's success."

"I noticed that too," Winston said. "She acted like she was the quarterback of the football team."

"Speaking of the quarterback—I'm surprised Ken isn't here," Lila said. "I guess he's trying to cheer up Jessica. I'm glad she has him right now."

For the first time since Jessica and Ken had started dating, Elizabeth didn't feel jealous. She, too, was glad that Jessica had Ken to talk to. She felt guilty not only because of Ken, but also because she hadn't really been there for Jessica when she had wanted to talk about Heather and the cheerleading problems she was having. *I'm the one who told her to make Heather a cocaptain in the first place*, she thought.

"I can't even imagine your sister not being a cheerleader," Todd said.

"I know what you mean," Winston agreed. "When I think of Jessica, I automatically think of cheerleading."

Elizabeth felt so far away from Jessica. The fact that she'd kept a secret from her created an enormous gulf between them. Usually when Jessica had a problem, Elizabeth was right there to bail her out. Because of the distance Elizabeth had created, she hadn't been there for her sister when Jessica had needed her the most. *Maybe I should just tell her about what happened between Ken and me,* Elizabeth thought. *Keeping a secret like this from her feels wrong, and if it goes on any longer, it could ruin our relationship for good!*

As soon as Ken dropped Jessica off at her house, she went right up to Elizabeth's room. She knew that Elizabeth would be at Lila's party and that her parents had gone to dinner with friends. She didn't know what she was looking for, but she was determined to find out more about her sister and Ken.

Jessica knew that Elizabeth always kept a diary of everything that happened to her. In the past Jessica would have thought her sister's life was too boring to read about, but now she was desperate to find her diary. *Apparently, there are things I never knew about Elizabeth,* Jessica thought as she felt a chill through her whole body.

Where does she keep that stupid diary? Jessica wondered as she searched Elizabeth's desk. She looked in the closet and on Elizabeth's bookshelf, but she found nothing. She got down on the floor and looked under Elizabeth's bed. *There it is,* she thought as she grabbed the red leather book and sat down on the bed.

Her hands were shaking as she opened the diary to the first page. She wasn't sure she really wanted to find out the truth about Ken. He'd made her so happy, and she hated to let go of that.

She also knew that if she didn't find out what happened, the doubts and suspicion would always haunt her.

Jessica skimmed through the first few pages of the diary, and it appeared to be mostly about the books Elizabeth was reading or the tests she was studying for. *How typical of Elizabeth to write down every boring little detail of her boring life,* Jessica thought as she continued to flip the pages.

Then her eyes settled on three letters: K-E-N! And to Jessica's horror his name was all over the diary! Her hands were shaking, and she felt the sweat start to form on her brow.

Ken called me this afternoon, and we went to a movie tonight. It almost seemed like a Saturday-night date, but of course he's just looking after me like Todd asked him to. Still, when he dropped me off at my house afterward, I wasn't expecting to feel the way I did as I looked into his eyes to say good-bye. . . .

Jessica's eyes skipped ahead frantically to more passages about Ken. As painful as it was to read about her sister's feelings for Ken, she couldn't resist.

The backyard was dark, and we slipped eagerly into the shadows. Without another word Ken folded his arms around me, lifting me slightly so his mouth could find mine. I kissed him hungrily, my fingers tangling in his hair. Meanwhile, his hands were on my neck, my shoulders, my back. We couldn't seem to stop touching each other—maybe because for weeks we'd been dying to do this, but holding back.

Jessica dropped the diary onto the floor and collapsed onto Elizabeth's bed in tears. It was true—Elizabeth had had an affair with Ken while Todd had been in Vermont. Jessica's feelings were so jumbled up and confused that she didn't know which emotion was stronger—her jealousy, or the feeling of being betrayed by a sister who had kept a secret from her.

This has truly been the worst day of my life, Jessica thought. *I'm not a cheerleader anymore, and the person I thought was becoming my new boyfriend had an affair with my sister!*

THE POM-POM WARS

Written by
Kate William

Created by
FRANCINE PASCAL

BANTAM BOOKS
NEW YORK • TORONTO • LONDON • SYDNEY • AUCKLAND

To Jean and Burt Rubin

THE POM-POM WARS

Jessica Wakefield sat on the edge of her twin sister Elizabeth's neatly made bed, a clothbound notebook gripped in her hands. "I don't believe it," she said to herself, staring at the diary with wide, shocked eyes. "Liz and Ken—a hot and heavy fling—and I never even knew about it?"

The night before, hidden under Elizabeth's pillow, Jessica had found a small picture frame holding a strip of black-and-white photo-booth snapshots. Not terribly interesting, Jessica thought, until she realized that the boy Elizabeth was smooching with in the photos was Ken Matthews, not Elizabeth's longtime steady, Todd Wilkins! The same Ken Matthews who just so happened to be Jessica's new boyfriend.

The pictures weren't dated. Dying to know more, Jessica had taken the next opportunity to sneak into her sister's bedroom and search Elizabeth's diary for clues.

She'd expected a brief mention of Ken somewhere to explain the photo, along the lines of, "A bunch of us went out and Ken and I got silly in the photo booth. I've always had a crush on him, he's such a hunk, but of course he'd never be interested in me—he's more Jessica's type." Instead . . .

Propping a pillow against the headboard of Elizabeth's bed, Jessica leaned back and rested the diary against her tucked-up knees. Flipping back a few pages, she reread the first journal entry that related to Ken. Elizabeth had written it just a few weeks after Todd and his family moved from Sweet Valley, California, to Burlington, Vermont, leaving behind a—supposedly—heartbroken Elizabeth.

"Ken called me this afternoon, and we went to a movie tonight," recorded Elizabeth. "It almost seemed like a Saturday-night date, but of course he's just looking after me like Todd asked him to. Still, when we said good night, I was startled by the way I felt as I looked into his eyes. If I didn't know better, Diary, I'd think I was falling for Ken. . . ."

Jessica turned the page. "I can't give in to these feelings." Elizabeth had underlined the word "can't" about ten times. "He's Todd's best friend!"

But Elizabeth did give in, and this was where the diary really started to get juicy. Jessica scowled. It would be fun to read, if the boy Elizabeth was writing about was anyone but Ken . . . ! Half of her wanted to hurl the diary across the room; the other half couldn't tear her eyes from the page. She had to read each and every gory detail.

"I almost don't want to write this down,"

Elizabeth confessed. "I hope no one ever finds out about it. I can't believe I let myself get so carried away. . . ."

It made Jessica squirm to read her sister's swooning account of her first kiss with Ken. "We couldn't seem to stop touching each other, maybe because for weeks we'd been dying to do this, but holding back. Where will this end, Diary? There's no going back now. . . ."

On the next page Elizabeth was overcome with remorse. "Todd called. He doesn't seem to suspect anything. Why should he? I'm his girlfriend and Ken's his best buddy. If he can't trust us, who can he trust? I decided there was one surefire way to get rid of the guilt: Stay away from Ken. Who was I kidding? I might as well tell the ocean to stop crashing on the shore."

Jessica snorted. " 'Tell the ocean to stop crashing on the shore'? Ugh, Liz, you are so corny. How did Ken stand it?"

Despite her disgust she kept reading, captivated by this tale of forbidden love. "We met at the beach again tonight," Elizabeth wrote. "I told my family I was going over to Olivia's to study for the French test. Diary, I've never felt so bad—and so good—at the same time. Ken kissed me like no one's ever kissed me before. . . ."

Jessica's blue-green eyes flashed with jealousy. How dare he kiss Elizabeth like that! Ken was supposed to be in love with her, Jessica. Had he really said outrageously mushy things to Elizabeth, like, "You're the sweetest, most beautiful girl I know, I think about you every minute of the day, I adore you"?

"This was ages ago," Jessica reminded herself. "Liz and Ken momentarily lost their minds, that's all."

The affair seemed to go on forever, though. It had lasted only a few weeks, but Elizabeth spent pages and pages describing every secret rendezvous, every delicious stolen glance and kiss. Jessica pored over the diary, scandalized at the thought of her usually upright and honest sister doing so much lying and sneaking around. "I'm trying really hard to act normal around Ken at school so no one guesses what's going on between us. Luckily even Jessica doesn't seem to suspect anything, and she's got a nose for these things."

"Well!" Jessica declared indignantly. "Excuse me for not having such a devious mind that I could even imagine you'd be such a cheating two-timer!"

She dropped the diary on the bed and closed her eyes, suddenly feeling drained. *First I quit the cheerleading squad, and now this. What a night!*

The disturbing image of Elizabeth and Ken in a passionate embrace faded from Jessica's mind. It was replaced by an equally disturbing image from a key moment in that afternoon's football game against Claremont. Just as Jessica had been about to lead her squad into one of their standard school-spirit routines, her new cocaptain, Heather Mallone, had called out a cheer Jessica had never even heard of. While the other girls pranced and shouted, whirling and shaking their pom-poms and dazzling the crowd with their fancy footwork, Jessica had just stood there with her own arms hanging limp at her side, looking and feeling like a total idiot. The home-team fans had leaped to their feet in thunderous approval; Jessica had hurled her pom-poms to the ground and stalked off the field, the two words she shouted—"I quit!"—completely drowned out by the applause for Heather's snappy new routine.

"The day that girl drove into town in her little white Mazda Miata was the worst day of my life," Jessica grumbled bitterly. From the start blond, beautiful Heather Mallone had been a thorn in Jessica's side. Head cheerleader at her old school, Heather had bulldozed her way onto the SVH squad just as Robin Wilson, formerly a cocaptain, announced that her family was moving to Denver. Jessica had proposed that she remain the squad's sole captain. Instead the other girls had voted unanimously: They wanted Heather as cocaptain.

She brainwashed them, pure and simple, Jessica thought glumly, remembering how Heather had shown up one day with cute new practice uniforms for the whole team. *Putting us all on that gross wheat-germ-and-broccoli "Cheer to Win" diet, and bragging constantly about how her old squad were the state champions for ten years in a row.* "Grr," she growled out loud. "Just thinking about it . . . !"

It had been bad enough when Heather had been just the new girl on the squad, showing off her great jumps and combinations every chance she got. When the squad had named her cocaptain, in Jessica's opinion at least, they had created a monster. The first thing Heather did, one day when Jessica was sick and couldn't make practice, was to kick Maria Santelli and Sandy Bacon off the squad. "We've got to trim the fat if we want to make it to regionals," Heather had declared coldly. Jessica was the only one who had protested Heather's high-handed decision; blinded by dreams of glory, the other girls had backed Heather a hundred percent. *And now Heather's gotten rid of me, too,* Jessica thought, punching Elizabeth's pillow. *She knew how I'd react when she pulled that stunt at the game today—she knew she'd drive me right over the edge!*

It burned her to a crisp to think that Heather Mallone had gotten the last word—or rather, the last cheer. "If I'm not a cheerleader, I'm nothing and nobody," Jessica mourned. "All I've got is Ken, and it turns out Liz had him first!"

Reaching for Elizabeth's diary, Jessica reread the last few entries about Ken. Apparently, the stress of secrecy had finally gotten to the pair, and after repeatedly trying to stay apart and then running back into one another's arms, they had finally managed to make the resolution stick.

"I did it," Elizabeth wrote on a page that was smudged and crinkled by teardrops. "After school Ken and I went for a walk in the park, and I broke things off with him. We got pretty choked up, but I know deep in our hearts we both understood it was the only thing to do. I'm lonely and he's lonely, so we just kind of naturally turned to each other, but an actual out-in-the-open relationship would have been impossible and wrong. We could never have felt good about it. I think we'll be able to stay friends, though. There aren't any hard feelings. I'll always have a place for him in a secret part of my heart. And we promised each other: under no circumstances will we ever tell anyone about what happened between us. Never, ever."

Jessica closed the diary, a thoughtful expression on her face. One sentence of Elizabeth's in particular made a strong impression on her: "I'll always have a place for him in a secret part of my heart. . . ."

"That explains it," she deduced. "That's why Liz has been acting so weird lately and practically trying to talk me out of dating Ken. She's jealous!"

The realization gave Jessica a big emotional boost. It had definitely been unsettling to learn that her sister was once involved with Ken, but whatever had happened in the past, it was clear now that the only girl Ken got hot and bothered about was Jessica herself. *It must drive Liz crazy to see us together,* Jessica thought with a smug smile. *Serves her right!*

No, what was most interesting about Elizabeth's secret diary, Jessica decided, wasn't that Elizabeth had a fling with Ken Matthews. Jessica couldn't blame her sister for that—after all, Todd was three thousand miles away at the time, and Ken was the most adorable boy in Sweet Valley. No, it was that they'd managed to keep it a secret for all this time. *She never told me or Enid or anybody,* mused Jessica, *and I'm sure Ken didn't tell anyone, either.*

He certainly hasn't mentioned it to me! Which means Todd never found out that his supposedly devoted girlfriend cheated on him with his best friend.

Yes, that was very interesting, decided Jessica. Very interesting indeed!

"Poor Jessica," Elizabeth said to Todd as she dipped a tortilla chip into a bowl of spicy salsa. "Everyone's out celebrating the Gladiators' big victory, and she's sitting home alone!"

A party had spontaneously erupted at Winston Egbert's house, which was now packed with high-spirited Sweet Valley High football players, cheerleaders, and their friends. Standing by the refreshment table with Todd, Enid, Maria, and Sandy, Elizabeth glared across the room at the glamorous figure of Heather Mallone. "Jessica's sitting home by herself," Elizabeth repeated in a disgusted tone, "while Heather hogs all the glory."

"Talk about a guy magnet," said her best friend, Enid Rollins, tossing her auburn curls. "You'd think they'd be embarrassed to be seen drooling that way in public."

"It's not just the guys," Todd protested in defense of his gender. "Girls like her, too."

True, the crowd gathered around Heather was coed. "You're right," Elizabeth conceded, dipping another chip, "and that's the worst part. I can't believe Jessica's old cheerleading friends, especially Amy, aren't showing more loyalty to her. Instead, they're kissing up to Heather worse than ever!"

"They expect her to lead them straight to the cheerleading nationals," Maria Santelli reminded Elizabeth, "and I hate to say it, but I really think she can do it."

Elizabeth shook her head. "Maybe, but if you ask me, there are more important things than just winning competitions. I thought cheerleading was supposed to be about having a good time. Whatever happened to team spirit and good sportsmanship?"

"That's not Heather's philosophy," said Sandy with a sigh of resignation. "She's out to get what she wants, and if anyone stands in the way . . ." She drew her index finger across her throat to illustrate her point.

"Heather gave me and Sandy the boot because she thought we were holding back the squad," said Maria. "She had to find another way to get rid of Jessica, though."

"And now she has total control of the squad," concluded Sandy. "Talk about sly!"

Elizabeth poured herself a cup of soda, still fuming on her sister's behalf. Personally, she didn't see the attraction of cheerleading, but she knew it was important to Jessica; it was one of the few hobbies, besides shopping and boys, that her sister really got into body and soul.

Elizabeth remembered how happy Jessica had been the day the squad voted her cocaptain. *I didn't get it,* she admitted to herself. *How could anyone be that excited about something as silly as cheerleading?* In Elizabeth's opinion girls should have better things to do than hop around in short skirts, cheering on the boys' teams. Of course, at Sweet Valley High the cheerleaders performed at both boys' and girls' games, but still . . . Jessica was such a great athlete—she could have easily made the tennis or softball or gymnastics teams. But no, it had to be cheerleading.

This difference in attitude was typical of the sixteen-year-old twin sisters. They were identical in appearance, with the same slim, athletic figures, honey-blond hair, turquoise eyes, and sun-warmed complexions, but no one who knew them well ever mixed them up . . . unless, that is, Elizabeth and Jessica wanted to be mixed up! They'd swapped identities on more than one occasion, but for the most part Elizabeth was happy to be the thoughtful, sensible, serious twin, and Jessica was happy to be the carefree, outrageous, irresponsible twin.

Of course, both girls knew that their personalities were more complex than that, but their reputations had a basis in truth. In addition to being a conscientious student, Elizabeth spent a good deal of her free time writing articles for the SVH newspaper, *The Oracle.* She finished her homework before making phone calls, and if she had a big test the next day, she resisted the temptation to blow off studying in favor of a movie or beach date with Todd. Jessica, on the other hand, reversed these priorities; her social life always came first. As for worrying about the future—college, a career—she was too busy enjoying the present!

I always thought I'd be psyched if Jessica quit cheerleading and put her energy into something more meaningful, Elizabeth reflected now, *but it shouldn't have happened like this. . . .*

"So you weren't able to talk Jess into coming to the party, either?"

Elizabeth blinked up at the speaker, startled from her reverie, and her cheeks flushed hot pink. Ken Matthews, the blond, well-built quarterback of the Sweet Valley High football team, and Jessica's current boyfriend, was smiling down at her. Jessica's current boyfriend . . . and once upon a time Elizabeth's secret love . . .

Elizabeth glanced quickly at Todd and was relieved to see he hadn't noted her telltale blush. "Uh, no. She said she didn't feel like talking to anybody, and she especially didn't want to run the risk of bumping into Heather."

As if on cue, Heather herself flounced up to the refreshment table. She was no longer in her cheerleading uniform, but the tight black dress she wore was just as short, revealing plenty of long, suntanned leg and quite a bit of shoulder and cleavage, too.

"Too bad about your sister," Heather said in passing to Elizabeth. "I guess she wasn't cut out to be a cheerleader. I'd say today's game separated the women from the girls, wouldn't you?"

Before Elizabeth could make a retort, Heather sashayed off with a cup of fruit punch. "The nerve of that girl!" she exclaimed.

"She's a monster," agreed Maria. "Poor Jessica never stood a chance."

Ken ran a hand through his bright-blond hair.

"I hate to see someone like Heather get the better of Jessica," he declared. "If only there were something I could do to cheer her up!"

"Just don't use the word 'cheer' around her," suggested Enid.

"There's gotta be something." Todd winked at Ken. "And if anyone can figure out what it is, it's you."

The others laughed. Elizabeth, meanwhile, felt as if the false smile she wore might crack her face in half. *I'm surprised they don't see right through me,* she thought. But, then, it wasn't always that hard to keep a big secret. She and Ken had successfully hidden their clandestine romance from the whole school—no one ever found out. *We wore masks,* she remembered. *We became actors, reading lines from a carefully crafted script.*

And now, after thinking that her relationship with Ken was over and done with, safely locked away in the past, Elizabeth found the old, confusing feelings crowding back to the surface. She watched Ken's face as he talked to Todd and Aaron and Bruce about a highlight of the football game. It was a handsome face, and an honest, open face . . . a face that, just a moment before, had been glowing with sincere concern and affection for Jessica. *He's not wearing a mask anymore,* Elizabeth thought. *I'm the only one who still has something to hide. . . .*

Safe in the knowledge that her sister would be out late, Jessica continued reading Elizabeth's diary. After breaking up with Ken, Elizabeth had started dating Jeffrey French. But then Todd's family moved back to Sweet Valley, and Elizabeth had to choose between Jeffrey and Todd. The diary was better than a romance novel!

When the phone rang, Jessica jumped guiltily, the diary flying from her hands. Leaping to her feet, she returned the notebook to its hiding place, then grabbed the receiver. "Hello?"

"Jess, it's me."

Despite her mood, Ken's deep, husky voice sent a happy shiver up Jessica's spine. "Hi, there."

"How are you feeling?" he asked, raising his voice in order to be heard over the noisy buzz of a party in the background.

"Still pretty crummy," she admitted.

"Well, I know you said you wanted to be left alone, but I have a proposition for you."

"What kind of proposition?"

"Meet me outside your house in ten minutes and you'll find out."

"Oh, come on. Tell me!" Jessica begged.

"Ten minutes, OK?" said Ken.

"It can't wait until tomorrow?"

"Nope, and I can't wait, either. I'm too nuts about you to waste a Saturday night apart!"

Jessica smiled. "When you put it that way . . . !"

Exactly ten minutes later Ken's white Toyota pulled up in front of the Wakefields' house on Calico Drive. Jessica was standing on the sidewalk, ready to hop into the passenger seat. "So, what's so urgent?" she asked him.

Ken gave her a swift kiss and then sat back again, smiling at her with sparkling eyes. "I've been thinking," he began eagerly, "about cheerleading."

"You've been thinking about cheerleading?" Jessica groaned. "Can we change the subject before I throw up?"

"I know you're depressed because you won't be cheering anymore, but this is the thing. There's no reason you have to stop doing what you like to do just because you're not on the squad anymore."

"Oh, really?" Jessica cocked an eyebrow. "Yes, I suppose you're right. I could cheerlead by myself in my backyard. Boy, that would be a riot," she said sarcastically. "Meanwhile, that bimbo Heather Mallone will be cheering with my squad in front of my school!"

"You don't need them," Ken persisted. "That's my point. You should start your own squad!"

"Start my own squad?" Jessica's jaw dropped. "You're kidding."

Ken shook his head. "I've never been more serious."

"Then you're just plain crazy. Start my own squad," Jessica repeated, laughing. "OK, imagine if you'd quit the football team and I told you, 'No prob, just start your own team!' "

"Why not?" Ken countered. "Give me one good reason it wouldn't work."

"OK, first of all, there's always been only one official cheerleading squad at Sweet Valley High. I mean, there are probably rules about that sort of thing."

"New clubs form all the time," argued Ken. "If you don't ask, how do you know they won't let you start up another squad?"

"Maybe," Jessica conceded. "But anyone who's any good is already on Heather's squad."

"Not true," said Ken. "There are tons of girls out there who'd like to cheer and would probably be good at it. Every time the squad has a vacancy, you get dozens of girls trying out for that one spot, right?"

"But what about uniforms? Where would we practice?"

"The cheerleaders have always had to buy their own uniforms," Ken pointed out. "As for practicing, come on. All those athletic fields? If you were willing to practice before instead of after school, you could take your pick."

"It could be done," Jessica finally had to admit. Despite herself, she was starting to get a little excited.

"You can do anything if you want it bad enough."

"My very own cheerleading squad." Jessica couldn't help it—a big grin spread across her face. "I won't have a cocaptain, not Heather or anyone else. I'll call all the shots—I'll be totally in charge!"

"Queen Jessica," Ken agreed.

"I'll write all new cheers—it won't be the same old stuff," she continued. "I'll do a talent search and hold my own tryouts. All new girls, a whole new attitude!"

Ken clapped. "That's the spirit!"

"Oh, Ken!" Jessica flung her arms around his

neck and gazed up at him with starry eyes. "You are just the sweetest, most adorable guy in the whole world, did you know that?"

"No, I didn't know that," he teased, wrapping his muscular arms around her slender waist. "Tell me again."

"You are just the sweetest, most . . ."

Ken silenced Jessica with a tender yet passionate kiss on the lips. *Everybody thinks my sister's such a brain,* Jessica thought as the kiss deepened and she abandoned herself to the delicious sensation. *But if you ask me, she's an idiot for letting Ken Matthews slip through her fingers!*

"You seem quiet," Todd observed to Elizabeth as he drove her home after the party. "Something on your mind?"

"Oh . . ." Elizabeth shrugged, looking away from him out the passenger-side window. "I guess I'm just still steaming about Heather. I kept telling Jessica to work with her, be flexible and open to new ideas and all that, but now I understand exactly how Heather made her feel and why she quit. That girl is a monster!"

"She's horrid," Todd agreed as he turned onto Calico Drive, "but Jessica will bounce back. She always does." The BMW rolled to a stop in front of her house. Killing the engine and the lights, he reached for Elizabeth. "Come here," he said softly.

Elizabeth let Todd pull her close and shut her eyes as he started pressing light kisses on her forehead, her temples, her cheekbones. But no matter how hard she tried, she couldn't give him her full attention. Her mind kept wandering, and it was leading her to the most disturbing places.

Jessica and Ken park like this now. Ken kisses Jessica like this. . . . Just thinking about it made Elizabeth's toes curl with envy. *I could be sitting in a white Toyota instead of a black BMW. I could be kissing Ken Matthews instead of Todd Wilkins. . . .*

Placing her hands on either side of Todd's face, Elizabeth gave him a kiss so boldly passionate, it made his eyes pop open in surprise. But it didn't work . . . not for her, anyway.

Elizabeth was still hiding it from Todd, but she couldn't hide it from herself. Lately Todd, the big love of her life, the boy for whom she'd given up all others, left her stone cold. She was starting to wonder: When she gave up Ken in order to save her relationship with Todd, did she choose the wrong boy?

Chapter 2

"Whoa, better call the *Sweet Valley News*," said eighteen-year-old Steven Wakefield with a teasing grin. "It's Sunday and she's out of bed before noon. I think this qualifies as a miracle!"

Jessica tightened the belt on her bathrobe as she entered the sunny Spanish-tiled kitchen. She stuck her tongue out at her handsome older brother, a prelaw student at the state university who often came home on weekends. "You've just forgotten what it's like to be young and fun and have a social life. Reading the business section of the newspaper—you look just like Dad!"

Over at the counter Mr. Wakefield was ladling batter into the waffle maker. "I get the feeling I was just insulted," he said, pretending to be hurt. "What's the matter with looking like ol' Dad?"

"Just kidding." Crossing the kitchen, Jessica stood on tiptoes to give her tall father a kiss on the cheek. "Steven's lucky he looks like you."

"If you think flattery will get you the first waffle, you're absolutely right," Mr. Wakefield said.

Jessica smiled. "You're easy, Dad."

She greeted her mother with a kiss, too. "I didn't expect you to be in such a good mood," Mrs. Wakefield admitted, giving her daughter an affectionate hug and then returning to the task of slicing a juicy cantaloupe. "You were pretty down in the dumps yesterday after the football game."

"Since then I've gotten a whole new perspective on the cheerleading situation," explained Jessica as she poured herself a cup of hot lemon-scented tea. "Ken had the absolute best idea."

"Let's hear it," said Steven, putting the business section aside in favor of the funnies.

"Well . . ." Jessica leaned back against the counter, facing her parents and brother. "I guess I don't have to remind you of all the underhanded things Heather Mallone has done since she moved to Sweet Valley."

"We've been hearing about it on a daily basis," Mr. Wakefield agreed, flipping the first crisp, golden waffle onto a serving plate.

"Because of her I quit the squad yesterday, and there's no way I'm going back as long as she's in charge."

"And it sounds like she's there to stay," observed Mrs. Wakefield. "So what did Ken propose?"

"I form my own squad," said Jessica, her eyes shining. "She stole the old one from me, but she can't stop me from doing what I do best. I know I can get Maria and Sandy, and probably Lila, too, and then I'll audition a bunch of new girls. We'll show Heather what school spirit's really all about!"

"I think it's a marvelous idea," Mrs. Wakefield enthused. "Good for Ken. Good for you!"

"So you're going to start your own squad, from scratch." A mischievous smile creased Ned Wakefield's face. "Why, you should recruit your sister!"

At that moment Elizabeth appeared in the doorway. "Recruit me for what?" she mumbled sleepily, stretching her arms over her head and yawning.

Jessica tilted her head to one side, considering her father's suggestion. "You know, Dad," she mused, "you might be onto something. Think about the publicity we'd get with identical twins on the team!"

Steven snorted. Mrs. Wakefield smothered a smile.

"Recruit me for what?" Elizabeth repeated, still a little foggy.

Steven shook imaginary pom-poms. "Yay, team. Go, fight, win!" he cheered.

Elizabeth squinted at him suspiciously. Both her parents were now laughing openly. "Wait a minute. You're not talking about me cheerleading, are you?"

Her brother held up his hands, protesting his innocence. "Hey, I didn't start this."

Elizabeth whirled to face Jessica. "How many

times do I have to tell you I'd rather floss with barbed wire than be a cheerleader? Girls should play sports on their own, not just sit on the sidelines cheering on the guys!"

Jessica rolled her eyes; she'd heard this speech before.

"Besides," concluded Elizabeth, "you're not even on the squad anymore. How could you recruit anyone?"

"Never underestimate the powers of Jessica Wakefield," intoned Steven mysteriously.

Elizabeth looked to her parents for illumination. "Jessica's thinking of forming her own cheerleading squad," Mrs. Wakefield explained, "so she's in the market for athletic talent, and you naturally came to mind."

Elizabeth raised her eyebrows at Jessica. "Your own squad?"

Jessica smiled smugly. "Isn't it brilliant? Talk about the best revenge!" Her dimple deepened. "And it was all Ken's idea, can you believe it? I didn't think it could work, but he talked me into it. He really believes in me, and he wants more than anything to see me happy. Isn't that just so sweet?"

"Very," said Elizabeth, flouncing over to the counter to help herself to a waffle. "But just forget about trying to talk me into having anything to do with anybody's cheerleading squad under any circumstances."

Jessica feigned nonchalance. "Suit yourself," she drawled. "I just thought you'd be happy for me. I mean, about the cheerleading, and about Ken. My life is so fantastic! I'm going to be the captain of my own cheerleading squad, and I'm in love with the most wonderful guy. . . ." Jessica was pleased to note that Elizabeth looked a bit green. "It was just so romantic last night, Liz. He swept me off for this spontaneous late date. I mean, I couldn't stay in a bad mood. And today we're spending the entire day together at this little secluded beach he knows about. He says it's very private."

Steven made a gagging noise. "Do you mind? I'm trying to eat."

"Well, have fun." Sloshing some maple syrup onto her waffle, Elizabeth picked up her plate and headed for the door.

Before Jessica could tag after her sister and torture her some more with further details of Ken's devotion, the telephone rang. Mrs. Wakefield picked it up. "Hello? Hi, Amy. Yes, she's standing right here."

She held the receiver out to Jessica, who stuck her lower lip out in a pout. "If she's calling to beg me to rejoin the squad, she's wasting her breath," Jessica mumbled as she took the phone, although she hoped Amy was calling to do just that. "What's up?" she asked curtly.

"Did you hear the thrilling news?" said Amy, her voice pitched high with excitement.

"Don't tell me," guessed Jessica. "Heather was hit by a truck!"

"Now, don't be that way," said Amy in a manner that Jessica found annoyingly patronizing. "No, silly, we're going to regionals!"

Jessica gripped the edge of the counter for support. "You're kidding!"

"Nope, we're really and truly going," said Amy. "The American Cheerleading Association scout was at yesterday's game, and he told Heather he was extremely impressed with us, and that we're definitely regionals material. 'Regionals material'—those were his exact words. How exciting is that?"

Just a few weeks earlier Jessica would have been doing handsprings over news like this. But now, to think the squad was going to regionals without her . . . "I'm just busting," she said, gritting her teeth.

"You know . . ." Amy's voice became conciliatory. "You could still be on Heather's squad if you really want to, Jess. I'm sure she'd take you back if you apologized and—"

"Heather's squad!" Jessica exploded. "She would take me back if I apologized! I don't think so!"

"Well, fine," said Amy, becoming huffy. "If you're going to be that way about it . . ."

"You bet I'm going to be that way about it," declared Jessica, slamming down the phone without even bothering to say good-bye.

The call from Amy had taken away Jessica's appetite. Abandoning her lukewarm, syrup-soaked waffle, she trooped after her sister. It wasn't like Elizabeth to be antisocial, but she'd retreated to the den to eat a solitary brunch in front of the TV. Jessica peeked in at her. *I really got her goat when I started gushing about Ken,* Jessica thought, an amused smile curving her lips. She sprinted out of the kitchen pretty darn fast—she just couldn't stand hearing about it!

Jessica reflected back on the dirt she'd discovered in Elizabeth's diary. She couldn't help being impressed that her boring, conservative, play-it-safe sister had played a role in such a melodramatic saga. First Todd had moved away—major heartbreak. Then Elizabeth had turned for comfort to Todd's best friend, Ken. Their friendship had blossomed unexpectedly into romance—major guilt. Unwilling to hurt Todd, Elizabeth and Ken had decided to do the right thing and forswear their secret love. Eventually, Todd had moved back to Sweet Valley, and he and Elizabeth had once again became a rock-solid steady couple. *But she never got over Ken,* Jessica surmised. *Not surprisingly, since he's a thousand times cuter and more fun than Todd!*

Jessica wondered what her sister's easygoing boyfriend would think if he found out that, unbeknownst to him, he'd been part of a love triangle involving his own best friend. Talk about fireworks!

She directed one last glance Elizabeth's way, then retreated back into the hallway. It gave her a feeling of power, having discovered this secret about her sister. *I know something about her that she doesn't know I know!* The question was how best to use this secret knowledge to her advantage. Because there was no doubt, at some time and in some way, she would use it. It was just too good an opportunity to waste!

• • •

"I'm having a tough time concentrating on this history assignment," Enid admitted to Elizabeth on Sunday afternoon. "The sun just feels so good, I keep drifting off."

The two girls were reclining on lounge chairs by the swimming pool in Elizabeth's backyard, attempting to combine homework with sunbathing. As she pushed the loosened straps of her bikini top to the side in order to bare her smooth, golden-bronze shoulders, Elizabeth glanced at Enid. Her friend was lying flat on her back, her face tilted to the sky. "Maybe if you sat up in your chair and opened your eyes," Elizabeth teased. "I find it a lot easier to read that way myself."

Enid giggled. "What a novel idea. You think of everything, don't you?"

Enid adjusted the back of her chair to a vertical position and opened her history book with a sigh. A moment later she closed it again. "I still can't concentrate," she declared. "I think I'll cool off with a dip in the pool."

"I'll join you," offered Elizabeth, happy for an excuse to toss her own book aside. She was having trouble concentrating, too, but for a different reason. . . .

Enid swam a few laps of the pool at a gentle crawl with Elizabeth backstroking beside her. Then the two girls hung off the ledge in the deep end, their legs floating. "So where's Jessica today?" Enid asked idly.

"She went to the beach with Ken," Elizabeth answered, hoping she sounded casual and uninterested.

Because she felt anything but. She remembered Jessica's smug announcement that morning: "We're spending the whole day together at this little secluded beach Ken knows about. He says it's very private. . . ."

The worst thing was, Elizabeth knew exactly what beach Jessica was talking about. It had to be the same one she and Ken went to when they were seeing each other secretly!

Elizabeth felt as if she might go crazy if she pictured Ken and Jessica alone on the beach together one more time. But she couldn't stop thinking about it, and despite the agony it caused her, she found she wanted to talk about it, too. "What do you think about those two, anyway?" she asked Enid. "I mean, about them as a couple."

"Oh, I think they're perfect together," said Enid, to Elizabeth's dismay. "The star quarterback and the head cheerleader. . . or rather, the ex–head cheerleader." She ducked her head backward into the water to wet her hair. "They're both blond and gorgeous and outgoing and popular, and they really seem to be nuts about each other. This could be the guy Jessica gets serious about, don't you think?"

"I suppose." Elizabeth trailed her fingers in the water, then drew her hand back quickly when she realized she'd been sketching the initials "K.M." "Then again, in a day or two she could blow him off and get interested in someone new. You know how she is."

"Not everyone's cut out for monogamy," Enid

agreed. "But don't you think it's also partly a question of finding the right person? I mean, you and Todd have been together for a long time partly because that's your style, but mostly because you're totally right for each other. If Todd had turned out to be a different guy, you might be into dating around like Jessica."

Elizabeth pushed off from the side of the pool, rolling onto her back. Enid paddled after her. "You're probably right," Elizabeth said after splashing around for a moment. "I mean, don't get the wrong idea," she added. "I'm happy for Jessica, it's just that . . ."

What a liar! she thought to herself. *You're not happy for Jessica at all!* "What am I saying?" she burst out. "To tell you the truth, Enid, seeing Jessica and Ken together . . . it makes me feel . . . oh, I don't know."

Enid was always a good listener; now she waited patiently for Elizabeth to finish her thought. Elizabeth gazed at her friend's face, unsure. *I could just tell her everything, she considered. God, it would feel so good to get this off my chest! And Enid's always wonderful at helping me put things in perspective. . . .*

"You see . . ." Suddenly Elizabeth couldn't quite bring herself to do it. After so much time had passed, it would just be too hard to explain the whole complicated, sordid story. And what if Enid thought Elizabeth was horrible for going behind Todd's back like that, for lying to everyone, including Enid herself?

Late at night your emotions more easily get the upper hand, Elizabeth thought, remembering the tumult of feelings she'd experienced the previous night at the party, and then when she'd said good night to Todd, and then again when she was alone in her room. But in the bright light of day . . . The sun seemed to be trying to chase her secret feelings back into their hiding place. And maybe that's where they belonged.

"It's just a little weird, that's all," said Elizabeth. "I mean, Jessica's so moony about Ken because their relationship is new, and it sort of makes me feel like Todd and I are boring, you know?"

Enid nodded. "There's nothing quite like that brand-new-infatuation stuff," she said, "but you and Todd have something even better. Deeper, you know? It's real—it's stood the test of time."

"Yeah, you're right," agreed Elizabeth with false brightness. "You're absolutely right." Turning away from Enid, she swam to the ladder and climbed out of the pool. As she dried herself off, she made a decision. *I'll just have to keep it inside,* she told herself firmly, *and try harder to be happy with Todd, and happy for Jess and Ken.* Because Todd was her boyfriend, and Ken was her sister's boyfriend, and the sooner she got that straight in her mind, the better off she'd be.

Ken chased Jessica to the water's edge. She squealed with laughter as he picked her up easily and slung her over his shoulder fireman style, then waded with her into the surf. She beat playfully against his back with her fists, but she wasn't trying too hard to get free.

A big wave rolled in, knocking Ken off balance. "Whoa!" he shouted. "Looks like we're going for a swim!"

They both got a thorough dunking. Jessica spluttered to the surface, laughing. Ken scooped her up in his arms, and she put her own arms around his neck. They bobbed in the water that way, gazing adoringly into each other's eyes.

"You look like a sea monster," she teased, plucking a piece of seaweed from his hair.

"And you look like a mermaid," he said, giving her a kiss.

His lips were wet and salty and delicious. "Umm," murmured Jessica. "Let's try that again. . . ."

A few minutes later, after toweling off and reapplying suntan lotion to each other's bodies, they were lying face-to-face in a pleasant tangle of limbs on the beach blanket. "How come when I see other couples acting all mushy like this, I think it's nauseating," said Jessica, nuzzling her nose against Ken's, "but when we do it, it's so much fun?"

He laughed. "Good question." He nibbled on her ear. "But it is fun, isn't it?"

Jessica sighed with pure happiness. "Um-hm."

"Anyway, that's why I brought you here, so we'd have privacy. I mean, just in case we couldn't keep our hands off each other or something. I mean, I sort of anticipated that that might be the case," he added with a sexy smile, "especially if you happened to be wearing a totally hot black string bikini."

"Sorry to be such a temptress," said Jessica.

Ken's grin widened. "Don't be sorry, I'm loving every minute of it."

Cuddling closer, Jessica rested her head on Ken's shoulder. For a moment they lay peacefully, listening to the lulling sound of the waves crashing on the shore. "I guess it really doesn't matter how we behave," she commented, "since there's no one here to see us, anyway."

"It's just you and me," Ken agreed. "We're the only two people in the entire world."

"Umm." Jessica rubbed her cheek against his neck. *That's the way it is when you're in love,* she thought. *Everything and everyone else seems to disappear. . . .*

Jessica's brain hadn't been completely erased, though. Suddenly the image of Ken and Elizabeth cuddling on a beach blanket popped, in an unwelcome fashion, into her mind. "So how many other girls have you brought to this secret beach?" she teased, hoping to coax a confession out of Ken.

"None. You're the first."

Jessica laughed. "Oh, c'mon. I bet you came here with Terri."

She could feel Ken shaking his head. "Nope."

"Not even with Terri?"

Ken and Terri Adams, the petite, pretty assistant manager of the Sweet Valley High football team, had been a steady couple for quite a while. They'd broken up not long before Ken had started showing an interest in Jessica. "Not even with Terri," Ken confirmed.

"There must have been someone." Propping herself up on one elbow, Jessica lightly traced a pattern on Ken's chest with her fingernail. "You can tell me. I won't get jealous."

Ken laughed. "Sorry to disappoint you, but I don't have that many skeletons in my closet. I guess I was saving myself for you."

Putting both arms around her, he pulled her close again. His mouth found hers, and he began kissing her hungrily . . . a kiss that left no room for doubt. She hadn't been able to trick him into saying anything about Elizabeth, but Jessica decided it really didn't matter. No matter what Elizabeth might be feeling, it was obvious Ken wasn't hung up on the past.

They stayed at the beach until the sun was low in the sky, a fiery red ball poised to drop into the western sea. "Are you hungry?" Ken asked as he pointed the Toyota back toward town. "I was just thinking I could go for a burger and shake."

"Sounds good to me. You can really work up an appetite lying on a beach blanket all day, huh?"

He flashed a smile at her. "All that heavy breathing burns a lot of calories."

Jessica rolled down her window, shaking her salty tangled hair in the wind. She couldn't seem to stop smiling. "This was a great day," she shouted to Ken over the pulse of the radio, "but for once in my life, I'm not sorry the weekend's almost over. Tomorrow at school I'm going to start recruiting my new cheerleading squad!"

Ken turned into the Dairi Burger parking lot. "I bet you won't have any trouble finding girls who want to cheer."

"But I'm only going to take the cream of the crop," said Jessica. "How do you think Elizabeth would be as a cheerleader?"

"Elizabeth?" Ken's eyebrows shot up. "As in, your sister?" Jessica nodded and Ken burst out laughing. "Elizabeth, a cheerleader," he repeated. "Sorry, I just can't picture it."

"I think she'd be great," argued Jessica.

"Yeah, but does she want to cheer?"

"It doesn't matter what she wants," said Jessica. "It's what I want!"

They were both laughing until, at the same instant, they spotted the white Mazda Miata convertible with the "CHRLDER" license plates. "Yuck," grumbled Jessica.

Ken put the key back in the ignition. "We could go someplace else," he offered.

"No," said Jessica. She wasn't about to let Heather Mallone scare her away from her longtime favorite hangout. "This is fine. Yesterday I thought I never wanted to lay eyes on Heather Mallone again, but now I actually wouldn't mind having a word with her."

There was no doubt that Heather had set out to take Sweet Valley by storm and that she was succeeding. As Ken and Jessica entered the Dairi Burger, their eyes were drawn immediately to a big table in the center of the restaurant crowded with laughing, chattering kids. Heather sat surrounded by some of her new, admiring friends, a gang of very popular SVH seniors.

"Let's do take-out," Ken said in a low voice to Jessica. "Maybe you don't mind her, but she makes me sick."

They had to walk by Heather's table to reach the take-out counter. As they approached, the table fell silent.

Jessica felt all eyes on her, including Heather's. With her shoulders straight and her chin up, she met Heather's smirking, triumphant gaze head-on.

She thinks I'm just going to slink by all miserable and groveling, realized Jessica. *Boy, does she have me figured wrong!*

Instead of following Ken to the counter, Jessica pivoted on her heel and marched right up to Heather. "Congratulations, Heather," she said sweetly. "I hear you're taking your squad to regionals."

Heather blinked, surprised. Then she regained her composure. "That's right," she purred, obviously expecting Jessica to beg to be allowed back onto the squad.

"Well, good luck in the competition," said Jessica in the same bright, careless tone.

Tossing her hair, Jessica sauntered over to Ken. She knew Heather was staring after her. *Good luck is right,* she thought with a secret smile. *You're going to need it!*

Jessica knocked on Elizabeth's door when she got home. "Come in," Elizabeth called.

Elizabeth was sitting on her bed, a spiral notebook open on her lap. Jessica bounced onto the bed next to her. "Did you have a nice day?" she asked her sister.

Elizabeth shrugged. "Average." There was a pause. Jessica waited patiently. At last Elizabeth asked reluctantly, "How 'bout you?"

"Oh, it was divine." Jessica closed her eyes rapturously. "Ken is just . . ." She shook her head, dimpling coyly. "I don't think there are words to describe what it's like being with him. I mean, it's just . . . he's just . . . Oh, Liz, you can't even imagine."

Elizabeth tapped her pen on the notebook. "Do you mind?" she said sharply. "I'm kind of busy."

Jessica ignored this none-too-subtle hint. "I asked Ken about you," she told her sister.

Elizabeth's eyes bugged slightly; she looked as if she'd just swallowed something wriggly. "What . . . what about me?"

Jessica stifled a giggle. "I asked him if he thought you'd be a good cheerleader," she replied, all innocence.

Elizabeth sank back against the pillows. "Oh, cheerleading. Well . . . what did he say?"

Jessica didn't hesitate to put words in Ken's mouth. "Oh, he said you were probably too bookwormy to be a cheerleader."

"Oh, really." Elizabeth's tone grew huffy. "That's one way of putting it, I suppose. Another way of putting it is that I wouldn't be caught dead doing it."

"Really?" Jessica tilted her head to one side. "You mean, you've never wanted even a teeny, weeny bit to be on the sidelines cheering for Todd on the basketball court, or say . . . Ken on the football field?"

Two spots of red stained Elizabeth's cheeks. "OK, Jess," she snapped, slamming her notebook shut. "I'm going to say this one more time and one time only, so listen good. I—will—not—under—any—circumstances—be—on—your—new—cheerleading—squad!"

"OK, OK." Laughing, Jessica put her hands up in an "I surrender" pose. "It's your choice, Liz, of course."

"You bet it's my choice," Elizabeth called after her as Jessica disappeared into the bathroom that connected their bedrooms.

In her own room Jessica went straight for the telephone. In quick succession she dialed three phone numbers: Lila's, Maria's, and Sandy's.

She had the same conversation with each girl. "Meet me tomorrow before homeroom," she instructed her friends. "I've got something extremely important and top secret to discuss with you!"

Next Jessica called Ken for a lovey-dovey good-night chat. Then she showered, spent a few token minutes on homework, and got ready for bed.

Switching off the light on her nightstand, she cuddled under the covers, smiling happily to herself. She planned to have very satisfying dreams, about steaming up some car windows with Ken . . . and about knocking Heather Mallone and her lousy cheerleading squad right out of the regionals competition.

Chapter 3

Lila, Maria, and Sandy met Jessica by her locker Monday morning before school started. As soon as they were all there, Jessica whisked them into the girls' room for a private conference.

"So what's going on?" Lila demanded, whipping out a lipstick as she leaned close to the mirror to examine her flawless makeup.

"Yeah, what's the big secret?" asked Maria, fluffing her long brown hair with her fingers.

"I have a proposition for you," declared Jessica. Sandy was wearing a short denim skirt; Jessica eyed her calves critically, checking for muscle tone. "I hope you've been working out lately, Sandy, even though Heather kicked you off the squad."

Sandy wrinkled her nose, her hazel eyes puzzled. "Actually, I've kind of been blobbing out. I was just so sick of that totally obsessive diet-and-fitness regimen Heather had us on, I figured I deserved a break."

Jessica turned to Maria. "I've been on a couple long bike rides, but that's about it," Maria said. "Why? What's this all about?"

"My new cheerleading squad, that's what this is all about!" said Jessica.

Lila froze with the lipstick an inch from her pursed lips. "Your new what?"

"Cheerleading squad," repeated Jessica, taking a small bottle of cologne from her purse and spritzing the base of her throat. "Ken helped me see that there was absolutely no reason I should let an upstart like Heather Mallone put an end to my cheering career. So I'm forming my own squad, and I'm counting on you three to be the foundation."

"Oh, Jessica!" squealed Sandy. She and Maria crowded close, bouncing up and down with excitement. "What a great idea!"

Lila finished painting her mouth, then tucked the lipstick back into her bag. "What's the point?" she drawled.

"What's the point?" said Jessica indignantly. "The point is this is my school and my sport, and if anyone deserves to go to regionals, it's me. And you two," she added, turning to Maria and Sandy. "Why should we be shut out from the glory we all worked hard for?"

"I'm with you one hundred percent," declared Maria.

"Me, too," said Sandy.

Jessica looked at Lila. "Sorry," said Lila. "There's a reason I quit the squad myself ages ago. Cheerleading is a bore, and the uniforms are tacky."

"It is not a bore!" Jessica protested. "And the uniforms don't have to be tacky. We're a new squad—we can buy the hottest, cutest uniforms out there."

"So, OK," Lila said, playing the devil's advocate. "So let's say the four of us have spiffy uniforms. We're still only four girls—hardly enough for a squad."

"I said you guys would be the foundation of the squad," Jessica pointed out. "You'll have to help me recruit the best dancers and gymnasts in the school. I know there's lots of talent out there just waiting to be tapped."

"Dancers and gymnasts?" Lila remained skeptical. "What do they know about cheerleading?"

"Nothing," Jessica said cheerfully. "But they'll have what it takes to turn into cheerleaders—strength, agility, grace, limberness, rhythm. We're just going to have to practice like mad and then get an audience with the ACA scout to get a slot in regionals." She shrugged. "Piece of cake!"

Lila had to laugh. "That's what I love about you, Wakefield. You're from another planet, but you act like you own this one. OK, sign me on."

"Hooray!" Maria gave Lila a hug. "We'll be cheering together again, Li. This is going to be so much fun!"

Jessica clapped her hands. "Enough of the love fest. We have business to attend to. First things first. Who should we recruit?"

All four agreed that two of their schoolmates were must-haves: Patty Gilbert and Jade Wu, two dancers who'd starred in the SVH variety show. "Patty especially would be great because she's so good at choreography," Jessica commented. "All right, we'll go after those two at lunch."

"If we can get them both, that'll bring us to six," said Maria. "Still a little skimpy."

"I'd prefer seven or eight," agreed Jessica.

"How about your sister?" suggested Sandy. "I always thought she'd be a terrific cheerleader."

"Funny you should say that," said Jessica. "Liz is on my list, too."

Lila laughed out loud. "You're kidding. Liz a cheerleader?"

Jessica brushed some blusher on her cheeks. "Why not?"

"You'll never get her on the team," Lila predicted.

"Wanna bet?"

"Sure, what'll it be?"

"Let's see. . . ." Jessica snapped the blusher compact shut. "How about since we were just talking about uniforms, whoever loses buys new uniforms for the entire squad?"

"Yow!" exclaimed Lila. "That would set you back big-time, Wakefield. You must be pretty sure of yourself."

Jessica smiled. "Oh, I am."

Lila narrowed her eyes suspiciously. "Hmm. Well, I still say your sister would rather be eaten alive by red ants than lift a pom-pom. You're on!"

Lila held out one perfectly manicured hand. Taking it, Jessica gave it a firm shake. Then she slung her arms around Maria and Sandy's shoulders and steered them back out into the hallway. "Are you ready?" she asked, her eyes sparkling. "Are you psyched?"

Maria and Sandy bobbed their heads. "You better believe it!" they chorused.

At lunchtime Jessica hunted down sophomore Jade Wu at a corner table with her boyfriend David Prentiss. "Jade, I need to talk to you about something," Jessica announced in an important and mysterious tone.

At the same time, Maria rounded up Patty Gilbert, who'd been sitting with her cousin Tracy, Tracy's boyfriend, Andy, DeeDee Gordon, and Bill Chase.

Jessica and Maria hustled the two girls outside to the courtyard. Patty's and Jade's jaws dropped when they heard Jessica's invitation. "Cheerleading?" said Patty, her big brown eyes widening. "Gee, Jess, it was sweet of you to think of me, but the cheerleading thing—no offense, but it never really appealed to me."

"I don't think I'd have the time," said Jade, ducking her head shyly. "What with dance class three afternoons a week . . ."

"Maybe you've never been into cheerleading, but this is going to be a whole new ball game," said Jessica earnestly, looking from Patty to Jade and back again. "I want my squad to be different, innovative. That's why I need your dance and choreography skills. This is our chance to experiment, to bring a whole new look and style to the art of cheerleading!"

Patty smiled thoughtfully. "When you put it that way, it sounds like a challenge. It sounds like fun."

Jessica and Maria both smiled encouragingly at Jade. "Dance class is pretty formal and structured," Jade reflected. "Maybe . . . maybe I'll give it a try."

Jessica gave her an impetuous hug. "That's all I'm asking," she said. "Just show up at our first practice at the far end of the football field tomorrow morning before school. And spread the word. I want you two especially, but everybody's welcome to show up at practice and try out!"

Back inside the cafeteria, Jessica and Maria joined Lila and Sandy. "My new squad is almost complete. Patty and Jade are onboard!" Jessica sang triumphantly.

"They've agreed to come to practice tomorrow morning, anyway," said Maria. "How'd you make out with Elizabeth?"

"About like we expected," Lila reported. "Let me see if I can remember her exact words: 'I'd rather walk down Main Street naked than put on a cheerleading uniform.'"

Jessica lifted her shoulders in a careless shrug. "Obviously you didn't take the right approach."

"Face it," said Lila smugly. "Your sister isn't going to join the cause. The rest of us will need uniforms, though. You'd better start looking for a part-time job to pay for them!"

Jessica just smiled. She had an idea about how to coerce Elizabeth onto the new cheerleading squad. *Lila just doesn't have the right leverage,* Jessica thought. *I'm going to ask Elizabeth in such a way that she just won't be able to say no!*

By the end of lunch period the rumor had spread like wildfire around the Sweet Valley High cafeteria. Dozens of girls of all shapes and sizes, freshmen through seniors, crowded around Jessica's table, pressing her for information.

"Is it true, Jessica? You're starting your own cheerleading squad?" sophomore Stacie Cabot asked excitedly.

"Can anyone come to the practices?" pert, slender Lisa Walton wanted to know.

"What if you don't have any experience?" asked Alicia Benson.

"When are tryouts?" Jennifer Morris wondered. "How many girls are you going to pick?"

Jessica fielded the questions with a feeling of pleased self-importance, basking in the glory of having all eyes in the room upon her.

All eyes . . . including those of Heather Mallone.

Heather was sitting with what was left of the old cheerleading squad. After glancing disdainfully at Jessica, Heather leaned over to whisper something in Amy's ear. Amy laughed hysterically.

The laughter didn't bother Jessica one bit. *If she's cracking jokes, then it proves she really feels threatened.*

And Heather had a very good reason to feel

threatened, Jessica decided as she surveyed the huge pool of potential talent surrounding her. All the eager faces and bodies made her realize that her dream really could come true. It wasn't just talk.

Jessica Wakefield's cheerleading squad was on its way!

Elizabeth was cooking dinner when Jessica breezed into the kitchen late that afternoon. "Yum, smells good," Jessica commented, leaning over the saucepan and taking a deep, appreciative sniff. "Chili and corn bread, my favorite."

"Wanna set the table?" asked Elizabeth.

"Sure." Opening a drawer, Jessica grabbed a handful of silverware, then turned back to her sister. "So it's pretty exciting, huh? Having everybody buzzing about my new cheerleading squad."

"It's the talk of the town," Elizabeth agreed, tasting the chili and then adding a few more shakes of cayenne.

"It looks like tons of people are planning to come to practice and tryouts," Jessica continued, "which is good, because then I can afford to be very selective."

"I'm sure some of the girls will turn out to be really good."

"So how about you?"

"How about me what?"

Jessica smiled. "You know. Have you given it some more thought? Will you come to cheerleading practice tomorrow morning?"

"I swear, Jess," exclaimed Elizabeth as she

stirred the chili. "You're completely dense, did you know that? How many times are you going to make me tell you that I have absolutely no desire—as in zero, zilch—to be a cheerleader?"

"Maybe I just haven't phrased the question in quite the right way," mused Jessica.

"It doesn't matter how you phrase it," Elizabeth declared. "The answer is always going to be no."

"No, no, let me try one more time," said Jessica. Putting down the silverware, she folded her arms across her chest and looked Elizabeth straight in the eye. Both her tone and expression grew more serious. "How about this: Please be on my cheerleading squad, Liz, or else . . . I'll tell Todd about your fling with Ken."

"You'll what?" Elizabeth dropped the ladle into the chili.

Jessica smiled. "You heard me."

A fiery flush swept across Elizabeth's face. She felt as if she'd just swallowed a chili pepper whole. "I heard you, but I can't believe . . . How did you—Ken didn't . . . ?"

Elizabeth bit off her question, realizing that she'd basically just acknowledged her guilt. Jessica was still smiling like a cat that held a mouse between its paws. "No, Ken didn't tell me," Jessica assured her sister. "A couple of days ago totally by accident I stumbled upon those photo-booth pictures of you and Ken hidden under your pillow."

"Oh, those." A wave of relief washed over Elizabeth. If that was all the evidence Jessica had against her . . . "Why, those don't mean anything.

We were just fooling around. Ken and I never—"

"And then I read your diary."

"You what?"

"I read your diary," Jessica repeated cheerfully. "I had no idea it was going to be so steamy, Liz! I mean, there I was back then stupidly trying to get you interested in meeting a new guy after Todd moved, and it turns out the whole time you were already cheating on him with Ken!"

"I wasn't—I didn't—" Elizabeth spluttered.

"Yes, you did." Jessica grinned. "You did, and then you came home and wrote about it. In great detail."

Elizabeth was speechless with fury. "I can't believe you read—and now you're going to—"

Jessica supplied the term cheerfully. "Blackmail you. So, what'll it be, Liz? Will you be on my squad, or should I call Todd right now?"

Elizabeth sucked in a hot, angry breath. "Jessica Wakefield, this is the meanest, nastiest, most underhanded thing you've ever done!"

Jessica shrugged off the criticism. "You should know," she said, her eyes sparkling wickedly. "I mean, when it comes to underhanded, you wrote the book . . . or should I say the diary? So." She posed the question one last time. "What'll it be?"

Elizabeth realized she didn't have a choice. Her sister had her between a rock and a hard place. The thought of putting on a cheerleading uniform and jumping around with Jessica and a bunch of other giddy females made her skin crawl. But the thought of Todd finding out about Ken . . .

"All right," Elizabeth choked out. "I'll be on your squad. But I'll get you back for this, Jessica. Mark my words!"

Smiling, Jessica reached for the phone. Elizabeth's hand shot out to stop her. "You said you wouldn't call Todd if I agreed!" she cried. "We just made a deal!"

Jessica laughed at Elizabeth's panic. "Chill out—I'm just calling Lila. She'll want to hear about this. I mean, not all of it," she teased, "just the part about your joining the team."

Jessica punched in Lila's number. "Hello, Li?" she said a moment later. "I'm at home with Liz, and she has something she wants to tell you."

Jessica held the receiver out to Elizabeth. "Go on, tell her," she hissed.

Elizabeth took the phone reluctantly. "Hi, Lila," she said stiffly. "Um, yeah, I do have some news. I've decided I'd like to try out for Jessica's new cheerleading squad." There was a pause; Jessica guessed that Lila was ranting on the other end. "What can I say?" Elizabeth finally concluded. "I changed my mind."

Jessica grabbed the phone from her sister. "What do you think of that, Li?" she asked sweetly.

"What are you doing to her?" Lila demanded. "Is she tied up? Are you torturing her?"

"I guess Liz has always had a secret dream to be a cheerleader." Jessica glanced at her sister, whose face was still red with fury. "So, Lila . . ." Reaching into her backpack, Jessica pulled out a copy of the latest Cheer Ahead catalog, which she and Lila had been looking through during school that day. "I think the little red-and-white numbers on page fifty-four look pretty hot. You can order mine in size six!"

Turning her back on Jessica, Elizabeth stomped across the kitchen to stand at the stove, furiously stirring her pot of chili. Whistling cheerfully to herself, Jessica sauntered out into the hall.

She paused in front of the mirror hanging over the table in the entryway. She high-fived herself, smiling at her reflection. *Way to go, Wakefield!*

Chapter 4

Elizabeth was dreaming that Mr. Collins, her favorite English teacher and the adviser to *The Oracle,* had taken the computers and typewriters out of the newspaper office. "From now on we're not going to print the news," he announced, passing out pom-poms to the whole staff. "We're going to cheer it!"

In her dream Elizabeth stared in horrified disbelief at Mr. Collins. She could barely hear him because of the buzzing in her head. . . . What was that awful noise . . . ?

The covers went flying as Elizabeth sat bolt upright, her heart pounding. It was still dark out, but the clock radio on her nightstand was blaring loudly. She swatted the off button with a desperate, irritated gesture. "Six A.M.," she muttered, throwing back the covers and climbing out of bed. "I can't believe I'm doing this!"

Shuffling to her closet, she wrapped herself in her bathrobe. In the bathroom she splashed cold water onto her face. Now wide awake, she blinked at herself in the mirror. *I should have told Todd right off the bat about Ken. But now it's too late; he'd never understand why I waited this long, and my diabolical sister is going to use it to blackmail me for the rest of my life!*

At the bottom of the staircase Elizabeth glanced out the window in the front hall and shivered. The first light of dawn was just warming the eastern sky, but it looked damp and chilly outside. *As if cheerleading isn't an insult in and of itself,* she thought bitterly, *we have to practice in the middle of the night?*

She trudged into the kitchen, her slippers making protesting slapping sounds on the tile floor. Jessica, already dressed in hot-pink leggings and a bulky sweatshirt, stood at the counter measuring something into the blender. When Elizabeth appeared, Jessica tapped the lid onto the blender and hit the power button.

Elizabeth put her hands over her ears. "Do you have to do that?" she complained. "Some sensible people in this house may still be trying to sleep!"

Jessica flashed her sister a peppy, encouraging smile. "A good breakfast is very important," she declared. "Power drinks, my own special recipe. Low cal, high protein, and delicious." Stopping the blender, she dipped a finger in to sample her concoction. "Umm, taste." She poured a glass for

Elizabeth and then one for herself. "This certainly beats Heather's disgusting lettuce-and-wheat-germ diet!"

Elizabeth frowned at the thick beige liquid. "What's in it?"

"Yogurt, banana, strawberries, a splash of o.j., and this high-energy protein powder I bought at the health-food store. And try one of these." Jessica held out a basket with a cloth napkin over it. "Buttermilk bran muffins with apple and raisins. I made them last night."

Setting a good example, Jessica took a big swig of her power drink. Grudgingly, Elizabeth lifted the glass to her lips. "Do you like it?" Jessica asked hopefully.

The drink wasn't half-bad, but Elizabeth wasn't about to admit that. "Does it matter if I like it?"

"Oh, come on, Liz," Jessica said in a cajoling tone as she slipped an arm around her sister's waist and gave her a squeeze. "Now that we've come to this arrangement, why not make the best of it? It could really be a lot of fun. Look." Skipping across the kitchen, Jessica bent to pull something out of a large canvas sack. "Here are your practice pom-poms. Aren't they adorable? Aren't you getting psyched?"

Jessica pressed the red-and-white pom-poms into Elizabeth's hands. *My very own pom-poms,* Elizabeth thought, staring down distastefully at the emblems of her degradation. *I never thought the day would come . . . !*

Just touching them made Elizabeth's whole

body twitch. She tossed the pom-poms aside in disgust.

The gesture was lost on Jessica. "Oh, Liz." She clasped her hands together, her eyes starry. "Just seeing you with those pom-poms . . . You're going to make the most beautiful cheerleader! I can't tell you how often I've dreamed of this, of you and me, cheering together side by side. I'm so happy!"

Elizabeth was not happy, but Jessica didn't pause to give her a chance to express her feelings either way. "Cheerleading is a blast. It's my favorite thing in the whole world, and you're just going to love it. I promise!"

Elizabeth gave her sister a dirty look. Then she drained the rest of her power drink, placed the empty glass on the counter with a clunk, and marched out into the hall and up the stairs to take a shower and get dressed for practice.

Despite the early hour the Sweet Valley High football field was swarming with would-be cheerleaders. Jessica scanned the crowd excitedly. "Amanda Hayes and Sara Eastbourne," she said to Lila, pointing. "They're both fantastic dancers."

"They take class with Mr. Krezenski," remarked Lila, naming the world-famous dancer who had a studio in Sweet Valley. "Supposedly he's pretty tough."

"That means they're disciplined." Jessica nodded with approval. "They know how to work hard. I like that."

Elizabeth was sitting cross-legged on the ground a short distance from the other girls. "Liz looks totally unpsyched," observed Lila. "What kind of thumbscrews did you put on her to get her here?"

"She's here," Jessica said. "That's all that counts."

"It's great to see Lisa Walton," said Maria, "and Mandy and Patsy and Jennifer. And look! Danielle Alexander. Isn't she a ballet dancer?"

"This is sure going to be interesting," predicted Sandy.

Practice pom-poms in hand, Jessica waved her arms at the crowd of chattering girls. When they were all facing her and attentively silent, she flashed a big, welcoming smile. "Thanks for turning out!" she boomed in her best cheerleader's voice. "It's great to see so many people. Start stretching out, OK? And I'll tell you what I've got in mind for the week ahead."

Some of the girls wore sweatshirts over leotards and tights, while others were dressed in shorts and T-shirts. They all started stretching out their leg muscles, twisting at the waist, and loosening up their shoulders. Patty Gilbert, wearing flowered Capri tights and a matching cropped sport top, dropped to the ground in a perfect Chinese split. Jessica beamed.

"We'll meet out here every morning this week at the same time," she began, "and on Friday I'll hold official tryouts. I'm shooting for a squad of eight or ten girls—it all depends on how you do. So let's get fired up!"

Her words were greeted by an enthusiastic cheer. Jessica took a bow, then clapped for silence. "OK. Not including Lila, Maria, and Sandy, how many of you have cheerleading experience? Let's see some hands."

Not one hand was raised. "Hmm. Well, OK. How many of you have tried out for the squad before—the old squad?"

Three hands went up this time. Jessica nodded. "Right, I remember. How about the rest of you? Do we have any gymnasts out there?"

A number of hands went up in response to this question, and quite a few more when Jessica asked about dance—jazz, modern, and ballet. "You're all going to be super, I just know it," she concluded. "Now, what I'd like everyone to do is to spread out on the field in a line facing me. Sandy, Maria, Lila, and I are going to run through some basic moves for you, and then I want to see you give it a try."

Bending, she hit the play button on the portable tape player she'd brought with her. As the catchy beat of a popular song began pulsing out of the speakers, Jessica started moving her feet from side to side and clapping her hands rhythmically. Lila, Maria, and Sandy joined in.

"First, the feet," Jessica called out. "We can sway from side to side"—she demonstrated the motion—"or rock back and forth. We can lunge with one foot forward like this, and hop back. As for our hands"—she dropped her pom-poms—"we can make fists, blades, cups, and fans.

Different hand positions go with different arm movements. We use our arms dramatically—watch me sweep, thrust, punch, and slice—to create rhythm and balance, and to catch the crowd's attention."

Jessica had matched each term with a gesture, and she was pleased to see most of the girls successfully imitating her movements. She got them all sidestepping and snapping their fingers, then clapping. "As you know," she hollered, "cheerleading is about building excitement in the teams and the fans. You've gotta have the jumps, but you've also gotta have grace and style and a killer smile." She grinned widely. "And lung power. Let's hear it—let's hear you yell!"

She shouted a cheer and the girls on the field echoed her. "I can't hear you!" Jessica called teasingly, cupping a hand to her ear. "What did you say?"

"Go, fight, do it right, WIN!" the girls hollered.

All the girls were moving to the music, shaking their shoulders and clapping and smiling. Patty, Jade, Lisa Walton, Stacie Cabot, Mandy Farmer, Danielle Alexander, Jennifer Morris, Patsy Webber, Alicia Benson, Aline Montgomery, April Dawson, Leslie Decker, and, of course, Elizabeth. *What a great bunch!* Jessica thought. *I'm going to have the hottest cheerleading squad in the history of California. No, make that the history of the world!*

Fifteen minutes later she was tearing out her hair. "Great, you can do a perfect cartwheel, but that's just not going to cut it," she said to Alicia. "We need to see you do a round-off, back handspring. Spot her, Lila, would you? And Jade!"

Jessica turned to Jade Wu. "Let's see you try that back crunch again."

Obediently, Jade bounced into the air, arching her back as if trying to touch her heels to the back of her head. Jessica shook her head. "Higher," she commanded. "Get some vertical. Jump!"

She whirled to face Danielle next. "Try that spread-eagle one more time."

Danielle flung her long blond hair back, her face determined, and then launched herself into the air. "No, no, no," Jessica moaned. "This isn't *Swan Lake*! Bounce off both feet—put some spring into it, and smile!"

Danielle grimaced. "I'm trying, but it doesn't come naturally," she grumbled. "Especially the smiling part!"

Jessica stepped back to get the big picture. Sara and Amanda both had great rhythm and lots of personality, but neither of them could jump more than a foot in the air if her life depended on it; gymnasts Lisa and Leslie could both do flips from a standing position, but when it came to stringing the jumps together with dance steps, they started tripping over their own feet; Danielle was clearly never going to be as comfortable in sneakers as she was in toe shoes; April, Jennifer, and Mandy were simply hopeless.

"Patsy Webber looks good," Lila said to Jessica,

"and she used to live in France. She'd really add some style, you know?"

Jessica watched as the tall, slender girl with the striking green eyes and short coppery-red hair attempted a split. Patsy got stuck halfway to the ground. "Are you kidding?" exploded Jessica, feeling as if she were about to burst a blood vessel. "She's about as limber as a plank of wood!"

"She needs some work," Lila conceded.

"All right. All right!" Jessica bellowed, turning off the music abruptly. The girls all froze. "All right," she repeated in a calmer tone, making herself smile. "Another thing that's crucial in cheering is coordination, and by that I mean doing your arm movements, footwork, and jumps in sync with the rest of the squad. It's all got to flow—you have to start thinking of yourselves as part of one body. If I'm sliding right, everyone's sliding right. If I go down in a split, everyone's going down, one after the other, without missing a beat. Right now I want you to pair up and work on performing side-by-side herkies."

The girls were all staring blankly at Jessica. "Go on and get started!" she commanded.

Still, no one budged. Then Patty cleared her throat. "Um, what's a herky?"

"What's a herky?" said Jessica in disbelief. "What's a herky?" Her voice rose to an indignant screech. "Are you trying to tell me that not one of you knows what a herky is, one of the most basic cheerleading jumps? Not one of you bothered to study up a little before coming to practice? Not one of you—"

She was so frustrated, she couldn't even get the words out. "Well, you'll just have to . . . you'll just have to . . ." she sputtered. She hurled her pompoms onto the ground, preparing to stalk off the field. "Figure it out yourself!"

Elizabeth had been keeping a low profile, practicing the jumps by herself on the fringes of the crowd. Now, along with the others, she stared in shocked silence at Jessica's retreating back. *Wow, what a blowup. So much for Jessica's dream team!*

The girls began milling about, murmuring among themselves. Standing in a tight huddle, Lila, Maria, and Sandy appeared to be debating what to do next.

Patty Gilbert threw her hands in the air. "I don't know why Jessica bothered recruiting us for the new squad," she grumbled, "if she's not even willing to take the trouble to train us!"

As the girls began to disperse in confusion and disappointment, Elizabeth darted forward. "Wait!" she called. "Don't leave."

When the girls were gathered around her, Elizabeth gave them all a reassuring smile. "I know that sounded a little harsh," she said apologetically. "Jessica's pretty worked up about all this, and it looks like the excitement got the better of her. Having her own squad is a lot of responsibility—she's going to be learning some things from scratch just like you guys are. So don't give up, OK? Come back tomorrow, same time, same place."

Elizabeth's speech was received with nods and smiles. Relieved, she lifted a hand to wave good-bye as the girls headed across the field toward the school building.

I can't believe I did that. Elizabeth shook her head, disgusted by her own helpfulness. *I can't believe she threw a tantrum and I saved her skin.* Not that it wasn't typical! She bent to tie the lace of her sneaker, an ironic smile on her face. *Jessica bites off more than she can chew, and I end up covering for her. She really owes me. Boy, does she owe me!*

When Jessica turned to storm off the field, she was mortified to discover Ken standing just a few yards away. "Oh, God, I can't believe you saw that!" she exclaimed, flushing.

"Rough practice?" he inquired, slinging an arm around her shoulders.

"You could say that. How did I ever think this could work? Being a good gymnast or dancer simply does not automatically make you a good cheerleader. These girls are total novices. Not that the Sweet Valley squad was ever championship material, but at least everyone knew what a herky was!"

"They'll get it together," Ken predicted, massaging her shoulders with strong fingers. "It'll just take some time."

"Yeah, like a year," said Jessica. "The problem is, we only have a week or so if we want to get an audience with the ACA scout and qualify for regionals! Oh, it's impossible." She fought the urge to burst into tears. "You saw them, Ken. Even Maria and Sandy have lost their edge since Heather kicked them off the squad. What am I going to do?"

"I have one word for you." Ken held up his index finger. "Visualization."

Jessica blinked. "Run that by me again?"

"Visualization," Ken repeated. "It's my quarterbacking secret. If I want to complete a pass, I have to be able to see it in my mind's eye first, and feel my body executing it before I even move a muscle. And when I call plays? I've taught myself to use my brain in a certain way, to visualize where each player will be, how he'll move, how we'll all move together as one entity." He grinned wryly. "Sounds kooky, huh?"

"Visualization." Jessica was unconvinced. "Isn't that what just happened back on the field, when I looked at all those girls and realized they stunk?"

Ken laughed. "No, visualization isn't seeing what's there, it's seeing what you want to be there. It's focusing on images of perfection and internalizing them. I'm telling you, Jess, it's the only way you'll get your squad up to speed in such a short time."

"Visualization, huh?" Jessica's expression brightened hopefully. "You really think so?"

"You can get videos for pretty much every sport—I bet they have them for cheerleading, too."

"What do I have to lose? I'll try it," Jessica decided. She smiled, her eyes twinkling mischievously. "In fact, I'm trying it right now. I'm visualizing . . . you and me at Miller's Point."

Ken grinned as he pulled her close for a kiss. "Funny, I was visualizing the exact same thing!"

"You're pulling my leg," Todd said to Elizabeth that day during lunch. "You went to Jessica's cheerleading practice this morning?"

Enid was also gaping in astonishment at Elizabeth. "What possessed you?" she asked.

Elizabeth shrugged as she took her cheese, sprouts, and tomato sandwich out of her lunch bag. She didn't want this to turn into a big deal. "Does it really strike you as that bizarre?"

"Yes, because you've always hated cheerleading," said Enid, twisting the cap off a bottle of apple juice. "Just yesterday you totally bit Lila's head off when she asked you about trying out for the new team."

"I changed my mind," Elizabeth said somewhat defensively. "Jessica really needs my help, so . . ."

"Yeah, but we're talking about cheerleading, not homework or something." Todd laughed. "Is she paying you or what?"

Elizabeth cracked a weak smile, not wanting him to guess how close he was to the truth. "I'm sure she'll find a way to return the favor."

"I still can't picture it." Enid giggled into her straw, blowing bubbles in her soda. "Liz in a short skirt shaking some pom-poms!"

Todd grinned at Elizabeth. "I can picture it," he teased. "Yow."

"Well, I really admire you." Enid was clearly still trying to smother a smile. "I mean, this whole sisterhood thing, the way you and Jessica always come through for each other. It's pretty inspiring."

Inspiring, my—Elizabeth took a bite of her sandwich, even though she had absolutely no appetite. She couldn't admit it to Todd and Enid, but frankly, "the whole sisterhood thing" made her sick.

"So you're really going to try to do it," said a voice dripping with disdain.

Jessica was standing in the hot-lunch line with Ken. Now she turned, tray in hand.

As always, Heather looked perfect: her thick mane of icy-blond hair fell in glamorous waves, her makeup was understated but flawless, the bright turquoise scoop-necked dress clung to her curves, silver jewelry set off her suntan—even her sandals looked Italian, Jessica thought, and very expensive. *Not to mention the pedicure! I hate her. I really hate her!*

"Actually, I'm not going to try to do it," replied Jessica coolly. "I'm just plain going to do it."

"In your dreams." Heather's smug smile got under Jessica's skin like fingernails scratching a blackboard. "I heard your first practice was . . . rough, to put it politely."

Jessica's face flamed. "That's why it's called practice. When the time comes for the real thing—"

"And when will that be?" Heather countered. She laughed dismissively. "You'll never pull a squad together, Jessica, and even if you do, what's the point? You don't have a school to cheer for—I'm in charge of the one and only Sweet Valley High cheerleading squad. And nothing's going to change that!"

"I guess we'll see, won't we?" Jessica challenged. "We'll see who has the best squad—we'll see whose school this really is!" Tossing her hair, she turned a haughty profile to Heather. "Come on, Ken. We're holding up the line."

Out of the corner of her eye, Jessica saw Heather stalk away. "Good for you," Ken murmured in her ear. "Good for you, standing up for yourself and for your squad!"

Jessica forced herself to smile with confident nonchalance. Deep inside, though, she was shaking like a palm frond in the wind. She had laughed them off, but Heather's words had really hit home. "You'll never pull a squad together, and even if you do, what's the point? You don't have a school to cheer for. . . ."

For a second Jessica squeezed her eyes closed, remembering that morning's disastrous practice. I'm staking my reputation on my new squad, but what if we fall flat on our faces? It was too terrible to contemplate, but the possibility was there—she had to face it. Heather might be right; Jessica might be setting herself up for a humiliation even worse than that of being elbowed off the old squad.

Chapter 5

"Hi, guys," Jessica said to Amy, Annie Whitman, and Jean West on Tuesday as she put her lunch tray down on their table. "It looks like the coast is clear—no sign of Heather," she joked. "OK if I sit with you?"

The three girls exchanged uncomfortable glances. Jessica, busily peeling an orange, was oblivious. "I never see you guys anymore—Heather totally monopolizes you," she complained. "But I want you to know that I'm not holding a grudge—about this whole cheerleading thing, I mean. I'll still be your friend even though you're cheering with Heather instead of me!"

It was a pretty magnanimous statement, and Jessica expected Amy, Jean, and Annie to be grateful. Instead they looked as if someone had poisoned their lunches. "What's the matter, Amy?" asked Jessica. "Don't tell me you're bent because

I'm starting my own squad and didn't ask you to be on it. Of course if you want to try out, you're welcome—"

"It's not that," said Amy, tossing an anxious glance over her shoulder. "It's just . . ." Instead of completing her sentence, she started packing up what was left of her lunch.

"It's just what?" pressed Jessica.

Amy sighed. "Heather would get mad if she saw us . . . you know."

"No, I do not know," said Jessica.

Amy looked to Annie for help. "We don't want to jeopardize our positions on the squad," Annie explained. "So it's probably better if we . . ."

The three girls rose to their feet. Jessica stared at them. "You're kidding!" she exclaimed. "Are you saying you won't even have lunch with me because of what Heather might think?"

"It's nothing personal," Amy assured her.

"Baloney!" said Jessica. "C'mon, Jean. You have more sense than that. Are you afraid of Heather, too?"

"Sorry, Jessica." Jean lowered her eyelashes, embarrassed. "Better safe than sorry."

Amy, Jean, and Annie scurried off. *They couldn't get away from me fast enough—you'd think I was a leper or something!* thought Jessica indignantly.

She couldn't believe it—ditched by some of her closest friends! *Or at least they used to be my friends, until Heather stole them.* Suddenly Jessica felt like crying; she bit into a juicy orange section to hide the fact that her lower lip was trembling.

She was hurt by Amy, Annie, and Jean's rejection, but it also made her more determined than ever to throw herself heart and soul into her new cheerleading squad. *I'll show Heather,* thought Jessica. *I'll show them all!*

"There," said Elizabeth on Tuesday afternoon as she removed a sheet of paper from the printer in the *Oracle* office. As well as writing occasional feature stories, she had her own weekly byline called "Personal Profiles." "My column's finished. Do you want to look at it, Penny?"

"I'm sure it's fine." Penny Ayala, the newspaper's lanky, fair-haired editor in chief and one of Elizabeth's closest friends, quickly skimmed the piece. "And I'm glad you're done, because I have another assignment for you."

"What's that?" asked Elizabeth, curious.

"We need a story about Jessica's new squad battling Heather's for cheerleading supremacy at Sweet Valley High," said Penny, her hazel eyes twinkling, "and who better to write it than someone on the inside?"

Elizabeth turned away and started sticking notebooks and papers into her backpack. "I know I don't often turn down an assignment, but if it's OK, I'd rather not do this one," she told Penny.

"Why not?"

Sweeping a strand of silky blond hair back from her forehead, Elizabeth faced Penny again. "Oh . . . I don't know. Maybe I'm too . . . biased. Yeah, I don't think I could write an objective article about something I'm so intimately involved in."

"But it doesn't have to be objective." Penny laughed. "We're talking about cheerleading, not politics! Just make it entertaining. Talk to Jessica, talk to Heather. . . ."

"That's the thing." Elizabeth snapped her fingers, glad to have stumbled upon an airtight excuse. "Heather wouldn't grant me an interview in a million years. Jessica and I are public enemy number one as far as she's concerned."

"So forget the Heather-Jessica angle. Talk to the girls on the two squads. Get their perspectives."

Elizabeth slung her backpack over her shoulder. "OK," she agreed reluctantly. "I'll give it some thought."

She was on her way out the door when Penny called after her, "Hey, Liz, I even have a title for your story. 'The Pom-pom Wars.' Catchy, huh?"

"The Pom-pom Wars," Elizabeth thought grimly as she walked down the hallway toward the main lobby. *Spare me, please!*

Halfway to the student parking lot, she remembered that she'd told Todd she'd stop by the gym when she was done at the newspaper office—he was playing in an intramural basketball tournament. She hesitated for a moment, about to turn back, and then continued on to the parking lot. *I just don't feel like cheering him on,* she decided. *I mean, I used to like it, when it was just for fun. But now that I'm trying to get into the cheerleading mentality . . .*

"Todd Wilkins, he's our man," Elizabeth muttered out loud. "If he can't do it, no one can!" *Ugh. What have I gotten myself into!*

As Elizabeth neared the Jeep, she noticed that a familiar white Toyota was parked just two spaces away. Not only that, but someone had just climbed into the Toyota's driver's seat and was belting himself in.

Ken rolled down the window and smiled at her. "Hey, how're you doing, Liz?"

She walked past the Jeep to stand somewhat awkwardly next to Ken's car. "Oh, I'm OK, I guess."

"I wanted to tell you, I think it's great that you've joined Jessica's cheerleading squad."

"Oh, yeah, well . . ." Elizabeth lifted her shoulders.

"I know it's not really your thing," said Ken. "Jessica thinks you're the best sister in the world for doing it."

Elizabeth gave him a brittle smile. "Does she? I don't suppose she told you that . . ."

She paused. Ken waited expectantly, a friendly, innocent light in his eyes. *He doesn't know,* Elizabeth realized. *He doesn't know Jessica found out about us, that she's blackmailing me.* ". . . that she had to twist my arm," she concluded somewhat lamely.

Ken chuckled. "She's mastered the art of persuasion, that's for sure." He turned the key in the ignition, and the Toyota's engine rumbled to life. "See you around, Liz."

"So long."

Elizabeth settled herself into the Jeep, watching Ken's car in the rearview mirror until it disappeared. She realized her pulse was racing, and when she checked her reflection in the mirror, her cheeks were pink and her eyes bright. *How can Ken have that effect on me?* she wondered irritably as she backed out of the parking space. It wasn't even a good conversation!

But he did have that effect on her . . . no doubt about it.

The black BMW rumbled to a stop just a few feet short of the guardrail at Miller's Point, a dead-end road in the hills above Sweet Valley. Todd let the engine die, then switched off the headlights.

For a few minutes he and Elizabeth sat in comfortable silence, gazing out at the velvety-blue night sky, the lights of the town twinkling in the valley, and in the distance the Pacific glinting silver in the moonlight.

Todd slipped an arm behind Elizabeth's shoulders. Automatically, she shifted in her seat, turning to face him. Gently, he placed a hand on each side of her face. She closed her eyes as he began to kiss her.

"Liz."

Elizabeth blinked. "Liz," Todd repeated.

"Hmm. What's the matter?"

He pulled back from her slightly and peered into her face, a puzzled frown creasing his forehead. "Nothing's the matter . . . with me." He dropped his eyes. "But I can tell you're not into it."

Elizabeth bit her lip. There was no point pretending her reponse to Todd's kisses hadn't been lukewarm at best. "I'm just . . . I don't know," she mumbled.

"Is something wrong?" Todd asked, a note of fear entering his voice. "Is it me?"

"Oh, no, of course not," Elizabeth hurried to assure him, even though there was something wrong, and it *was* him, in part.

"Because I've been getting the feeling lately," continued Todd, looking straight ahead through the windshield, "that you're . . . bored or something. With me. With our relationship."

"That's simply not true," declared Elizabeth, tugging on his arm until he turned toward her again. "I've been kind of busy and preoccupied, that's all. And tonight . . ." She stifled a yawn. "I'm just plain exhausted. I was up before dawn for cheerleading practice," she reminded him with a wry smile.

Todd gazed down at her, studying her face. She tried her best to look loving and sincere.

At last the worried expression left his eyes. He folded her in a tight hug. "Sorry to be so paranoid," he whispered into her hair. "I'm just so crazy about you. I don't know what I'd do if you stopped loving me."

Todd's mouth found hers and once again they were kissing. This time Elizabeth made an effort to be more responsive. It wasn't that hard. As she tangled her fingers in Todd's hair, she imagined it was blond instead of brown; she pretended she was running her hands over another boy's shoulders, rubbing another boy's broad, hard, sexy back. . . .

When Todd started up the car a while later and did a U-turn to head home, Elizabeth found herself feeling incredibly guilty. Not only had she lied to Todd again, saying there was nothing wrong, but she'd convinced him that nothing was wrong by pretending she was with another guy! It was almost as bad as actually cheating!

And the worst part was Todd still didn't suspect a thing. He was humming to the song on the radio, the corner of his mouth curved slightly upward in a soft smile.

As they bumped back onto the main road, the headlights of another car crossed theirs. The car was turning off at Miller's Point; curious, Elizabeth glanced over to see if it was anyone she knew.

There were two people in the white Toyota—two blond heads, his and hers, one with short hair, one with long. Ken and Jessica, in quest of a romantic interlude. *Why does it bother me so much, and when is it going to stop bothering me?* Elizabeth wondered, a sick, sharp pain in her chest. When am I going to forget about Ken?

As soon as Ken dropped her off, Jessica pounded up the stairs and rapped on her sister's door. "Can I come in?"

"I'm about to go to sleep," Elizabeth replied, her tone discouraging.

Jessica pushed open the door and charged in

anyway. "But you're not asleep yet!" she observed cheerfully.

Elizabeth was reading in bed. She scowled at her sister. "I'd like to be."

"Well, I personally am never going to be able to fall asleep," Jessica declared, ignoring her sister's broad hint to get lost. "I'm just tingling from head to toe, you know? My whole body is like . . ." She dropped onto Elizabeth's bed, bouncing. "I was with Ken," she explained, a sly smile in her eyes. "He just gets me so . . ." She nudged Elizabeth's knee under the covers. "Well, you remember."

"I'm afraid not," Elizabeth said coldly, looking back down at her book.

"Oh, come on, Liz," Jessica teased. "I read your diary, or did you forget?" She didn't like thinking about Ken kissing her sister, but it definitely made her feel a lot better to remind Elizabeth repeatedly that these days Ken was kissing her. "Isn't he a great kisser? He has the best lips. Not too hard and not too soft. I hate guys with squishy lips, don't you? But Ken's are perfect. Umm—just thinking about it!"

Elizabeth slammed her book shut. "OK, I'm ready to turn my light out. Do you mind?"

Jessica grinned impishly. "No, I'm not leaving until you admit that Ken Matthews is the best kisser of any boy you ever went out with, including Todd."

"I can't believe how infantile you are!" cried Elizabeth. "Will you just get out of my face?"

"Admit it," Jessica pressed. "Ken's the best kisser."

Elizabeth shook her head stubbornly. "To tell you the truth, I hardly remember," she said, reaching for the light switch. "Good night, Jessica."

The room was plunged into darkness. "Night, Liz," said Jessica, rising. "Oh, I almost forgot—I'm holding an extra practice tomorrow afternoon, here at our house. I ordered a visualization video from Cheer Ahead, and they're sending it overnight mail—we're all going to watch it together. And don't think you don't have anything to learn from this, Liz, just because your jumps are already pretty good. I want to see you put your whole heart and soul into this. You're a cheerleader now—be proud!"

Her face buried in her pillow, Elizabeth grumbled something inaudible. Something profane, probably, Jessica thought with a grin. "Sleep tight, Liz," she said. "And try to dream about cheerleading, OK?"

There was a muffled click as Jessica shut the door to the bathroom behind her. Elizabeth kicked the covers off, then pulled them back again; she tossed from one side to the other, trying to get comfortable. But her eyes were wide open in the dark, and suddenly she wasn't the least bit tired.

Jessica had gone to her own room, but her words seemed to linger in Elizabeth's. "I'm tingling from head to toe. . . . Admit it, Ken's the best kisser. . . ."

Elizabeth had said she didn't remember. But that was yet another lie. She put her hands to her cheeks, feeling how red and hot her face was. The trouble was she did remember what it was like to kiss Ken—all too well.

Reaching up, Elizabeth turned the lamp on her nightstand back on. She swung her legs over the side of the bed and crossed to her desk. She'd hidden her diaries in the bottom drawer, under a pile of old school notebooks. *Not that that stopped Jessica!* she thought bitterly.

She took one of the volumes of the diary back to bed. Propping up her pillows, she sat up with the covers pulled over her lap and let the diary fall open in her hands. As if the emotions recorded there were especially strong and vibrant, it opened automatically to a page on which she'd written about Ken.

Elizabeth read the entry: "I can't believe I let myself get so carried away. . . . Diary, I've never felt so bad—and so good—at the same time. Ken kissed me like no one's ever kissed me before. . . ."

She'd written Ken's name over and over in the margins, the pen biting deep into the paper. The journal was so intense, so personal. *And Jessica read it—she read it all!* Elizabeth thought, feeling angry and violated. "I shouldn't have written about it," she murmured out loud to herself. "I should have kept it to myself, locked in my heart. It was our secret, Ken's and mine."

With a sigh Elizabeth returned the diary to the desk drawer. Lying in the dark again, she wrapped her arms tightly around a pillow. Right before she drifted off to sleep, the thought flashed across her mind: *Oh, Ken, if I could only hold you in my arms one more time. . . .*

The dream was bizarre and yet vivid. Elizabeth sat on a throne on a stage. First Heather Mallone and the SVH cheerleaders revved up the audience as the marching band performed a lively tune. Then Todd and Ken appeared, both dressed in their sports uniforms. One at a time they walked across the stage toward her, bowed to her, and then bent to kiss her, once, twice, three times. Elizabeth considered each kiss carefully, and then the scores flashed onto the scoreboard. Ken received two 5.9's and a perfect 6; the cheerleaders hopped about, cymbals clashed, the audience cheered lustily. But Todd—Todd's performance disappointed everyone, including Elizabeth. She wanted to be generous, but she simply couldn't score him higher than two 4's and a 3.8.

Her lips still burning from Ken's dream kisses, Elizabeth opened her eyes to the gray light of dawn spilling into her shadowy bedroom. *This is terrible,* she thought, reflecting on the dream, and then remembering her date with Todd the night before. *I'm obsessing about Ken even more than I did back when we were involved with each other!*

It had to stop—that much was clear. But how? How to get over Ken the second time around?

That's the whole problem, Elizabeth realized. *I can't expect to get over Ken a second time when maybe I never entirely got over him the first time.*

She recalled the conversation she'd had a few days earlier with Mr. Collins. She'd asked for advice on behalf of a romantically confused "friend," and Mr. Collins had said, "It sounds like whoever she is still has some unresolved feelings for this other guy. She should try to work those feelings out before they destroy her relationship with her boyfriend."

Mr. Collins was right—he's always right, Elizabeth recognized. Harboring these secret feelings wasn't fair to Todd, or to herself. But how on earth was she supposed to "resolve" them? How could she find out how she really felt about Ken Matthews when he was happily dating her own twin sister?

Chapter 6

"No offense, but I don't think this is going to work," Patty said to Jessica on Wednesday after school. "How can just watching a tape on TV improve our skills?"

"I agree," said Elizabeth. "Wouldn't the time be better spent practicing?"

At Jessica's request, all the girls interested in trying out for her cheerleading squad had gathered at the Wakefields' house after school. Jessica herded them into the den. "The woman I talked to on the phone yesterday promised me this would make a huge difference," she said, doing her best to hide her own skepticism. "All kinds of athletes use these visualization tapes—tennis players, golfers, football quarterbacks . . ." She winked at Elizabeth. "Let's just give it a try, OK?"

Lila continued to grumble as the girls sat down in a circle facing the TV. "It sounds like New Age hocus-pocus to me."

"Tell me about it," Jessica hissed in Lila's ear as she tore the shrink-wrap off the video. "But I'm desperate!"

She stuck the tape in the VCR. Immediately a peppy musical theme blared over the speakers. Then two girls in tight, short orange-and-black cheerleading uniforms bounced into view. "Hi!" one of the girls chirped. "I'm Rosita and this is Amber, and we're cocaptains of the Fort Bridger, Texas, cheer squad, last year's national high-school champions!"

"And we're here to show you some of our best stuff," Amber piped in, "so your squad can start capitalizing on its own best qualities and talents to become the best you can possibly be!"

This perky announcement was met with groans from the Sweet Valley girls. "I think I'm going to be sick," mumbled Elizabeth.

"I bet they came in first because their uniforms are so skimpy," speculated Maria.

Jessica felt like gagging, too, but she wasn't about to let her squad quit before they even really got started. She whistled for silence. "C'mon, keep quiet! They take cheerleading seriously in Texas—I bet we can learn a lot from these girls."

The visualization video lasted twenty minutes. Amber, Rosita, and their teammates ran through a series of jumps, dance steps, and combinations, filmed from a variety of angles and sometimes in slow motion. There was very little narration; instead a musical sound track set the mood. In spite of herself Jessica found herself tapping her foot and snapping her fingers. Every now and then one of her muscles twitched; she realized she was literally itching to get out there and try some of the jumps. *Look at the height she's getting on that stag leap!* Jessica marveled silently, staring enraptured at the screen. *I never thought to try that arm position—doesn't that look sharp!*

When the tape ended, Jessica hit the rewind button and they watched it again. After the second time she rewound the tape and turned off the TV The girls rose to their feet, stretching. "So what did you think?" Jessica asked eagerly. "Wasn't that cool? I saw a bunch of stuff the second time through that I didn't even notice the first time—I started focusing on their footwork, you know?"

Lila, Jade, and Patty nodded; a couple other girls shrugged. The rest were looking at their watches and edging toward the door. "Well . . ." Jessica said, thinking maybe she should be satisfied with the fact that they weren't griping and complaining anymore, "let's think about what we saw, OK? Let it sink into your brain. Tomorrow we'll practice twice, before and after school. And then I guess we'll see if this visualization stuff is all it's cracked up to be!"

"Thanks for letting me interview you, Heather," Elizabeth said. "This will definitely make my story more rounded."

She'd cornered Heather in the lunch line, and after a momentary show of reluctance, Heather had agreed to step out to the courtyard for five minutes or so. They sat side by side on a bench; Elizabeth's pen was poised over her notebook.

"So you're writing an article about Jessica's new cheerleading squad," Heather said with a sniff.

"It's called 'The Pom-pom Wars,'" Elizabeth told her.

Heather laughed heartily. "That's hilarious. Really, Liz, you have a great sense of humor, using the word 'war' when you know it's going to be more like an overthrow."

"So you don't think Jessica will succeed at forming her own cheerleading team?"

Heather shrugged. "Maybe she'll form a team, but I honestly don't expect any competition from them—or should I say you? Anybody can mail-order cheerleading uniforms, but looking cute is no substitute for talent."

Elizabeth bristled at this thinly veiled insult. "Back to Jessica's motivation," she said, a bit more aggressively. "You antagonized Jessica until she felt she had no other option but to quit the squad, right?"

"That's one version of the story," said Heather.

"And before that, you got rid of Sandy and Maria," Elizabeth pressed. "That leaves you with a squad of just four. Do you really think four girls can represent the entire Sweet Valley High student body? Do you really think being cutthroat and elitist is a good way to exhibit school spirit?"

"It's not the purpose of the cheerleaders to 'represent' the student body,'" said Heather coldly. "Our job is to be the very best—that's how you build pride in your school, not by encouraging mediocrity."

Elizabeth scrawled a few last words and then slammed her notebook shut. She didn't think she could keep a lid on her temper if she had to spend another minute with Heather Mallone. "Thanks for your time, Heather," she said, rising.

"No problem." Heather also got to her feet. Flinging her long blond hair over her shoulder, she tapped Elizabeth's notebook with a sharp cherry-red fingernail. "And I'm glad to see you haven't quit the newspaper because of cheerleading. You wouldn't want to put all your eggs in Jessica's flimsy basket!"

Pivoting on one high heel, Heather breezed back into the cafeteria. Elizabeth followed, her eyes blazing with suppressed fury.

She found Jessica sitting alone at a corner table. "Let me guess," Jessica said when she saw her sister's face. "You just had a conversation with Heather Mallone."

"She's the worst!" Elizabeth exclaimed.

Jessica rolled her eyes. "Tell me about it."

Elizabeth sat down. "I mean, of all the unpleasant, self-centered, ice-cold—"

Jessica laughed. "I hope that's the way you're going to describe her in your newspaper article!"

"I'm tempted to, let me tell you," said Elizabeth.

Jessica had been writing something on a piece of notebook paper. "What's that?" Elizabeth asked.

"I'm trying to write a new cheer," said Jessica,

turning the paper so Elizabeth could see her scribbles. "But I'm not feeling terribly inspired. Every time I picture those girls jumping . . ." She grimaced.

"So you do the best with what you've got," said Elizabeth. "You look for ways to make them look better than they are."

Jessica snorted. "I'm a cheerleader, not a magician! And right now I feel dumb, dumb, dumb. I've been sitting here for fifteen minutes, and I can't think of any words to rhyme with 'beat.'"

"Heat," suggested Elizabeth. "Meet, greet, feet, neat, cheat, seat, treat—"

"Whoa, hold on!" exclaimed Jessica, laughing. "Let me write these down." She jotted down the words and then looked up at her sister with a grateful smile. "Thanks a lot, Liz. You're a lifesaver."

"I'd be happy to help you write the cheer," Elizabeth offered, "if you explain the code you're using."

"Really?" Jessica looked surprised and pleased. "You'd do that? I mean, even though I—um—coerced you into doing this?"

"Talking to Heather led me to the conclusion that your new squad is the best thing that could have happened to cheerleading at Sweet Valley High," declared Elizabeth. She smiled wryly. "Of course, the second-best thing would've been if you'd left me out of it!"

"You know," Lila said to Jessica on Thursday afternoon, "I hate to say it, but I think they're looking better. I think that dumb visualization tape actually helped!"

Pom-poms on their hips, Lila and Jessica stood at the edge of the athletic field watching the other girls practice. Jade sprang onto Patty's shoulders, then jumped off, executing a perfect side banana before landing lightly on her feet. Meanwhile, Sara and Amanda were spotting each other for round-off, back-handspring runs. Lisa, Stacie, and Jennifer were attempting jumps they'd been afraid to try the day before. Even Elizabeth, Maria, and Sandy, whose jumps were already technically strong, seemed to be performing their moves with added zest and style.

"Putting it all together will be the hard part." Jessica felt her spirits lift. "But I *am* starting to think there's some hope!"

"Having her at the other end of the field really cramps my style, though," commented Lila. "Doesn't it make you self-conscious?"

Jessica's gaze shifted along with Lila's. A hundred yards away Heather was practicing with her squad. At the moment she had stopped to watch Jessica's group, her arms folded across her chest and a disdainful smile on her lips.

Heather said something to Amy, who laughed loudly. Then they turned away and to rejoin their squad. Heather clapped her hands and shouted; the girls fell into line and like clockwork, chanting loudly, pranced their way through a lively, complicated cheer. Every jump and step was elegant, athletic, precise; the whole look was polished and tight. As much as she would have liked to find fault, Jessica couldn't spot a single error. *Championship material*, she thought gloomily. *They're as good as Rosita and Amber and the Fort Bridger girls!*

"Thank God she didn't see us practicing before the visualization video, huh?" said Lila.

"We're making progress, but there are a lot of rough edges," Jessica agreed dismally. "We have a long way to go. A long way."

"Liz, could you help me for a minute?" Jade called.

Elizabeth dropped her pom-poms and hurried to Jade's side. "What's up?"

"I'm working on my trojan," Jade explained, "and I think I have the leg positions down. One leg is tucked up and bent at the knee while the other is extended straight back, toe pointed. But I can't remember where my arms are supposed to be."

As Elizabeth demonstrated the jump for Jade, she realized someone was watching them. When she turned to see who it was, her heart did a round-off, back handspring.

Ken, wearing sweatpants and a cutoff T-shirt over his football shoulder pads, stood at the edge of the field, his helmet cradled under one arm. He lifted a hand in a wave; Elizabeth waved back.

Then she saw him smile; he put a hand to his mouth and shouted something. "Looking good, Jess!"

Jess. Elizabeth turned back to Jade, swallowing her disappointment. *Of course he wasn't looking at you,* she chastised herself. He was waving and smiling at Jessica—Jessica was his girlfriend, not Elizabeth.

As she left Jade practicing on her own, Elizabeth repeated the silent lecture. *He's not here to watch me, he's not here to watch me. He doesn't think about me anymore—as far as he's concerned, we're ancient history.*

It didn't help a whole lot. Elizabeth still felt the adrenaline surging through her veins; she was buoyed up on a wave of energy and excitement, just because she knew Ken was near. Taking a deep breath, she launched into a tumbling run: round-off, back handspring, back handspring.

After landing the second back handspring, she shot straight into the air in a perfect split jump. Then she dropped to earth, squatting on one knee with her breath coming fast, pom-poms at her waist.

She heard someone clapping and cheering. "Liz, that was fantastic!"

It was Jessica. Hopping up, Elizabeth glanced over at her sister as she shook out the muscles in her legs.

Ken stood at Jessica's side, an arm around her waist. They both gave Elizabeth a thumbs-up sign. Elizabeth smiled, feeling light-headed from her exertion and from the knowledge that, no matter how casually and how briefly, Ken's eyes had rested on her. The chant in her brain changed. *He was watching me, he was watching me . . .*

• • •

On Friday afternoon Jessica pressed the play button on her portable tape player and then dashed over to line up with her cheerleading squad. She'd made final cuts and only the cream of the crop remained: herself and Elizabeth, Lila, Maria, Sandy, Jade, Patty, and Sara. And in their beautiful new red-and-white uniforms, compliments of Lila, they looked sharp and professional. As the fast-paced music started—Patty and Jade had picked out the songs—the line shimmied sideways, arms flying and pom-poms shaking. "We're turning on the heat!" Jessica and the other girls yelled. "We're the team to beat!"

In quick succession each girl in line stepped forward and performed a jump. Lila did a fabulous side-kick, Y-leap combination; Patty did a double herky no problem; Elizabeth's trojan-crunch combination was textbook perfect; and Jade, the last to go, amazed them all by landing her jump in a split.

Jessica couldn't contain her enthusiasm. She threw her pom-poms in the air, shouting joyfully, "That's it, you guys. You've got it!"

With double practices every day, and the constant reminder of Heather's squad's perfection at the other end of the field—the standard to meet and beat—it had been an emotional, exhausting week. Now the girls jumped up and down, hugging each other. Retrieving her pom-poms, Jessica waved them triumphantly. "Let's hear it. Give me a V!" she cried, grinning broadly. "For visualization!"

• • •

"Congratulations. I knew you could do it!" Ken exclaimed, striding toward her. "You really whipped the squad into shape. You guys look awesome!"

Elizabeth was standing slightly apart from Jessica and the other girls. She froze, her eyes widening. "Ken, it's—"

"A miracle," he said, wrapping his arms around her. His T-shirt was damp with sweat; he smelled like fresh-cut grass and some musky deodorant. A shiver ran down Elizabeth's spine. "I'm so proud of you, Jess, I could just . . ."

Ken drew her nearer, lowering his face to hers. He was about to kiss her . . .

Elizabeth stiffened and Ken stopped, his lips just inches from hers. For a split second they stared into each other's eyes, startled, and then they quickly stepped away from one another, laughing awkwardly. "Sorry about that," Ken murmured, his face reddening. "I didn't mean . . . I thought you were . . ."

"Easy mistake to make," Elizabeth assured him, her own cheeks flaming. "Don't worry about it—happens all the time."

Patting her on the arm, Ken hurried off to find the girl he'd meant to kiss. Elizabeth stood looking after him, still blushing. She realized her whole body was trembling. Ken always did have that effect on her. . . .

A short distance away Ken grabbed Jessica by the waist and lifted her high into the air, then lowered her to the ground again so he could plant a big kiss on her lips. Elizabeth turned away from the sight. She wanted to forget that Ken belonged to Jessica now—she wanted to treasure the feeling he'd left her with.

Because she couldn't deny it. She loved Todd, and she wanted to be loyal to him, but at that moment he was the furthest thing from her mind. Elizabeth hugged herself, savoring the memory. She couldn't deny how wonderful it had felt to be in Ken's arms again, even by accident, even just for a moment.

"You'd better not make that mistake too often," Jessica teased. "I know we look a lot alike, but by now you're supposed to know who's who!"

"It's the cheerleading uniforms," Ken protested. "And from a distance, from the side . . ."

Ken reached out to hug her again, tickling her. Jessica laughed. *How silly!* she thought to herself. A second before, when she'd seen Ken hug Elizabeth, she'd actually felt a flash of jealousy. They looked so good together, and she couldn't help wondering, Did they feel good together? Jessica was pretty sure Elizabeth still pined for Ken; did Ken still carry a secret torch for Elizabeth?

Of course he doesn't, she told herself as Ken's lips met hers in a sweet, searching kiss. She could feel him focusing on her, head to toe, his whole body and soul. They were so full of love for each other, sometimes Jessica thought they would spontaneously combust. No, there wasn't any room in

Ken's heart for those old forbidden feelings for Elizabeth.

Jessica gave Ken a last peck on the cheek. "We're going to run through the new routine one more time. Watch us, OK?"

"You bet," he said with a loving smile.

Jessica fairly floated across the grass. *This is what it's all about,* she thought happily as she turned up the volume on the tape player so that the music was really blasting.

She had her identity back. She was Jessica Wakefield, captain of the hottest cheerleading squad in Sweet Valley. And while she was ready to cheer her heart out for all the Sweet Valley High athletes, she knew she would shine brightest when the football team was on the field . . . and she was cheering for Ken.

"I can't believe it," Amy gasped. "Those can't be the same girls we saw practicing earlier in the week!"

Heather's eyes were also fixed on the rival squad. As Jessica and her team shimmied and shouted their way through a flashy routine, Heather nearly swallowed her gum. "They're good," she admitted grudgingly. "They're very good."

Annie had come to stand next to them. "It's the choreography," she remarked. "It's really jazzy and fresh. Patty and Jade must have helped her with it."

"Should we be worried?" asked Jean, nibbling her fingernails nervously. "I mean, what if they're not just good—what if they're better?"

Heather sniffed. "I have to give Jessica credit for making passable cheerleaders out of that motley crew. They are good, but they're not better. Besides"—a gloating smile wreathed her face—"I know something Jessica doesn't know."

"What's that?" asked Amy.

"There's a rule that only one team from each school can go to regionals," Heather replied, "and we've already been picked to represent Sweet Valley!"

"Phew!" Amy exclaimed, relieved. "For a minute there I was starting to sweat."

Jessica's squad was forming a pyramid. Heather watched, still smirking as she waited for them to lose their balance and tumble to the ground.

They didn't fall, but Heather decided it didn't matter. What good was a perfect pyramid going to do them? "It's really too bad they've wasted so much time," she drawled dismissively, snapping her gum as she turned her back on Jessica's squad. "Boy, is Jessica going to be burned when she finds out her team isn't even eligible for regionals!"

It was pitiful, really, that Jessica had even tried to start a new squad, decided Heather. Clearly Jessica just hadn't gotten the message yet. She wasn't the most popular girl at Sweet Valley High anymore—she wasn't the one setting the pace, the fashion. It was Heather's turn.

Chapter 7

"What do you mean, only one squad from a school can enter the regional cheerleading competition?" Jessica said to Lila over the phone on Saturday morning.

Still dressed in her robe and slippers, Jessica had been standing at the sink rinsing her cereal bowl when the phone rang. Now, holding the receiver between her ear and shoulder, she turned off the water and dried her hands on a dish towel.

"Just what I said. Only one squad can go per school—or to put it another way, each school is allowed to sponsor only one squad as its official representative. It's right here on page twenty-two of the ACA rule book."

"That can't be right," Jessica exclaimed. "It's not fair!"

"Rules aren't always fair," Lila pointed out. "I wouldn't have stumbled upon it myself if Heather dearest hadn't called a few minutes ago to casually suggest that I check out page twenty-two."

Jessica stamped her foot. "She is just so darned cocky, isn't she? She's so sure she can just laugh at us, that we're not a threat. I'm calling Mr. Jenkins."

"The American Cheerleading Association scout?"

"Yep. Maybe they don't enforce this particular rule, or maybe I can talk him into making an exception. He lives in Palisades, right?"

"Bridgewater, I think."

As soon as she hung up on Lila, Jessica dialed Bridgewater information. Elizabeth strolled into the room while Jessica was jotting Mr. Jenkins's number down.

"I'm calling Mr. Jenkins," Jessica informed her sister. "Wish me luck!"

A moment later she was speaking with the ACA scout who'd been so impressed with Heather and the rest of the Sweet Valley High squad at the game a week ago. "Mr. Jenkins, I'd like to find out about arranging an audition with you," Jessica announced. "My name is Jessica Wakefield, and I'm the captain of a new cheer squad at Sweet Valley High."

Elizabeth watched with interest as Jessica shook her head. "I was on Heather Mallone's squad—I mean, that was my squad! But I'm not anymore—I've formed my own team."

Now Jessica was nodding. "That's right. We're just getting started, but we're great, I don't mind saying. We have a really unique look and style, and I think you'll agree we're better than Heather's squad and we should be the ones representing Sweet Valley High at regionals—"

For a moment Jessica was silent while Mr. Jenkins talked. Then she burst out, "But if you'd just come to Sweet Valley and take a look. . . . I understand. I'm sorry, too. Good-bye."

Jessica replaced the receiver, her jaw clenched tight. "He didn't buy it, huh?" guessed Elizabeth.

"He said he's very busy scouting all the schools in the area." Jessica heaved a frustrated sigh. "He already visited SVH once and he doesn't plan on returning."

Elizabeth took a carton of orange juice from the refrigerator and gave it a shake before pouring herself a glass. "So he didn't say it was impossible for your squad to go in place of Heather's," she observed. "It was more a question of his not going to the trouble to check us out and make a comparison."

"Same difference."

Elizabeth tilted her head to one side. "Is it?"

"What are you getting at?"

Elizabeth shrugged. "I don't know. I guess I'm just surprised that you'd give up so easily. Maybe this isn't that important to you, after all."

"But it is!" Jessica cried. "I'd do anything to go to regionals, but what's the point if I can't get an audience with Mr. Jenkins?"

Elizabeth sipped her juice. "Like I said, I'm just surprised that you're giving up so easily."

Jessica stared at her sister. Then, slowly, a light brightened behind her eyes. She snapped her fingers. "I've got an idea!"

Elizabeth smiled. "I was wondering when your scheming brain would shift into high gear."

"Run upstairs and put on your cheerleading uniform," Jessica ordered, "while I call the rest of the squad."

"What's the plan?" asked Elizabeth.

Her sister grinned. "If the regional scout won't come to Jessica Wakefield, Jessica Wakefield will just have to go to the regional scout!"

"Mrs. Jenkins?" Jessica said to the attractive thirty-something woman who answered the front door of the stucco ranch house in Bridgewater.

Jessica was wearing her red-and-white cheerleading uniform; the rest of the squad, also in uniform and with pom-poms in hand, were lined up on the walk behind her. Mrs. Jenkins blinked at the sight. "Yes?"

"Is Mr. Jenkins home?" Jessica inquired.

"He's gone out to do a few errands," Mrs. Jenkins replied. "He should be back any minute, though. Can I help you?"

"Oh, no, thanks," said Jessica with a sweet smile. "But if it's OK, we'll just wait for him. Outside," she added quickly, smothering a giggle when she saw Mrs. Jenkins's look of horror at the prospect of having eight cheerleaders in her living room.

"That's fine," Mrs. Jenkins said, visibly relieved. "Have a nice—"

She started to close the door. "One more thing," Jessica called after her. "What kind of car does your husband drive?"

Mrs. Jenkins wrinkled her forehead, puzzled. "It's a red Honda Civic. Now if you'll excuse me . . ."

Hopping down from the front stoop, Jessica hustled her cheerleaders onto the Jenkinses' lawn. "He'll be home any minute," she informed the squad, "so as soon as we see a red Honda Civic, I want everyone to—"

"Look!" Maria pointed up the street. "I think that's him now!"

"All right, let's go!" shouted Jessica, hitting a button on the tape player and snatching up her pom-poms. "You know what we have to do!"

In a flash Maria, Sandy, and Elizabeth had boosted Patty and Sara onto their shoulders; Jessica and Lila then helped Jade scramble to the top. An impressive standing pyramid greeted Mr. Jenkins as he pulled into the driveway.

Flanking the pyramid, Jessica and Lila started stamping their feet and chanting. "We've got the beat and our team's got the heat. We will defeat any rivals we meet. . . ."

Mr. Jenkins had climbed out of his parked car and was standing at the edge of the lawn, grocery bags in his arms, watching Jessica and her squad perform. Bending quickly, Jessica cranked up the volume on the tape player.

The tempo of the music grew faster and more electrifying. Jade, Patty, and Sara had hopped down from the pyramid, and now the whole line of girls was whirling and leaping in turn. The routine built to its climax. In pairs the girls darted forward to perform their final stunts: Lila and Jade did no-hands cartwheels, landing in splits; Maria and Sandy did round-off, back handsprings; Sara and Patty each did a flip, one front and one back, and then shot into the air again in perfect stag leaps; and finally Jessica and Elizabeth did spread-eagles, landing front and center in side-by-side Chinese splits.

Mr. Jenkins put down the grocery bags so he could applaud. "Bravo!" he yelled, whistling. "Good show!"

Jessica hopped to her feet and trotted over to him, panting from the exertion. The other girls pressed close behind her. "What did you think, honestly?" Jessica asked with an eager smile after introducing herself.

"It's a dazzling routine," said Mr. Jenkins. "Highly technical and very original."

"I've incorporated some modern-dance choreography into it," said Jessica. "I think it makes us one of a kind."

"And I like the twin factor," he continued, beaming at the Wakefield sisters. Jessica elbowed Elizabeth in the ribs. "Yes, all in all this is one of the most impressive routines I've seen all season."

"So you'll give us a slot in regionals?" Jessica concluded, her eyes shining.

Mr. Jenkins's smile faded. "I'm afraid not," he said regretfully. "We've been over this, Jessica—you know the rules. Only one team from a school can compete, and although your squad is terrific, I've already granted a spot to Heather's squad. They earned it."

"They stole it," Jessica muttered under her breath. "It should have been ours!"

Mr. Jenkins patted her on the shoulder, then bent to retrieve his groceries. "Try again next year, girls," he called before disappearing into the house.

Jessica hurled her pom-poms onto the grass, her face crumpling. Elizabeth slipped an arm around her sister's shoulders. Lila, Maria, Sandy, Jade, Patty, and Sara all looked at each other, their eyes shadowed with disappointment.

"I'm—I'm sorry," Jessica stuttered, putting a hand to her eyes to dash away the tears. "I led you guys to think we could go all the way, and now it turns out we're not going any further than Mr. Jenkins's front yard. I wasted your time. I'm really, really sorry."

Her shoulders drooping and her chin on her chest, Jessica trudged toward the Jeep, alone.

"What a bummer," said Sara, her sigh weighted with disappointment. "Poor Jessica. She really had her heart set on this, didn't she?"

The eight girls were driving back to Sweet Valley; Lila, Maria, and Sandy were in the Jeep with Jessica, while Elizabeth, Sara, and Jade rode in Patty's Chevy Nova.

The Jeep was leading, but Jessica, usually a speedy driver, was setting a funeral-procession pace. "She staked all her hopes on going to regionals," agreed Elizabeth. "She didn't want to feel that Heather had beaten her, you know? She wanted another chance to compete with her, on neutral ground. But I guess now she's going to have to hang up her pom-poms once and for all."

"It's really a shame," declared Patty, flipping on her turn signal as they neared an intersection. "I mean, I'll be the first to admit it—I was totally skeptical when she first approached me about cheering. But this past week I've really come to appreciate how demanding a sport it is. Not to mention fun!"

"I feel like I've really been stretched in new ways," agreed Jade. "I loved having a chance to get creative with my dance training, athleticize it, you know? Until I started cheerleading practice this week, I really had no idea how strong I was, how much I was capable of."

Elizabeth, sitting in the backseat, rested her arms on the seat in front of her. "I guess there's not much any of us can do but wait until next year, like Mr. Jenkins said. Maybe Jessica will find a way to get some kind of official status for her squad, or maybe you guys could try out for Heather's squad."

Sara wrinkled her nose. "I would never cheer for Heather," she pronounced.

"Her whole philosophy is based on excluding people," said Jade, "whereas Jessica really reached out to bring a whole new range of talents into her squad."

Elizabeth nodded. "That's true. In the past the cheerleaders were a pretty tight group. We've cracked the clique wide open!"

"Yeah, well," said Patty, reaching down to the

radio to give the dial a spin, "easy come, easy go."

Patty had tuned in to a local station. A game was being broadcast. "The SVH football game against El Carro!" Elizabeth realized, leaning forward to hear.

"I guess while we cheered for Mr. Jenkins, Heather and her squad were cheering for the Gladiators," said Sara.

"What's the score?" asked Jade.

The four girls listened until the announcer said, "As the first half winds down, the Gladiators have fallen behind twenty-eight to six. It looks like it's going to be a romp for El Carro High."

Patty turned off the radio in disgust. "They're getting trounced."

"Watch out!" Elizabeth cried.

Ahead of them Jessica had braked suddenly. Patty skidded to a halt, nearly rear-ending the Jeep. "What the—" she exclaimed.

Now Jessica was signaling, about to pull into the parking lot of a convenience store. Lila hung out the passenger-side window, beckoning urgently for Patty to follow.

"What's going on?" Jade wondered.

"Let's find out," said Patty, trailing the Jeep into the parking lot.

As soon as the Jeep was parked, Jessica, Lila, Maria, and Sandy poured out. They were quickly joined by Elizabeth and the others.

"You guys ready for another performance?" Jessica asked.

"What are you talking about?" said Elizabeth.

"The football game," explained Jessica. "Were you listening?"

"Sweet Valley's losing," said Patty. "There doesn't seem to be much point in stopping by for the second half."

"We're all going to stop by," Jessica told her. "The Gladiators could use our help."

"What are you talking about?" Elizabeth repeated.

Jessica grinned. "I'm talking about cheerleading. I'm talking about how we've practiced hard all week and now it's time to show the world what we can do!"

"You want us to go down to the field and perform?" said Elizabeth in disbelief.

Jessica nodded. "We're in uniform and we're all warmed up," she pointed out. "What's to stop us?"

The other girls began buzzing excitedly. Only Elizabeth protested. "But, Jess, we can't do that! We're not the real squad!"

"Oh, no?" Jessica lifted her chin, her eyes flashing with pride and determination. "I think we should let the fans decide. C'mon!" She waved the girls back to the cars. "It's almost halftime—we'd better hurry!"

Jessica was already settling into the driver's seat of the Jeep, revving the engine. Elizabeth had no choice but to pile back into Patty's Nova. She found her heart racing with anticipation. *This is the real thing,* Elizabeth thought, sparked by Jessica's fire. *We're going to cheer in front of the whole school!*

• • •

The stands at the football field were packed with fans, but the mood, on the Sweet Valley side at least, was solemn. "We're just in time," Jessica hissed as she and the other girls darted under the home-team bleachers. "Only one minute till halftime. Stay right here, and don't let anyone see you!"

Jessica had put on a denim jacket over her cheerleading uniform. Donning dark sunglasses as well, she jogged quickly up the steps and ducked into the sound booth at the top of the stands. The announcer, busy recapping highlights of the game so far, didn't even notice her. The girl sitting in front of the broadcasting controls, however, waved Jessica to a halt. "Hey, what are you doing in here?"

"There's been a change," Jessica said breathlessly. "The cheerleading music, at halftime?" Taking a cassette from her jacket pocket, she pressed it into the girl's hand. "Play this instead."

"Are you sure?" the girl asked. "Who authorized—"

"Just play it," Jessica said firmly. "It'll be all right, I promise."

Before the girl could ask any more questions, Jessica dashed back out of the booth.

Underneath the bleachers she found her squad huddled in a tight knot. "All of a sudden I'm really nervous," Jade confessed.

"We've never performed in front an audience before," said Sara, her teeth chattering.

"What if we forget our moves?" wondered Patty.

"You won't forget—you'll be brilliant," Jessica declared, bundling them into a big hug. Elizabeth proffered the canvas equipment bag, and Jessica reached in to hand pom-poms all around. "When the music starts . . ." She looked upward, her lips moving in a rapid prayer. "And please, please let it start. . . . When it starts, just let out all the stops. Go for it. We've got nothing to lose!"

They all turned to face the football field through the slats of the bleachers. The scoreboard was in plain view as the last seconds of the first half ticked down. "Ten, nine, eight, seven, six," Jessica murmured, her heart beginning to thump like a kettledrum. "Five, four, three, two, one. That's our cue!"

The two football teams started to trot off the field. On the opposite side of the field, the El Carro cheerleaders were getting ready to perform. Heather and her squad bent to retrieve their pom-poms, brushed dust off their skirts, smoothed their hair.

As Jessica's squad stormed the field, she heard a murmur start up in the stands. Then the music started: her music, the tape she'd put together with Patty and Jade's help.

Before Heather had time to react, Jessica's squad was lined up on the field facing the home-team bleachers. The Sweet Valley fans quickly figured out what they were seeing and began hooting their approval. The squad launched straight into their routine, smiling at the crowd and yelling at the top of their lungs. "We've got the beat and our team's got the heat," Jessica shouted. "We will defeat any rivals we meet!"

The music had a jazzy, irresistible rhythm. Jessica's squad clapped energetically, and soon the fans were clapping with them. The sound was deafening.

One by one, Jessica and her team performed their dazzling airborne combinations. Each time one of the girls landed a jump, the crowd roared. By the time the routine reached its stirring climax, the fans were on their feet, waving banners and tossing confetti.

Jessica landed her last jump and sank to the earth in a split. The squad held their pose while the audience applauded wildly. The Sweet Valley High football team had jogged back onto the field to watch the performance; to Jessica's delight, Ken had seen it all. But that was nothing compared to the satisfaction she got from watching Heather's reaction.

For the first time since she'd moved to Sweet Valley, confident, beautiful Heather Mallone appeared to be at a total loss. She stood on the sidelines, her squad lined up behind her, pom-poms on her hips and her mouth hanging open. Jessica grinned and waved at the crowd, blowing kisses and laughing. *Mirror, mirror on the wall,* she thought, giddy with triumph. *Now who's got the fairest cheerleading squad of all?*

• • •

As usual, the Dairi Burger was packed to the rafters after the football game. When Jessica walked in with Ken, they were immediately besieged by friends. "Really awesome, Wakefield!" boomed Bruce Patman, planting a kiss on Jessica's cheek and then slugging Ken playfully in the shoulder.

"You guys were great," echoed Bruce's girlfriend, Pamela Robertson. "You should be out there all the time!"

"Weren't they fantastic?" Ken agreed, his arm firmly around Jessica's shoulders. "I've always thought cheerleaders played an important role, but I never realized they could do that much to fire a team up."

"The final score tells the whole story," said Scottie Trost, the Gladiators' wide receiver. "Thirty-four to twenty-eight—what a comeback!"

Jessica beamed. "Well, we can't take all the credit," she said modestly. "You guys played a great game."

"I'm telling you, we couldn't have done it without you," Ken insisted, giving her a big kiss. "Seeing you back on the field, Jess—it was just like old times."

"It was better than old times," declared Todd, giving Elizabeth a squeeze. "Thanks to all the new talent Jessica recruited!"

The moment was perfect . . . until Amy, who'd been huddled in a booth with her boyfriend, Barry Rork, charged over to Jessica. "How could you do that to us?" she demanded tearfully.

"Heather didn't give me much of a choice—besides, she did it to me first," replied Jessica. "You said it yourself the other day, Amy—nothing personal, right?"

"It is personal. You made me look like an idiot in front of the whole school!"

Jessica smiled. "So how did it feel?"

Amy shook her head. "I can't believe you're taking pleasure in this." A tear streaked down her cheek. "I guess this means we're not friends anymore!"

Before Jessica could reason with her, Amy bolted from the restaurant. Jessica shrugged. Amy's outburst had tarnished the moment, but only slightly. As more and more people poured into the Dairi Burger, Jessica continued to be surrounded by admiring schoolmates and barraged with compliments. Everyone preferred her squad to Heather's, no contest. Heather, meanwhile, was nowhere to be seen—as soon as the game ended, she'd headed home in a sulk.

"So is it true, Jessica?" Zack Johnson, a Gladiators' linebacker, wanted to know. "Are you guys really the new squad? Are you taking over from Heather?"

"Well, I don't know," said Jessica coyly. "Do you think we should?"

The answer was a resounding "yes." All around her Jessica's friends were toasting her with milk shakes and soft drinks. "Here's to Jessica, Liz, Lila, Maria, Sandy, Jade, Patty, and Sara," said Ken, his blue eyes glowing with love and pride. "The best cheerleaders in the history of Sweet Valley High!"

The praise was like candy; Jessica couldn't get enough of it. *I'm back where I belong,* she thought happily, remembering the day Heather Mallone had walked into the Dairi Burger and begun the process of trying to elbow Jessica out of her place at the top of the SVH social hierarchy.

She had the winning quarterback at her side; they were the couple of the hour. Yes, Jessica was back in the spotlight. Now she just had to make sure she stayed there.

Chapter 8

At the start of lunch period on Monday, Jessica hurried straight to the principal's office. As usual, Rosemary, Mr. Cooper's secretary, was barricading the door like a dragon guarding a treasure trove. *Like anyone actually wants to go in there!* Jessica thought.

Rosemary peered at Jessica through her bifocals. "Do you have an appointment, dear?"

"No, but I need to speak to . . ." Jessica caught herself just in time from saying "Chrome Dome," the student body's irreverent nickname for the bald principal. ". . . to Mr. Cooper as soon as possible. Make that immediately, as in right now. It's extremely urgent!"

Rosemary raised her wispy, overplucked eyebrows. "Well, let me see if he can squeeze you in before his appointment in the faculty lunch room," she offered in a grudging tone, as if she were doing

Jessica the biggest favor in the history of the world.

Rosemary buzzed Mr. Cooper and mumbled something incoherent. Then she looked at Jessica, her head bobbing on her skinny neck. "The principal will see you now," she said formally.

Circling Rosemary's desk, Jessica pushed open the door to Chrome Dome Cooper's office. "Hi, Mr. Cooper," she said cheerfully.

"Jessica, it's good to see you." The round-faced principal stood up and waved her into a chair facing his desk. "What can I do for you today?"

Jessica sat down, folding her hands on her lap. "It's about cheerleading, sir."

"Ah." Seated again, Chrome Dome propped his elbows on the desk and tented his fingers under his double chin. "Cheerleading."

"As you may know, I quit the varsity squad about ten days ago because of . . . personality differences with Heather Mallone, the new cocaptain," Jessica explained. "I decided to form my own squad, and all last week we practiced like crazy. We knew the old squad—Heather's squad—was going to regionals, and we thought we could go, too. But it turns out that only one team per school can go."

"Oh, that's too bad, too bad," clucked Chrome Dome.

"The thing is, Mr. Cooper," said Jessica, leaning forward in her chair. Suddenly her eyes were blazing. "It's not fair that Heather's squad should automatically get to go to regionals. The cheerleading competition is about school spirit, and I think my squad has more of that. She formed her team by kicking people out—I formed mine by inviting people in. And I just know that if the student body could vote on which squad they want to represent them at regionals, mine would win hands down!"

It was a stirring speech and Chrome Dome was clearly affected. "Well, I'll tell you, Jessica," he said, rubbing his bald head until it was shinier than ever, "I was at the game on Saturday, and I thought your squad was terrific, just terrific. Now, that's not to say I approved of your just bursting onto the scene without getting permission first, but on the other hand, the fans loved it, they definitely loved it. The team loved it—they turned the tables on El Carro and pulled off a victory. Yes, it showed school spirit all right—clearly you girls have plenty of that."

"So you think it's a good idea?" Jessica asked eagerly. "Having the whole school vote?"

"I think it's an excellent idea," he confirmed, thumping a fist on his desk for emphasis, "a very sound, democratic idea. Yes, the students should vote, because, after all, it should be their cheerleading squad competing at regionals—not yours or Heather's but Sweet Valley High's."

"I couldn't agree more," declared Jessica.

"We'll have a—what shall we call it?—a cheer-off tomorrow," Mr. Cooper suggested. "Both teams can display their talents in front of the entire student body. After school, of course."

"Of course!" Jessica agreed, springing to her feet. "Oh, thanks, Mr. Cooper. Thanks so much!"

In her joy she was almost tempted to kiss old Chrome Dome on his polished pink head. Almost.

"I think 'The Pom-pom Wars' story came out great," Penny said to Elizabeth before the *Oracle* staff meeting got started during lunch period. "Do you think you could do a follow-up story? I mean, it was so exciting, the way Jessica's squad charged onto the field at halftime of the football game on Saturday. Personally, I always thought the cheerleaders were just there for decoration, but that performance changed my mind."

Hitching herself onto a table, Elizabeth swung her feet, kicking them against the table legs. "I'm afraid the follow-up would be kind of anticlimactic," she replied. "The pom-pom wars seem to be over. Heather's team won."

Elizabeth told Penny about the unsuccessful visit to the ACA scout's home. "He told us to try again next year. Jessica was pretty bummed, as you might expect. She felt better after that halftime stunt, but I don't see how it can change anything. Heather's squad is going to regionals and we're not—that's the bottom line."

At that moment Mr. Collins entered the room, and Elizabeth and Penny turned their attention to him. The meeting was brief—Mr. Collins reviewed some upcoming deadlines and then demonstrated a few additional tricks for using INFOMAX, the new on-line computer database. Elizabeth took some notes and asked a couple of questions. As soon as the meeting was over, the other students disappeared, eager to get to the cafeteria to grab a bite before the bell rang. Only Elizabeth stayed behind, experimenting with INFOMAX.

Mr. Collins had taken a seat at a desk in order to look over the first draft of a feature article for Olivia Davidson, the *Oracle*'s arts editor. When Elizabeth turned off her computer a few minutes later and got to her feet, he smiled across the room at her. "I wanted to congratulate you on your newfound talent, Liz." He smiled, the corners of his sky-blue eyes crinkling. "Teddy and I were at the game on Saturday, and we were both very impressed. Teddy couldn't wait to boast to his friends that not only does his favorite baby-sitter tell the best stories, but she can do cartwheels and back flips, too!"

Elizabeth laughed. Mr. Collins, one of her favorite teachers at Sweet Valley High, was a divorced single parent, and she often baby-sat for his six-year-old son. "I have to admit I was having a blast out there," she confessed. "It's really a fun sport—I'm starting to see why Jessica's so into it."

"Just don't overdo it," Mr. Collins cautioned. "I don't want you showing up with a sprained wrist or something."

"I'd type with my toes if I had to," Elizabeth joked. "Anything to get the story out!"

Mr. Collins tipped his chair backward and gazed at her, his smile more thoughtful. "I've been meaning to talk to you about something, Liz—something else. Remember that story you told me about your friend, the one who fell for her boyfriend's best friend when her boyfriend was out of town?"

Elizabeth felt a blush crawl up her neck to her face. "Um, yeah. What—what about it?"

"Well, I was wondering if your friend had any luck resolving the issue."

"Actually . . ." Elizabeth ducked her head, hiding behind a curtain of blond hair. "Actually, I'd say if anything, the situation is worse. You see, my friend's girlfriend, the one who's dating the other guy now, found out that my friend used to be involved with her—the second girl's—new boyfriend. Are you following me?"

"I think so," said Mr. Collins. "So, what happened?"

"Nothing, really. But now my friend's more confused than ever. She's still thinking about that other guy, but at the same time she's also incredibly worried that her boyfriend will find out about what happened in the past."

"What tangled webs we weave, eh?" said Mr. Collins, raking a hand through his strawberry-blond hair. "This is the thing, Liz. You asked for my advice . . . for your friend . . . but later I realized I left out the most important part. The honesty-is-the-best-policy part."

"Oh, that," Elizabeth said wryly.

Mr. Collins smiled. "It's a pretty useful all-purpose moral to just about any story," he remarked. "My point in this case is that your friend has a pretty compelling reason to do the right thing. If she doesn't tell her boyfriend about the other guy, the guilt is going to eat her alive."

Immediately Elizabeth felt the truth of Mr. Collins's words in the depths of her heart. *He's right—I am being eaten alive,* she thought.

"Honesty is the best policy," Elizabeth said softly. "Thanks, Mr. Collins. I'll discuss this with my friend right away. It'll be hard, but she'll just have to find a way to bring it up with her boyfriend. He might get upset, but down the road their relationship will be stronger, right? I mean, because they were honest with each other?"

"There's no guarantee, but perhaps he'll understand," said Mr. Collins. "The important thing is, she'll be able to live with herself."

"Right." Elizabeth put a hand on the doorknob, then turned back. "Thanks. Or did I say that already?"

"It's nothing." Mr. Collins lifted his hands, smiling. "Free advice, all day, any day."

Elizabeth laughed. "See ya, Mr. Collins."

"Take it easy, Liz."

As she walked down the corridor toward the cafeteria, Elizabeth mulled over Mr. Collins's wise words. *Honesty is the best policy,* she repeated to herself, trying to work up her courage to confront Todd. She'd do it that very afternoon—they had a date to go out for pizza. *Honesty is the best policy, honesty is the best policy . . .*

As Elizabeth approached the swinging door to the cafeteria, the loudspeaker system crackled. The vice principal briskly ran through the usual array of lunchtime announcements, and then there was some static and Chrome Dome himself came on the air. Elizabeth stopped in her tracks to listen.

"Ahem, I have one additional piece of news to share with you," Mr. Cooper said, clearing his throat. "Tomorrow after school there will be a special assembly in the gym. The entire student body is invited to view routines performed by the two cheerleading squads captained by Heather Mallone and Jessica Wakefield, respectively, and then to vote on which squad should represent Sweet Valley High at the regionals competition."

Chrome Dome's remaining words were drowned out by the uproar in the cafeteria. Elizabeth pushed into the crowded lunchroom; the din of voices was deafening.

"Is it true?" students were demanding of each other. "A cheer-off? Wow, cool, what a great idea!"

"I'm for Jessica's squad one hundred percent," Elizabeth heard someone say.

"No way, Heather's squad is much better," another voice argued. "She's in a class by herself—she's dynamite."

Everyone had an opinion. "Kicking Maria and Sandy off the squad—that was her first mistake." "I really hope this puts her in her place." "But what makes Jessica think she can just take over the whole way sports are run at SVH?" "Her squad was better, though. Don't those girls deserve a shot at the championship?"

"Jessica!" Elizabeth shouted when she spotted her twin.

Jessica waved happily. "Come on over here,

Liz," she called. "Help me out with this press conference!"

Once again Jessica was surrounded by schoolmates plying her with questions and compliments. Elizabeth stepped to her sister's side.

"It's pretty clear why we have an edge," Jessica told her fans, slipping an arm around Elizabeth's waist. "The old squad used to have one Wakefield twin, but now it has none—while my squad has two!"

Elizabeth rolled her eyes, laughing. "Modest as always," she teased Jessica.

"Hey, I have no regrets," Jessica said. "Modesty's not about to get us to regionals."

"Nothing will get you to regionals," a voice snapped harshly.

Elizabeth and Jessica both whirled. Heather had marched up behind them. Bright spots of color stood out on her fair cheeks; Elizabeth almost expected to see steam shoot from her ears.

"Oh, good, Heather, there you are," said Jessica, her tone silky smooth. "You know, I just love that dress—I saw the exact same one at Lisette's, but I didn't buy it because I didn't think the color would be good on a blonde. Anyhow, Mr. Cooper wants to meet with the two of us to talk about the procedure for the cheer-off tomorrow. Can you spare a few minutes before practice this afternoon?"

"Do I have a choice?" Heather spat out angrily.

"Sure, you have a choice," said Jessica with a playful grin. "You could choose to boycott the cheer-off—to forfeit. Then my squad could save our energy for regionals!"

"Forget it," declared Heather. "We'll be at the cheer-off, and we'll prove to the whole world that you're just looking for attention. You don't have the real stuff. You don't have what it takes to win at regionals, but we do."

"I guess our fellow students will decide, won't they?" said Jessica with admirable coolness.

"They'll decide, and you'll be sorry," Heather predicted, turning on her heel and flouncing off.

Elizabeth and Jessica stared after Heather. Then they looked at one another and burst out laughing. "A week ago I would have been scared to death of that girl," said Jessica, "but not anymore. I think she's starting to show her true colors, and finally I'm not the only one who's able to see them!"

"What is it, Liz?" asked Enid on Monday afternoon. "You sounded frantic on the phone, so I drove as fast as I could."

In half an hour Todd would be picking up Elizabeth for their pizza date. After much agonizing Elizabeth had decided she couldn't go through with her honesty-is-the-best-policy plan without practicing her confession first.

Now she ushered Enid into the front hall. "Thanks for dropping everything to come over," said Elizabeth. "I can't tell you how much I appreciate it, you're just the best friend and I'd be lost without you—"

Enid held up a hand. "Whoa, Liz, you're babbling. Slow down!"

Elizabeth took a deep breath. "OK, let's—I think Jessica is out back by the pool. Let's go upstairs."

She led the way to her bedroom. Once inside, she closed and locked the door. Enid laughed. "Liz, you're acting like you're about to brief me about an undercover spy mission. What's going on?"

Enid sat down on the edge of Elizabeth's bed; Elizabeth perched on the desk chair. "I have to tell you something," Elizabeth began, "that I would have told you a long time ago, except I decided not to tell anyone. We decided. But now I realize I should have told someone in particular—Todd, not you—but before I tell him, I thought I'd tell you."

She paused to take a breath and realized her hands were shaking. "Liz, you're not making sense," Enid said, her voice soothing. "Start at the beginning, OK?"

"OK." Elizabeth's eyes shifted to the desk drawer where the diary was hidden. *I could just let her read it,* she thought somewhat illogically. *I could just let everyone read it—we could print excerpts in* The Oracle!

"It started when Todd moved to Vermont," Elizabeth related. "Remember how lonely I was? I thought I'd die without him. And then after a while I realized I was going to make it, but I was pretty sure I'd never find another boy to love for as long as I lived."

"I remember," said Enid with an encouraging smile. "You met Jeffrey, though, and then Todd moved back. So you weren't lonely forever."

Elizabeth nodded. "But before Todd moved back, before Jeffrey . . ." She gulped; her voice dropped to a whisper. "There was someone else."

Enid gaped. "Someone else? You're kidding!"

"I wish I were," said Elizabeth.

"Who?"

Elizabeth counted to ten in her head. She knew Enid was going to fall off the bed when she heard this. "Ken Matthews."

Enid did practically topple over with astonishment. "Ken Matthews?" she repeated, her voice a surprised squeak. "But no one ever—how did you—where—when—I can't believe it!"

"We were really careful," Elizabeth explained. "We steered clear of each other in school, and all our 'dates' were to places no one was likely to spot us. It was a secret from everybody."

"Because you were still Todd's girlfriend, and Ken was Todd's best friend," said Enid.

Elizabeth nodded glumly. "So do you despise me?"

"Oh, of course not." Enid's eyes were warm with sympathy. "Things like that happen, you know? Todd dated other girls while he lived in Vermont—he was open about that."

"That's just it," exclaimed Elizabeth. "He was open and I wasn't. At least I wasn't open about Ken. I told Todd about my dates with Nicholas Morrow and later about Jeffrey, but Ken . . . that was different. I knew he'd be crushed."

"So even after he moved back to Sweet Valley and you two started going out again, you didn't tell him," Enid deduced.

Elizabeth shook her head. "At that point I figured what he didn't know couldn't hurt him." She laughed humorlessly. "Now, *there's* a motto for people who don't buy into the 'honesty is the best policy' philosophy!"

"And now it's bothering you," said Enid, "and you think you should come clean with Todd."

"It is bothering me." Elizabeth twisted a strand of hair around her right index finger. "But it's complicated, because it's bothering me for a bunch of different reasons in a bunch of different ways."

Enid's eyes glittered with sudden understanding. "Oh, I see," she said. "Jessica and Ken! You're not jealous, are you?"

Elizabeth decided now wasn't the time to go into all the pathetic details of her current emotional crisis. "'Jealousy' isn't really the right word," she said evasively. "Jessica found out about me and Ken—that's basically what got me rethinking all of this."

"She found out and she didn't kill you?" Enid asked in amazement. "What I mean is, she found out and she didn't immediately blab to everybody in Sweet Valley?"

"Doesn't sound like Jessica, does it?" agreed Elizabeth with a grim smile. "I bet this sounds like Jessica, though."

She told Enid about Jessica's blackmailing

strategy. Enid slapped her hand on the bed. "I knew there had to be some weird reason why you decided to join Jessica's squad! Boy, that's low. That's really low!"

"It's no worse than I deserve," said Elizabeth, "and the upside is that I don't hate cheerleading as much as I expected to. If nothing else, it's great exercise. But the whole mess made me realize that this secret isn't good for my mental health. So when Todd and I go out tonight . . ."

Enid reached forward to pat Elizabeth on the knee. "It's the right thing to do, Liz. I'm behind you all the way."

Just thinking about the scene with Todd made Elizabeth want to throw up. "Do you think he'll be mad? What if he storms out of Guido's Pizza Palace? What if he decides he never wants to see me again?"

Elizabeth was on the verge of hysterical tears. "Calm down," Enid advised. "I bet anything it won't happen that way. He'll be shocked, sure, and hurt. He may need to take some time to himself to think about it, figure out how he feels. But then he'll realize that in the grand scheme of things, it's just kind of a blip."

"A blip."

"Right, a blip. The fact is, it didn't amount to anything between you and Ken. You went back to being just friends. And your motives for keeping the whole thing from Todd were pretty pure—you didn't want to hurt his feelings."

Pretty pure—I doubt that! thought Elizabeth.

But she wanted to see the situation the way Enid did. "If the roles were reversed," she said, "if I moved away and Todd went out with you, and then I found out about it a million years later . . ." She wrinkled her nose. "I don't know how I'd feel."

Enid laughed. "You've obviously been thinking too much about this, and now we're talking it to death. You'll psyche yourself out. Just do it."

Enid gave Elizabeth's hand a reaffirming squeeze. Elizabeth made her mind go blank, and then she let one simple idea enter. *I'll tell Todd and then it will all be over,* she thought.

She nodded, feeling strengthened by Enid's support and her own inner resolve. "I will," she declared. "I'll do it."

"You're really packing away that pizza," Todd observed an hour later as they sat opposite each other in a booth at Guido's Pizza Palace. "I'm glad we ordered a large!"

"We had a grueling practice this afternoon," said Elizabeth, reaching for another thick slice of the Guido's special. "As you can imagine, Jessica isn't taking the slightest chance of losing the cheer-off tomorrow. We ran through our routine about a hundred times."

"Speaking of the cheer-off," said Todd, reaching for another piece of pizza himself, "Winston, Ken, and I were talking, and we thought maybe we'd make flyers and banners promoting your squad." He grinned sheepishly. "Just a bunch of proud boyfriends demonstrating our support."

Elizabeth's spine stiffened at the mention of Ken's name, especially in the context of "boyfriends." She managed to crack a weak smile. "That's really . . . sweet."

"Well, I can't speak for the other guys, but I'm always psyched to find a way to show you how much I love you."

"Oh, Todd," Elizabeth mumbled, dropping her eyes.

Quickly, she took a sip of her soda so he wouldn't see her chin tremble. *Oh, Todd . . . why do you have to make this so hard?*

Since arriving at the restaurant, she'd been waiting for an opportunity to bring up the subject of her and Ken. After talking with Enid, she'd felt pumped up and ready. She couldn't wait to have a clean slate with Todd, to free herself from the weight that had been settling more and more heavily upon her heart—and to free herself from Jessica. Once Todd knew everything, Jessica wouldn't have any power over her.

But so far the right moment hadn't presented itself. *I can't just say, "Pass the Parmesan—oh, and by the way, I was in love with your buddy Ken Matthews once."*

"Speak of the devil," said Todd, his eyes directed at a point behind Elizabeth. He waved. "Hey, Matthews, Jess. Over here."

Elizabeth turned, then groaned silently. Jessica and Ken were strolling toward their booth.

"What a surprise," Jessica said with a grin. "We didn't expect to see you."

"How's it going?" Ken asked.

"Pretty good. Have a seat," invited Todd.

"Sure, we'd be—" Ken started to say.

"Actually," Jessica interrupted, "you guys look like you're almost through." She winked broadly at her sister. "And I see a nice table for two by the waterfall that has our name on it. Catch you later."

As he passed the booth, Ken gave Todd a high five. Elizabeth sank back in her seat, swallowing her relief. What a close call. . . .

Todd was watching Ken and Jessica walk away. "You know," he said when the pair was out of earshot, "I don't really understand what Ken sees in Jessica, but I've got to say this much—she's really making him happy."

Elizabeth nodded dumbly. Only a blind person could have missed Ken and Jessica's starry-eyed glow, not to mention Jessica's slightly rumpled hair. They'd probably stopped at Miller's Point on their way over. . . .

"He's really in love—he finally met the right girl," continued Todd. "Can you believe it? I mean, the guy has dated a lot of girls, a lot of really cute, nice girls, too. But the other day he told me he'd only been in love once before."

"Once before, huh?" Elizabeth felt her face go pale and then flush hotly. She knew in her gut who that other girl was. *Once before . . . with me.*

"Nobody deserves more for something good to happen to him." Todd refilled their glasses from the pitcher of soda. "He's a great guy, you know? I'm pretty lucky to have a best friend like him."

"You are," Elizabeth murmured.

"I mean, I'd do anything for him, and I know he'd do anything for me." Todd looked straight into Elizabeth's eyes. "Loyalty. That's what friendship is all about, right?"

Elizabeth felt as if she'd been stripped naked, as if her soul lay bare and exposed on the table. But Todd didn't seem to see anything out of the ordinary; he was smiling at her. "Right," she said, her voice little more than a whisper.

She ate the rest of her pizza in silence, listening to Todd chat about possible banner slogans for the cheer-off. *I can't tell him,* she realized, the pizza she'd eaten sitting heavy as a stone in her stomach. *I can't tell him that his best friend, as well as his girlfriend, betrayed him in the worst way imaginable. God, how could I have thought even for a moment that that was the right thing to do?*

Elizabeth remembered Mr. Collins's comment when she'd filled him in on the latest installment of "her friend's" problem. "What tangled webs we weave. . . ."

The web was too tangled, and no matter how she looked at the situation, Elizabeth simply couldn't see a way to extricate herself. Her relationship with Todd wasn't the only thing at stake; there was also Todd and Ken's friendship to consider. And first and last, there were her stubbornly strong feelings for Ken. . . .

Enid had characterized Ken and Elizabeth's long-ago secret fling as a "blip," and Elizabeth hadn't bothered to argue the point. "When you look at the big picture," Enid had said, "it's just not that important."

But a blip was something that came and went with no aftereffects, whereas Elizabeth's feelings for Ken had reasserted themselves until they were as all-consuming as anything else in the big picture of her life.

No, I absolutely can't under any circumstances tell him, Elizabeth concluded once and for all, gazing dismally across the table at Todd's cheerful, innocent face. *Sorry, Mr. Collins, but I guess I'm just going to have to be eaten alive!*

Chapter 9

At school on Tuesday morning Jessica tossed a few books into her locker and dug around for the notebook she needed for her first class. Then she slammed the locker door and plunged into the crowd of jostling students.

She couldn't help strutting just a little. The cheerleaders on both squads were wearing their uniforms, as was traditional the day of a big game, and she was pleasantly conscious that all eyes were on her in her short, perky red-and-white outfit. She walked along with a happy bounce. The cheer-off was still hours away, but already her leg muscles felt coiled, supple, strong. *When it comes to cheerleading, I'm the best there is,* she thought, brimming with confidence. *Heather may be hot, but I'm volcanic.*

"Jess. Jess, wait up!"

Jessica stepped out of the traffic and turned to

look behind her, an expectant smile on her face. Amy, also dressed in her cheerleading uniform, was hurrying toward her.

When she saw who had called out to her, the smile on Jessica's face faded. "Oh, it's you," she grumbled.

"Jessica, can we talk?" asked Amy, her own expression conciliatory.

Jessica shrugged. "Yes, I believe we both have the capability of speech," she said haughtily.

"Oh, don't be a pain, you know what I mean." Amy grabbed Jessica's arm and gave it a yank. "Just give me a chance to say one thing, OK?"

With a show of reluctance Jessica followed Amy into the girls' room. Once there, she folded her arms across her chest and lifted her chin, her manner completely unreceptive.

"You don't have to look so fierce," Amy began, tucking a strand of silky ash-blond hair behind one ear. "I just wanted to apologize."

Jessica blinked. "Apologize?"

Amy nodded. "I was really out of control at the Dairi Burger on Saturday night. I didn't mean what I said."

"You sure sounded like you meant it."

"It was the heat of the moment. I mean, you totally humiliated us. I was still feeling pretty burned. But afterward, when I thought about it for a while, I realized you were totally in the right. We deserved it."

"Well, Amy, that's very big of you to say so," observed Jessica graciously.

"Isn't it, though?" They smiled at each other. "The thing is, even though we're on rival squads, I want us to still be friends. I don't care if it ticks Heather off. I'll understand if you still have hard feelings toward me, but I want you to know I don't have any hard feelings toward you. In fact, I'm proud of you. It took a lot of gumption to go out there and form your own squad, and you guys are good. Not as good as us," she hurried to add, "but still, pretty darned good!"

Amy's slate-gray eyes sparkled with earnest tears; Jessica felt her own eyes grow moist. The two girls exchanged a quick hug. "Thanks, Amy," Jessica said, sniffling. "I can't tell you how much better I feel."

"Me, too." Amy fumbled in her purse for a tissue and blew her nose loudly. "It's really a relief to know that no matter who wins the cheer-off this afternoon, we'll still be friends."

"Right," said Jessica, although there was no doubt in her mind which squad was going to win the cheer-off . . . and reign supreme at Sweet Valley High forevermore. She grinned slyly. "And maybe if you're really nice to me, Amy, next year I'll let you try out for my squad!"

By lunchtime the entire school was decorated with streamers, balloons, posters, and pennants proclaiming the superior talent, beauty, and popularity of the two rival cheerleading squads. Amy's boyfriend, Barry Rork, and Annie's boyfriend, Tony Esteban, had printed up dozens of posters with a huge blowup picture of Heather and her squad; Todd, Ken, and Winston, meanwhile, were spearheading the "campaign" on behalf of Jessica's squad, with help from Sandy's boyfriend, Manuel, and Jade's boyfriend, David. They'd spent all night making buttons and banners urging the student body to "Send Jessica's team to Regionals!"

Elizabeth carried her tray through the cafeteria to an empty table, feeling almost embarrassed by the hoopla that had grown up around the cheer-off. *And having to wear this uniform to school!* she thought, glancing down at her long tanned legs emerging from underneath the very short, flirty skirt. *Unbelievable. Absolutely unbelievable!*

Enid stopped Elizabeth. "Liz, Jessica's waving to us," she told her friend. "There's a whole bunch of people sitting at a table over—"

"I don't think I'm up to it," Elizabeth cut in. "Is it OK with you if we steer clear of the fuss?"

"Sure, whatever you want," Enid said agreeably.

They sat at a small corner table, facing each other. "I was going to call you last night, to see how it went with Todd," Enid said, her fork poised over her plate of macaroni and cheese. "I saw you two together this morning before school, and you looked like normal. So everything's fine?"

Elizabeth squeezed a packet of low-cal dressing onto her chef's salad. "Everything's the same," she corrected her friend, making a wry face. "I chickened out. I didn't tell him about Ken."

"Oh, Liz. What happened?"

Elizabeth gave Enid a rundown of the previous

evening's scene at Guido's Pizza Palace. "I know what it's like to try to screw up your courage to initiate a conversation like that. Wouldn't you know Jess and Ken would walk in at just the wrong moment?" Enid commiserated.

"Maybe it was just the right moment," Elizabeth reflected. "Maybe it's better for some skeletons to stay in the closet, so to speak."

"I know you're concerned about hurting Todd's feelings, and you should be. But what about you?" asked Enid. "What about your peace of mind?"

Before Elizabeth could answer, somebody tapped her urgently on her shoulder. A moment later her twin sister was literally dragging her out of her chair. "Come on, Liz," chirped Jessica. "I need you!"

"What's going on?" Elizabeth demanded as Jessica pulled her through the cafeteria. Then she saw why Jessica "needed" her. "Oh, Jess," Elizabeth groaned. "Could you leave me out of this?"

"Leave you out of this? Are you kidding?" said Jessica. "Liz, you're part of the squad. You're one of our shining stars!"

A crowd had formed around a couple of tables that had been pushed together. All the trays had been cleared off, and in their place stood Lila, Maria, Sandy, Jade, Patty, and Sara. As the twins approached, the other girls began tapping their feet and clapping.

Jessica jumped lightly up onto the table, hauling Elizabeth after her. Then she cupped her hands around her mouth megaphone style. "We just wanted to make sure you're all getting psyched," she called out to the crowd.

There were cheers and whistles, as well as a few scattered boos from Heather supporters. Todd caught Elizabeth's eye and grinned proudly; Elizabeth tried to smile and look as if she were enjoying herself when in reality she wished she could crawl under the table and disappear.

"And that you're planning to come to the cheer-off and vote for your favorite cheerleaders!" Jessica continued.

The din grew louder. People started chanting Jessica's squad's signature cheer. "We've got the beat and our team's got the heat. . . ."

Jessica, in her element, started clapping and stamping along with her squad. Reluctantly, Elizabeth followed suit. After marching around the table waving a pro-Jessica banner, Winston grabbed some of the guys standing nearby and formed an impromptu all-male kick line. Someone released a bunch of red and white helium balloons. Elizabeth couldn't help laughing. She had to say one thing for the great cheer-off—it was shaping into one of the biggest events in recent Sweet Valley High history. *Maybe I'll be writing a follow-up article after all!* she thought.

The SVH gymnasium after school on Tuesday looked like halftime at the Super Bowl. The bleachers were packed with students waving banners and balloons; the air was snowy with confetti. On opposite sides of the basketball court, the two cheerleading squads were warming up.

As Jessica stretched her Achilles tendons and then lowered herself carefully into a split, her eyes followed Ken, who was dashing up and down in front of the bleachers, handing out flyers urging people to pick Jessica's squad. A glow of love softened her face. *He's really nuts about me,* she thought, wanting to laugh out loud. *And I'm really nuts about him. This whole thing just feels so . . . nice! How did it happen? Why didn't it happen sooner?*

She didn't really want to question it; she was just glad that she and Ken had found each other. *And I suppose I have Elizabeth to thank as much as anyone,* Jessica thought with secret amusement, *for letting Ken go so he'd be free to fall in love with me!*

Just then Mr. Cooper and Coach Schultz, the SVH athletic director, strode onto the basketball court, microphones in hand. "We're just about ready to begin the cheer-off," Coach Schultz announced, his deep, scratchy voice resounding throughout the gym. "We flipped a coin, and Jessica Wakefield's squad will perform first. One more minute, girls, and then you're on!"

Jessica bounced to her feet and quickly gathered her squad around. "So who's nervous?" she asked when they were in a huddle. All seven girls raised their hands. Jessica laughed. "That's OK. Being a little nervous gets the adrenaline flowing and keeps you on your toes."

"I'm worried about performing on the hard

floor," confessed Jade. "We've only practiced outside on the grass. This surface feels different!"

"It's not that different," Jessica assured her. "You'll be fine, all of you." She flashed a wide, encouraging smile. "Now, I'm counting on you to get me to regionals, OK?"

The squad closed in tight for a group hug. Then they clapped their hands loudly, gave a shout, picked up their pom-poms, and trotted into position facing the bleachers.

As they waited for their music to start, Jessica felt her heartbeat quicken in anticipation. Ken was sitting front and center, a red-and-white banner in his hand; he caught her eye and winked. A surge of adrenaline flooded Jessica's veins, and then the music began.

For a few minutes Jessica wasn't aware of anything or anyone other than the seven girls she was performing with—it was as if Mr. Cooper and Coach Schultz, Heather's squad, and the hundreds of students packed in the bleachers ceased to exist. The only thing she could hear or feel was the music and her body responding to it; her entire being was concentrated on the act of keeping in sync with her squad and performing her arm movements, footwork, and jumps with flair and precision.

The routine ended with each girl performing her most dramatic and polished jump combination, and then they piled themselves into a pyramid. As Jessica and Lila boosted Jade to the top and then took their places at the side to support the girls at the bottom, the crowd leaped to its feet in a standing ovation.

The applause was thunderous; Jessica curtsied, a huge smile lighting up her face. Jade hopped down, followed by Patty and Sara; then all eight girls fell on each other, hugging and laughing. "We did it!" Maria cried.

"Not a single mistake!" exclaimed Lila.

"There's no way Heather can beat that, no way," declared Jessica, her cheeks flushed with triumph. "We're going to regionals, you guys. I'm sure of it!"

The crowd was still shouting and stomping with approval as Jessica and her squad trotted over to the bench. As soon as they sat down, Todd and Ken plied them with towels and bottles of water. Elizabeth took a towel from Todd. As she blotted the perspiration from her forehead, she surreptitiously sneaked a glance at her sister and Ken. Ken was standing behind Jessica, rubbing her shoulders and whispering something in her ear. Jessica's eyes were closed; she leaned into Ken, a blissful smile on her face. *At this moment she has everything she's ever wanted—her life is perfect,* Elizabeth thought, an unaccountable flash of jealousy piercing her heart. *What kind of crummy sister am I? Why can't I be happy for her?*

Coach Schultz was speaking into the microphone again. "That's a pretty enthusiastic response for Jessica's squad," he observed in a hearty tone. "Now, don't wear yourselves out, because there's another very fine cheerleading squad waiting to perform for you. Let me present to you Heather Mallone, Amy Sutton, Jean West, and Annie Whitman!"

If Heather was nervous, it didn't show. Elizabeth sat up straighter; so did Jessica and the rest of her squad. Suddenly, the giddy smiles disappeared. Even Jessica had started chewing her nails. Elizabeth's mouth went dry; she took a slug of water. *We did our very best, but we can't take victory for granted,* she thought, wiping another bead of sweat from her forehead.

The music started, and Heather and her squad launched into a spunky, playful routine, the kind of routine that makes people start tapping their feet and clapping to the beat. They, too, had been busy the previous week; it was an all-new routine, as fresh and original as anything Elizabeth had ever seen. *It's as good as our routine,* she realized, gulping. *Maybe even better.*

And there was no doubt that Heather, Amy, Jean, and Annie were the cream of the old SVH cheerleading crop. No one could kick higher, spin faster, or jump, cartwheel, and flip with more pizzazz. They were athletic, sexy, and sharp. The audience loved them.

Their routine complete, Heather and her squad posed for the crowd, waving like beauty-pageant contestants. A few people threw tissue-wrapped bouquets of flowers. Elizabeth glanced at her twin; Jessica was pale as a ghost.

Chrome Dome Cooper waved for silence. When the crowd simmered down, he cleared his throat. "Ahem. We've seen both squads perform, and if I may say so myself, our high school appears to have a surplus of talent. What show-stopping numbers! Now for the vote."

Elizabeth slid over on the bench so she could squeeze her sister's hand; Jessica's fingers were as cold as ice.

Chrome Dome continued. "Instead of taking a hand count, we're going to ask you to vote with your feet. Those of you who support Jessica's squad, gather over at this bleacher"—he pointed one way—"and those of you voting for Heather's squad, assemble over here. Ready, set, go!"

A rowdy melee ensued, with students scrambling down from one bleacher to race over to the opposite side of the gym. For the first minute or two, it looked as if more people were piling onto Jessica's bleacher. The healthy glow returned to Jessica's complexion; she smiled joyfully. "It's looking good," she whispered excitedly to Elizabeth. "It's looking really good!"

But by the time everyone had settled down again in their new seats, the numbers appeared to have evened out. Elizabeth, Jessica, and the other girls watched with bated breath as Mr. Cooper and Coach Schultz each headed over to one of the bleachers to quickly count heads.

Afterward, the two men met in the middle of the basketball court and exchanged a few words. Elizabeth saw both sets of bushy eyebrows shoot up in disbelief. *It can't be,* she thought.

Shaking his head, Mr. Cooper returned to the

microphone. "The impossible appears to have happened," he informed the crowd. "I counted the exact same number of votes for Jessica's squad as Coach Schultz counted for Heather's. It's a tie!"

Jessica's jaw dropped. "A tie?" she exclaimed incredulously.

"Who will get to go to regionals?" Patty wondered.

"Look!" Elizabeth was pointing toward the center of the court. "Isn't that Mr. Jenkins, the ACA scout?"

Jessica whirled to see. A man had emerged from the audience to join Mr. Cooper and Coach Schultz. "None other," Jessica confirmed, surprised.

"Do you suppose he'll cast the deciding vote?" asked Sandy.

The three men conferred for a moment. Then, beaming, Mr. Cooper presented Mr. Jenkins to the student body. "Mr. Jenkins attended this historic event as an official representative of the American Cheerleading Association," the principal proclaimed, "and as such, he is ready to propose a delightful solution to our difficult dilemma. Mr. Jenkins?"

Mr. Jenkins took the microphone. "I came today prepared to congratulate the winning squad on earning a regionals berth," he said, "and I'm happy to say that despite the tie vote, I can still do that. There's no reason any of this talent should go to waste. Sweet Valley High can compete in regionals if the two teams merge, with Jessica Wakefield and Heather Mallone serving as cocaptains once more. Congratulations, girls! You're all going to regionals!"

Both squads had been paralyzed with suspense. Now they exploded joyfully, dashing across the court to congratulate each other. Annie hugged Maria; Sandy hugged Jean; Amy hugged Elizabeth. After all the animosity and competition, everyone was thrilled to be reunited.

That is, everyone but Jessica and Heather. Jessica hung back, her feet rooted to the floor. On the other side of the basketball court, Heather also was refusing to budge. Even from a distance Jessica could see her archenemy's face contort with fury.

Go to regionals . . . with Heather? Cocaptains again . . . with Heather? *Never!* Jessica thought, her hands tightening into fists. *Never, ever, ever!*

Heather bolted toward the cluster of jumping, laughing cheerleaders; Jessica charged forward as well. She didn't know what Heather was going to say, but she wanted to make sure her team understood in no uncertain terms that a merger was out of the question. Out of the question.

"I'm sorry Mr. Jenkins got your hopes up," Heather growled through clenched teeth as she collared Annie, Amy, and Jean, "because we're not going to regionals. I would rather cheer barefoot on hot coals than cheer with that girl!"

Heather hustled her squad away from Jessica's. Jessica faced her own squad, her eyes flashing sparks. "I'm sorry, too," she said, choking on the words, "but we're not going to regionals, either. I would rather cheer naked in Siberia than cheer with that girl!"

"But, Jessica!" cried Maria. "We've been practicing so hard! It could work if you'd only—"

"I said no, and that's final!" barked Jessica. Blinded by tears of anger and disappointment, she turned her back on her squad and walked away.

The dream of competing at regionals had turned to dust.

Chapter 10

Slowly, the Sweet Valley High gymnasium emptied out. After pronouncing their ultimatums, both Jessica and Heather had stormed off. Mr. Jenkins had long since thrown up his hands and headed home, as had Coach Schultz and Chrome Dome Cooper. Only the members of the two cheerleading squads remained, standing in the middle of the basketball court and staring dejectedly at each other.

"It's not fair," Amy burst out, stamping her foot. "Why should it be up to them to decide if we go to regionals or not?"

"We've all worked too hard to just let it go," Jade agreed, an uncharacteristic intensity in her soft voice.

"I can't believe I spent all that money on cheerleading uniforms for nothing," bemoaned Lila.

"I was dying to go to regionals," confessed

Annie, her green eyes glittering with unshed tears. "I've dreamed of this for years, ever since I first started cheerleading."

Maria put a comforting arm around Annie's shoulder. "We all have," she said sadly.

When Jessica flounced out of the gym in a tantrum, and it became clear that the new cheerleading squad had crashed before it even got off the ground, Elizabeth expected to feel relieved. After all, she hadn't wanted to be a cheerleader; there were other, more important things she could be doing with her free time, like writing for *The Oracle*. But now, to her surprise, she found herself feeling as cheated and disappointed as the rest of the girls.

"You're right," she said. "It's not fair, it's not fair at all. Heather and Jessica are our captains, but that shouldn't give them total control over our destiny. We should all have a say in this—we can't let them get away with being so high-handed!"

"But if Mr. Jenkins says we can only go to regionals if the two squads merge with Jessica and Heather as cocaptains, but Jessica and Heather refuse to be cocaptains . . . where does that leave us?" asked Sandy.

"I'll tell you one thing, I'm going to make Jessica pay me back for these uniforms," Lila was muttering under her breath.

"Maybe if either Jessica or Heather would agree to step down," hypothesized Sara.

"Those two? No way, they're too stubborn," said Amy.

"Never in a million years," confirmed Maria.

Sara sighed. "It was just a thought."

Patty turned to Elizabeth. "Liz, you know Jessica better than anyone. Can't you think of a way to work this out?"

Elizabeth frowned, her brow creased with concentration. "There has to be an answer," she agreed. "But what is it?"

Jean heaved a defeated sigh. "It's hopeless," she said mournfully. "'Bye, everybody. I'm going home."

One by one the cheerleaders gathered up their pom-poms and walked with slumped shoulders and heavy footsteps toward the gym exit. "Just give me some time," Elizabeth called after them. "I know I'll think of something."

There were a couple nods, a few halfhearted waves, but Elizabeth could tell the girls didn't put much faith in the prospect of Elizabeth or anyone coming up with a scheme for reconciling Heather and Jessica.

Maybe Jean's right, maybe it is hopeless, Elizabeth concluded wearily as she climbed into the driver's seat of the Jeep. But even as she entertained this thought just for a second, Elizabeth felt her spine stiffen with protest. The word "hopeless" wasn't part of her vocabulary. She'd always taken pride in finishing what she started; she wasn't a quitter.

"Every problem has a solution," Elizabeth said out loud to herself. That is, every problem except this thing with Ken and Todd. . . .

She backed the Jeep out of the parking space. "This problem has a solution," she corrected herself, "and I'll find out what it is. I'll think of something. . . ."

"What's going on?" Jessica asked suspiciously.

It was the day after the disastrous cheer-off, and in homeroom Elizabeth had mysteriously informed Jessica that the cheerleaders were meeting in the library during lunch period.

"The cheerleaders are having a meeting?" Jessica had squeaked. "But I didn't call it—I don't even officially have a squad anymore . . . wait a minute. Did Heather call it?"

"We called it ourselves," answered Elizabeth. "Both squads together. Everyone except Heather, that is. So be there!"

When Jessica entered the conference room, Elizabeth and the other girls were clustered with their heads close together, whispering. They all looked at her, their expressions not nearly as solemn as Jessica expected. A few of the girls were even smiling. *As if everything's hunky-dory!* Jessica thought. *As if we're going to regionals or something!* "What's going on?" she asked bluntly.

Amy cleared her throat, sounding for all the world like Chrome Dome Cooper. "Ahem. We have an announcement to make," she said in an important tone. "We—the combined cheerleading squads—would like to go to regionals." She lifted a hand before Jessica could protest. "And we want you to be our sole captain."

Jessica dropped into a chair, astonished. "The sole captain? But what about . . ."

"Heather has agreed to stay on the squad but to step down as captain," Elizabeth interjected. "It was a tough sell, let me tell you, but finally we made her see that it was in everybody's best interest. After all, you were here first—you have seniority, and by right you should be the one leading Sweet Valley High to regionals."

"You're kidding," Jessica gasped.

"We're dead serious." Lila grinned. "Isn't it great?"

As the news slowly sank into her brain, a smile began to spread across Jessica's face. "Boy, I wish I'd been there to hear Heather resign," she murmured. "I'm the captain. I'm the captain and we're going to regionals!"

"So you'll take responsibility for all of us?" asked Annie.

"Well, I'll tell you the truth." Jessica leaned back in the chair and clasped her hands behind her head, reveling in her newly bestowed power. "I'd be happier if Heather were off the squad altogether."

"We know you don't like her, but you have to admit we need her," said Jean.

"She's done a lot for cheerleading at SVH," Amy chimed in. "Without her talent, her spark, her new ideas, we'd never have caught Mr. Jenkins's eye in the first place."

It was true; Jessica couldn't argue. Reluctantly, she nodded her head. "I guess you're right."

"You really don't know," Elizabeth told her sister, "what a feat it was getting Heather to agree to stay on the squad but not be the captain. I mean, you know how ambitious she is."

Jessica beamed. "And now she's going to be taking orders from me!"

"Don't make her bitter by gloating," Elizabeth advised. "Since you won, you can afford to be generous. At practice this afternoon, two thirty on the atheltic field, let her think she's still calling the shots."

"Sure," agreed Jessica, her manner smug and self-satisfied. "I'll humor her a little."

"This is great," exclaimed Amy, reaching across the table to clasp Jessica's hand. "We'll be cheering together again, Jess. And we're going to regionals!"

As the other girls applauded, Jessica indulged in a little fantasy. She was on stage at regionals, accepting the first-prize trophy, flanked by the rest of her squad . . . including Heather, now just one of the girls. *I'm back on top,* Jessica thought exuberantly, *where I belong!*

At two fifteen all the cheerleaders with the exception of Jessica were gathered outside on the athletic field, waiting for Heather. Nervously, Maria looked at her wristwatch. "What if Heather's late?" she asked. "What if Jessica shows up early? Maybe we should have told her two forty-five instead of two thirty, to give ourselves extra time."

"Don't worry," Elizabeth said soothingly, although she, too, was growing nervous. "We have the situation under control."

"And here comes Heather now," drawled Lila.

Heather strode across the grass toward them, dressed in turquoise bike shorts, a big white T-shirt, and sneakers. She was not smiling. "What's the story?" she asked without preamble. "Who called this practice?"

"We did," said Elizabeth.

Heather cocked an eyebrow at Elizabeth. "You? You're not on my squad."

"Yes, I am," Elizabeth said serenely.

Heather put her hands on her hips and opened her mouth. Amy intervened quickly. "The two squads are combining like Mr. Jenkins suggested," she explained, "so we can go to regionals. And we want you to be our sole captain."

Heather blinked. "Me?"

"You," confirmed Jean. "You're the one who deserves credit for turning the squad around."

"But what about Wakefield?" demanded Heather. She glanced at Elizabeth. "I mean, the other Wakefield."

"She's agreed to step down in favor of your leadership," said Lila. "She'll still be on the squad, of course, but she'll just be a regular member rather than a cocaptain."

Heather shook her long blond hair, amazed. "She really agreed to all this?"

"She's committed to seeing the SVH cheerleaders go as far as they can go," said Elizabeth, "and we finally made her see that this arrangement was the best way to make sure not only that we get to regionals but that we win regionals."

A triumphant smile illuminated Heather's face. "Who'd have thought that girl would show so much sense?" she said snidely.

"So you'll do it?" asked Maria. "You'll be our captain?"

Heather tipped her head to one side, considering. "I probably don't need to tell you that I'd be happier if Jessica was off the squad altogether."

Elizabeth exchanged a glance with Amy and they both stifled a giggle. "No, you don't have to tell us that," said Amy. "But you have to admit, we'd be nothing without the new girls Jessica recruited and trained."

"And the new girls won't cheer without Jessica," declared Patty.

"Also, the twin factor will be a big plus at regionals," added Sandy. "Mr. Jenkins was just wild about it."

"Yep, we need Jessica," Amy concluded. "No two ways about it."

"Well . . . OK," said Heather grudgingly. "Jessica stays. But I notice she's late for practice."

Once again Elizabeth had to smother a grin. "Oh, she'll be here any minute now."

"She's probably just a little embarrassed," Amy surmised. "I mean, it was kind of a blow to her pride, giving up the captaincy and all. You probably shouldn't rub her nose in it. Let her think she's still in charge."

Heather nodded knowingly, and this time Elizabeth had to turn away to hide her smile. "We did it!" she whispered, surreptitiously high-fiving Lila. "We fooled them both."

"It was ridiculously easy," Lila whispered back. "I guess we're lucky those two have such huge egos!"

The Wakefields' doorbell rang at about five thirty, and Elizabeth trotted downstairs to answer it. When she saw who was standing on the front step, her cheeks flushed scarlet. "Oh, hi, Ken," she said. "Um, come on in."

"Hey, Liz." Ken stepped in the hall. "Could you tell Jessica I'm here? We're driving up to Las Palmas Canyon for a picnic."

"Oh." Elizabeth pictured her sister and Ken standing above the breathtaking gorge at sunset, their arms around each other. The thought made her sick to her stomach. "Yeah, sure," she choked out, turning to dash back up the stairs. "She'll be right down."

When she got to Jessica's room, though, she heard the shower running. She shouted something to her sister and then slowly returned to the front hallway. "She'll be a few more minutes," she informed Ken. "Uh . . ." She couldn't just leave him standing there in the hall. "I was just about to start dinner. Can I get you something to drink? Iced tea, maybe?"

"That would be great," said Ken, following her to the kitchen.

As soon as they entered the kitchen, Elizabeth realized it wasn't the most neutral place for her and Ken to hang out. *Does he remember?* she wondered, shooting a glance at him out of the corner of her eye as she opened the fridge to remove the pitcher of iced tea. *Does he remember that we were in the kitchen making sub sandwiches for a party at my house the first time we kissed? Does he remember taking the plate from my hand and pulling me outside to the patio where it was dark?*

Her own heart was pounding from the memory, but Ken appeared completely at ease and oblivious. Elizabeth poured two glasses of iced tea, topped them with slivers of lemon, and handed one to Ken. "Jess and I got home only about half an hour ago," she explained, "and I got the first shower. Cheerleading practice ran kind of late."

"I heard all about it from Jess," said Ken. Tipping back his head, he swallowed half the tea in one gulp. Elizabeth caught herself staring at his throat and tore her eyes away. "The two squads have combined and she's the captain. I've never seen her more psyched about anything. But how'd you pull it off?" He smiled. "How'd you handle Heather the Horrible?"

Elizabeth smiled back. "Well . . ." Suddenly she was bursting to tell him the truth. "Do you really want to know?"

Ken nodded. "I'm dying to know."

"It's a bit of a conspiracy," Elizabeth admitted, "and you have to promise not to tell Jessica."

"I promise," said Ken, his eyes bright with curiosity.

"First we met with Jessica, and then we met

with Heather, and . . ." Elizabeth recounted the two cheerleader meetings held earlier that day.

Ken burst out laughing. "You mean Jessica thinks she's the captain and Heather thinks she's the captain, but in reality they're both captains only they don't know it?"

Elizabeth grinned. "Pretty sly, huh?"

Ken shook his head ruefully. "Boy, when Jess finds out . . ."

"She won't find out till regionals, and by then either we'll have won or lost and it won't matter," said Elizabeth. "The point is just to go and show our stuff. After that she and Heather are free to battle it out."

"Liz, Liz," said Ken, clucking his tongue. "Who'd have thought you could be so devious?"

Elizabeth dropped her eyes, smiling. *Don't you remember? Don't you remember when we both had to be devious, when we had to sneak around and tell lies in order to be together, but it was worth it because we couldn't stand to be apart?*

"Ken, I—"

At that instant Jessica breezed into the kitchen, her blond hair still damp from the shower, looking fresh and sexy in sage-colored linen shorts and a crisp white tank top. "Here you are," she said to Ken, hurrying forward to greet him with a big hug and kiss. "Has Liz been telling you what a marvelous cheerleading captain I am?"

"As a matter of fact, yes," said Ken, winking at Elizabeth over Jessica's head. "That's the very topic we were discussing."

Jessica linked her arm through Ken's and propelled him toward the door. "See ya later," she said to her sister. Now it was Jessica's turn to wink. "Don't wait up for me, OK?"

Elizabeth waved good-bye. When she was alone, she leaned back against the kitchen counter, sipping her iced tea with a contemplative expression on her face. Her pulse was still racing because of how close she'd come to confessing to Ken that she still had feelings for him. *I'm glad Jess came along when she did,* Elizabeth thought. *At least . . . I think I'm glad.*

Yes, I am glad, she decided a moment later. It was clear that for Ken their romance was long over. Just because she was insanely confused, why make things more complicated for him?

Insanely confused . . . and incredibly attracted. Elizabeth shivered pleasantly, thinking about Ken and how sweet and adorable he was . . . and that wink! *We have a secret again, him and me,* she thought, hugging herself and smiling. The balance of power had shifted again, slightly in her favor this time. *I know something Jessica doesn't know, for a change!*

Chapter 11

"This isn't going to work," Jessica pronounced at Thursday's cheerleading practice. She tossed her ponytail, eyes blazing. "I'm telling you, I'm this close to strangling that girl!"

Jessica had written a new cheer the night before, and she'd just spent fifteen minutes trying to demonstrate it to the other girls on the squad. But every thirty seconds Heather interrupted her to make a criticism or suggest a change.

"She just likes to . . . express her opinion," said Amy, her tone conciliatory.

"That's putting it mildly," snapped Jessica. "It's like she thinks she's still captain or something. She's driving me crazy!"

Amy glanced over her shoulder at where the rest of the squad was standing around on the grass. "Just try to mellow out, OK?" she advised Jessica. "I know you want to give Heather a piece of your mind, but we don't want to drive her off the squad."

"We don't?" said Jessica testily.

Amy gave her friend's ponytail a playful tweak. "Come on. Take a deep breath and count to ten. We only have a couple more practice sessions before regionals on Saturday, and we can't afford to waste time being mad at each other. We already tried that back when we were two separate squads, remember?"

Jessica rolled her eyes, but she did as Amy said. "One, two, three . . ." she grumbled.

Amy patted her on the back. "Good for you, Jess. You really are the stuff that great cheerleading captains are made of."

They strolled back over to the rest of the squad. "OK," Jessica sang out, her voice falsely cheerful. "How 'bout we hold off on that number for a while? Let's run through the routine that Patty and Jade helped me choreograph. It shouldn't take the rest of you—Amy, Jean, Annie, and Heather—long to pick it up."

Practice pom-poms in hand, the girls lined up on the field. Jessica started the tape player. "Now, the first move," she shouted above the music, "is a sideways dance step that goes like this—"

Jessica started to demonstrate the step. All the other girls followed suit . . . with the exception of Heather.

Angrily, Jessica hit the off button on the tape player. "Now what?" she demanded of Heather, who was standing with her feet rooted to the ground and her pom-poms hanging limp at her sides.

"This just seems like the right time to tell you," said Heather in her snottiest tone, "that I don't really like this cheer."

The nerve of this girl! "You don't like this cheer," Jessica repeated in disbelief. "For your information, this cheer almost won us the cheer-off two days ago."

"'Almost' is the key word," declared Heather. "And you can take my word for it, it won't win us the regionals competition."

Jessica folded her arms across her chest. "Oh, really. And why is that?"

"Because of that dance stuff you're so into," said Heather. "There's too much of it."

Jessica glanced at Patty and Jade, her eyebrows elevated as if to say, Can you believe this garbage?

"I don't think there's too much of it," said Patty.

"Well, yeah." Heather laughed harshly. "Because you put it there, right?"

"It adds elegance," Jade spoke up. "And it's just as technically hard as doing athletic jumps—I think the regionals judges will appreciate that."

"Don't count on it." Heather's know-it-all tone made the hairs on Jessica's arms stand on end. "I've been to regionals with the team from my old school—I've won regionals. I've been to state—I've won state. And the judges are traditionalists. They welcome a certain amount of innovation, but they definitely don't favor routines that have been . . . diluted."

"Dance does not dilute the routine!" cried Patty.

"I like it the way it is," agreed Sara.

"Well, I personally think that if Heather says we should change it—" began Jean.

Suddenly all the girls were talking at once. Everyone had an opinion, and everyone's opinion was different. The bickering voices lifted higher and higher. . . .

"Stop it!" Jessica screeched. "Just shut up, would you?"

The rest of the cheerleaders stared at her. "I think . . ." Jessica began.

She was about to say, "I think you should keep your fat mouth shut from now on if you want to cheer on my squad, Heather Mallone!" Instead, after clearing her throat and making a massive effort to suppress her temper, she said, "I think that's enough for today. See you guys back out here tomorrow afternoon."

She walked away quickly, not trusting herself to talk to anyone. As she neared the edge of the field, she saw that Ken had been standing there watching. "Pretty good show, huh?" she greeted him morosely.

"Better than female mud wrestling," Ken joked.

He put his arm around her, and she leaned into him with a frustrated sigh. "I just don't know how we're going to pull things together in time for regionals on Saturday."

"You will."

Jessica looked up at him. "How do you know?"

"Because I just know. I know you and I know what you can do, and you can do this."

"Really? You really think so?"

Ken smiled down into her eyes. "I wouldn't say it if I didn't mean it."

"Oh, Ken," whispered Jessica. Twining her fingers in his hair, she pulled his face close to hers for a kiss. "Just knowing you believe in me makes me feel so much better. It makes me feel like I can do anything."

"So kiss me, then," he whispered as his lips met hers.

Despite the resolution that Elizabeth coaxed from Jessica to be calm and tolerant, Friday afternoon's practice was even worse than Thursday's. Every other sentence out of Heather's mouth began, "At my old school we did it like this," which predictably led to constant bickering with Jessica. And with the larger combined squad of twelve girls, choreographing the routines had become a more complex task.

"I don't have a good feeling about this," Annie said to Elizabeth as they took a water break. Annie rubbed her stomach gingerly. "I think it's giving me an ulcer."

"There's so much tension in the air, you could cut it with a knife," Elizabeth agreed, bending over the water fountain.

"I'm mostly afraid that one of them will get so steamed, she'll yell, 'Look, I'm the captain here so we'll do it my way,' and then the other will say,

'What are you talking about, I'm the captain!' and then the you-know-what will really hit the fan."

Elizabeth laughed as they walked back onto the field. "Can you imagine the explosion? They'd feel the shock waves all the way up in San Francisco!"

Both Heather and Jessica shot Elizabeth and Annie dirty looks as they rejoined the squad. "You just missed a very important demonstration," Jessica said somewhat snappishly. "Next time, if you don't mind, you might wait until the whole squad is dismissed for a water break."

"Well, excuse me," Elizabeth said, trying to lighten Jessica up with a smile. Her sister didn't smile back.

"I think we should practice that kick-lunge-hop-jump combination a few more times," Heather suggested, imperiously waving the girls into position.

"We've run through it about a zillion times already," Jessica disagreed.

"And it's still rough," countered Heather. "They'll laugh us off the stage at regionals if we can't even synchronize our kicks!"

"OK." Jessica and Heather flanked the line of cheerleaders. All twelve girls stood at attention, their practice pom-poms on their hips. "Ready, set, go."

Along with the others Elizabeth swung her right leg skyward, toe pointed. Then she lunged forward, hopped to bring her feet back together, and sprang up into a spread-eagle. Out of the corners of her eyes, she'd been able to see the rest of the squad, and it looked pretty good. But Heather still wasn't satisfied.

"Patty, your spread-eagle was about two feet higher than everyone else—this isn't the Olympics gymnastics floor routine. And Sandy, did you ever hear about pointing your toe?" Heather shook her head in disgust. "No wonder I didn't want you on my squad," she grumbled, under her breath but still loud enough to be heard.

Jessica stared at Heather, her mouth hanging open. Tears welled up in Sandy's eyes; she ran over to the water fountain to hide them.

"Sorry," Patty said, her voice tight. "I'll try to be more moderate next time."

"You'd better do more than try," advised Heather. She turned to Maria and gave her the eyeball up and down. "And meanwhile, your jump had no elevation whatsoever. Have you put on a few pounds?"

Maria looked stricken. Her hands went automatically to her slender waist. "I don't think—"

"Would you stop criticizing my squad?" Jessica burst out.

"In case you haven't noticed," Heather retorted, "your squad has supposedly combined with my squad, and that means everyone should be performing to the same high standards, but if your squad can't cut it—"

"We know there are still a lot of rough edges," Elizabeth quickly interjected, before the subject of who was really boss could come up, "and we're trying our best, we really are. Thanks for the feedback, Heather. I think it will help us fine-tune the routine for regionals."

"Well, I don't need to remind you that regionals are tomorrow," Heather said, somewhat less huffily.

"No, you don't need to remind us," said Jessica. "All right, let's shift gears. Everybody partner up and practice your jumps—spot and coach each other."

Elizabeth and Maria moved off to a vacant part of the field and spent a few moments catching their breath and stretching. "That was a close call," Maria remarked, sliding onto the grass in a split and flattening her torso forward on top of her extended leg. Balancing on one foot, Elizabeth bent the other leg at the knee and lifted it behind her, then reached back to grab the ankle. "I have to admit I'm starting to worry. We haven't even decided on which routines to perform at the competition tomorrow!"

"Maybe it would have been better to choose one of the two squads to go to regionals," said Maria. "Then SVH would have had a shot at the trophy. As it is, if we can't even work as a team, what chance do we have of winning?"

Elizabeth couldn't think of a good answer to Maria's question. In silence the two girls resumed practicing their jumps. Elizabeth was intensely aware of Ken, who had stopped at the edge of the field on his way to the locker room to watch the cheerleaders. The possibility that his eyes might rest on her energized Elizabeth to jump to new heights, and when at one point Ken tossed a wave her way and shouted, "Looking good, Liz!" she thought she would split in two from joy.

Just knowing Ken will be in the audience is all the motivation I'll need to perform at my peak tomorrow, Elizabeth thought as she returned Ken's casual wave. *But what about the rest of the squad?*

Jessica glanced over at Ken just in time to see him waving and grinning at Elizabeth. For a moment something about the scene struck her as sinister. It was almost as if, for a split second, the world turned upside down and inside out. Instead of dating Jessica, Ken was dating Elizabeth. They'd gone public with their torrid romance instead of keeping it a secret. Elizabeth had never got back together with Todd; she'd been with Ken all along. . . .

Jessica shook her head. *It didn't happen that way,* she reminded herself as Ken walked across the grass toward her. Jessica smiled at him, her eyes shining with love. *Of course it didn't happen that way! He broke up with Liz, he got over her, and now he's with me. Me and only me.*

Ken swept her up in his arms. The warmth of his embrace almost banished the tiny niggling doubt that had stolen into Jessica's heart. Almost. She just couldn't help thinking about how different things might have been. . . .

"I can't believe you're going to eat that," Ken said Friday night as he and Jessica sat down at one of the small round wrought-iron tables at Casey's

Ice Cream Parlor in the Sweet Valley Mall.

Jessica studied her mountainous double-fudge sundae with whipped cream and nuts. "Three flavors of ice cream," she declared blissfully. "It is sinful!"

"I wanted to give you a treat the night before regionals," said Ken, "fuel you up, but if you eat all that, you'll never get off the ground tomorrow."

Jessica laughed. "Don't worry. I'm so nervous, I'm burning calories like crazy. This'll only last me for about half an hour."

Ken spooned into his own smaller sundae. "You shouldn't be nervous. You're the best there is—you'll knock the socks off the regionals judges."

Jessica beamed at him. "You really think so?"

"I really think so."

Jessica nudged Ken's foot with hers under the table. "I know I'll feel inspired because you'll be there watching me."

Ken nudged her back. "It's about time I had a chance to cheer for you."

For a full minute they smiled into each other's eyes while their ice cream started to melt. Finally Jessica broke the spell. "I can't believe we're so moony!" she said, laughing.

"Yeah, how did this happen?" kidded Ken, pretending to be shocked. "I don't usually get this way over girls."

"But I'm not just any girl," Jessica reminded him playfully.

"No, you're not," he agreed, reaching across the table to put his hand on hers. "You're one in a million."

Jessica opened her mouth, about to make a joke about how she couldn't actually be one in a million since she had an identical twin, but then she stopped herself. *Why bring up the subject of Elizabeth and how much alike we are?* she thought. No, she didn't want Ken thinking about her sister—she wanted Ken thinking about her.

At the same time, since they were having such a lovey-dovey, confessional chat, this did seem like a convenient opportunity to pry a little. . . .

"I really feel close to you," Jessica told Ken, her eyelashes lowered shyly. "I don't think . . . I don't think I've ever liked anyone this much." She giggled, her cheeks turning bright pink. "God, I can't believe I said that!"

Ken squeezed her hand. His eyes were deep with answering emotion. "I'm glad you did," he murmured huskily, "because I feel the same way about you."

"It has happened pretty fast, though, hasn't it?"

Ken nodded. "Maybe it's because we were good friends for a long time first, I mean before we . . . you know."

"So we didn't have to spend a lot of time in that getting-to-know-each-other phase, because we already did."

"Something like that."

"But part of the fun of this is that even though we've been friends for ages, now that we're going out, I'm learning new things about you all the time," said Jessica.

"Like . . ."

"Like your favorite flavor of ice cream is mocha chip, and even though everyone thinks you're just a jock, you want to study premed in college, and you arrange your T-shirts by order of color in your dresser drawer, and on at least one occasion you've gone skinny-dipping after dark at Secca Lake."

Ken laughed. "Now, don't let all this top-secret, classified information get around."

"What else should I know about you?" asked Jessica. "Any other deep, dark secrets?"

"Sorry to disappoint you. That T-shirt stuff is about as deep and dark as it gets."

"So there's nothing you want to tell me, about your . . . past," Jessica hinted delicately.

Ken shook his head. "Well, I do have one big regret," he admitted.

"You do?" Jessica leaned forward, her eyes wide. Could this be it? Was he finally going to tell her about Elizabeth?

"Yes." Ken rattled his spoon around in his empty ice-cream dish. "I regret that I didn't realize sooner that all the other nice, fun, pretty girls at Sweet Valley High can't hold a candle to Jessica Wakefield."

Jessica was disappointed that Ken hadn't spilled his guts about Elizabeth, but she couldn't be too disappointed when he said something as incredibly sweet as that. *He's protecting Elizabeth's privacy and reputation—he's so chivalrous!* "Things happen when they're supposed to, you know?" she said softly. "I think we found each other at just the right time."

"I couldn't agree more."

Ken slid his chair around the table so he could give Jessica a kiss. She rested her head against his shoulder. "It's funny, I don't feel nervous about tomorrow anymore," she told him.

"That's because you're with the king of visualization," he explained. "And right now I'm visualizing you leading the Sweet Valley High team to victory at regionals!"

"Did I ever tell you," Todd said as he and Elizabeth approached Casey's, "that ice cream the night before a big game is the secret to my success on the court?"

Elizabeth laughed. "Oh, really?"

"During basketball season there's always a carton of fudge swirl in the freezer. Once my dad finished it off and forgot to buy more, so I didn't get my good-luck bowl of ice cream before bed. I missed an easy basket in the last couple seconds of the game, and we lost by one point."

"I never knew you were so superstitious!" Elizabeth put her arm around Todd's waist and tickled him. "And I thought your big secret was wearing your good-luck underwear."

He grinned. "Well, that, too."

The moment they walked into Casey's, the smile faded from Elizabeth's face. Suddenly she wasn't in the mood for ice cream—her appetite had been instantly ruined.

Todd waved to Jessica and Ken. "Hi, you two."

Elizabeth forced herself to smile at them. "Fancy meeting you here."

"Getting some of that good-luck ice cream?" Ken called to Todd.

Todd nodded. "You bet. I'm treating Liz."

Knowing Todd would be disappointed if she told him she didn't want anything, Elizabeth ordered a small dish of strawberry. "That's all?" he asked.

She shrugged. "I'm kind of . . . keyed up. I don't think my stomach can handle more than one scoop."

They snagged the last empty table, which fortunately was on the opposite side of the ice-cream parlor from Jessica and Ken. *Maybe they'll leave soon,* Elizabeth thought. Then she might be able to relax and enjoy Todd's company.

"This really is a big thing, going to regionals," he remarked. "I'm proud of you, Liz."

"Thanks."

"It won't make you nervous, having me there watching?"

"Of course not." She swept the hair back from her forehead and smiled. "It'll be nice knowing there are some friendly faces in the audience."

"There'll be a bunch," Todd promised. "I'm going with Ken and Winston. We wouldn't miss it for the world."

"Well, I hope we don't let you down," she said, glancing sideways at Jessica and Ken. Although they'd long since finished their ice cream, the two didn't appear to be in a hurry to leave. *God, I can't believe they're doing that in public!* thought Elizabeth as her sister and Ken smooched. She counted silently in her head, timing the lip-lock. Ten seconds. Eleven, twelve, thirteen . . .

"You won't let us down," Todd was saying. "Even if you don't win the title—and I'm confident you will, by the way—just to compete in regionals is an honor. You're the first squad from SVH ever to qualify! And you personally have been cheering for only two weeks. It's really an incredible achievement, Liz."

"Uh, yeah," she mumbled, tearing her eyes away from Jessica and Ken. "Thanks."

Todd had other caring, supportive words for her, and Elizabeth tried to look attentive as he spoke. But she couldn't think about cheerleading regionals . . . not when Jessica and Ken were just a few tables away winning the make-out regionals!

Chapter 12

It was a misty gray dawn as the cheerleaders gathered in the parking lot at Sweet Valley High to carpool to Carver City, where the regionals competition was being held. Jessica rubbed her upper arms and stamped her feet; even in a bulky sweatshirt and sweatpants, she felt chilled to the bone. "I don't think I've ever had to wake up this early in my life," she complained. "The sun isn't even up!"

Maria yawned widely. "At least you slept. I was so nervous, I didn't close my eyes all night."

"I slept, but I had this horrible nightmare," said Annie, hugging her sports duffel to her chest. "We went onstage at regionals, and halfway through the routine I realized I was wearing underwear and nothing else!"

Jessica and Maria giggled. "I've had that dream," said Maria, "except usually I'm doing something for the student council, like addressing an all-school assembly, and I step up to the podium in the auditorium and—"

Just then a white Mazda Miata peeled into the parking lot. Heather hopped out, looking well rested and perfectly groomed. "I'm glad everyone was punctual. Are you ready?" she greeted the other girls. Her manner was so chirpy, Jessica wanted to smack her. "Are you psyched?"

The group gave a small cheer. "OK, let's hit the road," suggested Jessica. "Liz and I can take two people in the Jeep."

"There's room in my car, too," offered Patty.

"Whoever's left over can ride with me," said Amy.

The drive to Carver City, about forty-five minutes north of Sweet Valley, seemed to pass in a blink. As Elizabeth pulled into the lot adjacent to the high-school athletic complex, Jessica's whole body started to tremble. "Ohmigod, look at all the cars," she said, her teeth chattering. "The Whitehead Academy van—they always have the sharpest uniforms, not to mention the fact that their coach used to choreograph routines for the state university squad." She spotted another van and gulped. "And Springbrook High. They've won regionals two years in a row! Oh, Liz, let's go back home. We don't have a prayer!"

"We do so," Elizabeth declared, setting the parking brake.

Sandy leaned forward from the backseat to give Jessica's shoulder a squeeze. "It doesn't matter who won regionals last year. What counts is who's the best today."

"And that's going to be us!" Jean chimed in.

The twins, Sandy, and Jean joined the rest of the squad, and together they marched into the gymnasium. A loud, colorful spectacle met their eyes. Heather was the only one who seemed completely calm and unconcerned—the rest of the girls froze in their tracks.

There were girls everywhere. Brightly colored banners marked off the space where each squad would practice; scanning the gym, Jessica spotted Springbrook High, Whitehead Academy, Fort Carroll, Lawrence, Palisades, San Pedro, Ramsbury. Her teeth started chattering again. "I . . . don't . . . think . . . I . . . can . . . go . . . through . . . with . . ."

Elizabeth gave her sister a shove from behind. "There's nothing to be afraid of, silly." She grinned. "We've got an edge, remember? The twin factor!"

As they made their way to a corner of the gym where there was still some floor space, Jessica checked out the competition. The Whitehead Wildcats, already dressed in their black-and-red uniforms, were gathered in a huddle around their famous coach. A few feet beyond them the San Pedro squad launched into a routine with a fireworks explosion of spectacular sequenced jumps. Jessica paused to watch, then wished she hadn't. It only made her more insecure.

We haven't even decided which routines we're going to perform, she thought, hurrying after the rest of the squad. *We're doomed!*

When Jessica caught up to the others, Heather had already stripped off her sweats and was stretching out. After a few minutes of limbering exercises, the Sweet Valley girls formed a circle. "Why don't we warm up with the school-spirit cheer," Jessica suggested, "and then we can work on the dance number, since that's the one that's been giving us trouble."

To her relief Heather just nodded. *She's keeping her place, finally!* Jessica thought.

The girls fanned out, spacing themselves an arm's length apart. "OK," Jessica shouted, "on the count of three, stomp, clap, yell, and then the wave—spread-eagles in sequence starting with Jade on the far left, and then back crunches for the wave going back the other way. Don't let yourself get caught behind—each girl takes off exactly one beat after the girl next to her. Ready? One, two—"

"Wait a minute," Heather interrupted.

Jessica glared at her. "Do you have something to add?"

"I have something to subtract, actually," she said. "Let's scrap the second wave and save our energy for later in the cheer."

"But it doesn't look balanced if you only do it going one way," Jessica argued. "And besides, didn't you see those girls from San Pedro High? We have to start out with something flashy—we can't play it safe if we want to win!"

"It's hardly playing it safe," Heather countered stubbornly. "I don't want to be out of breath when we go into the star formation for our next jump after the 'Rally, Sweet Valley' yell."

"Well, maybe you're not in as good shape as you

think you are, Heather, if you're knocked out after a double wave," Jessica said sarcastically.

"And maybe you don't know anything about winning a regionals competition if you think a double wave is the answer to all our problems," Heather retorted.

Jessica felt something snap in her brain. Suddenly someone was yelling at Heather at the top of her lungs . . . and Jessica recognized her own voice. "What gives you the right to call all the shots, Heather? We don't need your advice—we were doing just fine until you came along!"

"You were getting nowhere until I came along!" Heather shouted back.

Simultaneously both Jessica and Heather threw down their pom-poms. "I've had it!" Jessica exclaimed.

"Forget it, she's impossible!" Heather declared.

Heather started to stomp in the direction of the water fountain; Jessica was ready to head back out to the parking lot and rev up the Jeep for the trip home. Before either girl could take a step, Amy put her thumb and index finger to her lips and let out a piercing whistle.

Jessica and Heather stopped in their tracks and stared at her. "*You've* had it?" Amy said to them. "What about the rest of us? How do you think we feel?"

Elizabeth stepped to Amy's side. "This self-centered showboating has gone on long enough," she asserted sternly.

Lila joined Elizabeth and Amy. "Right. Either

you two shut up and start working together, or you're both off the squad and we're performing without you!"

One by one the rest of the squad lined up behind Lila, Amy, and Elizabeth. "Are you with us?" Amy demanded.

Jessica hung her head. "I'm with you," she muttered, glancing at Heather out of the corner of her eye.

Heather nodded contritely. "Me, too."

"OK," said Elizabeth. "Then let's practice this cheer, once with a single wave and once with the double wave. Then we can decide which feels best."

After they'd performed the routine the second time, Jessica turned to Heather. "I think you're right about the—" she started to say.

Heather had opened her mouth at the same moment. "Maybe the double wave does work—"

They both burst out laughing. *It's going to be OK*, Jessica thought.

Miraculously, once Heather and Jessica were back on speaking terms, it took only a few minutes to work out the final kinks in their second routine. After cooling off they retreated into the locker room to change into their uniforms, put on makeup, and brush their hair; then they regrouped once more in the gym.

Jessica was reading the printed program; now she checked the clock on the wall. "The first team is about to perform," she said. "Since we go last, let's rest up for a while and watch."

While they'd been practicing, the bleachers had filled up. As the other girls hurried off, Elizabeth paused to scan the crowd, hoping to spot some friends from Sweet Valley High. Just then someone stepped up behind her and slipped his arms around her waist.

Elizabeth let out a startled gasp; the boy was lightly kissing the back of her neck. He was so close, she could smell the fresh, citrusy scent of his aftershave.

"Hey, Jess," Ken whispered into Elizabeth's ear. "There's a meteor shower tonight. How about we take a blanket down to our secluded beach and catch some falling stars to celebrate your regionals victory?"

Elizabeth's first impulse was to push Ken away, tell him that once again he'd made an understandable mistake. They'd laugh about it, and Ken would run ahead to catch up with Jessica. Then another impulse took over. . . .

I'll tell Jessica that Ken mentioned the meteor shower and the beach and then dashed off again before I could tell him he had the wrong twin, Elizabeth decided as she closed her eyes and leaned back against Ken's broad chest. *She'll have her date tonight with Ken, and what she doesn't know won't hurt her. . . .*

"That sounds great," Elizabeth murmured. "What an incentive to win!"

"I have to head home as soon as the competition's over," Ken said, his arms tightening around her, "so here's your victory hug in advance. I'm with you all the way, Jess!"

"Thanks, Ken," Elizabeth whispered.

Ken kissed her on the cheek and then disappeared into the crowd. Elizabeth stood for a moment, one hand lifted to where Ken's lips had touched her skin. When she refocused, she realized that someone was staring at her.

Heather had retraced her steps to hustle along anyone who was lagging. "Come on, Liz," she called sharply. "Lawrence High is already halfway through their first routine!"

Elizabeth scurried after Heather, her face flaming. *Did she see?* she wondered anxiously. *No, she couldn't have. I would've noticed her sooner.* Elizabeth took comfort in this thought, even though she knew it wasn't necessarily true. While Ken's arms were around her, she hadn't been aware of anything; Todd himself could have been standing right in front of her, and she probably wouldn't have noticed!

"Gosh, they're really good," gushed Lila, nervously twisting a strand of her hair. "Did you see the height on that team stag leap?"

"And it was perfectly timed," said Annie, shaking her head. "What a landing—not one girl misstepped."

The Ramsbury Rockets landed their final jumps in the form of a big *R*, held the pose for a moment, and then waved energetically at the audience. The applause was loud and enthusiastic.

"The crowd liked that a lot," said Jessica, biting her fingernails.

"The judges liked it, too." Heather pointed. "See? They're smiling and whispering to each other. I bet they mark Ramsbury even higher than Springbrook!"

A minute or two passed in tense, expectant silence, and then the point total for the Ramsbury squad flashed on the scoreboard. "They've moved into first place!" squealed Amy.

Jessica grabbed Elizabeth's arm for support. "I think I'm going to pass out. I think I'm starting to hyperventilate!"

"You can't pass out, because after the next team it's our turn," Elizabeth said pragmatically. "Just take slow, steady breaths, Jess. Like this. In, out. In, out."

Jessica breathed in and out as instructed. Then she smiled weakly. "I feel better."

Elizabeth patted her on the back. "I think you're going to make it."

"Thanks for being so calm and sensible, Liz." Jessica gave her sister a spontaneous hug. "Where would I be without you?"

"Passed out or hyperventilating," Lila joked.

"Or both," said Amy.

The spotlight was now on the Fort Carroll cheerleaders, the second-to-last squad to perform. The eight girls trotted to the middle of the basketball court, their ponytails bouncing. Half wore flouncy pleated purple skirts with cropped white sweaters, and the other half wore white skirts with purple sweaters. "Cute uniforms," commented Jessica.

"They look sharp," agreed Elizabeth.

The Fort Carroll team performed their musical number first. It was technically strong, but not that original, Jessica was happy to note. Their second routine was more of the same, a traditional fight cheer with lots of stomping and clapping and a smattering of well-executed jump combinations. "Good but not great," Heather pronounced when they were through.

Sure enough, Fort Carroll's point total was slightly lower than Ramsbury's. "Ramsbury's the team to beat," Jessica said.

Heather nodded. "And Sweet Valley's the team to beat them!"

The two girls looked each other straight in the eye. For the first time since she'd met Heather, Jessica didn't hate and resent her; she felt camaraderie and, of all things, trust. *I can count on her,* Jessica thought. *We'll never be best buddies, but when it comes to cheerleading, she's a pro. She'll pull out all the stops—she'll blow the judges away.*

Jessica smiled; Heather grinned. "So," Jessica said to the rest of the squad. "Everybody ready?"

They didn't even have time for one last pep talk. "And now, last but not least, Sweet Valley High!" the announcer boomed.

As she jogged out onto the court with Heather and the other girls and felt the energy pulsing from the audience, Jessica's nervousness melted away, and her love of the limelight asserted itself full force. She smiled broadly, radiating pure joy in the moment. *This is it! We're on!*

They'd opted to start with their shorter school-spirit yell, saving the innovative dance routine for their finale. As she sprang into motion, kicking, swaying, clapping, twirling, jumping, shouting, Jessica was aware of the other girls in the squad, aware that they were watching her out of the corner of their eyes, using her as their guide. She felt her body respond to the demands she made of it—she knew she'd never looked stronger, crisper, more in control.

The regionals audience enjoyed the first routine; they went wild over the second. As the Sweet Valley High squad struck their final pose, Jessica glanced at Heather. Heather was breathing hard, but she was beaming. "We were brilliant!" she mouthed to Jessica.

Pom-poms on their hips, Jessica and the others waited for their score. The judges put their heads together; they conferred for what seemed to Jessica like a year. "We were the best," she murmured to herself. "At least, I think we were. But Ramsbury was awfully good. Maybe we didn't quite cut it. Sara was a teeny bit behind on that last jump. Oh, I can't stand it!"

The judges appeared to have reached a consensus. Clutching each other for support, her teammates stared at the scoreboard; Jessica covered her eyes.

Then the crowd let out a roar of approval; Jessica felt someone grab her and shake her.

"We did it!" Lila screeched. "We won!"

The Sweet Valley High squad exploded into the air, tossing their pom-poms and shouting with joy. Jessica grabbed Amy and twirled her around. "Do you see that?" she whooped. "Do you see those scores?"

They quieted down as the judges presented the runners-up trophy to a disappointed but gracious Ramsbury squad. Then it was Sweet Valley's turn. Jessica's heart started pounding as the head judge spoke into the microphone. "And now we're pleased to present the grand-prize trophy to the team that will be representing our region at the State Cheerleading Championships. On behalf of your squad, will Sweet Valley High cocaptains Heather Mallone and Jessica Wakefield please step to the podium?"

Jessica took a step forward and then halted, her mouth falling open. "Cocaptains?" she yelped, shooting an accusing look at Heather. "I thought I was the captain!"

Heather glared back at her. "No, I'm the captain. They told me you agreed to step down."

Jessica shook her head. "They told me *you* agreed to step down!"

The judges and everyone else in the gym were still waiting for Jessica and Heather to accept the trophy. Elizabeth tried to propel her sister forward. "Don't blow it now!" Elizabeth hissed.

Jessica put her hands on her hips, refusing to budge. "Forget it," she fumed. She couldn't believe how badly she'd been duped. "If you want her to be your captain, I quit."

"If you want her to be your captain, I quit," Heather echoed.

Amy stepped forward. "If you two won't agree once and for all to be cocaptains, we all quit," she announced, her voice loud and firm. "Either we all go to state, or none of us goes!"

The rest of the squad nodded, clearly backing Amy in her ultimatum a hundred percent. Reluctantly, Jessica turned to face Heather.

Heather extended her hand. "Truce."

Jessica shook Heather's hand. "Truce."

A moment later the two cocaptains were each holding a handle of the heavy silver trophy while the crowd gave them a standing ovation. Suddenly the reality hit Jessica and she burst into tears of joy. "We won!" she cried, flinging her free arm around her twin sister.

"We won!" Elizabeth agreed, her own eyes shining with the thrill of victory. "We're going to state!"

Chapter 13

"I still can't believe it," sang Jessica, dancing across the kitchen in a giddy circle. She grabbed Elizabeth, whirling her around, too. "We won regionals. It's official—Sweet Valley High cheerleaders are the best!"

"You were great," Elizabeth told her sister truthfully. "It couldn't have happened without you, Jess. All the girls think so."

"Then why did you play that mean trick on me?" asked Jessica, pretending to pout. "Faking me out that I was the only captain, and then doing the same thing to Heather."

"Because we knew it was the only way to keep you both on the squad since you were too stubborn to serve as cocaptains." Elizabeth smiled. "And it worked, didn't it?"

Jessica laughed. "You're right. I guess I can't be too mad about it! And Heather's starting to come around. I'm never going to like that girl, but I can put up with her. At least until we win states and then nationals!"

"That's the spirit!" said Elizabeth as she ripped open a bag of pretzels and offered them to her sister.

Jessica shook her head at the pretzels and then reached for the phone. "I'm going to call Ken and then—"

Elizabeth slapped the heel of her hand to her forehead. "I almost forgot," she exclaimed. "Ken gave me a message for you."

Jessica's eyebrows lifted in surprise. "He did?"

Elizabeth nodded. *Is my face turning red?* she wondered. *Can Jessica tell that Ken held me in his arms and whispered the message in my ear?* "Well, he thought he was talking to you," explained Elizabeth, laughing to hide her discomfort. "He was kind of in a hurry—he didn't realize—"

"Spit it out," Jessica commanded. "What did he say?"

"He said . . ." *Say it: He wants to take you to your private beach and watch the shooting stars.* "He won't be able to see you tonight because he has some family party to go to. But he's really proud of you and he'll call you tomorrow."

Elizabeth regretted the lie as soon as it left her lips, but she couldn't call the words back. They were out there; she'd set the wheels in motion.

"Oh." Jessica's face fell with disappointment. Then it brightened again. "Well, in that case, I guess I'll party at Lila's with the cheerleaders. Her parents are ordering in a ton of great food—Lila's inviting a bunch of people. Want to go with me?"

Elizabeth patted her mouth, faking a huge yawn. "I'm beat—I might just curl up in bed with a book."

"Suit yourself." Jessica grabbed a set of keys off the counter. "Then you won't be needing the Jeep?"

"Nope. It's all yours."

As soon as the door shut behind Jessica, Elizabeth sank back against the counter, her knees buckling. *I can't believe I did that!* she thought, amazed at her own duplicity. But it wasn't what she'd already done that most astonished Elizabeth. It was what she was intending to do.

Picking up the phone, she dialed Todd's number. "Hi, it's me, Liz," she said when he answered. "I'm going to have to cancel our date tonight. I'm so wiped out from regionals—I think I'll just take a long, hot bath and go to bed early. But I'll see you tomorrow, OK?"

After hanging up she sprinted into the hall and up the stairs. Instead of entering her own bedroom, however, she barged into Jessica's, making a beeline for the closet. As usual, Jessica's wardrobe was in total disarray, with clothes lying knee-deep on the closet floor and dangling haphazardly off hangers. *Something casual but sexy,* Elizabeth thought, rummaging through Jessica's blouses and tank tops. *Something that won't get too wrinkled when I'm lying on the sand with Ken. . . .*

After choosing a pair of gauzy white trousers

and a clingy crocheted top, she glanced at her watch to see how much time she had to get ready. Then she laughed out loud. *What a dead give-away!* she thought, quickly unbuckling the leather strap from her wrist.

Because Jessica never wears a watch. And if I want Ken to think I'm Jessica—and that's the only way I'm going to be able to get close to him—I'd better make sure I get every detail just right. . . .

There were no other cars in the parking lot by the beach when Ken's white Toyota pulled in. "Good," he said, shooting a sexy smile at Elizabeth. "Looks like we'll have the ocean and stars all to ourselves, Jess."

A shiver of anticipation chased up Elizabeth's spine. "Good," she echoed, her voice as soft and caressing as the night breeze.

Ken slung the beach blanket over his shoulder. Hand in hand, he and Elizabeth scrambled over the grassy dune. Before them a sliver of sand gleamed like silver in the moonlight; a crescent of foam marked the waterline.

They stood for a moment, drinking in the peaceful, magical scene. Ken's fingers tightened around Elizabeth's; she returned the pressure. *It's been so long,* she thought, her whole body electrified by Ken's touch, *so long since I was with Ken, since I was with any boy but Todd. . . .*

Quickly Elizabeth forced the thought of Todd out of her mind. She didn't want to feel guilty; she wanted to feel good.

Ken spread the blanket on the sand in the shelter of a dune. He sat down, and Elizabeth lowered herself gingerly beside him. Then he settled onto his back, one arm extended so that Elizabeth could rest her head on his shoulder. They lay side by side, their faces to the velvety-black, star-speckled sky. "There's supposed to be a meteor shower tonight," he told her, pointing upwards. "If we look to the northwest."

As if on cue, a tiny bright object streaked across the sky, then fizzled and disappeared. "There!" exclaimed Ken. "Did you see it?"

"Yes!" An instant later another shooting star appeared, and then another. "It's like fireworks!" Elizabeth breathed.

Ken shifted so that he was lying on his side. His other arm went around Elizabeth, pulling her toward him. Suddenly they were face-to-face, so close Elizabeth could feel the heat of Ken's body. Ken brushed the hair back from her face; her heart started to pound. *He's going to kiss me,* she thought, breathless with desire. At last . . .

Elizabeth closed her eyes. Ken's lips found hers; she pressed her body against his, responding eagerly. The kiss grew longer, deeper. . . .

Something was wrong. Elizabeth's dream was coming true: She was kissing Ken Matthews again, something she'd been thinking about night and day for weeks. But somehow it wasn't quite the way she'd remembered it—it wasn't nearly as exciting as her fantasies. She kept kissing Ken, waiting in vain for the familiar fiery passion of old to ignite her soul, but it didn't happen. Instead Elizabeth felt a fuzzy, affectionate warmth overlaid by a sudden, confusing sorrow. *Todd,* she thought. *I miss Todd. I want to be with Todd, not Ken!*

At that moment Ken pulled back from Elizabeth. She could see his eyes searching hers in the moonlight. "Jess?" he asked, puzzled. "No, wait. It's . . . Liz?"

They jumped apart, sitting up. Ken stared at Elizabeth in shock; Elizabeth covered her face with her hands to hide her shame and embarrassment. "I'm so sorry," she said, her voice cracking. "I can't imagine what you must think of me. Oh, God, how could I have . . ."

She started to cry. Ken patted her back gently. "Ssh. Take it easy. You freaked me out for a minute there, but it's OK, Liz. Just tell me what's going on."

Elizabeth tried to collect herself. "It's just . . ." There was nothing for it but to tell Ken the whole horrible truth. "I've been going crazy with jealousy since you and Jessica started dating," Elizabeth confessed, her cheeks stained scarlet with humiliation. "I wanted to be happy for her, but I couldn't, and it made me realize that I had all sorts of feelings for you that I'd never really dealt with—I just shoved them into this deep, secret place in my heart and figured eventually they'd die off. I've just been . . . I haven't enjoyed being with Todd at all for weeks. And so I wanted to find out if I really was still in love with you, and this seemed like the only way, but now I see it was a terrible mistake, and what would Jessica think if she could see us like this, not to mention Todd!"

A fresh spate of tears flooded from Elizabeth's eyes. Ken hugged her against his shoulder, murmuring soothingly. "It's not the end of the world," he said with a laugh. "Really, Liz. We didn't do anything so terrible. We kissed and then we both discovered it was a mistake. Hardly a major sin. And besides"—he held her away so that he could gaze earnestly into her eyes—"since we're playing true confessions, I've got to admit that I didn't get over you right away, either. What drew me to Jessica at first was the fact that she was your identical twin sister. I could almost pretend she was you."

"But . . . but you love Jessica," Elizabeth whispered.

Ken nodded. "I do. It didn't take long to figure out that I didn't want to pretend, that what I like best about Jess are the qualities that make her uniquely her. She's the Wakefield for me. Which isn't to say that I don't have fond memories of my time with you," Ken hurried to add, "even though the circumstances were kind of painful."

Elizabeth drew in a long breath, then let it out in a heartfelt sigh. "Boy," she said, brushing the tears from her cheeks. "I really made a fool of myself, huh? Throwing myself at you like that—I feel like such an idiot!"

"You shouldn't," insisted Ken. In the moonlight she could see him smile. "If anything, I'm flattered."

"So we can still be friends?"

Ken found Elizabeth's hand and gave it a firm squeeze. "Of course. The best of friends, always. You're a really special person, Liz."

Ken gave her a swift hug and then they hopped to their feet. Elizabeth almost floated back to the car, she felt so lighthearted with relief. *I'm not in love with Ken!* she thought happily. *I was just delirious, dumb, dizzy. Todd's the one for me—always has been, always will be.* Now she did feel something spark in her soul . . . the rekindling of her love for Todd. She could hardly wait to be back in his arms again.

"Great party, Li," said Amy as she filled her plate with Chinese food at the buffet table set up on the patio next to the Fowler Crest swimming pool.

"Don't I always throw great parties?" Lila snapped her fingers to the beat of the rock music blasting from the outdoor speakers. "I mean, can you even imagine uttering the words, 'Mediocre party, Li'?"

Jessica laughed. "You get extra points this time for spontaneity."

Lila smiled as she looked around the backyard, which was decorated with multicolored balloons, mounds of fresh flowers, and an enormous banner reading "Congratulations, SVH Cheerleaders!" "To tell you the truth," she confided, "it wasn't that spontaneous. Mom and Dad figured we'd need a party whether we won or lost. I think if you turn the banner over, it says, 'Sorry you blew it' or something like that."

Using tongs, Jessica placed a plump egg roll on her plate. She was spooning out sweet-and-sour and hot-mustard sauces when Heather strolled up.

"Hi, Jess," Heather said in her usual la-di-da tone.

Jessica's jaw tightened. *No, I'm never going to like this girl*, she thought, *but I have to be nice.* She smiled stiffly. "Hi, Heather. Having a good time?"

"Oh, sure," said Heather. "Although, I must say, I'm so used to winning competitions that I take it a little bit for granted, you know?"

"Umm," murmured Jessica, resisting the urge to give Heather a pinch. *Be nice, be nice!*

"So where's your sister?" Heather asked as she picked up a plate from the buffet.

"I guess she didn't feel like partying," said Jessica. "She's probably doing something truly exciting, like reading in bed."

"Hmm. Or maybe she's out with that adorable blond boy, Ken the quarterback."

"Ken is my boyfriend," Jessica corrected Heather. "Liz goes out with that adorable brown-haired boy, Todd the basketball player."

Heather raised her eyebrows. "Oh, really? But I could have sworn I saw Ken and Liz . . ." The sentence trailed off suggestively. "Maybe it wasn't the way it looked," she concluded.

Jessica stared at Heather. Then she dropped her plate on the buffet table with a clatter. "Excuse me," she mumbled. "I need to make a phone call."

Heather was smiling as Jessica took off across the patio. Dozens of questions raced through Jessica's mind, but she wasn't about to ask Heather and give her the pleasure of realizing she'd caught her off guard. She saw them . . . where? Doing what? Jessica wondered. "Maybe it wasn't the way it looked. . . ." well, what did it look like?

Charging through the French doors, she hurried to the nearest telephone. She dialed her own home number, praying that Elizabeth would answer quickly. *If she's reading in bed, she should pick it up by the second or third ring,* Jessica thought. Even if she's in the bathroom, she'd get it by the fourth or fifth. The phone rang six times, and then the answering machine picked up. "Sorry we're not able to take your call right now, but if you leave your name and number after the tone . . ."

Jessica slammed down the receiver. "Where is she?" she asked out loud.

Todd. Yes, maybe the answer was that simple. Jessica dialed Todd's number. "Oh, Todd, you're home," she said when he answered the phone. "It's Jessica. Is Liz over at your house by any chance?"

"No," said Todd. Jessica could hear the drone of an action movie in the background. "She said she was tired and wanted to go to bed early. Is something wrong?"

"Oh." Jessica chewed her lip. "No, I was just going to try to talk her into coming over to the party at Lila's. I just assumed she'd be with you—I'll try my house. Thanks."

So Liz is out, but not with Todd, surmised Jessica as she raced through the marble hall of Fowler Crest and out the front door.

By the time she got home, she'd decided that there was nothing ominous about Elizabeth's not answering the phone. She was probably in the bathtub, running water, and didn't hear it, or else she'd turned off the ringer so she could sleep. Don't be so paranoid! Jessica let herself into the house and ran up the stairs two at a time. "Liz?" she called. "Are you there?"

Her sister's bedroom door was open a crack and the light was out. Jessica pushed the door open, reaching for the switch. The light blinked on, revealing a neatly made bed—the room was empty.

"And she's not in the bathroom," Jessica murmured as she cut through it to her own room. "And she wasn't downstairs, so where . . ."

Her eyes came to rest on her closet. The louvered doors were open, which wasn't unusual. But for some reason Jessica suddenly felt a strong hunch. *Liz was in here. She took something from my closet!*

It took her only a second to determine what was missing: her favorite new pants and top, which she'd hung up carefully, not wanting them to get crumpled like the rest of her clothes. Jessica stood in front of her closet, an empty hanger clutched in her hand. *Elizabeth lied to both me and Todd, and then she went somewhere wearing one of my outfits . . . why?*

Suddenly Jessica remembered the message

Elizabeth had given her from Ken. "He couldn't go out with me tonight because he had other plans," Jessica murmured. Her heart contracted into a small, scared fist. "With his family, supposedly. But what if he's really out with . . ."

She couldn't bring herself to voice her suspicion aloud, but the more she thought about it, the more she was convinced that it was true. Hadn't Elizabeth vowed to get Jessica back for blackmailing her into joining the cheerleading squad?

A picture flashed into Jessica's brain, of Elizabeth and Ken talking and laughing in the kitchen the other day when Jessica had walked in. *As if they had some private joke,* thought Jessica. They certainly didn't seem to feel awkward around each other because of what had happened between them in the past. But, of course, they wouldn't feel awkward if they'd gotten involved again in the present, if all that thwarted passion Elizabeth had written about in her diary had come back to life!

"I can't believe she did this to me," Jessica sobbed, tears streaming down her face. "My own twin sister. Pretending to be happy for me when the whole time she was just waiting for a chance to steal Ken back!"

"I feel so much better having cleared things up with you," Elizabeth told Ken as they drove back to Sweet Valley, "but I'm still going to feel guilty about Todd's not knowing."

"Maybe it's time to tell him," said Ken. "I bet

we end up laughing about it—it all happened so long ago, it's just no big deal. And I'll tell Jessica, too."

"Actually, you don't need to do that," said Elizabeth. "She found out."

"You're kidding!" Ken looked at her, surprised. "You told her?"

Elizabeth made a wry face. "Not exactly. She read my diary."

Ken burst out laughing. "Sounds like Jess, all right. So, was she upset? I can't believe she didn't mention it to me!"

"A little shocked, but no, I wouldn't say she was upset." Magnanimously, Elizabeth decided not to tell Ken about the blackmailing angle. "I guess she doesn't view me as a romantic threat."

"Tell you what," said Ken. "Let's go over to Todd's right now. We can get this off our chests once and for all. Won't that feel good?"

Elizabeth nodded. "I suppose I'll have to tell him about tonight's fiasco, too."

Ken shot her a conspiratorial glance. "We could edit the transcript a little."

She laughed. "OK. You're right. Let's get it over with!"

Ken turned the Toyota onto Country Club Drive in the elegant hill section of Sweet Valley. Elizabeth hurriedly practiced her speech to Todd in her head. *I've been meaning to tell you . . . couldn't get up the courage . . . confused, lonely, but never stopped caring for you . . .*

They drove down the Wilkinses' long, winding

driveway. Then Ken let out an exclamation, jolting Elizabeth from her thoughts. "The Jeep! What the . . ."

Elizabeth stared. Sure enough, a familiar white Jeep was parked in front of the house. "Jessica must be here," she said, her forehead crinkling. "I can't imagine why. Unless . . ."

Ken turned to her. "Unless . . . what?"

Instead of answering Elizabeth sprang out of the car and hurried to the front step, Ken close at her heels. *No,* she thought, her hand trembling as she rang the bell. *She promised she wouldn't tell him. Unless somehow she found out about my twin switch tonight. . . .*

Ken joined Elizabeth as the front door swung open to reveal Todd and Jessica standing side by side. Immediately Elizabeth knew that her worst fears had been realized. Jessica's face was teary and vengeful; Todd was pale, stunned.

And Jessica was holding Elizabeth's diary clutched to her chest.

"You didn't," Elizabeth gasped.

"I didn't do anything," cried Jessica. "It was you, Liz!"

The two mismatched couples stared at each other. Ken hung his head, stricken with guilt. Elizabeth forced herself to meet Todd's eyes, then looked away when she saw the ocean of hurt there. Hurt that she herself had inflicted.

"What have I done?" she whispered, her own eyes filling with bitter tears. "What have I done?"

• • •

"Look, Wilkins, Jessica. We can explain," Ken said.

"I bet," snarled Todd.

Jessica took a step forward, her eyes on Ken's face; Todd, meanwhile, retreated into the hall. After one last agonized glance at Elizabeth, he slammed the door with all his might.

The sound echoed throughout the quiet night. Elizabeth jumped as if she'd been shot, her hand going to her heart. Then she turned on her heel and ran, blinded by tears, toward the Jeep.

Jessica and Ken were left alone. She stood with her arms folded, her shoulders shaking with suppressed sobs. "Jessica." Ken stretched out a hand toward her. "It's OK. Please don't—"

"Get away from me!" she cried. "Don't touch me. Don't come near me!"

"But we have to talk," he said, his voice vibrating with emotion. "You have to give me a chance to—"

"To what?" She stared at him through a wild tangle of blond hair. "To tell me more lies?" She pointed toward the Jeep. "There's the girl you really love—the one you never stopped loving. Why don't you go to her?"

"No," Ken said hoarsely. "Jessica, it's you I—"

"Stop," she sobbed, covering her ears. "I won't listen. I can't trust you or believe you. And I wanted to, I really did. I loved . . ."

Ken reached for her again. Whirling, Jessica ran away from him into the dark night.

The happiest day of her life had turned into a

waking nightmare. Elizabeth had exacted her revenge for being blackmailed onto the squad. Jessica's dream of winning regionals had come true, but the price was too high. . . . It had cost her the boy she loved.

Don't miss Sweet Valley High 114: **"V" FOR VICTORY**, *the last book in this sensational three-part mini-series*

"V" FOR VICTORY

Written by
Kate William

Created by
FRANCINE PASCAL

BANTAM BOOKS
NEW YORK • TORONTO • LONDON • SYDNEY • AUCKLAND

To Anders Johansson

"I don't think I can take another minute of this!" Jessica Wakefield exclaimed on Saturday afternoon, her body tense with anticipation as the awards ceremony of the State Cheerleading Championships in Santa Barbara reached its climax. Jessica and her squad at Sweet Valley High were competing at State for the first time, and it looked as if they had a chance to take home the title.

"I know," whispered Amy Sutton, her slate-gray eyes flashing with excitement. "I think I'm going to explode."

"Well, at least it's finally show time," Jessica said, tightening her blond ponytail on top of her head and adjusting her sunglasses. They'd been sitting in the hot afternoon sun for nearly an hour while a series of merit awards were distributed. Now only the winning squads remained to be announced.

"Attention, everybody!" called Victoria Knox, the state representative of the American Cheerleading Association. "The ACA is proud to present the top three cheerleading squads in the state of California. We recognize these squads as representing excellence in all cheerleading categories, including athletic ability, artistic impression, and most important, school spirit. And now the envelope, please!"

The girls fidgeted nervously as an athletic-looking young woman in blue nylon shorts and a white T-shirt ran out onto the field. "Thank you." Ms. Knox smiled as the woman handed her an oversize envelope. She cupped her hand around the microphone and spoke into it. "Please hold your applause until all the teams have been named."

"Why don't they just get on with it?" complained Lila Fowler, swinging her heavy mane of long brown hair over her shoulders.

"Lila, shh!" said Jessica, straining to hear Ms. Knox's voice.

"For their flawless execution and athletic prowess, the third-place award goes to Sacramento High," announced Ms. Knox, holding up a small copper trophy in the shape of a cheerleader.

The audience remained quiet, but the Sacramento squad let out an enthusiastic shout.

Amy leaned over to Jessica. "I can't believe it," she breathed. "Sacramento came in third!"

Jessica flashed her an optimistic smile and held up crossed fingers. The Sacramento squad had seemed like their most imposing opponent. The girls from Sacramento had put on an extremely impressive athletic performance, finishing with a spectacular display of team jumps. "Maybe their routine was too technical," whispered Jessica to Amy.

Ms. Knox's voice boomed out across the field. "And for impressive tumbling, innovative choreography, and an abundance of spirit, the second place winner is—"

Jessica held her breath as Ms. Knox fumbled with the envelope, praying her school wouldn't be named. "Laguna High from Laguna Beach, California! Girls, please come onto the field to accept your awards."

"We're going to win!" Jessica whispered excitedly to Lila, her cheeks flushed with excitement as the captains of the placing squads ran onto the field.

"La-di-da!" said Lila, twirling a red-and-white pom-pom in the air.

Jessica rolled her eyes. "You could at least pretend you're excited," she said. She knew that Lila had agreed to be on the squad only because she was Jessica's best friend. Lila had been on the team a long time ago, but she had quit, claiming that cheerleading was a boring, useless activity.

"Well, this is it, guys!" squealed Annie Whitman, her green eyes sparkling. "It's all or nothing now."

Patty Gilbert, Jade Wu, and Sara Eastbourne, all talented dancers, took up a quiet cheer. "SVH! SVH! SVH!" they intoned together.

Jessica looked around at her squad as the others

picked up the cheer, chanting softly and clapping rhythmically. All the girls were caught up in the excitement of the moment. Sandy Bacon and her best friend, Jean West, were huddled together, holding on to each other for support. Maria Santelli and Annie Whitman were tapping on the bleachers in time with the cheer. Even her twin sister, Elizabeth, seemed to be sharing in the enthusiasm. Jessica felt a swell of pride as she took in the squad she had put together. They had performed to perfection this afternoon, she thought with satisfaction, and they deserved to win.

Jessica held her breath as the announcer ripped open the envelope containing the first-place winners. A drumroll began from the far end of the field, and Jessica could feel her heart beating in time with it. "And now," intoned Ms. Knox, speaking in an enticingly slow voice, "the—number one—cheerleading squad—in the entire state of California is . . . Sweet Valley High!"

The crowd roared and jumped up spontaneously. Jessica was elated, swept up in the excitement as she was pulled up to her feet with the crowd. "C'mon, guys!" Jessica exclaimed, waving to her teammates to follow her down the bleachers. Jessica felt a rush of energy as the girls ran across the field, waving their pom-poms in the air. She almost couldn't believe it was true. Her squad had won the state championships! They were better than all of the cheerleading squads in California! They were going to nationals for the first time ever!

Suddenly her cocaptain, Heather Mallone, shoved past her and sprinted to the podium ahead of the rest of the girls. For a moment Jessica had forgotten that she had to share her glory with her archrival, the beautiful new girl in town who had taken over her squad and was trying to take over the entire school. *How typical,* thought Jessica, wondering what kind of stunt Heather was going to pull.

"Congratulations," said Ms. Knox, holding out a gold statuette as Heather reached the podium, the other girls behind her. Heather accepted the trophy graciously as warm applause filled the stadium. Jessica steamed as she watched Heather grab the microphone and stand poised in the middle of the field, waiting for the crowd to settle down. *She's just basking in the attention, isn't she?* thought Jessica to herself bitterly.

Heather cleared her throat and flashed a big-toothed white smile at the audience. "I just want to thank everybody on my squad for all their hard work," she said, flipping her blond hair with a shake of her head.

My squad! thought Jessica in indignation. *She* was the official captain of the squad. *She* was the one who had carried her squad through weeks and weeks of training the entire year. Heather had been cocaptain for only a few weeks. "Can you believe her?" whispered Jessica to Amy in indignation.

"Jessica, please," said Amy. "This isn't the time to sharpen your claws." She turned her attention back to Heather, a rapturous smile plastered on her face. Jessica gritted her teeth, seething in frustration.

"But most of all, I want to thank *you*," continued Heather in her annoyingly sexy voice, extending her hand in a gracious gesture, "you—the judges, the audience, and our friends, for recognizing my squad for what it is—the best in the state and soon to be the best in the nation!"

Jessica's face burned as the crowd cheered in appreciation. All the Sweet Valley High cheerleaders were crowded around the podium, jumping and screaming. Jessica couldn't believe it. Was the entire squad blind? She moved forward to take the mike and make a speech of her own when the roar of the crowd interrupted her.

"Com-bo jump! Com-bo jump!" yelled the audience, calling for a replay of Heather's famous combination jump, the jump with which they had finished their routine.

Jessica stared aghast as Heather put on a dazzling solo display. She performed her combination jump with aplomb, pulling off a flawless triple herky and Y-leap combination. Then she ran across the field and performed a series of back flips, finishing off with a perfect landing in the splits.

"Bravo! Bravo!" yelled the crowd, hooting and cheering for more. Jessica couldn't stand one more moment of Heather's sickening display. She slipped away from the circle of cheering girls and darted across the field toward the goalpost. She looked back to see if anybody had noticed her leave, but the girls seemed oblivious, completely entranced with the nauseating spectacle Heather was making of herself.

Well, victory isn't as sweet as I imagined, Jessica thought, ducking into the deserted gym. She couldn't stand sharing the spotlight with Heather. *Sharing it!* thought Jessica wryly as she made her way across the stadium. *Having it stolen right out from under me is more like it.* She almost wished they had lost just so she could have seen Heather humiliated.

Ever since beautiful blond Heather Mallone had stepped into the Dairi Burger, she'd been making Jessica's life a living nightmare. Heather had apparently been the big star of the cheerleading squad at her old high school, Thomas Jefferson High, in Reno, Nevada. And she had decided to be the star of her *new* school as well, thought Jessica with annoyance. She had arrived on the scene at exactly the same time that Jessica's old cocaptain, Robin Wilson, had moved out of town. Not only had the girls voted unanimously to let Heather join the squad, but they had voted her in as cocaptain as well.

That's when everything started falling apart. Heather had taken over the squad like an army invading foreign territory—she had introduced new cheers, new uniforms, and even a new diet-and-exercise program. And the girls had eaten it up. Even though the uniforms were cheap and skimpy, the diet unrealistic, and the exercise plan like a military regime, the girls had followed her every step of the way—all because she promised to lead them to nationals. She had undercut Jessica's authority at every turn, making Jessica look like the enemy and turning all the girls against her.

Jessica seethed as she ticked off Heather's offenses in her mind. One day at practice while Jessica was sick at home, Heather had even had the audacity to fire Maria and Sandy, two of the most seasoned girls on the squad. Heather's irritating, singsong voice rang in her head. *"We all have to make sacrifices for the good of the team,"* she had said. Jessica had tried to rally the girls around her, but they had all stood behind Heather's decision to let Maria and Sandy go. Then, at the big game against Claremont, Heather had led the girls in a cheer that Jessica didn't even know. Jessica had just stood on the sidelines, humiliated, while her team pranced and cheered without her. That had been the last straw. "I quit!" Jessica had yelled, throwing down her pom-poms and flouncing off the field.

But Jessica Wakefield wasn't one to sit on the sidelines for long. So she had organized a squad of her own, recruiting her best friend, her sister, and a number of dancers at school. With a week of intense practice, she had put together a stellar squad, a squad that turned out to be so good, the American Cheerleading Association representative recommended combining the two squads for the state competition. She had Ken Matthews to thank for that. It had all been his idea.

Ken, thought Jessica glumly, walking out of the

silent gym and blinking at the bright sunlight. She sat down under a tree, feeling dejected despite the squad's victory. She felt as if she had lost everything that mattered to her. Not only had Heather stolen her squad, but her own sister, Elizabeth, had stolen her boyfriend.

Jessica had been thrilled to be dating handsome blond Ken Matthews, the well-built captain and quarterback of the Gladiators, the Sweet Valley High football team. She had expected her sister to be happy for her, too, but Elizabeth had been strangely pessimistic about the whole thing. She had kept warning Jessica to go slowly, and every chance she got, she had discouraged her being with Ken. It almost seemed as if she were trying to undermine their relationship.

And then one day Jessica discovered why. She was in Elizabeth's room when she happened upon a series of framed photos of Ken and Elizabeth in a photo booth—kissing. Driven by curiosity, Jessica had hunted out her sister's journal, only to discover that Ken and Elizabeth had had a secret fling while Elizabeth's longtime boyfriend and Ken's best friend, Todd Wilkins, was living in Vermont.

Jessica hadn't minded at first. She was surprised that Elizabeth had been so secretive about the whole thing, but it was all in the past. Ken was interested in her, and not her sister, now. But Elizabeth wasn't content with letting the past be the past. She wanted Ken back, and she wasn't going to let anything stop her. She had even gone so far as to pull a twin switch, going out on a date with Ken disguised as Jessica. Ken had fixed a romantic picnic, and they had shared a kiss at the beach. Ken hadn't even realized it was Elizabeth until he'd kissed her. Jessica's face blazed with the memory. How could Elizabeth have betrayed her like that? How could Ken have confused them?

Elizabeth Wakefield, her face creased with concern, watched Jessica run off the field. She jumped up to follow her but checked herself, remembering that she and Jessica weren't speaking.

"We did it!" yelled Annie Whitman, grabbing Maria Santelli around the waist and spinning her around.

"We're numero uno!" agreed Maria with a happy smile as Annie flung her in a circle.

Elizabeth backed away from the circle of girls hugging and congratulating each other. She was happy for the squad, but she couldn't care less about nationals. In fact, it was all a big pain. She had agreed to be on the squad in the first place only because Jessica had blackmailed her. After Jessica had discovered the truth about Elizabeth and Ken's fling, she had threatened to tell Todd everything if Elizabeth refused to be on her new squad. Elizabeth had hoped the squad would go to regionals, lose, and be done with it. Who would have thought they'd get this far?

"Hea-ther! Hea-ther!" yelled the girls, making a seat with their hands and lifting her in the air.

"Hey, Jessica, c'mon, you're the cocaptain!" shouted Annie, turning toward Elizabeth.

"What?" said Elizabeth, facing her with a startled expression on her face.

"C'mon, you guys, let's get Jess," said Annie to Maria and Sandy. "After all, there are two heroes here."

"No, no, I'm Elizabeth!" Elizabeth cried as the girls heaved her onto their shoulders. She struggled and tried to protest again, but the din of the crowd drowned her out.

Elizabeth sighed and relaxed, realizing she would have to ride it out. She forced a grin on her face, waving stiffly at the crowds as the girls carried her and Heather across the field.

"Jes-si-ca! Jes-si-ca!" yelled the girls, bouncing her in the air. Singing at the top of their lungs, they broke out into a round of "For She's a Jolly Good Fellow."

Elizabeth was mortified. Everybody could always tell her and Jessica apart. How could the girls have confused them? Jessica and Elizabeth might look identical, from their long golden-blond hair to their sparkling blue eyes to the matching dimples in their left cheeks, but that was where the similarities ended. In their styles and personality they were completely different. Jessica was on the wild side. She always wore funky clothes and tried out outrageous new hairstyles. Her look reflected her personality: Jessica liked to be seen. Jessica was happy as long as she was the center of the action, whether it be the center of a party, the center of a shopping mall, or the center of a beach. Elizabeth, on the other hand, preferred the periphery. While

Elizabeth liked having fun as much as her sister, she was more academic and socially minded. Elizabeth wrote a weekly column for *The Oracle*, the Sweet Valley High newspaper, and spent much of her spare time with her boyfriend, Todd Wilkins, or her best friend, Enid Rollins. Elizabeth was more conservative than her sister, preferring to wear comfortable clothing, her hair pulled back in a ponytail. From one look at them, from their styles to their demeanor, you could always tell them apart.

Well, thought Elizabeth as the girls paraded her and Heather across the field, *lately* I have *been acting more like Jessica than myself*. Not only did she *look* like Jessica in her cheerleading attire, but she'd been acting like her too. When Jessica had started dating Ken Matthews, Elizabeth had been consumed with jealousy. She had found herself acting completely out of character—wishing the worst for her sister, hoping she didn't enjoy herself, trying to sabotage her sister's dates.

And then she had pulled an uncharacteristically manipulative move. In a misguided effort to resolve her feelings for Ken, Elizabeth had disguised herself as Jessica and had gone out with him. Fortunately, when they had kissed, there had been no spark. Elizabeth had discovered then and there that the only person she wanted to be kissing was Todd. Ken had realized at the same moment that he was kissing Elizabeth, not Jessica. Elizabeth had explained everything, and Ken had been very understanding. They both had decided to go straight to Todd's to come clean about the fling they'd had when Todd was living in Vermont. But when she and Ken had driven up to Todd's house, they had found that Jessica had beaten them to it. Jessica had discovered Elizabeth's ploy and had driven straight over to Todd's, Elizabeth's diary in hand. Neither Jessica nor Todd had given them a chance to explain. Todd had broken up with her then and there. And she and Jessica hadn't spoken since. Elizabeth had never felt so alone in her life.

Finally Elizabeth saw the bleachers come into sight again. She heaved a sigh of relief as the girls deposited her onto the field. She had always known that she didn't want to be the center of attention, but this clinched it. Suddenly her face blanched as she noticed Jessica standing by the bleachers waiting for them, her arms crossed stiffly across her chest.

"Jessica!" Elizabeth exclaimed, speechless.

"What's wrong, Liz?" said Jessica, fire in her eyes. "It's not enough to steal my boyfriend, but you've got to steal my glory too?"

Elizabeth turned to face her, sputtering. "You . . . you don't understand," she said. But Jessica was already stomping across the field, her blond ponytail swishing behind her.

Chapter 2

"So tell us all about it, Elizabeth!" said Mrs. Wakefield brightly on Monday morning, setting down on the butcher-block table a bowl of granola and yogurt adorned with fresh strawberries. She laid a plateful of warm blueberry muffins next to it. In her pale-pink linen suit, Alice Wakefield looked as crisp and fresh as the balmy California day.

"About what?" mumbled Elizabeth, her nose stuck in her orange-juice glass.

"About your victory at State on Saturday!" Mrs. Wakefield said, pulling up a chair and giving Elizabeth her full attention.

"Oh, well, we won," muttered Elizabeth, averting her eyes. Her mother was acting especially chipper this morning, she thought, bustling around the sunny Wakefield kitchen preparing breakfast. Elizabeth usually appreciated her mother's good humor, but this morning she wasn't in the mood for it. She felt blacker than the bitter black coffee she was drinking.

"That's quite an achievement, isn't it?" said Mr. Wakefield, picking up the bowl of granola and serving them all. "The cheerleaders have never even gone to State before, right?"

"Quite an achievement," muttered Elizabeth sarcastically. "Winning the Nobel Peace Prize, that's an achievement. Being awarded the Purple Heart for bravery, that's an achievement. Winning a Pulitzer Prize, that's an achievement. Cheerleading? That's stupid."

"Elizabeth!" said Mrs. Wakefield sharply.

Elizabeth looked down at the table. Her outburst was completely out of character. "I'm sorry," she said, tears filling her eyes. *That was completely unnecessary,* Elizabeth thought, berating herself. Usually she could put up a pretty good front when things weren't going right, but today it didn't seem to be working. Elizabeth was dreading the day ahead. She was sure to come across Todd at school, and she had to face Jessica at cheerleading practice. The two people she loved most in the world weren't speaking to her, and it was all her fault. Tears clouded her vision again, and Elizabeth ducked her head, pressing a napkin to her eyes.

"That's all right, sweetie," said Mrs. Wakefield, patting her hand and looking at her with concern.

"Where's Jessica?" asked Mr. Wakefield, changing the subject abruptly. "Isn't she going to be late for school?"

"She's probably getting her beauty sleep," said Elizabeth wryly.

Just then Jessica came careening into the room, her sunglasses in hand and her book bag flung over her shoulder. "Hey, Mom, have you seen my pom-poms?" she asked in a rush.

Jessica looked particularly striking, thought Elizabeth. She was wearing a floral-print teal baby-doll dress that brought out the sparkle in her blue-green eyes and accentuated her honey-blond hair. *She's probably spent hours this morning preparing for all the attention she'll get at school today,* thought Elizabeth.

"They're in the den, dear," said Mrs. Wakefield tolerantly, "where you left them yesterday."

"Good morning, Dad," Jessica said, pointedly ignoring Elizabeth.

"Morning, sweetheart," Mr. Wakefield answered. Jessica grabbed a muffin for the road and ran out of the room. "See you later!" she called.

A few minutes later Elizabeth could hear Jessica rev the engine and pull away in the twins' Jeep. Usually Jessica and Elizabeth shared a ride to school, but ever since the incident with Ken, Jessica had taken to leaving without her.

"Well, Mom," Elizabeth said with a sigh, "it looks like you'll have to give me a ride to school on your way to work again."

"Drama-club member Bill Chase encountered high drama at Bridgewater's Shakespeare Festival last weekend," read Elizabeth, murmuring to herself as she skimmed the contents of her article on the computer screen. It was Monday after school and Elizabeth was at the *Oracle* office, putting the final touches on her "Personal Profiles" column for the week. She sat back and gnawed on a fingernail, thinking of an appropriate conclusion. "A dramatic finish to a dramatic event," she typed in quickly, adding the final period with a flourish. Elizabeth scrolled up and scanned the entire article quickly. Satisfied with the results, she pressed "save" and "print."

"Here you go, Penny," Elizabeth said, pulling the article from the printer and handing it to Penny Ayala, the lanky, fair-haired editor in chief of the newspaper and a good friend of Elizabeth's.

"Thanks, Liz," said Penny warmly, taking the page from her. She whistled softly as she perused the article. "Wow, you sure are on the ball. We don't need this until Wednesday."

"I know," said Elizabeth, "but I'm going to be busy with cheerleading practice all week." She made a face and Penny laughed. "In fact," Elizabeth said, glancing down at her watch, "I've got to run or I'm going to be late."

Elizabeth swung her book bag over her shoulder and rushed to the door.

"Whoa!" said a laughing voice.

"Mr. Collins!" Elizabeth exclaimed as she collided with the newspaper's faculty adviser at the door. She jumped out of his way quickly. "Sorry!" she said.

"That's all right, no harm done," said Mr. Collins

good-naturedly, walking into the office and dropping his briefcase on a chair. He rubbed his right arm. "I didn't really need this arm, anyway," he joked.

Elizabeth smiled. Mr. Collins always managed to cheer her up. Not only was Mr. Collins Elizabeth's favorite English teacher, but she considered him a friend as well.

"Actually, Liz, I'm glad I bumped into you," said Mr. Collins.

"And you did bump into me!" quipped Elizabeth.

Mr. Collins grinned as he popped open his briefcase. He rummaged through the papers and pulled out a list of story assignments. "Listen, Liz, I've got a favor to ask you."

"Sure," Elizabeth said amenably, hopping up on a stool by the drafting table. "Shoot."

"I need someone to write the front-page story for the upcoming edition, and we're a little shorthanded," explained Mr. Collins. "Olivia Davidson was supposed to write the coverage, but she's at home sick. And John Pfeifer is out on a sports beat, covering the tennis-team championships."

"I'd be happy to write the story," said Elizabeth agreeably. "When do you need it?"

"Actually, it's a bit of a rush," said Mr. Collins, an apologetic expression on his face. "We need to get the paper to press this afternoon."

Elizabeth calculated quickly. She could probably crank out the article in half an hour. With any luck the girls would probably still be limbering up when she arrived at the athletic field. She'd miss the warm-up exercises, but she'd be there in time for practice.

"So do you think you can manage it?" asked Mr. Collins, looking at her anxiously.

Elizabeth nodded. "Sure, no problem," she said.

"Great, great," said Mr. Collins, looking visibly relieved. "The article's a feature story on the cheerleading victory at State this weekend."

Elizabeth's jaw dropped. "The cheerleading victory at State?" she repeated.

"That's right," said Mr. Collins. "In fact, now that you've joined the squad, you're the perfect person to cover it." He patted her on the shoulder and walked away.

Elizabeth groaned as she headed back to the computer. She could easily envision what the story should be: a peppy, spirited article full of cheerleading puns and school spirit. She just couldn't imagine herself writing it.

Elizabeth flicked on the computer and stared at the blank screen, trying to summon the energy to write the appropriate coverage. What was there to say? she wondered. The SVH cheerleading squad went to State and they won. Finis, end of story. *OK, just get down the basic facts,* Elizabeth encouraged herself. *Start at the beginning.* She concentrated on the journalistic convention of packing all the newsworthy information into the first line. Who? The cheerleaders. What? The state championship. Where? Santa Barbara. When? Saturday. Why? She couldn't imagine.

Writing about cheerleading was even harder than doing it, thought Elizabeth with a sigh. She wouldn't have had such a problem writing a cheerleading article the week before. When Jessica had first coerced her into joining the squad, Elizabeth had been miserable. The thought of jumping around in a silly little skirt made her stomach turn. But then she found herself getting into it despite herself. She had actually enjoyed the challenge of preparing for the state championship. But now she was sick of it, and fighting with Jessica had taken every bit of the fun out of it.

Elizabeth put her head in her hands. Why did Mr. Collins have to assign her this story, of all things? Then she shook herself and sat upright, forcing herself to tackle the first line. "In an unprecedented event the Sweet Valley High cheerleading squad, cocaptained by Jessica Wakefield and Heather Mallone, championed a first-place victory at the state championships on Saturday at Santa Barbara." Hmm, this wasn't so hard, Elizabeth thought, continuing to type. "The cheerleaders will be competing in the national championship in Yosemite next weekend."

Forty-five minutes later Elizabeth was still sitting in front of the screen. She had managed to get down the basic facts, but she couldn't seem to infuse the article with the enthusiasm it warranted. Now she was almost an hour late for practice. Elizabeth felt like tearing her hair out. "I give up," she said finally, throwing up her hands. She quickly typed in a title—"*V* for Victory"—and printed out the article.

"Penny!" Elizabeth called. "Do you think you could help me out here for a minute?"

"Sure, one sec!" Penny said, crouched on the floor in front of a full-page spread. She carefully laid out the final photograph, smoothing it down with the back of her hand. Then she jumped up and joined Elizabeth.

"Penny, I need your help," said Elizabeth, raking a hand through her hair. "I'm writing this feature story about cheerleading that needs to get out today, and I've got to get to cheerleading practice. The story is late—no, *I'm* late, and I can't seem to get the cheerleading spirit into my practice—I mean, my story." She stopped, confused.

"OK, slow down and take a deep breath," Penny instructed. Elizabeth breathed in deeply, trying to calm herself.

"Now, start all over," Penny said. "What's the problem?"

"The problem is that I haven't finished this State cheerleading story and I'm late for practice. I've got down the basic facts, but it's lacking any flair—you know, school-spirit stuff," explained Elizabeth. "Do you think you could just add the finishing touches?"

"Consider it done!" said Penny, taking the article out of her hand. "I'd be happy to spice it up a bit."

"Penny, are you sure?" asked Elizabeth, biting her lip.

"Of course!" said Penny, taking a seat in front of the computer. She made a shooing motion with her hand. "Now get out of here!"

"Thanks, Penny," Elizabeth said, smiling gratefully. "I owe you one!"

"Just don't bang up your hands flipping," said Penny. "We need you here!"

I can't seem to do anything right these days, sighed Elizabeth as she flew into the girls' locker room to change into her cheerleading-practice attire. She had always prided herself on her work at the newspaper. Elizabeth never shirked her duty. No matter how tight the deadline, she always managed to complete her assignments. It was a commonplace around the office that in a crisis Elizabeth was the woman to get the job done. Usually she found herself taking up the slack, finishing up other people's work. But this time she'd had to pass her article off on Penny. And she was still late for cheerleading practice— over an hour late.

Jessica will probably think I'm late on purpose, thought Elizabeth as she slammed her locker door shut. But it was probably just as well that she missed the beginning of practice, she reasoned, trying to reassure herself. That way she wouldn't have to worry about talking—or not talking—to her sister.

When Elizabeth finally arrived in the gym in her cheerleading attire, however, the girls hadn't yet begun to practice. They were sitting together in a circle on the floor.

"Hi, Elizabeth!" Sandy Bacon and Jean West waved. Maria Santelli patted a place on the floor by her side for Elizabeth to sit down. Elizabeth smiled weakly and took a seat next to her.

"Oh, Liz, how gracious of you to show up," Jessica said sarcastically.

"Sorry," Elizabeth said. "I got held up at *The Oracle*."

"Well, you're going to have to rearrange your priorities if you plan to stay on the team," said Jessica in a patronizing tone.

Elizabeth gritted her teeth. As if she had any interest in staying on the team! She felt like screaming out for everyone to hear: "If you weren't blackmailing me, I wouldn't come near your stupid squad!" But of course Elizabeth couldn't say anything. Jessica had her over a barrel.

"Well," said Jessica, standing up. "Now that we're all *finally* here . . ." Emphasizing each word for Elizabeth's benefit, she paused meaningfully. "I guess we can begin."

Elizabeth was horrified. Had Jessica made the team wait an entire hour just to show her up? She felt a blush crawl slowly up her neck to her cheeks. "Were you all waiting for me?" Elizabeth whispered worriedly to Maria.

Maria shook her head emphatically. "Don't worry," she reassured her. "Jessica and Heather have been having a little debate."

Elizabeth raised her eyebrows and looked at her quizzically. "About costumes," Maria said, rolling her eyes.

Elizabeth couldn't help grinning.

"Do you mind?" said Jessica, glaring at both

of them. "We have business to take care of."

"Sorry, sorry," mumbled Elizabeth and Maria.

"Thank you!" Jessica said curtly. "Now, as you know, the national competition is being held in California this year—in Yosemite. I have just received the official roster of all the teams competing." She held up a piece of paper rolled up like a scroll. "I'll read off the names so we know what we're up against." Jessica unfurled the list and began to read aloud when Heather swiped it out of the air.

"Lemme see that!" Heather snarled.

Elizabeth was surprised at Heather's obvious aggressiveness. Heather usually hid her real motives behind a candy-coated smile and a gracious veneer. Jessica thought Heather was a calculating witch, and Elizabeth tended to agree with her. When Heather had first arrived, Elizabeth had tried to give her a chance. Heather had seemed like a very interesting and talented girl with a genuine love for cheerleading. Elizabeth had thought Jessica was just jealous of all the attention the new girl was receiving.

But after Heather had taken over the cheerleading squad, Elizabeth had changed her mind. First Heather had fired Maria and Sandy behind Jessica's back. Then she had slowly usurped Jessica's authority, finally causing her to quit her own squad. Heather might have a genuine goal to make the Sweet Valley High cheerleaders the best in the country, thought Elizabeth, but she didn't care whom she hurt in the process.

"Hey!" said Jessica, and tried to grab the list back, but Heather was oblivious. She was furiously scanning the list. Suddenly her face went white.

"Look! Thomas Jefferson High in Reno," exclaimed Amy Sutton, who had been reading over her shoulder. "That's your old team, Heather!"

"Of course it's my old team. Don't you think I know that?" snapped Heather.

An uncomfortable silence greeted her strange response. Amy coughed nervously and a few of the girls looked to Jessica for guidance.

Jessica shrugged and stared at Heather, her arms folded across her chest.

"Well," said Heather a moment later, pulling herself together, "I guess that somehow they're managing without me."

"I can't imagine how," said Jessica snidely, grabbing the list back from Heather and continuing to read aloud. "Brattleboro, Burlington, Evanston High, Hartford, Little Rock, Pawtucket, Riverdale, Tampa Bay . . ."

Elizabeth watched the exchange with interest. Heather still seemed to look a little blanched. *Something's up here,* Elizabeth thought, her reporter's nose sensing trouble.

"Well, another episode of the Jessica-Heather saga comes to a close," said Lila to Amy as she steered her lime-green Triumph into the parking lot of the Dairi Burger, Sweet Valley's most popular teen hangout. The girls had accomplished practically nothing at practice. Jessica and Heather couldn't agree on which cheers to practice, and they had finally given up and just discussed logistics concerning nationals. The girls had decided to stop in at the Dairi Burger for burgers and shakes to wind down after practice.

"The soap opera continues," said Amy, jumping out of the car and slamming the door. "Tune in next week for the rousing conclusion to our six-part miniseries: Jessica and Heather at the national competition."

Lila laughed and then shook her head ruefully. "If those two don't get it together," she said, "we're going to be the laughingstock of the competition."

"I know," Amy agreed as she crossed the lot with Lila.

"I never realized how competitive cheerleading is," Lila remarked. "I always thought cheerleaders just stood on the sidelines."

"Not around here, that's for sure," said Amy, running her fingers through her long blond hair.

"Wow, check out the scene," said Lila as they reached the wooden door of the Dairi Burger. The restaurant was hopping, as usual. It seemed like everybody from Sweet Valley High had decided to stop in at the Dairi Burger after practice. Members of the girls' cheerleading squad as well as the boys' football and basketball teams were converging on the door at once.

"Hey, there's Jessica and Elizabeth," said Amy, pointing to the front of the room.

"And there's Todd and Ken," said Lila, raising her eyebrows.

Amy and Lila watched as Jessica and Elizabeth grabbed the same table by mistake. They both mumbled something unintelligible and quickly moved to separate tables. At the same time, Todd and Ken sat down together, then quickly got up and moved unwittingly to Jessica and Elizabeth's separate tables.

"Can you believe this?" said Lila, watching with a bemused smile as a Charlie Chaplin–like scene ensued.

"Jessica!" said Ken, a shocked expression on his face.

"If you'll excuse me," said Jessica, jumping up.

"Elizabeth!" said Todd, anger and hurt creasing his features. He quickly shoved back his chair.

"Oh, no, please allow me," said Elizabeth, holding out a hand.

All four of them stood up together. Elizabeth and Jessica quickly took their own booths, and Ken and Todd sat back down at the separate tables. Now Jessica, Elizabeth, Todd, and Ken had taken the only available tables in the restaurant.

"Well, there's nowhere left to sit now," said Lila, her arms folded across her chest. "It will sure make life easier for everybody when the Bobbsey twins and their boyfriends are on speaking terms again."

"Hi, everybody!" Heather exclaimed, waltzing into the restaurant as Jessica sat down alone in a booth.

"Hi, Heather!" returned some seniors from the girls' tennis team seated near the front of the restaurant. A bunch of admiring sophomore girls waved from a table. "Look, Heather's here!" somebody said.

"The queen appears," mumbled Jessica to herself as Heather made her grand entrance. Annie Whitman, who idolized Heather, was close on her tail. Jessica groaned inwardly as a few of the guys whistled appreciatively. "Lookin' good!" yelled Bruce Patman.

Heather stood by the door and swept the restaurant with a regal gaze, savoring the attention she was receiving. She walked through the crowd slowly, which seemed to part like the Red Sea to make way for her. Finally she stopped by Jessica's table.

"Well, it looks like the Wakefields, et al., have taken over the restaurant," said Heather in a loud, patronizing tone, "so we'll have to sit with Jessie here."

Jessica bristled at the name "Jessie" but didn't rise to the bait.

"Please do," said Jessica, putting on a huge smile. Heather and Annie piled into the seat across from Jessica.

Lila and Amy followed suit, sliding into the booth on Jessica's side.

"Hey, Jess," said Lila teasingly, "playing musical chairs again?"

"Yeah, it's a really fun game," responded Jessica sardonically.

Just then the waitress appeared. All of the girls ordered shakes—except for Heather, of course, who ordered her signature Diet Coke with lemon and a straw—and they got a few orders of fries for the table.

"I can't believe we're going to be competing against your old squad," said Annie to Heather excitedly. "I'll bet they're no good without you. You were the captain, right?"

Jessica feigned a huge yawn. "Do we have to go through all this again? Haven't we heard enough about Heather's illustrious cheerleading career?" She went on in a singsong voice. "Heather was the captain of the Thomas Jefferson cheerleading squad. Thomas Jefferson won State for ten years straight. Heather *personally* took her team to State for two years in a row, and they won both years all because of her fabulous combinations. Heather won the award for best cheerleader in Reno her sophomore year, and—"

"Jessica's right," Heather said, interrupting her. "That's all ancient history. Now, if you'll all excuse me, I have to study for the French quiz tomorrow."

"But Heather," Annie protested, "your Diet Coke—"

"I'm not really thirsty," said Heather, jumping up abruptly and throwing some bills onto the table. "See you all tomorrow at practice." She grabbed her gym bag and made her way to the door.

"Heather passed up an opportunity to brag?" said Jessica, shocked at Heather's uncharacteristic behavior. "She must have a fever!"

"Je veux, tu veux, il/elle veut," recited Elizabeth,

her French book open in front of her. "I want, you want, he/she wants. *Je veux, tu veux, il/elle veut,*" she repeated. "*Je veux, je ne veux pas . . .*" Elizabeth's mind wandered off. *What I* want *is to have my sister and my boyfriend back*, she thought. *What I* don't want *is to study French verbs.*

It was Monday evening, and Elizabeth was hunched over her desk, trying to memorize the conjugations of irregular verbs for the French quiz in Ms. Dalton's class the next day. She'd been trying to study for an hour, but she couldn't concentrate. As soon as she tried to go over a verb in her head, she found herself repeating Todd's name, or Jessica's.

Elizabeth rubbed her weary eyes and made another stab at it. "*Je peux, tu peux, il/elle peut,*" she read. "I can, you can, he/she can. *Je peux, tu peux, il/elle peut, je peux . . . Non, je ne peux pas!*" she said finally, slamming the book shut.

It was time to talk to Jessica, Elizabeth realized. Until Elizabeth explained the situation to her, she wasn't going to have any peace. When Elizabeth and Ken had driven over to Todd's that fateful night the week before, Jessica hadn't given Elizabeth a chance to tell her side of the story. And since then Jessica had refused to speak to her—unless she had something particularly nasty to say. Elizabeth couldn't really blame her. Jessica thought Elizabeth had been trying to steal her boyfriend away from her. Somehow Elizabeth had to let her know that that wasn't the case.

Well, decided Elizabeth, just because Jessica

wasn't speaking to her didn't mean she couldn't speak to Jessica.

Elizabeth stood up with determination and swiftly crossed the bathroom adjoining the twins' rooms. Usually Jessica's door was wide open, but now it was shut.

Elizabeth tapped on the door softly. There was no response. Elizabeth knocked again. No answer.

Elizabeth pushed the door open and peeked in. Jessica was sitting cross-legged on the floor in the middle of what looked like an avalanche, scribbling something on a piece of paper.

"Don't you knock?" Jessica asked, repeating Elizabeth's favorite line.

"I did knock," Elizabeth said.

"Well, there's nobody here," said Jessica, scooting her legs around and turning her back on Elizabeth.

"What are you doing?" Elizabeth asked, venturing into the room. "Are you writing a cheer?"

"What I'm doing is not speaking to you," said Jessica childishly.

"Fine." Elizabeth sighed. "You don't have to say anything. But could you just listen for a few minutes?"

"I'll give you five minutes," Jessica said, flipping around and leaning against the bed, her arms folded squarely across her chest.

Elizabeth began pacing through the piles of clothing strewn about on the floor. "I want to explain about the other night," she began. "I know it looked bad, but it isn't as bad as you think. When you started dating Ken, I still had unresolved feelings for him. And I didn't feel happy for you, because I was jealous."

Elizabeth stopped and sat on the bed, waiting to see if Jessica would respond. Jessica just sat on the floor in silence, her eyes fixed on the bureau across the room. Elizabeth took a deep breath and plunged ahead. "So I pretended I was you so I could find out how I felt. And what I found out is that I felt nothing. And I want you to know that it was all my fault. Ken didn't know anything about it. He kissed me because he thought I was you. And he stopped as soon as he realized I wasn't."

Elizabeth slid off the bed and knelt down by Jessica, looking at her imploringly. "Jessica, you have to believe me. I wasn't trying to steal your boyfriend. I was just trying to seal off the past. So I could get over Ken. And so I could be happy for you."

Jessica stood up suddenly. "I don't want to hear another word of this," she said angrily, throwing her pen and pad on the bed. "I don't care what your intentions were. What if you had found out that you still had feelings for Ken, Liz?" Jessica kicked at the clothing on the floor. "Then what would you have done? Sneaked around again like you did when Todd was gone?" Jessica looked away in disgust. "You and Ken make me sick, with all your sneaking around. You two are meant for each other."

"But . . . but we're not sneaking around," Elizabeth protested.

Jessica ignored her. "And you know what else, Liz?" she sneered. "I don't believe you. I think you still have feelings for Ken. You couldn't stand to see me and Ken together, so you forced us to break up. And now you want me to be your friend again. Well, Liz, you can't have your cake and eat it too."

Tears began to trickle down Elizabeth's face as Jessica continued her diatribe.

"Look, Liz," Jessica spat out finally. "Why don't you just admit the truth? You wanted to get me back for blackmailing you, so you decided to steal my boyfriend." She fixed her sister with a piercing look. "Well, you won, Liz. Are you happy now?"

Elizabeth stared at her sister in shock, amazed that she didn't believe her. Her shock quickly turned to hurt as Elizabeth mentally replayed the angry accusations Jessica had thrown at her. But her hurt rapidly transformed into anger. Jessica had no right to act so high-and-mighty. She hadn't exactly been acting like an angel lately, thought Elizabeth self-righteously. Elizabeth had forgiven Jessica for blackmailing her. Not only had she forgiven her, but she had actually helped her out when she'd had trouble with the squad.

Well, decided Elizabeth stubbornly, she had made her effort. She wasn't going to beg for Jessica's forgiveness any longer. She was sick and tired of being a sap when it came to her sister. If Jessica wanted a fight, then she would get it.

"Well, if you don't believe me," Elizabeth said, standing up and speaking in a cold, removed tone, "then that's your business."

"I don't. Now, would you mind leaving?" Jessica asked. "Because your five minutes are up, and I'm not speaking to you any longer!"

"Well, that's fine with me," retorted Elizabeth. "Because I'm not speaking to you, either!" With that, she stormed out of the room, slamming the door behind her.

Chapter 3

"OK, guys, let's get psyched!" Jessica said on Tuesday afternoon at practice. "We've got three days to get in shape for nationals. We looked great at State, and we're going to look even better in Yosemite."

Jessica was determined to get the squad back on track. She and Heather had called for double practices all week, and the practice session that morning had been disastrous. The girls had wasted the entire morning trying to imitate Heather's combination jump—at Heather's suggestion, of course. Heather knew perfectly well that the other girls wouldn't be able to do it. It was just another opportunity for her to show off. But Jessica was determined not to waste any more time. She wasn't going to let Heather undermine her authority any further.

"So," continued Jessica, "Heather and I have come up with a schedule of our best routines for nationals. We'll start out with the combination we did at state. Now, everybody get in position for the 'Funky Monkey.'"

Jessica took her place in front as all the girls lined up behind her.

"C'mon everybody, do the 'Fun-ky Monkey'!" sang out Jessica, taking two steps to the right and turning in a circle.

"S-V-H's a-rockin', we're groovin' and we're hunky!" she called out.

All the girls joined in as Jessica led them through a series of intricate moves. "We're SVH, we're SVH," the girls called out, clapping their hands and hitting their thighs, "and we're funkin'."

"Fun-ky, fun-ky," chanted Jade Wu and Patty Gilbert, snapping their fingers on the sidelines.

"The Funky Monkey," finished the girls, shooting up in the air in stag leaps and coming down in unison in landing splits.

"Funky, funky!" said Jade and Patty again, putting on dark sunglasses and pointing at an imaginary audience.

The girls burst into laughter and collapsed onto the ground, repeating "funky, funky" and cocking their hands at the stands.

"Great, you guys!" exclaimed Jessica. "Now let's try it from the top one more time. This time I'll face you."

The girls got in line and Jessica assumed her position in front of them. "C'mon, everybody—" Suddenly Jessica stopped as she realized that Heather was sitting on the sidelines.

"Is there a problem?" asked Jessica, her voice flat.

"Oh, no, no problem," said Heather sweetly. "I thought I'd just sit out the warm-up."

"Here we go again," Lila sighed under her breath, sliding down to lean against the bench.

"The festivities begin," said Amy, joining Lila on the ground. She pulled off her ponytail holder and shook out her long blond hair.

Jessica shot them a warning look and fixed Heather with a steely stare. "This isn't a warm-up," said Jessica.

"Well, if you want to go ahead and repeat all our old cheers at nationals, that's fine with me," said Heather. "But I really don't think it's necessary for me to go through all of them again."

"Heather, as I recall," said Jessica through clenched teeth, "we decided *together* to perform these cheers at nationals."

"Oh, well, we must have just had a slight misunderstanding. I thought we were just choosing our best cheers. I never *dreamed* you'd want to repeat our old cheers for the national competition," said Heather, her tone sugar sweet.

"And I suppose you have a better suggestion," said Jessica, her voice strained.

"Obviously, if we want to win at nationals, we have to come up with an entirely new set of cheers," said Heather in a haughty tone.

"Which *you* just happen to have made up already," said Jessica.

"Well, I did come up with a few new routines

this weekend," said Heather. She flashed the girls an enthusiastic smile. "I'd love to show them to you. They're jazzy combinations, but technically complicated as well. If we could get them down, I think we'd really knock them dead at nationals."

"Heather, we have got exactly three days to prepare for the national competition. Three days," said Jessica, her voice strong. "We can either spend this time wisely perfecting our old cheers or waste it trying to learn brand-new ones. Perfection or mediocrity—it's your choice." Jessica faced Heather head-on, an unspoken challenge in her eyes.

"You're right, Jessica," said Heather sweetly. "We shouldn't take the chance. After all, better be safe than sorry, right? And we'll probably end up in the top ten anyway."

"I want to learn Heather's new cheers!" interjected Annie.

"Yeah," chimed in Jeanie. "Our routine's getting kind of old."

"I think Jessica's right," put in Lila, trying to help Jessica out. "It would be suicide to try to learn new cheers now."

"Well, why don't we take a vote?" suggested Elizabeth. *Always the diplomat,* thought Jessica, annoyed.

"OK, all in favor of learning new cheers, raise your hands," said Elizabeth. Jessica grimaced as half the squad raised their hands. "All in favor of doing our old cheers, raise your hands." Jessica held her breath as the rest of the girls raised their hands. It was a tie. Jessica threw up her hands in frustration. It was clearly impossible to get anything done with Heather around.

"Well, why don't we do half and half?" suggested Maria. "Half of our old cheers and half of our new cheers."

"That's fine with me," said Heather cheerfully. "But we have to make sure Jessica agrees. After all, she's the other captain."

Jessica was fuming. Now they were going to spend the entire week learning Heather's new cheers. And if she didn't agree to the idea, she would look like a spoilsport. "Sure, no problem," said Jessica shortly, her jaw clenched.

"Great!" said Heather, jumping up. "Now, first, I want to show you the 'Mambo Jamba.' It's a pretty sexy cheer, with a Latino influence."

Jessica gritted her teeth and got into line with the rest of the girls. She couldn't believe it. Heather had done it again.

Elizabeth flipped her gym bag over her shoulder and hurried out of the gym. Practice was finally over. She didn't know how much more of this cheerleading charade she could take. Not only were she and Jessica not speaking, but the cat fight between Heather and Jessica was getting unbearable.

Suddenly Elizabeth stopped dead in her tracks. Todd was coming her way from the opposite end of the football field on his way out of basketball practice. Elizabeth's heart started pounding in her chest. Todd looked so handsome in his blue sweats and white T-shirt. His strong, athletic frame was outlined by his clothes, and his dark-brown hair was ruffled from the wind.

Elizabeth instinctively turned back to the gym, but then she caught herself. This was the first time she'd seen Todd alone since they'd broken up. Because he'd refused to give her a chance to explain, she'd been too upset to pursue him. But he did deserve an explanation. She didn't blame him for being hurt. Elizabeth hesitated. She didn't have much of an explanation to give him. What if he wouldn't forgive her? Well, she decided, she could at least give it a try. She wasn't about to give him up without a fight.

"Todd!" called Elizabeth, hurrying up to him.

"Hi, Elizabeth," Todd said, his voice cold. He walked past her without even turning his head.

"Todd, please!" Elizabeth implored. "Just hear me out for a minute."

Todd turned and stopped, his arms folded across his chest.

Elizabeth stared at him. Now that she finally had his attention, she found herself at a loss for words. Todd took a step as if to walk off. "Wait!" Elizabeth said, catching his arm. Todd flinched and pulled away from her. Elizabeth, hurt, forged ahead anyway.

"I—I just want to apologize for seeing Ken while you were away in Vermont—and for not telling you about it," Elizabeth began. "I know how wrong it was, and I know how much I've hurt you. And I want to try to explain. . . ." Elizabeth hesitated and swallowed hard. "Todd, after you moved to Vermont, I had no intention of seeing Ken. I don't know how it happened. I guess we both missed you, and we turned to each other in your absence. But it didn't mean anything. And we should have told you about it right away when you came back. But I felt so confused and so guilty—" Tears came to Elizabeth's eyes. She'd always prided herself on her honesty. She glanced at Todd through her tears, but he looked unmoved, staring at her with unfathomable eyes.

"And then, when Jessica started seeing him, I felt—I felt confused again. Because I'd never really resolved my feelings for Ken." Elizabeth could see Todd visibly wince, and she took a deep breath. "So I went out with him just to see, to find out if there were feelings between us. And, Todd, I know it sounds horrible, but I wanted to be fair. I wanted to be fair to you and to us. I needed to know once and for all. Does that make any sense to you?" She looked up at him with pleading eyes, but his expression remained inscrutable.

"So, uh, when we were out on that date, we kissed," Elizabeth continued. "And there was nothing there. I realized then and there that the only person I wanted to be with was you. And now I'm afraid I've lost you forever. Todd, I'm so sorry about what I've done. I'll never cheat on you again. You're the one I love."

Elizabeth stopped and looked up at him, feeling completely vulnerable.

• • •

Todd was incredulous as he listened to Elizabeth ramble on. Did she think she could just say she was sorry and everything would be better? What kind of a fool did she think he was?

Todd had been deeply wounded, and his pride had taken a serious bruising. He had forgiven Elizabeth when she'd had a fling with Luke the summer she was in London. Of course, he'd had a little fling of his own. But this was different. She fooled around with his best friend! Behind his back!

He'd trusted them, Todd berated himself. To think he'd asked Ken to look after Elizabeth. *He sure did a good job looking after her,* Todd thought bitterly. And then they went out *again* when he was around! Well, Todd was sick of playing Mr. Nice Guy. Elizabeth couldn't get Ken, so now she wanted Todd back. But Todd wasn't going to play second fiddle to anybody, *especially* not to his best friend.

And now she was giving him this story about her date with Ken. That she didn't have any feelings for Ken. That she had been thinking about Todd the whole time. Well, maybe he had trusted her once, but he wasn't going to make the same mistake twice.

"Look, Elizabeth," said Todd finally, his voice even. "You can save your breath. You're not the person I thought you were, and I'm better off without you."

Elizabeth stared at him, openmouthed.

"Hope Ken likes your latest cheer," Todd bit out as he left.

Elizabeth watched him go, tears trickling down her cheeks. *I've lost the only boy I could ever really love,* she thought. *And it's all my fault.*

"The salsa routine?" said Heather on Thursday afternoon at practice, an incredulous look on her face. "For the grand finale? You've got to be kidding."

Jessica fought to keep her temper in check. She had come up with the funky salsa cheer by herself. It was the routine that her squad had presented at the cheer-off, the competition between Jessica's and Heather's squads to see which team would go to regionals. The students had loved it. And Mr. Jenkins, the ACA representative, had been so impressed with it that he had recommended combining the two squads for the regional competition.

"I suppose you'd rather do a cheer of your own," said Jessica. "For the sake of the team, of course."

"Well, I certainly don't care whose idea it is," said Heather with a small flip of her head. "It's just that the salsa routine is lacking a little *je ne sais quoi*, if you know what I mean."

"No, I'm afraid I don't," said Jessica flatly. "Care to translate, Mademoiselle Mallone?"

"Well, to be perfectly blunt, it's not jazzy enough," said Heather. "I mean, it's completely adequate. But it's not going to make the judges notice us. If we want to win at nationals, we've got to stand out. We've got to do something really special."

"Like one of your new cheers, for example?" Jessica said, her voice dripping with sarcasm.

"For example," said Heather, pretending not to notice Jessica's tone. "I was hoping we could do the new hip-hop routine I've been working on. It's sure to bring the house down."

"Cool!" exclaimed Jade Wu. "We could add some neat dance steps."

"Yeah," said Annie, "it'll be like a rap video."

"MTV, here we come," said Sandy, drawing a general laugh.

Jessica didn't bother putting it up for a vote. She knew what the girls would say. Heather had them so bamboozled that they would do anything she said. They thought she had the magic recipe for winning the national competition.

"Sure, great idea," said Jessica, thinking quickly. Before practice she had resolved not to let Heather take over, and she was still determined to meet that goal. "But before we start practice, I think we should decide on the uniforms we're going to wear for the grand finale."

The girls gathered around on the field while Jessica pulled out the sample uniforms she had ordered from Cheer Ahead, the sporting-clothes outfitter. They were standard red-and-white cheerleading outfits with a twist: matching full-body unitards. Jessica held them up for everyone to see. "Classic, beautiful, right?" said Jessica. "But look," she said, indicating the red Lycra unitards. "Catsuits for an added touch."

"They're fabulous!" said Lila.

"The catsuits are great!" breathed Amy. "We'll look so sharp when we're flipping."

"They're the latest," said Jessica, smiling with satisfaction. She handed the uniforms around for the girls to examine. They were met with approval by everybody.

When the uniform came around to Heather, she held it up in the air and wrinkled her nose delicately.

"What's wrong, Heather?" Jessica sneered. "Are the uniforms offending your senses?"

"No, of course not," replied Heather. "They're just a little, ah, traditional. It's just a little surprising, coming from you. You're usually so, um, faddy."

Jessica could feel her face burning. Not only was Heather insulting her uniforms, she was insulting her style as well. "Yeah, well, I always thought it was better to be faddy than cheap," said Jessica angrily.

"OK, you two," said Amy, holding up a hand. "Heather, why don't you show us your uniforms, and we'll decide together?"

"Well, I had these custom-made," said Heather, holding up a sample uniform. Jessica couldn't believe it. The uniforms consisted of tiny Lycra half tops and red-and-white-checked miniskirts that fell at the hip. Jessica couldn't imagine how they could possibly walk in them, let alone cheer in them.

"They're perfect," Annie Whitman breathed. "Hipsters for our hip-hop cheer!"

"They're great," agreed Maria. "We'll be the hippest squad around."

Elizabeth, as usual, put it to a vote. Jessica seethed as she watched the majority of hands go up in favor of Heather's uniforms. Only Lila, Amy, and Elizabeth stood by her.

"Oh, well, I really think we should use the cute little uniforms Jessica chose," Heather said after the votes had been cast. "After all, Jessica is the co-captain. And she went to so much trouble."

"Don't even consider it," said Jessica shortly. "Now, if you'll excuse me," she said, getting up abruptly, "I don't think I'm really necessary with hippy, hip-hop Heather around." Jessica turned and stalked off without looking back.

"Jessica! Wait!" came a male voice from across the field.

Jessica looked across the football field. It was Ken Matthews on his way from football practice. He was wearing a cutoff T-shirt over his shoulder pads and carrying a football helmet. Jessica turned her head and continued to stomp across the field, but her heart started pounding in spite of herself. Ken looked stronger and handsomer than ever in his football gear.

"Jessica!" Ken yelled again, running after her. "I want to talk to you!"

Well, I don't want to talk to you, thought Jessica stubbornly. Ken Matthews was a waste of her time. If he couldn't distinguish her from Elizabeth, then he obviously didn't feel anything for her in particular; he just liked her type.

Ken caught up to her and ran in front of her, blocking her path. Jessica stopped and faced him, her eyes a stony blue. "If you're looking for Elizabeth," she said in an icy tone, "she's still at practice." She turned on her heel and walked away.

Chapter 4

"On behalf of the entire school, I want to thank all the girls on the cheerleading squad for their continued support of our athletic teams," said Mr. Cooper, the principal, his loud voice booming across the auditorium.

Jessica fidgeted in her seat, anxious to get on the road. The weekend of the national competition had arrived, and the entire school was sending the team off in royal style. The school had organized a huge pep rally in the auditorium, to be followed by a parade out to the parking lot with the marching band playing. The auditorium was a festive sight. The walls were adorned with banners and pennants, and multicolored streamers and balloons hung from the bleachers.

"The cheerleading squad is the power behind the throne, the strength behind the success of our teams . . ." said Mr. Cooper.

Jessica yawned and leaned over to Lila. "Isn't he overdoing it a bit?" she whispered.

Lila rolled her eyes. "Yeah, old Chrome Dome's in fine form this morning," she said.

". . . behind the football team, the basketball team, the soccer team, and the track team," continued the principal. As he mentioned each sport, the teams stood up in blocks, yelling and hooting. "And they're a strength in and of themselves," finished Mr. Cooper. "For the first time in the history of Sweet Valley High, the girls' cheerleading squad has won the state competition. And for the first time in the history of our school, the cheerleading squad is competing in the national competition!"

The auditorium filled with the sounds of students hooting and cheering. "Way to go, cheerleaders!" "SVH all the way!" Streamers and confetti were thrown into the air, and the band broke into a rousing version of the school song.

After the band had finished, Mr. Cooper held up a hand for the audience to settle down. "And now I'd like to turn the mike over to Ken Matthews, the captain of the football team and Sweet Valley's star quarterback."

Whistles and catcalls accompanied Ken's trip across the auditorium.

"Please, cash contributions only," he said, grinning as he took the mike. The audience laughed and Ken paused, his face turning serious. He cleared his throat and spoke into the microphone. "This year we had an outstanding season. We won the divisional and regional championships, and more important, we beat the Big Mesa Bulls, our greatest rivals."

Ken paused while cheers filled the air. "And I just want to say, we couldn't have done it without the cheerleaders' support. We'd have been nothing without Jessica Wakefield and her squad cheering us on—behind us all the way through thick and thin."

Jessica's face flushed as Ken spoke. She felt as if he were speaking directly to her. She stole a glance in Heather's direction to see if she'd noticed she hadn't been mentioned. Heather was staring straight ahead, a pout marring her delicate features. She'd flirted with Ken the entire time Jessica was seeing him, but Ken hadn't paid any attention to her. Jessica felt a surge of satisfaction and turned her attention back to the floor.

"So to the entire cheerleading squad," Ken finished, "these are from all of us to all of you." Ken laid a bunch of red roses on the podium and walked off the stage.

The crowd roared. "Speech! Speech! Speech!" demanded the students.

Before Jessica could react, Heather was on her feet and racing across the auditorium. When she reached the podium, she gathered the roses under her arm and picked up the microphone. "On behalf of my squad, I'd like to thank you all for your tremendous support. . . ."

"It's unbelievable," Jessica said to Lila. "That girl's a real piece of work."

"She really is revolting," Lila agreed.

"This is too much," said Amy, leaning over. "Those roses were meant for you. Heather steals the show every time."

"Well, not this time," said Jessica resolutely, jumping out of her seat. Heather might have stolen the limelight at State, but Jessica wasn't going to sit on the sidelines this time, not in her own school. She quickly ran across the stage and joined Heather at the podium. Heather stared at her openmouthed as Jessica grabbed the mike.

"Sweet Valley High's cheerleading squad is the greatest in the entire state of California!" Jessica yelled. "And we're going to be the greatest in the nation. We're going to get out there and win this weekend—for our teams and for our school!"

The crowd roared its approval, rising to its feet and yelling. Jessica picked up the mike again and called the squad to the field. The girls ran onto the stage and gave an impressive performance of their new hip-hop routine. The crowd ate it up, tapping their feet and chanting to the music.

At the end of the routine Heather finished with an unexpected jump, a spectacular series of one-armed cartwheels followed by a no-hands back flip. Undaunted, Jessica followed with a dazzling jump of her own, a trojan-jump combination ending with a landing in the splits.

"Is this for real?" Lila said to Amy.

Amy rolled her eyes. "Just another episode of the Jessica-Heather show."

"Tune in tomorrow," Lila said with a sigh.

• • •

"Wow, that was quite a pep rally!" exclaimed Enid Rollins, Elizabeth's best friend, as she accompanied her to the parking lot.

"It really was, wasn't it?" said Elizabeth, her cheeks glowing. The excitement was intoxicating, and Elizabeth found herself swept up in it. The entire student body was accompanying the cheerleaders to the parking lot, and the energy in the crowd was palpable. The students had formed a parade, throwing streamers and cheering as they poured out of the building. The band was heading up the rear, playing a medley of victory songs.

"Is that the bus?" Enid gasped as they arrived at the vehicle designated to transport the cheerleaders to Yosemite.

"Pretty impressive, huh?" Elizabeth laughed. The cheerleaders had spent hours decorating the bus the night before. They had covered it in psychedelic colors and wild abstract designs. A banner streamed off the back, with the words SWEET VALLEY RULES! written in bold purple block letters.

"Well, have a great time!" Enid said. "It looks like this won't be as bad as you thought."

"Thanks, Enid!" said Elizabeth. "I'll call you first thing when we get back." She mounted the steps and waved cheerfully as Enid walked away.

Suddenly Elizabeth caught sight of Todd standing alone on the sidewalk. He cut a lonely figure, looking lost and forlorn at the far end of the parking lot. The pain of losing him washed over Elizabeth again, and she fought down a feeling of physical nausea. The horrible, judgmental words that Todd had thrown at her came back again, echoing in her head. *You're not the person I thought you were, you're not the person I thought you were.* Elizabeth shook her head hard, trying to rid it of the painful thoughts. She wrenched her eyes away from Todd and headed into the bus."SVH is number one! SVH is number one!" chanted a group of football players as they carried Jessica across the parking lot on their shoulders. Jessica beamed and she blew kisses to the crowd, basking in the glory of the moment.

As they reached the bus, Tim Nelson and Scott Trost deposited Jessica gently on the asphalt. Jessica hopped down and climbed up the steps, turning to wave at the crowd. The students whistled and cheered, yelling "Good luck!" and "Knock 'em dead, Jessica!"

Jessica mounted the steps and climbed into the front seat, feeling like a queen. She looked out the window and caught a glimpse of Ken Matthews staring longingly after the bus. Jessica felt a stab of regret as she remembered Ken's effort to talk to her earlier in the week. But she quickly banished the thought from her mind. *He's probably pining for Elizabeth. Well, I'll never speak to him ever again,* she vowed, blowing kisses at all her fans through the window.

As the bus pulled away, Todd kicked at the gravel in the parking lot, wondering for the thousandth time how his life had gotten so bad so fast.

One day he thought he was the luckiest guy in the world, with the best girlfriend and the greatest best friend—and the next day he lost them both, to each other!

Once again the images of Ken and Elizabeth came to his mind, tormenting him. He pictured them together while he'd been alone in Vermont—running on the beach, stopping for an intimate talk, kissing each other passionately. . . . Todd shook his head hard, forcing his thoughts in a different direction. He had to stop torturing himself like this.

Elizabeth looked so sad getting on the bus, thought Todd. And so beautiful. He knew she must be miserable going to nationals with the cheerleading squad. He wondered how Jessica had roped her into that one. He wished he had forgiven her, so he could have seen her off—and held her for a moment before she left. *But you were stubborn as usual,* Todd berated himself. Elizabeth had asked for his forgiveness and he'd refused. And now it was too late. She was leaving, and she wouldn't have anything to do with him. Feeling sorry for himself, Todd plodded back into the school building.

At the same time, Ken Matthews was slowly making his way toward the door of Sweet Valley High, lost in thoughts of his own. Jessica had created quite a stir at the pep rally. Her final jump had brought down the house. Jessica made cheerleading seem like an art, thought Ken with admiration. She was talented and beautiful—and feisty. Nobody pushed Jessica Wakefield around. *That's probably why I like her so much,* thought Ken. *She's strong and sexy—and I've let her slip through my fingers.*

Ken had tried to send Jessica a private message through his public speech, but she hadn't so much as glanced at him. *If only I'd told Todd about Elizabeth from the beginning, none of this would have happened,* Ken chided himself. *Todd and I would still be friends, Todd and Elizabeth would still be together, and Jessica . . . Jessica would still be mine.*

As Todd got up to the door, the crowd piling into the school bottlenecked. He felt somebody shoving him against the door. Todd turned and found himself face-to-face with Ken Matthews. Anger boiled up inside him as he confronted his back-stabbing friend.

"Hey, man, get off of me!" yelled Todd, placing his hands squarely on Ken's chest and shoving him away.

"I didn't touch you!" Ken shouted back. He pushed him back with all his might, sending Todd reeling against the brick wall of the school building. Students jumped out of their way, and the crowd formed a circle around them.

Todd's eyes bulged with rage. "Keep your hands to yourself!" he yelled. "Leave me and my girlfriend alone!" He hurtled forward and aimed his fist at Ken's face.

Ken warded off the blow. "It's not my fault if you can't keep a girlfriend!" shouted Ken, directing a blow at Todd's stomach. "Maybe you should blame Elizabeth and not me!" Todd jumped adeptly to the side and hopped back and forth as he faced his adversary, a savage look on his face.

The crowd around them began to chant. "Fight! Fight! Fight!"

"The Wakefield girls aren't worth all this trouble!" taunted Bruce Patman from the crowd.

Ken and Todd looked up simultaneously and charged at Bruce like enraged bulls, jumping on him and wrestling him to the ground.

"All right! All right! Break it up!" yelled Mr. Collins, arriving on the scene. He tried to pull the boys off Bruce, but the two of them were oblivious, rolling around on the ground as they tried to get Bruce locked in a pin. Tim Nelson and Robbie Hendricks went for Todd, while Tad Johnson and Scott Trost turned to Ken. Finally the four of them managed to wrench the boys away from Bruce.

As the football players held Todd and Ken back, Bruce stood up insolently and wiped the dirt off his jeans. "Girls got you a little worked up, huh?" Bruce said, a jeering challenge in his eyes.

"Lemme at him!" growled Todd, struggling with his captors. Ken swiped at the air in vain while Tad and Scott held him back.

"I'm afraid you two need to have a chat with the principal," Mr. Collins said, putting his hands on their shoulders. Todd and Ken stopped struggling, and the boys dropped their hold. "Follow me, please," said Mr. Collins, escorting them to Mr. Cooper's office. The boys followed him begrudgingly, both sullen and not speaking. Bruce snickered as they were led away.

"I do not tolerate fighting in my school," said Mr. Cooper, looking like a puffed-up bird sitting behind his solid-oak desk. "Sweet Valley High prides itself on offering the finest education and the highest-quality moral training. Here at Sweet Valley all the students adhere to a strict code of ethics. *All the students,*" Mr. Cooper repeated. "Is that clear?"

"Yes, sir," said Todd and Ken together, listening politely as the principal went on. "A gentleman settles his arguments with words, not weapons," boomed Mr. Cooper, raising a forefinger into the air. "The lash of the tongue is mightier than the thrust of the sword."

Todd and Ken nodded solemnly. Todd bit his lip and stared at the floor to prevent himself from smiling. Chrome Dome Cooper was famous for his stuffiness, and now he was outdoing himself. "The penalty for causing a ruckus in this school is not light, not light indeed. Now, do you know what that penalty is?" asked Mr. Cooper, fixing them both with a menacing stare. Todd and Ken shook their heads.

"Expulsion—*that* is the penalty for fighting in school," said Mr. Cooper. He slapped his hand on his desk for emphasis and stood up.

Both Todd and Ken hung their heads. *I wish he'd get to the point,* thought Todd.

"Now," said Mr. Cooper, dragging out his words and pacing around the office, "because you two both have outstanding records, I'm going to let you off easy this time. Just this one time, you understand?" He paused, cocking an eyebrow and looking in their direction. "I'm giving you both detention for the entire week."

"Yes, sir," Todd and Ken mumbled together.

"That's it. You're dismissed," said Mr. Cooper, sitting down again behind his desk and folding his hands underneath his double chin. "Run along now."

"Thank you, sir," said the boys, nodding deferentially as they stood up and walked out of the office.

"And don't let me hear anything about your fighting again!" Todd could hear Mr. Cooper call out after them.

Todd and Ken walked silently down the hallway.

"A real gentleman settles his arguments with words, not weapons," said Ken as soon as they had safely turned the corner, imitating Mr. Cooper's deep, grave voice.

Todd stuck a finger in the air. "The lash of the tongue is mightier than the thrust of the sword!" he exclaimed.

"Now, you boys have created quite a ruckus!" Ken went on in a booming voice.

"For which the punishment is very grave," continued Todd.

"Ten years in the federal penitentiary!" said Ken.

"To be followed by the death penalty!" added Todd. The two boys broke out into gales of laughter. Ken held up an open palm and Todd slapped him a high five.

Suddenly Ken dropped his hand and stood still. Todd stopped walking as he did, and an awkward silence filled the air.

Ken cleared his throat and looked serious. "Hey, man," he said, "I'm really sorry about what happened with Elizabeth. It was a mistake, and it didn't mean anything. We should have told you about it right away." Ken paused, and a pained look crossed his face. "I really messed everything up," he said. "Your relationship with Elizabeth, my relationship with Jessica—and our friendship."

"Well, you did mess things up a bit, but that's all in the past now," said Todd. "Apology accepted." He stuck out his hand for Ken to shake. "Let's call a truce."

Ken heaved a sigh of relief and clasped Todd's hand in his. He felt as if a huge burden had been lifted from him.

"But from now on, don't forget which twin is yours," Todd warned teasingly as they resumed walking down the hall.

"Don't worry about it. It'll never happen again," said Ken. "In fact, this is only solving half the problem. Now we've got to get you and Elizabeth back together."

"And although I'll never understand the attraction," replied Todd, "you and Jessica were obviously meant for each other."

"But there's not a lot we can do now with the girls all the way in Yosemite at nationals," said Ken.

"Hmm," Todd pondered. "Of course, we do have a three-day weekend."

Suddenly both of them stopped and looked at each other.

"Road trip?" said Ken, noting the glint in Todd's eye. "We'll take my car," said Todd, nodding. "I'll pick you up at four o'clock."

Chapter 5

"Wow, this is beautiful," Jessica said as the bus pulled through the gates of the national-cheerleading compound in Yosemite. The grounds were lush and sprawling, covered with huge redwood trees and luxurious flower beds.

"Like entering paradise," Lila said dryly. She rubbed her neck and stretched her arms above her head. "I thought we'd never get here." The bus ride had taken about six hours, and they hadn't made a single pit stop.

"Cheerleading paradise, in any case," said Amy, twisting around to face Jessica and Lila. "Have you ever seen so many cheerleaders in one place?"

"It's enough to make one sick," Lila said, propping her knees against the seat in front of her with an exaggerated sigh.

"Lila, *you're* enough to make one sick," said Jessica, elbowing her friend teasingly. "Now, get in the spirit of things," she commanded.

"Aye, aye, cocaptain," said Lila, giving Jessica a salute. She raised her arms above her head in a V formation, mocking their Victory cheer.

"Lila, you're hopeless," Jessica said, throwing up her hands and gazing out the window.

Jessica sucked in her breath as the bus weaved its way through the rolling hills of the cheerleading compound. "We're in the big league now," she said, taking in the landscape. The grounds were practically swarming with cheerleaders, each one seemingly more talented than the next. Squads from all over the country were practicing their routines with aplomb, jumping and flipping like pros.

"We really are," agreed Amy, her voice sounding awed. "Nobody's even noticed us."

"Or our wildly decorated bus," added Lila.

"Somehow I expected to make a splash when we arrived," mused Jessica. "We were sent off like celebrities when we left, and here we're invisible."

Suddenly things stood out in clear perspective for Jessica. In Sweet Valley they ruled. Now they were just one of the many teams from all over the country competing for the title of best cheerleading squad. Jessica pondered the gravity of it all. If they won, they would be the best cheerleaders in the entire country. Wouldn't that, in essence, make her the best cheerleader in the country—since she'd be the captain of the best team in the country?

"OK! Everybody up! Let's go!" Jessica's reverie was rudely interrupted by the grating sound of

Heather's irritating voice. Jessica's visions of glory came to a grinding halt as she remembered that she wasn't the captain of the cheerleading squad, but the cocaptain. Not only that, but Heather bane-of-Jessica's-existence was the other cocaptain. As long as she was cocaptain, she'd never be the best cheerleader in the country, thought Jessica, annoyed.

"Unload the bags first!" yelled Heather from up front, barking out orders like a drill sergeant. "Pom-pom bags, uniforms, hand 'em up!" Jessica's eyes narrowed as she watched Heather brazenly take charge. The girls obeyed her like a flock of sheep. Making a conveyor-belt formation, the girls stood up in the aisle and smoothly handed the supplies down the line. Heather took the bags as they were passed forward and threw them onto the lawn.

"OK, everybody off!" yelled Heather as soon as all the equipment was unloaded. She hopped out of the bus and stood by the door, shooing the cheerleaders out.

"She could use a whistle," whispered Lila to Jessica as they made their way down the aisle with the rest of the girls.

"Do you think she's going to strip-search us?" whispered Jessica back.

"Move it on out!" yelled Heather as Jessica and Lila approached the stairs. Jessica stopped and put her hand on the banister, fixing Heather with a steely stare. Their eyes met for one long moment, an unspoken challenge hanging in the air. Jessica's face set in determination. This was the most important event in her life, and she wasn't going to let Heather Mallone ruin it for her. She wasn't going to let her take over. More than ever she wanted to win, and more than ever she wished that bossy Heather Mallone had never shown her face at Sweet Valley High.

"Heather, I think we're all capable of getting off the bus by ourselves," said Jessica calmly. Deliberately moving at a maddeningly slow pace, she walked gracefully down the two big steps. She paused on the bottom step to wipe some imaginary dirt off her shoe. The she stood up and smiled at Heather as she stepped delicately to the ground.

"Here, Jess, why don't you carry these?" said Heather, throwing her an oversize duffel bag full of pom-poms as the girls gathered their supplies to head to their cabin.

Jessica caught the pom-poms in both arms and took a step back, recoiling from the force of the bag. "Heather, do you mind?" she snapped, glaring at her.

Suddenly a tall girl crashed into her, nearly mowing her over. "Hey!" Jessica said, stumbling. She quickly regained her balance and jumped out of the way. The girl just breezed by her, not even bothering to apologize.

Jessica leaned against the bus, the pom-pom bag held to her stomach. *Who's that?* she wondered, staring after the tall, beautiful brunette. With that kind of attitude she'd probably be tough competition. Jessica felt suddenly overwhelmed, like a small fish in a big pond.

"Jessica, are you coming?" yelled Heather. The sound of Heather's strident voice brought Jessica back to reality. Some random, pushy cheerleader was no problem for Jessica. Jessica was confident that she was more talented than all of the cheerleaders there combined. The only person in her way was Heather. And Jessica had to figure out a way to overcome the obstacle.

"We're almost there, guys!" said Elizabeth as she led the girls through the woods to the cabin they were sharing with the squad from Alabama. Jessica and Heather had gone to the main hall to check in, and Heather had put Elizabeth in charge of finding the cabin.

"What's it called? Holly House?" Maria asked, running up beside her.

"Hunter House," said Elizabeth, stopping to peer at the map that laid out the compound. "Shoot!" Elizabeth exclaimed as a breeze came up and whipped through the map, sending small ripples across it. She knelt down and smoothed out the map on the earth, securing it firmly with one knee. Holding her hair back from her face with one hand, Elizabeth examined the map carefully. "I think that's it," she said, pointing in the direction of a rustic log cabin up the hill.

"It's got an *H* on it," confirmed Maria. Elizabeth stood up and brushed off her knees, waving for the group to follow. Elizabeth and

Maria trudged up the hill with the girls close behind, panting from their trek through the woods.

"I wonder if this is part of the competition," said Jeanie breathlessly, leaning on Sandy for support.

"I hope not," responded Sandy, "because I think we'd lose."

"Hunter House," said Maria as they reached the cabin, reading the name printed on a cheerful diamond-shaped yellow sign hanging from the door.

Suddenly a face popped out the door. "Well, hi, y'all!" exclaimed a big freckle-faced southern girl, waving as the Sweet Valley High cheerleaders approached their cabin.

"C'mon in!" said another friendly-looking girl, propping the door of the cabin wide open. "We've been waitin' for you to arrive. Kept wonderin' where the girls from California were! I'm Wilhemina, and this is Peggy May."

"Hi, Wilhemina, I'm Elizabeth," said Elizabeth. She smiled at the superfriendly girl and walked into the airy bungalow.

"You can call me Will," continued the girl, chattering on by Elizabeth's side. "Or Willy, even. Do you go by Liz ever?"

"Sometimes my good friends call me Liz," said Elizabeth, forcing a smile. The girls seemed genuinely friendly, but Elizabeth wasn't in the mood for it. She just wanted to get through this weekend with as little interaction as possible and get home.

"We cleared out half the cabin for you," said a

girl with long blond ponytails high up on her head. "We took the right side," she said, pointing out their belongings. That was obvious, thought Elizabeth as she heaved her duffel bag onto a free bunk. The Alabama girls had already lavishly covered their side of the cabin with Braselton Bulldogs paraphernalia.

"You all psyched for a weekend of stiff competition?" said Wilhemina, hopping up eagerly onto Elizabeth's bunk and crossing her legs comfortably. Elizabeth groaned inwardly. Each one of these girls was more enthusiastic than the next. She couldn't believe she was going to have to spend an entire weekend pretending that she cared about cheerleading.

Elizabeth just nodded and began unpacking her bag. Fortunately, Wilhemina seemed to get the hint and jumped off her bed just as enthusiastically as she had arrived. "Hey, great uniforms!" she said, bounding over to Lila's bunk.

"Aren't they nice?" agreed Lila, holding up a stack of elegant one-piece uniforms. Half of the costumes were solid red and half were solid white. The necks and sleeves were trimmed with lace, and tiny bows ran down the bodice. The costume tapered in at the waist and flared out in a pleated skirt.

"Hey, I haven't seen these before," said Jeanie, running a finger over the soft cotton.

"Yeah, where did these come from?" asked Maria. All the girls gathered around Lila's bunk, picking up the uniforms and admiring them.

"I ordered them before we left. It's a surprise," said Lila with a smile. "I thought we could wear these for the grand finale and cool the Jessica-Heather rivalry a bit."

"That's a great idea," said Amy. "We can wear Jessica's uniforms for the salsa routine and Heather's for the hip-hop one."

"I don't think they're going to agree to it," said Elizabeth, coming over to the bunk.

"We'll just tell them it's been decided," said Lila. "Either they go along with it, or else we make them walk the plank." All the girls laughed.

"Sounds like y'all run a tight ship," said Wilhemina with a smile.

"Only when it's necessary," said Maria.

Jeanie stood up and surveyed the room, her hands on her hips. "Looks like you guys have gotten a jump on the decorating," she said to Wilhemina.

"Here, Jeanie, let's put this up," suggested Sandy, holding up a huge Sweet Valley High banner. The girls quickly hung it up, wrapping the string around knots in the wood. The other girls soon got involved, strewing their side of the room with Sweet Valley paraphernalia. They adorned the walls with Gladiator pennants and posters and stuck up red-and-white flags around the bunks. Elizabeth watched in astonishment as their half of the cabin was quickly transformed into a Sweet Valley High fan club.

Elizabeth turned her attention to the task at hand, trying to shut out the sounds of excited chatter. She felt completely divorced from the enthusiastic girls around her. The weekend stretched ahead of her endlessly. She couldn't imagine how she was going to get through this cheerleading extravaganza. She felt completely apathetic, unable even to summon enough energy to help with the decorations.

Giving in to her lassitude, Elizabeth methodically took her clothes out of her duffel bag and placed them in neat piles on the floor. Reaching into her cosmetic bag, she woodenly took out her toiletries one by one and placed them on the little nightstand by her bunk.

When she was done, she shook the bag to see if it was empty. Something clattered inside. Elizabeth fished around in her bag and pulled out the one remaining item. It was a little framed picture of Todd she habitually brought with her on trips. Elizabeth sat down on the bed, gazing at the picture. Todd's handsome face stared back at her, a loving expression in his warm brown eyes. With a sigh Elizabeth placed the picture carefully on the wooden nightstand.

"Hey, is that your boyfriend?" asked Wilhemina, popping up beside her. "He sure is cute!"

"Actually, he's not my boyfriend anymore," said Elizabeth sadly. She picked up the picture from the nightstand and put it back in her duffel bag.

Chapter 6

"Welcome to the Tenth Annual National Cheerleading Competition in Yosemite!" said the head of the American Cheerleading Association on Friday afternoon at orientation in the auditorium. She was a tall, athletic woman with short-cropped dark-brown hair and an engaging smile. She was dressed in a navy-blue suit, the signature apparel of the directors of the ACA. "I'm Zoe Balsam," she said with a smile. "I may look ancient to you, but I competed here not so long ago. The national competition was the highlight of my high-school career, and I hope it will be the same for you."

Jessica surveyed the crowd around her as the girls clapped. There were fifty squads competing at nationals, fifty squads comprising the most talented cheerleaders in the entire country. Each team was sitting in blocks, decked out in cheerleading attire representative of their school. Each squad seemed to have its own look, and they all appeared professional and polished. It looked as if they were going to have some serious competition.

"Nationals is a series of seven competitions spread out over three days," announced Ms. Balsam. "The event is broken down into three legs, each of which counts for one third of the total score. You will compete in the first leg on Saturday—a series of three competitions—and the second on Sunday—also a series of three competitions. On Monday is the grand finale, a concluding performance that counts equally for one third of the entire tournament."

Jessica calculated quickly in her head. "That means almost any team can steal on Monday," she said to Amy.

Amy nodded. "It's like the ice-skating program of the Olympics."

"Shh!" Heather said sharply, twisting around from her seat in front of them and giving them a warning look.

Jessica leaned over to Amy again. "It's hard to tell who's the director here," she said in a stage whisper.

Amy covered her mouth, stifling a giggle. Heather turned around and shot Jessica a dirty look.

"Heather, pay attention," said Jessica, pointing to the podium. "Ms. Balsam's speaking."

Heather flounced around in a huff.

"Weekend competitions will be held out in the field, weather permitting," continued Ms. Balsam.

"The grand finale will be held here, in the auditorium. That way the press will have easy access for pictures and interviews of the winning squads."

The press! Jessica thought. She pictured herself splashed across the front page of the *L.A. Times*, a headline reading, "Jessica Wakefield, Best Cheerleader in the Nation." She would give them an exclusive interview, with personal anecdotes and stories highlighting her cheerleading career. Maybe the talk shows would be interested as well, she thought.

"Each competition is worth one hundred points. The teams are judged in four categories: athletic ability, artistic impression, school spirit, and tumbling. Each category is worth twenty-five points," said Ms. Balsam. "And remember," she added, "each competition must include a classic double-herky combination and an original jump. The trojan-crunch combination is mandatory for every team in the final competition."

Jessica whistled under her breath. "Wow, this is complicated," she said to Lila.

Lila shook her head in amazement. "You'd think we were at the Olympics."

"I don't know how we're going to keep track of it," said Jessica.

"Do you mind?" Heather said, whirling around with fire in her eyes. "I am trying to listen."

Jessica rolled her eyes. If Heather continued to act like a den mother all weekend, the competition was going to be unbearable.

"You'll find the guidelines I have discussed so

far all laid out in the guidebook you can pick up on your way out. Dates and times of the competitions are listed as well," finished Ms. Balsam. "Good luck to all of you. I look forward to seeing you tomorrow on the field!"

The Sweet Valley High cheerleaders filed out of the auditorium with the rest of the participants. The entire squad was subdued, a little awed by the magnitude of the event.

"Did you check out the competition?" said Amy to Jessica on the way out of the auditorium. "These girls are hard core!"

Jessica nodded, but her mind wasn't on the competing squads. The only competition she was worried about was Heather.

Todd pulled his shiny black BMW around to the front of Sweet Valley High after school on Friday. His spirits were high. Before evening he would be with Elizabeth again. And he hoped she would forgive him for his bad behavior. He spotted Ken sitting on the bench with some of the football players and let forth two short beeps of the horn. Ken waved good-bye to his friends and jogged up to the car.

"We're in business, man," said Todd, leaning over to open the front door. He revved the engine as Ken folded his long frame into the passenger seat.

"Did you get the info?" asked Ken as Todd pulled out of the lot.

"It's all right here," said Todd, pointing to a tiny

corner of notebook paper sitting on the dashboard. He picked up the paper and waved it in the air with his left hand.

"Nice going, man," said Ken admiringly.

"Yep, everything we need is on these two sheets of paper," said Todd, grabbing the map of the greater-California area off the seat with his free hand. He waved the papers in the air, holding the steering wheel with his elbows.

"Whoa! Both hands on the wheel," said Ken, grabbing the address and map out of Todd's hands. "You drive, I'll direct."

"Yosemite," said Ken out loud, studying the address. "Did you have any problem getting the information?"

"No problem at all," said Todd cheerfully. "I told Mr. Collins I wanted to write to Elizabeth to wish her luck. He was happy to give me the address. He even asked me to send his good wishes as well."

"Brilliant," said Ken, unfolding the map and spreading it out on his lap. He traced his finger along the map, trying to locate the site of the cheerleading competition. "Yosemite is just north of Madera, right?"

Todd nodded. "If we take Route Forty-four, we should be there in about six hours."

"Just in time for a late-night snack with the girls," said Ken, grinning.

"Quick pit stop," said Todd, steering the car adeptly into the parking lot of a convenience store. He pulled up alongside the gas pumps and brought the car to a halt.

"I'll get some supplies," said Ken, jumping out of the car and running into the store. Todd filled up the tank with gas and handed the attendant his credit card. A few minutes later Ken emerged from the building, his arms loaded with a variety of junk food and sodas.

"We're on our way!" said Todd, donning a pair of sunglasses. "Yosemite, here we come!"

"Look out, ladies!" said Ken, giving Todd a high five.

Todd flipped on the radio, fiddling with the knob until he found a station he liked. With the radio blasting Todd turned onto Valley Crest Drive.

"Hey, there's Winston!" said Ken, pointing to the side of the road. Winston Egbert, affectionately known as the class clown, was walking down the sidewalk, balancing a few shopping bags in his arms. He looked even more awkward than usual up to his ears in groceries.

Todd pulled the car to the side of the road and came to a screeching halt by Winston.

"Come on, Egbert," said Todd, "this is the love mobile. We're taking take you to see Maria. Get in." Pretty brown-haired Maria Santelli was Winston's longtime girlfriend.

"What?" said Winston, lowering the groceries and peering out at the boys.

"We're going to the National Cheerleading Competition in Yosemite," explained Todd. "To see Jessica and Elizabeth and Maria—"

"And a couple hundred other girls," added Ken for effect. "C'mon!"

"Sorry, guys, can't," said Winston, shifting from one foot to the other as he juggled the bags in his arms. "I've got a bunch of groceries for my mother."

"Don't worry, she'll understand," Todd insisted. "You can call her when we get there."

"No, I really can't go," said Winston. "I've got to get these groceries home. And then I've got a bunch of chores to do. And there's this old movie on TV that I really want—"

But the boys weren't listening. Todd shut off the ignition and they both jumped out. Todd ran around to the backseat and opened it. "After you," said Ken magnanimously, gesturing to the seat.

"Oh, boy," said Winston, getting in reluctantly. Todd slammed the door after him, and the boys jumped back into the car. Todd put his foot on the gas and sped off toward the desert, tunes blaring.

"I think my mother's ice cream is melting," Winston said from the backseat.

"Got a spoon?" Ken asked.

"It's just all so excitin'!" enthused Wilhemina on Friday night at dinner in the huge cafeteria of the lodge.

"It sure ii-s," said Jessica mischievously, putting on a southern twang. Her blue-green eyes twinkled merrily as she smiled at Wilhemina.

Wilhemina laughed good-naturedly. "You know, Jess," she said, "you and your twin sister Elizabeth may come from California, but with your blond hair and blue eyes, you look like you belong in

Alabama! Why, with a little bit of fixin', we could make you two perfect southern belles."

"And we could change you and Peggy May into California beach bums!" said Jessica. She spoke for both herself and Elizabeth, but she didn't bother to look at her sister. "A few days on the beach, a couple of surfing lessons . . ." Jessica grinned, putting her arm around the easygoing girl's shoulder.

The other girls laughed, but Elizabeth just stared down at her plate, playing with her food. The turkey entrée looked good, but she had no appetite. Elizabeth felt completely out of her element. She was sitting at a table with two cheerleading squads in a roomful of hundreds of cheerleaders from around the country. Here she was in the center of Jessica's world, and she and Jessica weren't even speaking.

Elizabeth listened as the conversation swirled about her. The girls were all pumped up about the next day's events and were sizing up the competition.

"The Vermont girls look brutal," said Patty Gilbert, bringing a forkful of mashed potatoes to her lips. "They've got their routines timed to perfection."

Sara Eastbourne took a long gulp of lemonade. "And did you see the Texas Tigers, the team from San Antonio?"

"They came in second last year," put in Jeanie West. "I hear they're shoo-ins for the title this year."

"Not a chance," said Jessica, shaking her head firmly. "Not with us around."

"Oh, look, Heather," said Annie Whitman, pointing to the far corner of the cafeteria. "Your old squad from Reno is over there. Aren't you going to say hi?"

"No way." Heather snorted derisively. Annie raised one eyebrow and gave her an inquiring look.

Heather looked uncomfortable for a moment. "Well, they're the competition now," she explained, regaining her composure. "So, what do you think of the squad from Hawaii?" she asked, changing the subject quickly.

"They're not very impressive," said Lila with a dismissive wave of her hand. "I think they're just trying to win by looking good with their floral prints and colorful leis."

"That's true," agreed Amy. "They're pretty much all appearance and no substance."

"Yeah, but they have some great jumps," said Sandy Bacon.

"I saw them in a standing pyramid this afternoon," added Jade Wu.

Just then a stunning willowy girl with glossy brown hair appeared at the table. "Oh, hi," she said in a syrupy-sweet voice. "I just wanted to introduce myself. I'm Marissa James, the captain of the Reno squad. Heather here used to be on our team." The girls responded with a chorus of hellos.

"Hi, Marissa, long time no see," said Heather, smiling up at her. It seemed to Elizabeth that her smile didn't reach her eyes.

"How's it going, Heather?" said Marissa in a relaxed, friendly tone. "You know, it's just not the same at Reno since you, uh, since you—left."

"I'm sure," said Heather coolly. Heather sounded perfectly at ease, but the color seemed to drain from her face.

"You're the cocaptain, right?" said Marissa, leaning over to Elizabeth.

"Uh, no," said Elizabeth, her cheeks burning hotly. "My sister Jessica is the cocaptain." She indicated Jessica across the table.

"I think we met earlier at the bus," said Jessica in an unfriendly voice.

"Oh, did we?" said Marissa, showing no sign of recognition. "Well, you must be absolutely thrilled to be working with Heather," she said. "We really miss her at Reno. It's just not the same without her."

"I'm sure," said Jessica, her tone flat. "We really are thrilled to have her. Thrilled to pieces."

"Well, see you tomorrow." Marissa waved. "Good luck!"

"I hear she's the best cheerleader around," said Wilhemina as soon as Marissa was out of earshot.

"Yeah, everybody's been talking about her all day," added Peggy May. "She seems to have created quite a stir."

"She's definitely getting a lot of attention," put in Jeanie. "I saw a bunch of girls gathered around her earlier. It's like she's got a fan club."

"Well, I'm not surprised," said Maria. "She looks like a movie star."

Suddenly Heather scraped her chair back and stood up. "If you'll excuse me," she said, "I've got to get back to the cabin. I want to make sure our routine book for the weekend is in order." Annie opened her mouth to protest, but Heather was gone before she could say anything.

Elizabeth looked at her strangely as she left. Heather seemed to get all worked up whenever her old school was mentioned. Heather and Marissa must have a history, thought Elizabeth. Maybe Marissa hated working with her as much as Jessica did, she surmised.

A few minutes later Heather unlocked the door of the cabin and walked in alone, her heart pounding in her chest. She sat down hard on the bed and took a deep breath. Marissa James was going to try to make trouble for her, that was for sure. She'd been her greatest rival at Reno. Heather had been sole captain for two years in a row, and Marissa had despised her for it.

And to make it worse, the girls at Sweet Valley seemed overly interested in her history at Thomas Jefferson High. Especially Annie Whitman, who followed her around like a puppy. Heather looked at her watch. The girls would probably be back from dinner soon. If she went to bed early, they wouldn't be able to ask her any more questions, she decided.

Heather pulled down the covers on her bunk and gasped. Lying on her sheets was an ominous envelope across which her name was scrawled in bold black letters. Heather picked it up and opened it with shaking fingers. She pulled out a familiar newspaper clipping and stared at it unbelievingly, her whole body trembling. The headline read: "Kicky Captain Kicked Off Squad." Heather fell back on the bed and scanned the article:

> Heather Mallone, the much celebrated captain of the Thomas Jefferson High cheerleading squad, who led her team to State for two years in a row, has been dismissed from the squad due to a serious cheating incident. The authorities involved—

Heather couldn't bear to read more. She crumpled up the article and threw it onto the ground. Her worst fear had been realized. She had tried so hard to keep her past a secret, and now it looked as if somebody wanted it to come out. Heather was desperate to keep her cheerleading history to herself. She would do anything, she thought—anything. She just had to find out who did this and what they wanted.

Thinking twice, Heather picked up the article from the floor and smoothed it out again. She folded it carefully and put it back in its envelope. Suddenly a piece of paper fluttered to the ground. Heather snatched it up. It was a note: "Meet me outside in the clearing tonight at ten. I'll be waiting." The note was signed Marissa James. Heather shivered and slipped the small piece of paper into her bag.

"OK, guys, get ready to knock 'em dead!" exclaimed Jessica. The girls were in a huddle before the first competition on Saturday morning, and Jessica was giving them a pep talk. Everyone was wound up, and the excitement in the air was palpable. "Remember, arms straight, knees bent, chins up and out. And don't forget to smile, smile, smile."

All the girls put their arms in the middle of the circle, laying their hands on top of each other's. "One, two, three, SVH!" they yelled together. The girls let out a shout and threw their arms in the air.

"Girls, please take your seats in your sections in the bleachers!" came a booming voice over the loudspeaker. "Please take your seats! The first competition of the day will begin in fifteen minutes."

"All right, let's get moving!" said Heather in a

brassy tone, clapping her hands sharply. The girls followed as she led them to the Sweet Valley section in the stands. The competing squads were cordoned off in sections in the front half of the bleachers. The back half of the bleachers was devoted to members of the audience. The judges were lined up in special box seats in the front.

"Everybody's got today's program straight, right?" asked Jessica nervously as soon as they were all settled in the bleachers. The big moment had finally arrived, and she didn't want anything to go wrong. "We're doing the salsa routine first, the 'Mambo Jamba' this afternoon, and the 'Victory' combination at the end of the day."

"You've *got* to be kidding," said Heather, her voice dripping with disdain. "We're doing the salsa routine first?"

Jessica's temper flared. "Do you have a problem with that?" she demanded, her hands on her hips.

"Yes, I do," Heather asserted. "I think it's a mistake."

"And may I ask why?" Jessica asked, fixing Heather with a piercing stare.

"If we start out with the salsa routine, we're going to regret it," said Heather with a self-assured air. "I think we should do the 'Mambo Jamba' instead."

"I'm sure you do," said Jessica dryly. The salsa routine ended with a solo tumbling run by Jessica: a round-off followed by two back handsprings. The "Mambo Jamba," on the other hand, featured Heather's special combination jump. Obviously

Heather couldn't stand being out of the limelight for even one performance.

"The salsa routine is a nice upbeat number, but it's not technically complicated," Heather said. "The 'Mambo Jamba' is a showstopper. We'll catch the eyes of the judges right at the start."

"Heather, are you crazy?" asked Jessica in astonishment. "We can't just change the program at the last minute."

"Well, I made some last-minute adjustments last night," said Heather.

"Which you forgot to inform us about," said Jessica, folding her arms across her chest.

"I know, silly of me," said Heather, an apologetic smile on her face. "I didn't expect to fall asleep so fast."

"It's no big deal," said Patty Gilbert diplomatically. "We can just switch the order of the first two combinations."

"Look, guys," said Jessica. "It's our first performance, and we want to make a good impression. The salsa routine is our smoothest combination. We've been practicing it for weeks, and we've got it down to a science."

"Well, you know that first impressions are always the most important," said Heather. "If you want to play it safe and begin with a dud, that's fine with me. But I personally think we should start out with a bang."

"I'm for the 'Mambo Jamba,'" said Annie Whitman. "Heather's combination jump is the best we've got. Everybody will notice us from the start." Jessica fumed inwardly as Annie spoke.

"We'd better decide soon," said Elizabeth, looking at her watch nervously. "The competition starts in five minutes, and we're the third team to perform."

"Why don't we take a vote?" suggested Heather.

"Great idea!" said Annie.

Jessica gritted her teeth as Heather held the vote. "Whoever is in favor of the 'Mambo Jamba,' raise their hands," she said. Five sets of hands shot up immediately.

A small smile played on Jessica's lips as she counted the votes. It looked like seven to five in her favor. Then her smile faded as Maria, Sandy, and Jean slowly followed, lifting their arms awkwardly into the air. Only Lila, Amy, and Elizabeth's hands remained down. Jessica averted her eyes, feeling as if her friends had betrayed her.

"Well," said Heather, looking around with a self-satisfied smirk, "it looks like it's almost unanimous."

"OK, we'll start with the Mambo Jamba, then," said Jessica, swallowing her disappointment.

"Great!" Heather said. "I've got the tape right here."

What a coincidence, thought Jessica wryly as Heather jumped up and ran to the sound booth at the top of the bleachers to give the new tape to the controller.

Jessica stared at the field, seething in frustration. She barely noticed as the first two squads performed. Jessica didn't really care if they started with the "Mambo Jamba." It didn't matter to her one way or the other which combination they did first. But she was furious that Heather hadn't consulted her about it. And the squad had gone along with her, as usual. Heather just wanted to assert her power, thought Jessica in annoyance. And nobody even noticed it.

Jessica was so caught up in her thoughts that she didn't hear the announcer call their squad to the field.

"Jessica, c'mon!" urged Amy, by her side. "We're on!"

"Oh," said Jessica. She stood up and followed her squad down the bleachers, marching along with a stony look on her face.

"Jess," Amy said placatingly as they walked out to the field together, "Heather's jump is always a crowd pleaser, and she never, ever messes it up. It's guaranteed to win us this leg of the competition."

"All right, all right," Jessica grumbled, knowing deep down that Amy was probably right.

The girls took their positions in the center of the field and faced the judges. Suddenly the enormity of the situation hit her. They were about to perform in the first round of the national competition. Jessica stood tense and nervous as she waited for the music to start.

As the jazzy tune began to come through the loudspeaker, the girls began to move in time to the music; they swayed from side to side and lunged back and forth, shaking their pom-poms in the air. Jessica could feel the rhythm of the music throbbing through her body. Suddenly she forgot all about Heather and the audience and the judges. Her entire mind was filled with the pounding beat and the familiar steps.

Keeping in time with Jessica and Heather, the girls moved in perfect synchronicity. Jessica knew that they formed a uniform image, a whirlwind of fancy footwork and intricate moves. A hush seemed to sweep over the audience as the girls performed. The judges were motionless as well, riveted to the Sweet Valley High squad.

The beat changed, and the girls shifted to the athletic part of the program. They stood perfectly still for a beat, then launched into a series of side-by-side herkies. A round of applause greeted the difficult feat. Feeling a rush of adrenaline, the girls leaped into a trojan-crunch combination and followed it up with a spectacular team stag leap.

Jessica's mouth went dry as they approached the final, but most difficult, part of the program. She took a deep breath and leaped high into the air in a jumping split, dropping down to the ground on one knee, her pom-poms at her waist. Jade Wu followed, and in a wave pattern each girl leaped into the air in succession and dropped down to the earth. Jessica exhaled deeply as the last girl came down. Breathing heavily, the girls squatted on one knee in a line, their pom-poms held at their waists and radiant smiles on their faces.

Heather bounced up to the front of the group, getting in position for her combination jump. She stood poised and graceful in the middle of the field, commanding full attention. Suddenly she bounded across the field and jumped into the air in a perfect triple herky and Y-leap combination. As she landed, her foot slipped out from under her, and she tumbled across the field, somersaulting wildly. The crowd gasped audibly. Jessica sucked in her breath. She had never seen Heather make a mistake before. The judges jumped up to see if she was hurt. But like a pro, Heather got back up as if nothing had happened, continuing smoothly with the combination. She leaped into a series of energetic back flips. But her momentum seemed to give way before the last flip, preventing her from completing the rotation. Her arms flailed wildly, and she fell forward on her knees. Looking teary-eyed, she bounced up again and shot straight up in the air, landing in a crooked split.

A moment of silence followed the pathetic display, and then the crowd broke out into polite applause. The girls stood perfectly still, frozen smiles plastered on their faces.

"It's a disaster," Amy mumbled.

"A nightmare," agreed Lila.

"A total fiasco," said Jessica, speaking through clenched teeth, "and it's all Heather's fault."

"That was some night," Todd said, rubbing his neck as he maneuvered his BMW along the winding roads of the sleeping town on Saturday morning. The sun was just peeking out over the mountains, bathing the rustic landscape in a soft yellow glow.

"I feel like I've been through a war," agreed Ken, his voice still groggy with sleep. "We might as well have slept in a barracks." He yawned and stretched his arms above his head.

Todd felt as if he'd slept on a bed of Ping-Pong balls. The boys were all a little stiff from the lumpy beds at the Red Wood Hotel. They had arrived too late the evening before to go to the cheerleading compound, so they had found a hotel and called it a night.

"I think I'm going to be sick," complained Winston from the backseat of the car.

"Here, Winston, have some of these," said Ken, handing Winston a half-eaten bag of potato chips.

"Ugh, don't even put that near me," said Winston. The gallon of mocha-chip ice cream the boys had consumed on their way down wasn't helping matters, Todd thought. Their lack of sleep was compounded by collective bellyaches.

"I'll never eat again!" Winston vowed, raising his index finger in the air.

"At least not until lunchtime," said Ken with a laugh.

"Well, it's time to rally!" said Todd, flipping on the radio and picking up the speed. Despite his aching body and delicate stomach, Todd's spirits were soaring. In just a few minutes he would see Elizabeth again. He would finally have the chance to patch things up with her. He was also looking forward to watching the squad perform at the national competition.

"I can't wait to see the girls show their stuff," said Todd, voicing his thoughts aloud.

"Me neither," agreed Ken. "I'm psyched that we'll be there. The cheerleaders have been supporting our teams for years. It'll be nice to cheer them on for a change."

"I wonder if the competitions have started yet," mused Winston.

"I don't know, but we'll soon find out," said Todd excitedly as he spotted a huge stone arch marking the entranceway of the cheerleading compound. "That's it up ahead!" he said, pointing to the gates.

Todd cut his speed and coasted up the road to the entrance. Suddenly he pulled the car to a screeching halt. A foreboding placard greeted their arrival. The sign read: NO BOYS ALLOWED ON THE NATIONAL CHAMPIONSHIP GROUNDS.

"Oh, no!" despaired Todd.

"That's impossible!" lamented Ken.

"But that's discrimination!" protested Winston.

"That's right," said Todd in a determined voice. "And we're not going to let them get away with it." Todd wasn't exactly sure how they were going to do that, but he was sure they'd think of something. They had come too far to leave without putting up a fight.

"Follow me, men," said Todd, cutting the engine and hopping out of the car. Ken and Winston jumped out as well, and the three of them approached the entrance. Two official-looking guards in matching uniforms stood in front of the gates.

"Can I help you, boys?" asked one of the guards, a thin-faced man with a fuzzy mustache.

"Yes, sir," said Ken politely. "We're here to observe the competition."

"Can't you read?" asked the other guard in a gruff tone. His feet were planted widely on the ground, and his crossed arms rested lazily on his big belly.

"Sorry, fellows," said the first guard in a kindlier tone, "but no boys are permitted on the grounds during the national competition."

"But that's not fair!" protested Winston. "It's illegal to discriminate on grounds of race or gender."

"This ain't a job interview," said the second guard in a surly voice. "Boys don't belong at a girls' event. They just make trouble and mess everything up."

Todd thought quickly. "Well, actually, we're reporters for the *Hollywood Globe*," he said. He addressed his words to the first guard, who looked like the more reasonable of the two. "We've been assigned the national championship to cover for this week's front-page story."

"I see," he said, his expression dubious. He paused to think for a moment, twirling his mustache between his fingers.

Todd waited breathlessly for his response. Trying to look authentic, Ken quickly pulled his camera out of his backpack and began shooting pictures of the compound.

"Well," said the guard finally, rubbing his jaw

thoughtfully, "I'm sure the editors of your newspaper will understand when you explain the situation to them."

"You know, sir," Todd said, taking another stab at it, "this kind of coverage would be great press for the national championships."

"It would lend new prestige to the entire sport," added Ken for good measure.

"All right," said the guard. "Let's see your press passes."

"Press passes?" Todd repeated dumbly.

"As in ID cards for the *Hollywood Globe*," said the burly guard.

Todd gulped and looked at his friends for help. Ken jumped in and took over. "We left our press passes back at the office," he said smoothly, "and we'll be sure to bring them by later. But the thing is, we've really got to get into the compound now."

Todd decided to make a personal appeal. "You see, our girlfriends are in there," he said. "And we've got to see them. It's urgent."

The guards weren't impressed.

"Somehow I don't think that counts as an emergency," said the first guard, clearly getting impatient. "And I think your girlfriends are cheerleaders just like you're reporters for the *Hollywood Globe*."

"What's wrong, sonny?" asked the second guard, his jowly face leering. "Aren't there enough girls for you back in your high school?"

Todd opened his mouth to argue further, but the second guard waved him off. "Read my lips," he said, his voice slow and condescending. *"No—boys—allowed!"*

"I can't believe it," Jessica said, pacing back and forth in one of the spare rooms of the lodge late Saturday morning. "First Heather screws up and then she disappears." Heather had run off immediately following the first competition. Annie was gone as well. As soon as Heather had left, Annie had jumped up and followed her off the field, calling, "Heather! Heather!" Jessica shook her head. Annie's idol worship was really revolting.

"Do you want me to go find her?" asked Maria.

"No, we're better off without her," said Jessica, dismissing the suggestion with a wave of her hand. "Now," she said, facing the girls and rubbing her hands together. "We've got some important decisions to make. We're in a critical situation—an *extremely* critical situation."

For once Elizabeth had to agree with Jessica. The girls had been ranked fiftieth after the first competition. Jessica had called an emergency meeting immediately following the morning's fiasco.

"It's worse than critical," lamented Sandy Bacon dramatically. "It's the end of the world."

"We're going to be the laughingstock of the entire school," said Sara Eastbourne, flopping down on a couch on her back.

"We're ruined," echoed Jean West. "All our hard work for nothing. Hours and hours of practice. Days and days of preparation. And then—*poof!*"

She snapped her fingers in the air. "Two minutes, and it's all over."

"It's all over, is it?" Jessica said. Elizabeth looked at her sister suspiciously. Jessica had a familiar look in her eye. A look that meant trouble. Elizabeth could almost see the wheels clicking in Jessica's head. The morning's competition had been a total disaster, but Jessica wasn't one to give in easily. This was the first time the squad had met together without Heather, and Elizabeth was sure Jessica would find a way to turn the situation to her advantage.

"So you all just want to give up, huh?" said Jessica, fixing the girls with a challenging stare. "One setback and you just want to throw in the towel. Is that right, Jeanie?" Jessica asked, giving the girl a hard look.

"No, of course not," said Jeanie defensively.

"Is that what kind of team we are?" Jessica said, addressing all of them.

"No!" chorused the girls.

"Does the Sweet Valley High team just accept defeat without a fight?" said Jessica.

"No way!" yelled the girls, getting riled up.

"Who's number one?" shouted Jessica.

"SVH!" they yelled together.

"That's the spirit," said Jessica, her face breaking into a broad grin. She sat down on the floor and spoke quietly. "Now, I've got a plan," Jessica said. The girls gathered around and looked at her expectantly. "It's simple, but it'll work."

"Well?" Lila asked impatiently, tapping her cherry-red fingernails on the ottoman.

"We performed beautifully today, right?" said Jessica.

"Except for Heather's jumps," said Sandy.

"Or attempts at jumps," qualified Maria.

"Exactly," said Jessica. "So I hereby raise an official motion to have Heather voted off the squad. She's obviously collapsing under all the pressure. Right now we've still got a chance. We've got six more competitions to go. Either we make a comeback, or we let Heather bring us down."

Elizabeth's mouth dropped open. Jessica had protested wildly when Heather had kicked Maria and Sandy off the squad, and rightly so. And now here she was suggesting the same thing.

"I'm with Jessica," said Amy.

"Me too," agreed Lila.

"All in favor?" asked Jessica. Jessica looked around in satisfaction as one by one all the girls raised their hands. All except Elizabeth.

Jessica turned furious eyes to her sister, willing her to go along with the group. But Elizabeth refused to be bullied. "I'm not in favor!" she proclaimed, jumping up and facing the girls.

"We're a team, and the whole point of being a team is that you stick together," said Elizabeth, speaking in a strong voice. She addressed her words not to Jessica, but to the rest of the girls. "A squad is about good sportsmanship and camaraderie, about teamwork and solidarity."

The girls seemed distinctly uncomfortable as Elizabeth made her speech. Maria and Sandy fidgeted nervously; Jade and Patty stared down at the ground; Lila traced patterns in the woodwork with a finger.

"When you're a team, you stick together through thick and thin, and you don't kick people when they're down," Elizabeth continued, her voice becoming more impassioned as she spoke. "If we're not going to act like a team, then a title doesn't mean anything."

"Liz is right," said Maria, hanging her head. "Sandy and I were devastated when Heather kicked us off the squad."

"Yeah, you can't just throw people out if they make a mistake," Sandy put in.

The whole team begrudgingly agreed.

Jessica stood up. "We're going to regret this," she said, addressing the squad as a whole, but glaring at Elizabeth. "Mark my words, we're going to regret this." With that, she pivoted on her heel and marched out of the room.

"Man, I can't believe it!" said Todd, hitting his hand against the dashboard for the tenth time as the boys headed back to Sweet Valley on Saturday. He felt like screaming in frustration. They'd come all that way for nothing. "No boys allowed!" he said, shaking his head. "No boys allowed!"

"You can say that again!" said Winston with a grin. Todd smiled in spite of himself. He had been repeating "No boys allowed!" like a mantra for the last hour.

"No-o! Not again!" yelled Ken, making a motion to hang himself.

"What a total waste of time," Todd said in disgust.

"And money," added Ken.

"And ice cream," lamented Winston.

"How can they not allow boys in?" asked Todd, outraged. "Who could be in the audience?"

"A bunch of retired cheerleaders," said Ken.

"Or grade-school cheerleader wanna-bes," said Todd.

"Maybe they think we'd be a distraction," suggested Winston.

"Well, I can see that," said Ken. "After all, who could resist us?"

The boys lapsed into silence as Todd steered his black BMW down the busy Pacific Coast Highway. The blue-green ocean glittered off to their right in the distance, seagulls white specks on the horizon.

"Are we almost there?" asked Winston a few minutes later, shifting his lanky frame uncomfortably in the backseat.

"I think we're about halfway home," said Todd, trying to make out the road sign ahead of him. He managed to read the sign as they passed it. The sign said Cheer Ahead.

Suddenly Todd recalled the Cheer Ahead catalog he had seen at the Wakefields, the catalog from which Jessica had chosen the squad's uniforms. He slammed on the brakes. The car lurched forward, and the boys flew back against the seats.

"Oh, no!" said Winston.

"Oh, yes!" said Todd.

"Brilliant idea," said Ken.

• • •

"OK, you guys, now don't let this morning get you down," Jessica said, giving the girls a little pep talk before the second round of the competition on Saturday. "This routine features my jump," she reassured them, smiling sweetly at Heather, "so we won't have to worry about any mishaps."

For once Heather looked at a loss for words. She opened her mouth as if to respond but shut it quickly, looking the other way.

"And performing next is the squad from Sweet Valley, California!" boomed the announcer's voice.

"We're on!" said Maria.

"C'mon, guys!" Jessica said, running out to the field. The girls followed her enthusiastically, waving their pom-poms in the air.

Once in the center of the field, they spread out in a line, positioning themselves at arm's length from one other. As the lively samba beat began to pour out of the speakers, the girls started clapping their hands rhythmically in time with the music.

"How're we feelin?" Jessica yelled.

"Feelin' hot, hot, hot!" shouted the girls, stomping their feet and chanting with the music.

"How're you feeling?" Jessica roared, cupping her ear to the audience.

"Feelin' hot, hot, hot!" responded the crowd.

Fueled on by the audience's enthusiasm, the girls moved through the salsa routine flawlessly, shifting from jump to jump without a hitch. As the beat picked up, they sashayed into a jazzy dance number, swaying their hips and waving their arms in the air like flamenco dancers. The audience clapped along as the girls pranced across the field, performing an impressive display of fancy footwork.

Moving into position for their final jump, all the girls except Jessica leaped into the air at the same time and landed in Chinese splits with their feet touching. From an aerial view the girls formed a six-point star. A chorus of *oohs* and *aahs* could be heard from the crowd as they observed the star formation.

Jessica took a deep breath as she moved into position for her final jump: a tumbling run followed by a side-kick, Y-leap combination. Jessica tensed the muscles in her legs and sprang into action, moving through the jump flawlessly. The crowd burst into spontaneous applause as she finished the combination, hurtling her body high into the air in a Y leap and landing in the center of the star in a split.

The girls brought their legs together in unison and bent their knees. Jumping up, they moved into position for their final move: a five-four-three pyramid, their most impressive maneuver. "We've got the fever, we're hot, we can't be stopped!" chanted the girls, clapping and shouting as they hoisted each other onto their shoulders. Hopping up adeptly, Jessica, Elizabeth, and Patty climbed up the first two tiers and positioned themselves on top. Patty knelt in the middle, her pom-poms raised high. Balancing on one knee, Jessica and Elizabeth raised their arms in the air in L shapes.

"SVH!" yelled the girls. "We're hot, hot, hot!" The crowd roared its approval. Suddenly Jessica felt the pyramid sway. Out of the corner of her eye she saw Heather collapse at the bottom, causing a domino effect. One by one the girls fell. Finally the whole pyramid collapsed on top of Heather, and the girls toppled in a heap onto the ground.

The girls scrambled up and took their final positions, holding their heads high as the judges ranked them. Jessica stared unseeing at the bleachers, blinking back tears from her eyes. She had never been so mortified in all her life.

"I'm so sorry," Heather gasped out as they took their seats in the stands, a stricken look on her face. "It was an accident."

"Don't worry about it, Heather," said Annie, patting her hand in a comforting manner. "It could happen to any of us."

"But it didn't," Heather said, choking back a sob. "I'm so humiliated!" She jumped up and ran from the field, tears streaming down her face.

But Jessica didn't buy any of it. Heather wasn't humiliated. She was trying to humiliate Jessica. And it was working. It was clear as day what Heather was doing. She was deliberately sabotaging the competition just to make Jessica look bad. Jessica shook her head in amazement. She knew Heather was cutthroat, but she never thought she'd go this far for a personal vendetta. She would have never dreamed that Heather would sacrifice the entire competition just to embarrass her.

The girls quieted down as the judges read out

their scores: artistic impression: 20; school spirit: 25; athletic ability: 10; tumbling: 10. The color drained from Jessica's face as she digested the information. They had received a point total of 65 out of 100, one of the lowest scores of the day.

Shaking with suppressed fury, Jessica forced herself to look at the electronic scoreboard at the far end of the field. She scanned it quickly, her heart sinking as she made her way farther and farther down the list. Finally she spotted their squad listed third from the bottom. Jessica buried her head in her hands. Sweet Valley High was ranked forty-eighth in the competition.

"Don't go anywhere yet," Jessica said a moment later, addressing the squad. She wasn't planning to give up yet. It was time to take matters into her own hands. "I want everybody on the south side of the practice field immediately for a run-through of the 'Victory' combination. We're going to whip ourselves into shape for the next competition."

The girls begrudgingly stood up, grumbling among themselves. "Oh, what's the use?" Maria said. "We might as well throw in the towel now," muttered Sara. "Yeah, quitting's more respectable than losing," added Jean.

"Oh, one more thing," Jessica added as the girls began to trudge down the bleachers. They stopped and looked back. "I want to rechoreograph the final jump of the 'Victory' routine. Can somebody get the routine book from the cabin?"

"I'll go," Elizabeth offered, looking just as dejected as the rest of them.

Five minutes later the girls were gathered in the grass, going through the motions of stretching out and limbering up. They were a motley crew, thought Jessica, surveying the group. Shoulders sagging, Sara turned her head from side to side, stretching out her neck muscles. Amy sat spread-eagle, face-down in the grass with her arms stretched out in front of her. Jade and Patty were positioned directly across from each other for a dual stretch. Legs spread and toes touching, they moved as if rowing a boat in slow motion, slowly pulling the other down to the ground. Jean, Sandy, and Maria didn't even bother to make an effort. They lay flat on their backs on the grass, staring up at the sky in silence.

"OK, that's enough for now!" said Jessica, clapping her hands together. She gathered everybody around her.

"Girls," said Jessica, getting right to the point, "the situation is getting dire. There's only one problem at this point."

"Heather Mallone," supplied Amy.

Jessica nodded. "And there's only one solution."

"Can Heather," said Lila.

"Exactly," agreed Jessica.

"But we can't just cut Heather!" exclaimed Annie. "She's done so much for us. She brought a whole new approach to the squad—new cheers, new uniforms."

"Yeah," agreed Jade. "Heather makes us stand out."

"Well, the only way she's making us stand out now is by humiliating us," put in Amy.

"I don't know what kind of spell that girl has cast on you guys," Jessica said, her voice firm, "but if you remember, the ACA representative chose both my squad and Heather's squad to go to nationals. My squad stood out on its own—without Heather."

"Jessica's right," Lila chimed in. "The squads tied at the cheer-off."

"Well, what about what Elizabeth said?" worried Maria. "About team spirit and camaraderie?"

"And about sticking together when you're down?" added Sandy.

"Look, guys," said Jessica. "We gave Heather a second chance, and she blew it. I don't know what she's up to, but I don't think she's worried about team spirit at this point."

"Are you saying that Heather's doing this on purpose?" said Annie hotly. "She'd never do that."

"I'm not saying anything," said Jessica. "All I'm saying is that we have two choices at this point: We leave Heather in and we come in last place, or we get rid of her and do respectably, maybe even place. There's still time, you know. Now—all in favor?"

All the girls raised their hands, solemn looks on their faces. Annie hesitated and looked around, then slowly lifted her hand in the air.

"Looks like the ayes have it," said Lila.

"Good," Jessica said, rubbing her hands together. "It's decided, then. Heather's off the squad."

"But what do we do now?" asked Jeanie. "We haven't got a chance after the first two—"

Jessica held up a hand, cutting her off. "Now," she said, her eyes gleaming, "it's time to make our comeback."

Chapter 8

"I can't believe I'm shaving my legs, I can't believe I'm shaving my legs," Winston moaned again and again, holding a foamy, furry leg underneath the bathtub faucet. He brought the pink razor slowly up his muscular calf, wincing as clumps of hair fell into the tub.

It was Saturday afternoon, and the boys were back at the hotel, ready to don their new cheerleading costumes.

"Darnit!" Todd muttered as he poked himself in the eye with a mascara stick. He stood at the bathroom mirror, meticulously applying makeup. An array of cosmetics was splayed across the bathroom counter. Todd stood back and surveyed his handiwork. Something wasn't quite right.

"How did I let myself get talked into this?" Winston wondered aloud.

"Don't worry, Winston, it's all for a good cause," Todd reassured him.

"A good cause! A good cause!" mumbled Winston. "No cause is worth the hair on my legs." He held up a smooth white calf and moaned.

Todd squinted into the mirror, trying to ascertain the problem. The eyes, he decided finally, that was it. They needed a touch of color. He fumbled through the confusing assortment of jars, tubes, and ointments laid out on the counter. "Ken!" Todd said. "Can I borrow your blue eyeshadow?"

"Coming!" Ken called in a falsetto voice. A moment later he sashayed into the bathroom like a runway model, adorned in a classic cheerleading costume. "How do I look, dah-lings?" Ken drawled, his hands on his hips. He pirouetted slowly, pausing to exhibit the cheerleading outfit from a variety of angles. It was bright purple and yellow, with a V-necked sweater and a pleated skirt. A big, gold *S* was emblazoned on the sweater. Ken whirled in a circle, displaying the flare of the skirt.

Todd put his fingers to his lips and let out an approving whistle.

"Hubba, hubba!" said Winston, twisting around to watch the show.

"I always knew you'd make a great girl," said Todd with a grin.

"Here's your eyeshadow, honey," said Ken, batting his eyelashes at Todd. "But make sure to return it!" He pressed the compact into Todd's hand.

Suddenly Ken jumped with fright as he looked into Todd's face. He stood back and stared, his mouth agape.

Winston followed Ken's gaze. "Oh-mi-god!" he exclaimed.

"What, what?" Todd asked, looking from one to the other. Winston was staring openmouthed, and Ken had a look of horror on his face.

"Uh, Todd, we're trying to be cheerleaders, not cabaret dancers," Ken said.

"What do you mean?" Todd asked, studying his face in the mirror. He had outlined the rims of his eyes with a thick layer of purple eyeliner, creating the effect of a somewhat soulful raccoon face. The eyeliner then extended outward, curling upward from his lids to his brows. Thick layers of mascara coated his lashes, which sprung out like spider's legs. Two sharp lines of bright-pink blush highlighted his prominent cheekbones, and scarlet lipstick outlined his full, penciled lips.

"Oh, do you think I overdid it a bit?" Todd asked, biting his lip. He coughed as he tasted the artificial candy taste of lipstick on his tongue.

"Overdid it is being kind," said Ken.

"I think 'garish' is the word you're looking for," Winston added.

Todd's face fell. At this rate they'd never get to the cheerleading compound. There was no way they'd fool the guards. "I'm just not cut out for this," Todd said, throwing his arms into the air.

"OK, Todd, baby, don't despair. We're going to do you over." Ken fished around the counter and came up with a jar of makeup remover. He handed Todd the cream and a washcloth. "Now, first of all, get this stuff off."

Ken fiddled around with the makeup as Todd wiped gobs of it off his face. "Now, stick with me," Ken said, readying a jar of mauve blush and a makeup brush, "and we'll have you looking lovely in no time."

Jessica marched back to the cabin after her meeting with the girls, a determined air in her gait. Pine needles crackled underneath her feet as she strode through the woods, taking a circuitous route. She was going back to the cabin to break the news to Heather, and she didn't want to meet Elizabeth on the way.

Jessica practiced her speech in her head. "Heather, I've got some news for you," she said aloud. "The squad held a meeting, and we decided that it might be better for all of us if you agreed to sacrifice your position on the squad for the good of the team." No, too pointed. Heather wouldn't appreciate having her own words thrown in her face, and Jessica needed her cooperation. She tried a different tack. "Heather, maybe you shouldn't bother showing up for the competition this evening." Nah, too subtle. She might as well be direct. "Heather, you're off the squad." Jessica smiled as she repeated the words. She liked the sound of it.

Jessica was sure that Heather was going to put up a major fight, but she wasn't going to budge. According to the cheerleading bylaws, one cocaptain had complete autonomy in the absence of the other. In fact, when Jessica had protested after Heather had kicked Sandy and Maria off the squad, Heather had thrown that rule in her face. Well, she was going to get a taste of her own medicine now, thought Jessica in satisfaction. The squad had voted unanimously to kick Heather off the squad, and that was that. Jessica had followed the rules to a *T*, and there was nothing Heather could do about it.

The only problem was Elizabeth, thought Jessica as she climbed up the steep hill to the cabin. Jessica had left immediately following her pep talk, hoping to avoid Elizabeth until the third competition. She had left the girls in Lila's hands to run through the "Victory" routine. Fortunately, Elizabeth hadn't returned to the field in time. And Jessica hoped she had already left the cabin.

"Heather?" Jessica called, pushing open the wooden door of Hunter House.

"Hmm?" Heather said, turning her head. She was sitting in her bunk in the dark, her knees pulled up to her chest and her arms wrapped around them.

"We have to talk," Jessica said, marching into the room and flicking on the overhead light, a bulb hanging from a string in the peaked wooden ceiling.

"Sure," Heather said, blinking at the light. Her face was tear streaked and her eyes were red and puffy.

"Where's Elizabeth?" asked Jessica, looking around the room.

"She left a while ago," Heather said. "She was just here to pick something up."

"Good," Jessica said, pacing across the room, trying to determine how to handle the situation. She decided to get right to the point. "Heather, the squad took a vote this afternoon, and we voted unanimously to kick you off the team."

Heather opened her mouth, but Jessica went on. "And there's nothing you can do about it," she continued, fire in her eyes. "We aren't going to let you deliberately sabotage the SVH competition. The other girls may believe you've made some honest mistakes, but I know better. Your attempt to make me look foolish just isn't—"

"Jessica!" Heather interrupted her. Jessica's whole body tensed as she stopped to face her, anticipating a fight.

"It's fine," Heather said, waving a dismissive hand. "No problem."

Jessica looked at her suspiciously.

"Really," Heather said. "Don't worry about it."

"But—" Jessica sputtered, unable to believe her ears.

"Now, do you think I could be alone?" asked Heather gruffly, turning her back on Jessica.

"Uh, sure," said Jessica, turning out the light and walking out the door. How could Heather have made such a sudden about-face? wondered Jessica incredulously as she made her way back to the practice field.

"We were great!" Jessica enthused, slinging an arm around Lila and Amy as the girls walked to the cafeteria for dinner. They had just completed the third round, which sealed the first leg of the competition. The "Victory" routine had gone off without a hitch. They had cut Heather's jump from the end, and it hadn't even been noticed. The Sweet Valley High squad had come in fifth, boosting their overall ratings from forty-eighth to thirty-fifth place.

"Yeah, we're back on track!" agreed Amy. All the girls' spirits seemed visibly higher.

"We're on our way to vic-tory!" said Maria, performing the steps with which they had finished their routine. "S-U-C-C-E-S-S, that's the way we spell success!" she called out.

"V-I-C-T-O-R-Y, that's Sweet Valley's victory cry!" yelled Sandy and Jean. The three girls jumped into the air in a double herky and held their arms up in a V formation.

"I hate to put a damper on things," said Jade Wu, "but I don't think we stand a chance."

"What do you mean?" asked Maria in surprise.

"We may have been good, but we weren't good enough," said Jade, shaking her head. "If we want to place in the competition, we have to win every event."

"But we were perfect," protested Amy. "We executed every step flawlessly."

"Look, guys, let's face it," said Jade in a matter-of-fact tone, "without Heather we're ordinary."

Jessica wheeled on her. "What are you saying?" she demanded hotly, her arms folded across her chest.

Jade looked visibly uncomfortable. "I mean, we're

ordinary without Heather—just like without *you* we'd be ordinary," she said, trying to make amends.

"Well, I don't think we're ordinary," said Jessica in a huff. "And that kind of attitude isn't going to get us anywhere!" She stormed away from Jade and stalked toward the lodge alone.

Suddenly Jessica heard footsteps approaching from behind her. Elizabeth was marching up to her, a furious look on her face. Apparently Elizabeth had decided to break their vow of silence.

"How dare you make a unanimous decision without consulting me first!" Elizabeth ranted as she reached her. "How dare you hold a meeting and vote without me!"

"I didn't hold a meeting without you, Liz," Jessica scoffed. "You chose to go back to the cabin."

Elizabeth's eyes narrowed. "Jessica, you are as transparent as Plexiglas. You knew I'd offer to go back, and you made sure to vote without me."

"Oh, Liz, that's ridiculous," sneered Jessica. "Don't you think you're being a bit paranoid?"

"No, I don't!" said Elizabeth hotly. "I am sick and tired of being manipulated by you. It's totally against the cheerleading bylaws to make a squad decision without all the members present."

"So what do you want to do about it?" asked Jessica.

"I demand a revote!" Elizabeth said. "And if you don't agree, I'll take it to the head of the ACA!"

"Well, Liz, I don't think that's going to get you too far," said Jessica.

"And why not?" Elizabeth asked, sparks flying from her eyes. The two girls stopped and faced each other in open confrontation, identical icy stares coming from identical blue-green eyes.

"Because it's too late now, that's why," said Jessica. "I already told Heather about it, and she agreed not to be on the squad."

Elizabeth's mouth dropped open. "Heather agreed?!"

"That's right, Liz," said Jessica. "She wants to sacrifice her position in order to save the team."

Elizabeth was speechless. "Now, if you'll excuse me," said Jessica, brushing past her sister, "I'm kind of hungry."

"OK, just act natural," Todd said as the three boys padded across the grounds in full cheerleading regalia. They were outfitted in their purple-and-gold cheerleading costumes, complete with big white Keds and women's wigs.

"Oh, no problem," said Winston. "I *feel* natural. Only usually I prefer a sheerer shade of lipstick!"

Todd had to agree with Winston. He had never felt so awkward—or so ridiculous—in his whole life. But it looked as though their disguises were working so far. The boys had passed through the gates without incident. The guards had just waved them on.

A gust of wind blew up, and Ken raised his hand to his head, holding his wig in place. "Oh, did I mess up my hair?" he said.

Todd paused to check out Ken's wild, curly blond mane. "Not a strand out of place," he reassured him. "Your locks look lovely."

"And you make a fabulous brunette," Ken said.

"What about me, guys?" asked Winston, putting a hand to his short red bob.

Todd tried not to laugh as he took in Winston's attire. Winston's costume looked just like Todd's and Ken's, but his sweater had glittery sequins on it, as well as feather trim along the neckline. The store had run out of standard costumes, and Winston had had to take a special one.

"Well," Ken said diplomatically, "you won't win any beauty contests, but it works."

"I think that's the field up ahead," Todd said, pointing in front of him.

"I don't think I can go through with this," Winston said suddenly. "They're going to laugh us off the grounds."

Todd stepped back to survey Ken and Winston. "You guys look great," he said.

"You mean, you girls," corrected Ken.

"Right," said Todd, nodding. "From a distance you'd never suspect anything. You look like normal cheerleaders." Todd cocked his head to the side. "A little large, but besides that—"

"Well, here goes nothing," said Winston, taking a deep breath. They walked daintily under the bleachers and onto the field. It looked as if the stands were emptying out.

"Excuse me," Todd said in a feminine voice, stopping two girls, a blonde and a brunette, with big green *H's* monographed on their sweaters. "When is the next competition?"

The dark-haired girl looked at him strangely. "They're all over for the day," she said.

"We're all going to the lodge for dinner," said the blonde, looking the boys up and down.

"See you later!" said the brunette with a giggle, bouncing off with her girlfriend.

"Darnit!" Todd said. "We missed the competition."

"All dressed up and nowhere to go," lamented Ken.

"Do you see any of the SVH squad?" asked Todd, looking around the field. The boys scanned the field rapidly. Cheerleaders were milling about, but there was no sign of any of the Sweet Valley High cheerleaders.

"There are some girls in red-and-white uniforms down there," Todd said, shading his eyes from the glare of the setting sun.

"Nah, I don't think that's them," said Ken, squinting in the direction Todd indicated. "I don't recognize any girls from the squad."

"Excuse me, are you girls registered?" came an ominous voice from behind them.

The boys wheeled around to find an athletic-looking woman dressed in a blue suit. Todd gasped as he read the tag on the woman's jacket: Zoe Balsam, Director, ACA. They were face-to-face with the head of the American Cheerleading Association. Todd's heart began sounding a drumroll. It looked as if their visit to the American

Cheerleading Compound was going to be a short one.

"Uh, no, ma'am," squeaked Winston in a falsetto voice, patting his hair into place.

"Every cheerleading squad has to check in," said Ms. Balsam. "The security is extremely tight on the premises." A quizzical look crossed her face, and she scanned the list she held in her hands. "In fact, you can't compete without registering."

"We're just here to watch," explained Todd, putting his hands on his hips and adopting a feminine posture.

The woman looked at them suspiciously. "I haven't seen you girls yet. What are your names?"

"Uh, I'm Tilda Wilkins," said Todd, "and these are my squadmates, Kendall Matthews and . . ." Todd's voice trailed off as he searched for an appropriate name.

"I'm Winnie Egbert," said Winston, extending a dainty hand.

The woman still looked dubious as she shook Winston's hand. "And where are you from?" she asked.

"Uhh—" Ken stuttered, looking down at his sweater. "Sss—"

"Saskatchewan," Todd said, taking over. "We're from Saskatchewan, Canada."

"Well, girls, whether you're here to compete, train, or observe, you've got to be registered," said the director sternly.

"Yes, ma'am," said Ken. The boys turned and began briskly walking away.

"Girls!" yelled Ms. Balsam a few moments later.

"Oh, boy," muttered Winston. Todd held his breath as they looked back, waiting for her to blow the whistle on them.

"Registration's that way," she said, pointing to the right.

The boys quickly changed course and ran in the other direction, falling over one another in their haste. Todd risked a look back. Ms. Balsam was just standing there looking after them, shaking her head.

Chapter 9

"This way!" called Jessica, leading the squad in a run through the woods of the cheerleading compound early Sunday morning. The trail forked ahead of her, and she turned to the right, choosing a rigorous uphill path. The girls formed a procession as they followed the narrow trail through the dense redwoods. Lila ran directly behind Jessica, and Elizabeth brought up the rear.

The girls jogged along in silence for a few minutes as they maneuvered the difficult trail. The early-morning air was fresh and misty, and the sky was a clear gray-blue. All that could be heard in the stillness of the morning was the girls' breathing and the sounds of nature. Birds warbled and chirped, and a variety of invisible insects buzzed noisily. An occasional twig snapped as the girls trod upon the dewy earth.

Jessica breathed in the fresh air with satisfaction,

her aquamarine eyes bright with excitement. She was thrilled to have full control of the squad again. She had two days to lead the team to victory, and she was determined to do it. The squad had been up training since seven A.M. They had started with stretching exercises in the practice field and had followed up with a half hour of low-impact aerobic exercise. If they wanted to win all the competitions of the day, they had to be in the finest shape possible.

"I think—I'm—going—to pass out," panted Lila dramatically from behind Jessica.

"Have some water," offered Maria, passing forth a plastic canteen of fresh springwater.

"Thanks," breathed Lila, taking a long gulp as she jogged along the path. She wiped her brow with the arm of her T-shirt and passed the jug back.

"Water!" Jean cried from the back of the line. The girls handed the canteen down the line, each taking a swig in turn.

"Hey, Jess!" Lila called, adjusting the purple sweatband around her forehead to keep her hair off her face.

"Yeah?" Jessica asked, jogging along at a brisk pace.

"I think we need some inspiration," Lila said.

"Inspiration coming up," Jessica returned. The trail opened out into a grassy clearing in the woods. Jessica reduced her speed and trotted out into the meadow.

"Freedom!" exclaimed Maria, bouncing into a series of cartwheels in the clearing.

"Where—does she—get the—energy?" panted Amy, coming up to join Lila.

"Don't worry, the worst is over," Jessica encouraged the group, jogging along at a constant pace. "You guys are doing great! Now, everybody sing along!"

The girls clumped together as they left the woods, running in groups of twos and threes.

"I don't know but I been told!" yelled out Jessica.

"I don't know but I been told!" chorused the girls.

"SVH is good as gold!" shouted Jessica.

"SVH is good as gold!" returned the girls.

"I don't know, but it's been said!" chanted Jessica.

"I don't know but it's been said!" repeated the girls.

"The number one team's the white and red!" yelled Jessica.

"The number one team's the white and red!" echoed the girls.

"Sound off, sound off, YEAH!!" The girls cheered together, infused with new energy as they ran through the meadow.

Jessica clapped her hands together and took off toward the forest on the opposite side of the clearing. "I don't know but it's been said . . ." she yelled.

"Hey, I think I see them!" exclaimed Todd, catching a glimpse of the Sweet Valley High squad through the redwoods across the meadow. Todd,

Ken, and Winston, still in their cheerleading outfits, were jogging through the forest in search of the girls. They had been trailing them all morning. After catching sight of them leaving the practice field earlier, the boys had followed them at a distance into the woods.

"Are you sure that's them?" Ken asked, running up to Todd's side. His skirt whipped up in the wind and flew around his waist. "Yikes!" Ken exclaimed, patting it down quickly.

Todd peered through the trees, trying to make out the figures in the woods. All he could see was a blur of sweatpants and T-shirts. Perspiration trickled down his cheek, and Todd wiped it off with the back of his hand, smudging his makeup across his face.

"All my hard work!" Ken joked as he noticed the blotchy mess covering Todd's face.

"Ugh," Todd said, looking at the creamy pink blur on the back of his hand. "I don't know how girls can stand wearing all this gunk on their faces."

"It's one of the great unsolved mysteries," agreed Ken.

Suddenly the sounds of chanting wafted in their direction. The words were faint but distinct. "*I don't know but I been told!*" they heard.

"That's Jessica!" exclaimed Ken.

"C'mon!" Todd yelled, waving at Ken. The boys ran out into the meadow toward the forest opposite. They stopped and looked around them quickly. There was no sign of the girls anywhere.

"Shh!" said Ken, listening carefully. A faint

sound of chanting came from the far end of the forest.

"Follow the voices!" said Todd, taking off in the direction of the singing. The boys raced after him, trying to trace the sound of the girls' singing.

Fifteen minutes later they found themselves at their point of departure.

"We're in a maze," said Ken, shaking his head.

"The wind must throw the sound," said Winston.

"We'll never find them now," said Todd in a dejected tone, looking out into the clearing. He slid down a tree and slumped to the ground, resting his face in the cup of his hands.

"C'mon, Wilkins, don't give up so fast," said Ken.

"Yeah," said Winston, "don't tell me I'm dressed up like a drag queen for nothing."

"Hey, here they come!" said Ken, spotting the group through the trees. They could hear the sounds of footsteps approaching as the girls wound their way back through the woods, chanting all the while.

Todd jumped up, his heart beating fast. "OK, guys, let's hide behind the tree and try to get one of the girls' attention as they come by."

"Maybe I can distract Jessica," said Ken.

"That might be hard," said Winston. "I think she's playing drill sergeant."

The boys crouched behind the tree, ready to pounce on the girls as they jogged by. Suddenly they heard the sounds of footsteps approaching from the clearing in the other direction.

They turned quickly. Walking toward them from a distance was Zoe Balsam flanked by two large men. They were all wearing the navy-blue director's uniforms of the American Cheerleading Association.

"Oh, no, it's the head of the ACA!" despaired Todd.

"And some flight attendants!" added Winston.

"C'mon, let's get out of here!" urged Ken, jumping up and heading away from the directors.

"Wait!" Todd said, reaching out and stopping him. "We've got to keep going in the same direction or else we'll look suspicious."

"You're right," Ken said, nodding. The three of them took off at a slow jog, trying to appear normal.

Todd's pulse quickened as they approached the directors.

"Hello!" Ken and Todd called out, waving as they passed. Winston managed a short wave and tripped along after them.

"Good morning, girls!" returned the directors, waving and smiling as they passed by.

Jessica headed to the bathroom to shower after the run, deep in thought. The girls were still out on the practice field, doing a series of cool-down exercises under Lila's guidance. Jessica wondered how they'd fare during the second round of the competition without Heather. They'd done a great job at the third competition the day before, but that hadn't been good enough. Today they had to be better than great. They had to be extraordinary.

The words of Jade Wu came back to her: *Without Heather we're ordinary. Without Heather we're ordinary.* The comment had been haunting her all night. Jessica had scorned the idea, but Jade's words weren't lost on her. Before Heather had arrived at Sweet Valley, the cheerleading squad had been good, but not outstanding. They'd never competed in the regional competition before, not to mention state—or nationals. When Heather had come along, she had turned the team around. Jessica wondered, deep down, if Jade was right. Maybe Heather *was* the key to their success.

Jessica pushed open the door to the bathroom and heard the sounds of somebody weeping.

"Hey, are you OK?" she asked, peeping under the stall to see who it was. "Oh, it's you," she said, making a face as she recognized Heather's custom-made cheerleading shoes. She went to the sink and turned on the faucet to wash her hands.

Jessica could hear Heather sniff and blow her nose. "Go ahead," Heather said in an obstinate tone through the door. "Tell me how I ruined everything. Tell me how I humiliated the entire squad. Tell me how you hate me."

Jessica turned off the water and leaned back against the sink. Heather's sob story wasn't going to work on her. Heather had dug her own grave, and Jessica refused to pity her for it.

"OK," she said as Heather emerged from the

stall. "You ruined everything. You humiliated the entire squad. I—"

"Oh, stop it," Heather growled, coming out of the stall and turning to the sink to wash her hands. "If it weren't for me, you wouldn't even be here in the first place."

Jessica could feel the blood rush to her face. "You've got a lot of nerve!" she cried. "How dare you take any credit when you've as much as ruined our chances at nationals? Why don't you just admit the truth, Heather? You may be a great cheerleader, but you just can't cut it in the big leagues."

Heather opened her mouth as if to respond but quickly checked herself.

"Go ahead," Jessica goaded her. "Admit it. You're not good enough. You can't take the pressure."

"That is not true!" Heather said between clenched teeth.

"Oh, yeah?" Jessica said. "Then how do you explain your disastrous performances on the field today?"

"I had no choice," Heather said quietly. "I had to do it."

"I knew it!" Jessica exclaimed. "You messed up on purpose. You were trying to humiliate me."

"Oh, Jessica," said Heather scornfully. "This doesn't have anything to do with you. Contrary to what you may believe, the world doesn't revolve around you."

"It doesn't?" Jessica said, surprised. "What do you mean?"

Heather sighed. "It's kind of a long story."

A few minutes later they were sitting on their bunks in the deserted cabin. "OK, let's have it," said Jessica.

"Well, remember the girl you met at lunch from my old squad?" Heather began, getting up and pacing the room as she spoke.

How could I forget? thought Jessica, thinking of the tall, beautiful brunette who had practically run her over on their first day there. "Marissa James," Jessica confirmed.

Heather nodded. "Well, she heard from everyone that Sweet Valley would be Thomas Jefferson's biggest rival at the nationals. So in typical Marissa James style she decided to stop us."

"What do you mean?" It had never occurred to Jessica that anybody else but Heather was responsible for their problems. "But how did she plan to do it?"

"By blackmailing me to mess up the competition," Heather confessed.

"Blackmailing you?" said Jessica, aghast. "With what?"

"With this!" said Heather, pulling out the article.

Just at that moment the door swung open. "Jessica Wakefield, I have something to say to you," said Elizabeth, stomping through the door with a vehement look on her face. All the girls piled in behind her.

"Wait, listen—" began Jessica.

"No, you listen to me for once," interrupted Elizabeth, the words coming out in a flood. "You can't just push people around and get your own way all the time. You can't hold secret meetings and make important decisions without the input of all the members of the squad. We've been talking, and the whole team has agreed that it was unorthodox of you to vote without me. Your vote is officially null and void. If you want Heather off the squad, we *all* have to agree to it!"

Elizabeth stared at her sister, darts shooting from her eyes. The other girls shuffled nervously, waiting for a reprisal from Jessica.

"It's not necessary, Elizabeth," Heather said, slumping down on the bunk. "I've agreed not to be on the team."

"What are you talking about?" she asked, turning to face Heather.

"You had better tell them the whole story," Jessica said.

"What story?" Elizabeth asked.

Heather sighed. "I guess you should all hear this."

"Sounds juicy," Jessica heard Lila whisper to Amy as the two girls plopped down onto Lila's bunk. Jean, Maria, and Sandy piled onto Jean's bunk, leaning against the wood-slatted wall. The rest of the girls settled down on the floor in front of them.

When all eyes were turned toward Heather, she began to recount her tale.

"At TJ, I was the best cheerleader," Heather said. "I was the head of the squad, and I took our team to State for two years in a row."

Jessica sighed, then interrupted. "I think we've already heard all this before," she said.

"Do you mind?" asked Heather.

"OK, sorry. Go on," Jessica said.

Heather closed her eyes for a moment, as if to get hold of herself, and continued. "Well, it all happened around this time last year," she said. "We had just won at State, and we were preparing for nationals. Cheerleading was my life. It was all that mattered to me. I devoted so much time to cheerleading that my grades began to slide. Especially my math grade. The final exam was coming up, and I knew that I was going to fail. And if I failed, I would be kicked off the squad."

"So you cheated on the final," guessed Sandy.

"And you were kicked off the squad," added Jean.

"Right." Heather nodded.

"How did you manage to cheat on the test?" Amy asked.

"I, uh, got a copy of the exam before the final," Heather explained, bright-pink circles popping out on her cheeks. "And to make things even worse, I gave it to a few of my friends. That was how I got caught. We all had the same answers, and they weren't all right."

"How awful!" Annie exclaimed.

"Yeah, it was a big scandal, and my reputation at school was ruined. And in the entire town." She waved the article in the air as proof.

"Let's see," said Lila, stretching a hand out for the story. Lila skimmed it quickly and passed it on.

The girls murmured sympathetically as they read the incriminating account.

"But, Heather, we don't care about all that," said Annie, passing the story on to Maria. "You've already been punished as it is."

"Yeah, that's all in the past now," said Sara.

"Not exactly," said Heather. "You see, the first night at nationals, I found the article in my bed—planted by Marissa James."

The girls murmured in surprise.

"Marissa was my archenemy at TJ," explained Heather. "She wanted to be the captain for two years in a row, and the girls voted for me both years. So, anyway, Marissa told me that if I let Sweet Valley so much as *place* in a single competition, my secret would be out."

"She blackmailed you!" exclaimed Sara.

"That is despicable!" said Annie angrily. "That girl should be kicked out of the ACA."

"Well, it doesn't matter now," said Heather, her lips suddenly trembling as she spoke. "You know, when I came to Sweet Valley, I thought I'd have the chance to start over again. I thought I'd have a new beginning. But it looks like my past is destined to follow me around for the rest of my life."

"No, it's not!" objected Annie.

"That's ridiculous!" chimed in Sara. Jessica rolled her eyes. She couldn't believe how sympathetically the girls were responding. *You'd think that now at least they'd see Heather for what she really is,* she thought.

"You can still start over!" said Jean encouragingly.

"No, I can't," said Heather, shaking her head, "because I've ruined everything. I shouldn't have gone along with Marissa's scheme. I just couldn't bear the thought of my secret coming out." Tears trickled down her cheeks as she spoke. "I realize now that I should have told you all right away. I—I'm truly sorry. Now I hate myself, probably more than all of you hate me now."

"Why, Heather, that would be impossible," Jessica started to say, but she was interrupted by Patty Gilbert, who stood up and took the floor. Patty had been sitting with a pencil and paper during Heather's confession.

"Each round of the competition is worth one third of the total score, right?" said Patty. The girls nodded their heads. "And right now, we're thirty-fifth. It doesn't look like we can win. But if we come in first in all the competitions from now on, we can still place."

"Well, then," said Elizabeth. "Enough of this sitting around. Let's get out of here!"

"Wow, what a story!" said Lila, whistling under her breath. She and Jessica were walking to the field for the first competition of the day.

"I know," said Jessica. "The whole time I thought she was out to get me. And it turned out that Marissa James was out to get her." Jessica shook her head in wonder. "I never dreamed that somebody else was involved."

"You know, I almost feel sorry for her," said Lila.

"Well, I don't!" said Jessica emphatically. She ducked under a tree branch jutting out in the path. "I mean, it's too bad that she got kicked off her squad and suffered complete and utter humiliation." Jessica paused to savor the thought of it. "But that doesn't negate her heinous behavior the whole time she's been on the squad. And she should have told us right away about the blackmailing thing."

"I think the team feels pretty sympathetic toward her," said Lila. A fly buzzed noisily around her face, and she swatted it away.

"Wonders never cease," said Jessica. "I swear, that girl could rob them all and they'd thank her."

"Well, I think we should thank her for telling us the truth," said Lila. "I mean, when you're in that deep, it's hard to get out. Now we've still got a chance."

"Yeah," agreed Jessica, "we'll show Marissa James that Sweet Valley High can't be pushed around!"

Just then Marissa James approached them on the walk, looking fit and fashionable in a black Lycra unitard. Dark sunglasses were propped up on her head, holding back a thatch of rich auburn hair.

"Speak of the devil," Lila muttered under her breath.

"The devil is right," Jessica agreed.

"Oh, hi," Marissa said as she caught sight of them.

"Hi," Jessica and Lila returned, waving back unenthusiastically.

"So sorry you've all had such a rough time of it," she said as she passed, her voice dripping with false sympathy. "Oh, well, maybe next year!" she called.

"Or maybe *this* year," muttered Lila.

"I really hate that girl," said Jessica.

Chapter 10

"R-O-W-D-I-E, that's the way we spell row-die!" yelled Jessica, stamping her feet energetically as the squad launched into their standard school-spirit routine.

"Rowdie, let's get rowdie!" sang out the girls, hitting their hands against their thighs and stomping their feet in unison to the beat. It was the first competition of the day, and the Sweet Valley squad was performing brilliantly. The crowd was on its feet, clapping and stomping along with the music.

Jessica was beaming as she and Heather led the squad into the final leg of the routine. It was a jazzy dance number that Jade and Patty had choreographed. Clapping and shouting, the girls formed two lines facing each other, Jessica and Heather heading each row.

As the music shifted to an upbeat tempo, the girls sprang into action. Working in pairs, the girls did one-armed cartwheels toward each other in perfect succession. They followed with a line of front handsprings. As Heather and Jessica bounced back onto their heels, Jade and Patty performed a back crunch: a round-off followed by a back handspring. The other pairs quickly followed.

The last stunt was a front handspring followed by a spread-eagle jump with a landing in the splits. Heather and Jessica landed next to each other, and the other girls fanned out, forming a perfect *V*. "V-I-C-T-O-R-Y, that's Sweet Valley's battle cry!" they yelled, holding their arms up in the air in V shapes.

The audience applauded wildly, rising spontaneously to their feet.

Static filled the air, and a voice came over the loudspeaker. "Everybody please settle down," boomed the announcer. "Our last squad has performed. We'll have the results in just a moment."

The girls trotted off the field, out of breath but elated at the response to their performance.

"We did it!" said Jean as they took their seats in the bleachers.

"We were definitely not ordinary!" agreed Jade, laughing.

"The third-place winner in the first round of today's competition is the squad from Reno, Nevada!" boomed the announcer.

Jessica gritted her teeth as the Reno squad stood up and yelled out a cheer. Marissa's voice rang out loud and clear across the stadium as she led them in their school-spirit cheer. "Now we've really got to win," said Jessica to Lila, her voice determined.

The announcer's voice came over the loudspeaker again. "And the second-place prize goes to our most exotic squad—the Waikiki Pelicans all the way from Waikiki, Hawaii!"

Jessica grabbed on to Lila's hand for support as the audience applauded. This was their only chance. If they didn't win now, they were out of the competition for good.

"Jess!" Lila said, wriggling her hand. Jessica looked down. She was gripping Lila's hand so hard that her knuckles were turning white.

"Oh, sorry," she said, loosening her grip. Jessica closed her eyes and held her breath as the announcer continued.

"And our first-place winners—shocking us all with their amazing turnaround—the squad from Sweet Valley, California!" boomed the announcer.

The girls exploded with joy, hugging and high-fiving each other. Jessica glanced over at Heather. Heather looked back at her and winked. Jessica smiled. It looked as if everything was going to be OK after all.

"Do you think I could talk to you for a moment?" said Marissa James, yanking Heather away from the squad as the girls headed to lunch at the lodge.

"Sure," said Heather sweetly, pulling her arm away and stepping away from the group.

Marissa waited until the girls were out of earshot.

"Have you forgotten our little agreement?" she hissed. Her even features were contorted with rage, and she looked as if she were about to explode.

"No, Marissa, I haven't forgotten," said Heather evenly. "I've just decided it doesn't matter."

Marissa stared at her in astonishment.

"You see, I told my squad about the old Heather Mallone myself," Heather explained. "There's nothing you can say about me that they don't already know. Now you'll have to compete against the Sweet Valley squad in all their strength."

"You'll never win, you little weasel," Marissa snarled. "And I'll do everything in my power to make sure about that."

"I wouldn't waste my energy on our squad if I were you," Heather returned. "You'll need all of it for your own." Heather flipped her blond mane over her shoulders and walked calmly away.

"Are we all set?" Jessica asked on Sunday afternoon at the cabin as the girls got ready to leave for the second competition of the day. The event was scheduled to begin in half an hour, and the Braselton girls had already left for the field.

Jessica looked around at her squad proudly. They were dressed in Heather's tailor-made uniforms for their seventies disco routine. Both Heather and Jessica had agreed to wear Lila's uniforms for the grand finale. The girls were all decked out in red-and-white-checked hip-hugging skirts and half tops. Jessica had to admit they looked sharp.

"Ready to boogie down!" said Jeanie.

"Do the hustle!" sang Sandy. Everybody laughed as Jeanie and Sandy broke out into an exaggerated version of the dance. The girls were all pumped up from their victory in the morning, and they were ready to bring the house down again.

"Jean, you've got the pom-poms?" Jessica asked.

"Got 'em," said Jean, holding up the pom-pom bag.

"And Lila, you're bringing the routine book?" Jessica asked. Lila held it up in confirmation.

"I've got the music," offered Heather.

"OK, then!" Jessica said. She drew the girls toward her for a group hug. "Let's go get 'em!" she yelled. The girls clapped and let out a whoop.

Jessica slung her backpack over her back and bounced up to the door. She put her hand on the knob and pulled. It seemed to be stuck. "Wha—?" she said out loud, turning the knob and tugging at the door. It didn't budge. "I can't seem to get the door open," Jessica said.

"Let me try," Heather said, closing her hand firmly over the knob and pulling with all her might. The door wheezed in protest but didn't move. Heather took a deep breath and tried again, exerting all her force. Nothing. "How could the door be locked?" Heather asked, perplexed.

Jessica and Heather stared at each other in wonder, and then suddenly it dawned on them at the same time. "Marissa James," they said in unison.

Jessica turned and faced the girls. "It looks like Marissa James and her squad have been up to some mischief," she said. "The door's locked from the outside."

"And we're stuck in here," Heather added.

"Oh, no!" said Maria in despair, falling back onto a bunk.

"What are we going to do?" wailed Sandy.

"I don't know," said Heather, looking at her watch. "Our performance starts in half an hour. If we don't get to the field in time, we'll be automatically disqualified from the entire competition."

Jessica marched up to the door and yanked at it violently, a fierce expression on her face. The door stood firm. "Darnit!" Jessica cried, slamming her fist into the hard wood. It took her a moment to register the pain. "Oww!" she moaned, hopping around holding her hand.

"Jessica, are you OK?" asked Annie with concern, jumping up and running toward her.

"I'm fine, I'm fine," said Jessica, waving her away.

"Let's try the windows," Heather suggested, indicating the four windows lining the cabin walls. She quickly turned the handle of one of the windows and pulled. It didn't move. She braced her legs against the wall and yanked again, putting her whole body into it. Suddenly she went flying back across the room and fell onto a bunk, the handle in her hand. "Well, that one's out of the question," Heather said wryly, dropping the handle to the floor with a clatter.

The girls quickly made a circuit of the cabin, trying all the windows in succession, but their efforts were in vain. The windows were all sealed shut.

"I can't believe it," Heather muttered angrily, perching on the corner of a bunk. She stared at her watch, watching as the minutes ticked away. "All our work—"

"And now we don't even have a chance!" finished Annie.

"We're doomed," despaired Jean, dropping the bag of pom-poms onto the floor and slumping down on the ground.

"There must be *some* way we can get out of here," Jessica said in determination, looking around the wooden cabin frantically in search of an exit. She felt as if the wooden walls were closing in her. *Maybe they could break down the door*, she thought desperately. This was their only chance for a comeback. If they didn't compete now, her reputation as cocaptain was ruined. Suddenly her eyes lit upon the tiny window high on the wall at the back of the cabin. A crack of light shone through it. "That one's open!" Jessica exclaimed. All the girls followed her gaze.

"Jessica, are you crazy?" said Lila in wonder. "It's about two feet square."

"I bet Jade could get through it," said Jessica, indicating the slight, petite girl.

Jade looked nervous. "But it must be over twenty feet up," she said. "We'd need a ladder."

"Well, we're a cheerleading squad, aren't we?" said Jessica enthusiastically. "We make our own ladders!"

"Jessica's right!" enthused Heather. "We'll make a pyramid!" She stopped and thought for a moment, quickly measuring the space from the floor to the ceiling in her head. "I think we're going to have to do a four-three-two-one pyramid."

"A four-tiered pyramid!" breathed Elizabeth.

"Is that possible?" asked Sara.

"Usually not," admitted Heather. "But I think it's worth a try."

"Yeah, what have we got to lose?" added Jessica.

"Our lives, for one thing," said Elizabeth dryly.

"It is kind of dangerous," Heather agreed.

"So Heather and I will spot the pyramid on either side," Jessica said.

Heather nodded her head in agreement.

"Let's get moving, then!" said Lila, jumping up. "We've only got about fifteen minutes left."

"OK," said Jessica, surveying the squad, "biggest girls on the bottom and smallest on top." She quickly assigned positions. Patty, Lila, Amy, and Sara got down on the floor on all fours. Maria, Annie, and Elizabeth assumed their positions on top of them quickly, making the second tier.

"Everybody close in for support," said Heather. The girls shifted together, forming a tight fit. Jessica and Heather spotted Jean and Sandy as they climbed up the tiers. The pyramid swayed dangerously as they settled on top. Jessica and Heather quickly flanked the sides, holding the girls together. "Deep breath, everyone," said Jessica. "Steady!"

"Well, here goes," Jade said, biting her lip nervously.

Heather crouched down as Jade climbed onto her shoulders. Moving adeptly, Jade supported her full weight with her arms and swung her dancer's legs up onto Heather's shoulders. She stood and balanced carefully. Holding on to the ceiling for support, Jade placed her knees delicately on the third tier of the pyramid, careful to distribute her weight between Jean and Sandy equally. The girls held their breath as Jade released her hold on Heather. The pyramid stood.

"OK, guys," said Jessica in a soothing voice, "you look great. Now, just stay calm."

Jade reached up to the window carefully. Her fingers barely grazed the handle. She took a deep breath and stretched out on her knees, grabbing hold of the handle firmly. A triumphant grin spread across her face as she pulled the window open entirely.

"Heads up!" Sandy yelled as she felt the pyramid collapsing. Jade's hand slipped from the handle as her support began to give way. Jessica and Heather jumped to the sides, protecting the girls from the bunks as they slid down into a pile on the ground.

"Well, we did it," said Jade, peeking her head out from the mass of arms and legs. "We made a four-three-two-one pyramid."

The girls groaned and lay back in a heap on the floor.

• • •

"I've never seen so many cheerleaders in my entire life!" exclaimed Todd as he took in the scene before him. Todd, Ken, and Winston were seated at the far end of the bleachers, waiting for the second competition to begin. The field was bursting with groups of enthusiastic girls cheering and shouting as they practiced their routines. With all the squads in matching uniforms, the field had been transformed into a rainbow of colors.

"Me neither," Ken agreed. "Can you imagine having this many girls cheer you on at a game?"

"We'd win every point," said Todd.

"Girls, please take your seats!" yelled a voice over the loudspeakers. "The competition is about to begin!"

Todd, Ken, and Winston clustered together trying to look inconspicuous as the girls began filling the stands.

"Where do you think they are?" Todd asked, glancing down at his watch nervously. "The competition starts in five minutes." Todd looked over at the empty California section of the stands, a worried expression on his face.

"Every other team is here," said Ken, taking in the packed stands. Most of the squads were huddled together, giving pep talks and letting out small cheers.

"Don't worry, they'll be here," Winston reassured them. "They're probably doing warm-up exercises in the practice field."

"Unless they've passed out from their run this morning," said Todd.

"Well, you know Jessica," said Ken. "She wouldn't miss the competition for anything in the world. She's probably planning to make a grand entrance."

"She could be late, though," worried Todd. "Jessica doesn't wear a watch."

"But Elizabeth does," Ken pointed out.

"Please give a warm welcome to the Texas Tigers from San Antonio, Texas, our first squad to perform!" boomed the voice over the loudspeaker. The crowd clapped as a group of spirited girls in orange-and-black outfits bounced onto the field.

"They're starting!" Ken exclaimed in surprise.

Winston leafed through the program quickly, running a finger down the day's lineup. "Sweet Valley is the fifth team to perform in this competition."

"That gives the girls about ten minutes," said Todd. "We better go find them." The boys jumped up and tore down the bleachers, taking the steps two at a time.

"Why is everybody looking at us?" Todd asked as they trotted across the field, noting the funny looks they were drawing from the crowd. As they passed each squad, the cheerleaders seemed to gather together in groups, laughing and pointing.

"Don't worry about it, Todd," said Ken, holding on to his skirt as he ran. "We're popular, that's all."

"Whoa, mama!" yelled a girl from the audience, putting her fingers in her mouth and letting out a piercing whistle.

"Show us some leg!" hooted another girl.

"Oh, boy," moaned Winston, limping along after Ken and Todd. "I think they know who we are."

"Hey! Someone's coming!" Lila said, looking out the side window from her bunk. "Three cheerleaders. Three really funny-looking cheerleaders."

"Are they coming for us?" asked Maria.

"I hope so," said Lila.

The girls all piled onto Lila's bunk, shouting and waving out the window. "Help, help!" they yelled. "We're in here!"

"Let me see," said Jessica, trying to get a glimpse out the window. "Wow," she said. "The Amazon queens are coming."

Jessica leaned back against the wall, the relief evident on her face. "I can't believe it," she said. "We might make it to the competition after all."

Maria clambered up to the window, watching as two huge cheerleaders and one tall, skinny cheerleader lumbered toward the cabin. As she watched, the tall, skinny cheerleader's hair fell off. Maria gasped in shock.

"Oh-mi-god!" she screamed a moment later as Winston ran back to retrieve his wig. "It's Winston!" She waved a hand toward the others to look.

"And that's Ken and Todd!" Amy exclaimed.

Maria jumped off the bunk and ran to the door. She began knocking on it loudly, trying to get the boys' attention. Soon all of the girls had crowded around her. "Help, help!" they cried, pounding on the door as the boys approached.

"Don't worry, we're coming!" yelled Todd.

"Help is on the way!" added Ken, quickly unlocking the door and pushing it open. A throng of girls almost fell on top of them.

"Oh, hi, girls," said Ken with a smile, finding himself in a sea of cheerleaders.

"We might say the same thing!" exclaimed Maria as she took in the boys' lavishly made-up faces and cheerleading costumes.

All the girls started laughing as they got a glimpse of their liberators close-up.

"Where are you girls from?" asked Maria, noting the *S* on the boys' sweaters.

"Saskatchewan," Todd and Ken answered in unison.

"Saskatchewan!" responded Jeanie. "You came all the way from Canada!"

"I hear they're known for their husky cheerleaders," said Sandy.

"They've got some *sizable* talent there, don't they?" added Maria.

Maria's pun sent the girls into fresh gales of laughter. Everybody was laughing uproariously—except Jessica and Elizabeth, Maria noticed. They had both backed away from the group and were sitting on opposite bunks at the far end of the cabin. Obviously cheerleading costumes hadn't done the trick.

"All right, all right, that's enough," said Todd.

"Everybody up," said Ken. "You've got a performance to put on."

"I think the performance is already taking place," said Sandy merrily.

The girls stood up and gathered their bags, wiping away tears of laughter from their eyes.

"You know, Winston," said Maria, entwining her elbow in his and cuddling up to him. "I always did have a thing for redheads."

"You know what they say about us," said Winston with a goofy grin, hugging her closer to him and leaning down for a kiss. "We're fiery and passionate." Maria smiled as she wiped the lipstick from her lips.

"And hotheaded," added Sandy. "Maria, you better watch out."

"I think I'll take my chances," said Maria with a smile.

"Ken, who does your hair?" breathed Lila, sidling up to him. "That blond do is perfect with your eyes."

"Antonio," said Ken with mock seriousness. "But he's very expensive."

"Hey, Todd, want to borrow my lipstick?" asked Amy, holding out a bright-colored tube.

"Now, cut it out, you guys!" Todd said, shaking a pom-pom at all of them. "You have about a minute and a half to get onstage!"

Chapter 11

"And for the second time in a row, the number-one squad is Sweet Valley High!" boomed the announcer's voice over the loudspeaker system following the afternoon competition.

The crowd applauded enthusiastically as the band struck up a lively tune. The girls from the Sweet Valley squad went wild, jumping up and down with joy and throwing pom-poms in the air.

Jessica's knees buckled with relief, and she sat down hard on the bleachers. After all the excitement she suddenly felt drained. The girls had arrived on the field with about fifteen seconds to spare. They hadn't even had time for a pep talk. They had run straight onto the field and started their number. But they had been so pumped up with nervous energy that they had performed more brilliantly than ever.

"We did it!" yelled Sandy, grabbing Jeanie and flinging her around.

"We really pulled it off!" said Maria. "C'mon, Jess!" she said, grabbing Jessica by the hands and pulling her up. Jessica found herself caught up in a whirlwind of girls hugging and congratulating each other. Suddenly she felt herself being swung around by Heather.

As soon as Heather realized it was Jessica, she let go of her grip. Jessica and Heather looked at each other awkwardly for a moment, then shrugged and moved away. *Who would have ever thought I'd be hugging Heather?* pondered Jessica, shaking her head in amazement.

"The crowd went nuts over the disco stuff," said Maria as the girls began settling down.

"Yeah, and that jump by Heather really brought down the house!" said Annie. Jessica rankled at Annie's words. Heather, as usual, had virtually taken over the performance with her flashy dance-jump combination at the end of the routine. But it *had* been amazing, she had to admit.

"And we owe it all to the boys!" said Maria.

"Or the girls!" said Annie.

"They're getting more attention than anyone else here," said Jeanie.

"Well, of course they are," said Sandy. "Three boys in the midst of an all-girls event—what would you expect?"

"Yeah, all the girls are thrilled," said Lila.

"But the judges wouldn't be if they knew," said Maria. "I don't think the directors have caught on yet either."

"Lucky for us," put in Amy. "The boys really

saved us today. I thought it was all over."

"Let's go thank them," said Maria, slinging her bag over her shoulder and jumping up.

"Uh, I've got some stuff to take care of at the cabin," said Elizabeth quickly, hopping up and sprinting down the bleachers.

"Me too," Jessica said, taking off after her sister.

Amy and Maria looked at each other after the twins made their rapid exit.

"Something's got to be done about this," Maria said.

"Yeah," agreed Amy. "This is getting unbearable. We've got to get the twins back together—with each other and with their boyfriends."

"Let's go find the boys—I mean, the girls," suggested Maria.

Maria scanned the athletic field quickly. "I think they're over there, hiding from the crowds," she said, pointing across the field. Sure enough, the boys were huddled together at the far end of the field, trying to keep a low profile as hordes of cheerleaders streamed by them.

Amy and Maria ran down the bleachers and made their way across the field.

Maria couldn't help laughing as she took in Winston's attire. Her heart went out to him with love. With his long, skinny limbs and knobby knees, Winston always looked a little goofy. In his cheerleading outfit he looked ridiculous, like a bony stork dressed in a skirt.

Maria ran up to him and jumped into his arms.

Winston quickly unraveled himself, a horrified

expression on his face. "No public displays of affection as long as I'm a woman!" he said.

Maria clapped her hand to her mouth. "That's right!" she said, laughing. "What would the judges think!"

"You could be disqualified for intersquad affection," said Ken.

"Well, in your fancy outfits you *are* pretty hard to resist," said Maria.

"Yeah, what's with the plumage, Winston?" asked Amy.

"Are you going to the Oscars after this?" teased Maria.

"Well, you know, I really wanted to make a splash," said Winston.

"He thought he should go all out for Maria," added Todd.

"You're welcome to borrow *my* outfit sometime," said Ken, speaking in a high-pitched tone. He paused a moment to pose, putting a hand to his hair and shaking his blond curls. "But only if I can borrow yours. I love hip huggers."

"Oh, Ken, you're so lucky," said Todd in a high voice. "With my hips I'd never get away with it."

Everybody laughed.

Suddenly Todd turned serious as he noticed the rest of the Sweet Valley High cheerleaders making their way down the bleachers. "Hey, you guys, they're leaving!" Todd said. "We've got to catch up with Jessica and Elizabeth." Todd shaded his eyes with his hand as he tried to pick them out.

"Bad news, Todd," said Maria. "They already left."

"Bolted is more like it," Amy added.

Todd's face fell.

"Do you think it was the skirt?" Ken asked.

"Listen, you guys," said Amy. "You've got to get those two talking again."

"And get back together with them," added Maria. "They've been at each other's throats!"

Elizabeth walked through the woods alone on her way back to the cabin, laughing as she remembered how cute Todd looked in his little pleated skirt. She hugged her arms around herself, feeling a flood of warmth as she thought of Todd. The sun was shining brightly and the sky was a clear robin's-egg blue. A hummingbird whirred from a branch nearby. Elizabeth almost felt happy for a moment.

Then she remembered that she and Todd were broken up, and her high spirits evaporated instantly into the crisp afternoon air. Todd was no longer hers. She couldn't carry him around with her in her thoughts any longer. She couldn't dream of him anymore. She couldn't look forward to seeing him, to talking with him, laughing with him, lying in his arms. . . .

Why did he have to come here? Elizabeth thought in frustration, kicking at a pebble in the path. It was bad enough being broken up with him. Seeing him only made things worse. She wondered what he was doing there. He obviously hadn't come to see her. Todd had made it crystal clear that he wouldn't have anything to do with her. The pain of their conversation stung her again. Todd would never forgive her. And deservedly so, Elizabeth thought, hanging her head. She had betrayed his trust—and his love—with his best friend.

So what is he doing here? she wondered again. Maybe Ken wanted to make up with Jessica, and he had talked Todd into coming along. That was it, Elizabeth decided. Todd was trying to help out his best friend.

Well, Elizabeth thought sadly as she trudged up the hill to the cabin, *at least Ken and Todd are friends again.*

"I have no idea why Ken bothered to come all the way to Yosemite dressed like a transvestite," declared Jessica, "because I'm never going to have anything to do with him."

"Jessica, sometimes you can be so stubborn," Lila said, tucking a loose strand of hair behind her ear.

Jessica and Lila were sharing a banana split at the Crystal Ice Palace, an ice-cream parlor down the road from the cheerleading compound. They had sneaked away after the competition to get away from the gang.

"I am not being stubborn," said Jessica. She picked a maraschino cherry out of the whipped cream and popped it into her mouth. "I'm being completely reasonable."

Lila lifted a heaping spoonful of strawberry ice cream and hot fudge to her mouth. "Mpphh thnk mmpph formmmm mmph."

"What?" Jessica asked, cutting into a sliced banana with a spoon.

Lila dabbed her mouth with her napkin. "I said, I think you should forgive him."

"I thought that's what you said," said Jessica with a sigh. "I just can't imagine *why* you said it." Jessica speared the banana wedge with her knife and swirled it in the dish, smothering it with ice cream and hot fudge. Leaning over the dish, she popped her creation into her mouth. "Mmm!" she said, licking her lips. "This is yummy!"

"It ain't Casey's, but it'll do," said Lila. Casey's Ice Cream Parlor was a popular spot for dessert at the Valley Mall. It was Lila and Jessica's favorite place to take a break after a hard day of shopping.

Jessica wiped her mouth and leaned back in her chair, feeling dizzy from the ice cream she had just inhaled. "Here, you have the rest," she said, pushing the dish away from her.

"Thanks," Lila said, dipping a finger into the whipped cream.

"So, anyway," Jessica said. "You were trying to convince me to forgive Ken."

"You know, Jess, he didn't really do anything," Lila said.

"Yes, he did," insisted Jessica. "He went out on a date with my sister—a romantic date at the beach—*our* beach. And then he kissed her." Jessica shivered at the thought.

"But Jessica, he thought he was kissing you," said Lila.

"Exactly," said Jessica, putting her finger in the air. "Obviously I don't stand out." She leaned forward in her chair. "It's like that game show—*Kiss and Tell*—where the contestants have to guess who their partners are from a kiss." Jessica sat back in her chair, folding her hands together on her lap as if she had just made a brilliant point. "If Ken and I went on the show, he would get the consolation prize—a plastic pair of big red lips."

Lila rolled her eyes. "Fortunately for you, this isn't *Kiss and Tell*. It's real life."

Jessica shrugged her shoulders. "That's not the point. The point is that he couldn't distinguish between me and my sister—*in real life*," she said, emphasizing the last three words.

"Jessica, he realized immediately that he was kissing Elizabeth," Lila said, taking another stab at it. "And then he came to tell you right away." Lila brought a spoonful of chocolate ice cream and whipped cream to her mouth and pushed the ice cream to the middle of the table.

"Ken didn't tell me anything," Jessica said. "Elizabeth told me the whole sordid story."

"But that's because you wouldn't speak to him," Lila pointed out.

"Hmmph!" said Jessica stubbornly. "I don't care if he tried to tell me about it or not. If Ken can't distinguish me from my sister, then he must not really love me."

Lila waved a perfectly manicured hand in the air. "Fine, I give up," she said. She sat back and took a long drink of ice water.

"Good," said Jessica. But inside Jessica wondered if Lila was right. She missed Ken desperately. She wanted to be able to forgive him. But there was no way she was going to let him know it, she resolved, digging into the ice cream with a renewed fury.

Chapter 12

"OK, Liz, don't move," said Maria, sitting behind Elizabeth on her bunk as she twisted Elizabeth's hair into a French braid.

"Shoot!" Maria muttered as the silky strands slipped out of her hand. She unwound them and brushed out Elizabeth's thick hair again, separating it adroitly into three strands. Starting from the crown, she began weaving her hair into shiny golden-blond plaits.

Elizabeth sat perfectly still as she took in the commotion around her. The girls were all wearing red unitards as they got ready for the third competition, and it was like a circus in the cabin. The Alabama squad had already left for the field. As usual, the Sweet Valley squad was running a little late. The atmosphere was a bit frenetic, with girls running around frantically trying to get ready in time for the competition.

"Hey, Sandy, have you seen my lipstick?" asked Jean, sitting cross-legged on her bunk with a compact open in front of her.

"Here, use this," Sandy responded, sorting through her cosmetic bag. She tossed a tube through the air.

"Thanks," Jean said, catching the lipstick adeptly in one hand. She pursed her lips into a cupid bow and deftly outlined her mouth.

"Jessica, can I use the blow-dryer when you're done?" asked Sara, tapping Jessica on the shoulder. Jessica was bent over, drying her hair upside down. Her blond hair fell in a curtain around her face.

"What?" Jessica asked, straightening up and shutting off the dryer.

"I said, can I use the blow-dryer when you're done?" Sara repeated.

"Oh, sure," Jessica said, flipping her hair upside down and fluffing it around her face. Her cheeks were flushed a rosy pink from the heat, and her eyes sparkled brightly. Jessica smiled into the mirror on the wall, pleased with the effect. "Here, I think I'm done." She handed the blow-dryer to Sara.

Amy was rummaging around in the squad duffel bag, fishing for a medium-sized cheerleading costume.

"Hey, Amy, can you get one for me, too?" Lila asked, meticulously plucking her eyebrows. She carefully tweezed her left eyebrow into a thin, arched line.

"Sure," said Amy. She pulled out two red-and-white costumes and threw one to Lila. Lila swiped it out of the air with one hand and hopped up from the bunk.

"OK, girls," Jessica said, "five more minutes and we're out of here!"

Lila and Amy quickly pulled on their skirts.

"Oh-mi-god," said Amy, staring at the skirt lying in a heap around her feet.

"What the—?" muttered Lila as her skirt slipped to the floor.

All the commotion came to a sudden halt as the girls gathered around.

"Have you guys lost a lot of weight?" asked Sara.

"Let me see," said Maria, quickly pulling on a skirt. It dropped immediately to the floor. Maria kicked it up off the floor and examined it. "It's the elastic," she said. "It's missing."

One by one the girls tried on their skirts and watched as they fell to the floor. The elastic had been cut out of all of them.

"Looks like Marissa and her squad have struck," said Jessica grimly.

"Again," said Heather.

Jessica checked the door suddenly. It opened easily. "Well, we're not locked in this time," she said.

"We can get out, but we don't have anything to wear," said Sandy with a sigh, sliding down the wall dramatically and plopping down onto the pile of waistless skirts.

The girls were in a total panic.

"What are we going to do?" wailed Annie.

"Now we won't be able to compete!" despaired Jeanie.

"We can't let them get the best of us," determined Sara.

Soon all the girls were talking at once, complaining and throwing out suggestions.

"OK," said Jessica, taking charge. "Time for a squad powwow." All the girls piled onto her bed.

"Now, we've got three different uniforms left to wear," said Jessica. "Our standard SVH uniforms, the hip huggers, and our special outfits for the grand finale tomorrow."

"We can't wear the hip huggers again," said Heather. "I dropped them off at the lodge to be laundered this afternoon."

"What if we wore our outfits for tomorrow?" suggested Jade.

"Oh, that would be such a shame," said Patty. "We chose them especially for the grand finale."

"We can't wear them anyway," Jessica said, shaking her head. "They're locked away in the bus. We'd never get there in time."

The girls sat in silence for a moment, pondering the possibilities. They could hear the seconds slipping away with the quiet *tick tick tick* of Elizabeth's watch.

Suddenly Elizabeth jumped up. "I've got it!" she exclaimed. "The solution was in front of our noses the whole time."

"What?" asked Maria excitedly.

"We don't need those silly little skirts, anyway," Elizabeth said, always practical. "We're all wearing catsuits, right? Let's just cheer in those!"

"Y'all really did a bang-up job out there!" Wilhemina enthused after the final competition of the day. The Sweet Valley High squad had placed first for the third time in a row, and the Alabama girls were accompanying Jessica and Elizabeth to the lodge for dinner.

Elizabeth smiled graciously. "Thanks," she said.

"You sure are makin' a comeback," said Peggy May admiringly. "Why, I plum thought you'd drop out after the first two competitions."

"We thought we might drop out too," Elizabeth said.

"Y'all really knocked 'em dead in those sexy outfits!" exclaimed Wilhemina.

"I think it was that twin bit that really swayed the judges," put in Peggy May. "Why, that mirror routine was so darn real that I had to keep looking twice to make sure there were really two of you."

"Y'all looked like sheer angels," added Wilhemina.

Elizabeth smiled at the term. She and Jessica weren't exactly acting like angels these days. But she had to agree with the Alabama girls. The performance had climaxed with a mirror-image routine by Jessica and Elizabeth. Gesturing like mimes, the twins had faced one another and moved in sync, acting as if they were looking into a mirror. The crowd had gone mad with delight as the twins perfectly mirrored each other's steps, gestures, and jumps.

"I think it's the Reno squad you've really got to watch out for now," Wilhemina babbled on.

"Yeah, those girls have been on your tail all day," added Peggy May.

"I think you're right," agreed Elizabeth. "They're still ranked first overall."

Elizabeth noticed Jessica's jaw clench. She expected her to comment, but Jessica remained conspicuously quiet. She was clearly still giving Elizabeth the silent treatment. The rest of the squad had split immediately following the competition in an obvious effort to force the girls together. For once Elizabeth was thankful for the chatter of the Alabama girls so she didn't have to walk in silence with Jessica all the way to the lodge.

As they rounded the bend, Elizabeth noticed Ken, Todd, and Winston waving to them from afar, decked out in their cheerleading uniforms. In spite of herself, Elizabeth's heart did a little trojan crunch at the sight of Todd. The boys were gesturing wildly, signaling for them to come over. Elizabeth couldn't bear the thought of facing Todd or of watching Ken attempt to win Jessica over. The color high in her cheeks, she carefully averted her gaze, as did Jessica.

But the boys' attempts hadn't gotten past the Alabama girls. "Darlin's, looks like those big girls over there are trying to get y'all's attention," said Wilhemina.

Jessica and Elizabeth looked over at Ken and Todd gesturing frantically from the top of the hill. They both waved back casually and kept on walking.

"What squad are those girls on?" Peggy May asked. "They sure are hearty lookin'."

Jessica and Elizabeth looked back and noticed the boys running after them. Winston's skirt kept flying up, revealing a pair of gangly, muscular legs. He was trying desperately to hold it down as he ran. Suddenly he tripped over a loose shoelace and clutched at Ken and Todd for support, causing all three of them to tumble to the ground.

Not being able to contain themselves any longer, Jessica and Elizabeth burst out laughing. "Oh-mi-god!" Jessica cried, tears running down her face. "Did you see Win—" Elizabeth gasped. "He—" They were laughing so hard they had to stop walking.

The Alabama girls stopped and stared at the twins in confusion. "Why, whatever is the matter?" asked one of the girls.

"Nothing, nothing," said Elizabeth, making a superhuman effort to control her laughter. "Those, uh, girls just took a tumble, that's all."

Jessica waved the girls away. "Go on ahead without us," she said. "We'll just be a minute."

As soon as the Alabama girls were out of sight, Jessica and Elizabeth burst out laughing again.

"I have never—" gasped Elizabeth with laughter, barely able to get the words out, "seen anything—so ludicrous—in my whole life—!"

"Did you see Winston?" asked Jessica, choking back her laughter.

"He looked like a bird with his skirt flapping in

the air!" Elizabeth burst out, fluttering her hands like wings. "He was ready to soar away!"

"And then he flew right into the boys!" exclaimed Jessica. "And they all went down."

Elizabeth nodded. "It was a crash landing," she said solemnly, sending Jessica into fresh peals of laughter.

Elizabeth couldn't resist taking another peek at the boys. Winston was crouched down with his skirt flying around his waist, trying to tie his shoelace. Todd was standing up, wiping the dirt off his knees. Ken was darting along the ground chasing after his wig, which had gotten caught in a gust of wind.

"Oh, oh!" cried Jessica, holding on to her stomach.

"He's chasing his hair!" Elizabeth cried.

"His beautiful blond locks!" yelped Jessica.

The twins burst out into a cataclysmic fit of laughter. They were laughing so hard that they had to hold on to each other for support. They rolled and shook, tears streaming down their faces. When one of them started to calm down, the other would start giggling, sending them both into a fresh round of laughter. Finally they sniffed and wiped their eyes, managing to settle down.

"Can you believe how hysterical the boys look dressed like cheerleaders?" said Jessica.

"It's a sight I thought I'd never see," said Elizabeth.

"Todd looks like a supermodel with his sleek brunette mane," said Jessica.

"And Ken looks like a Kewpie doll with those blond curls!" said Elizabeth. "He—"

Suddenly it struck Elizabeth that she and Jessica were talking again. Her voice trailed off as she realized that they were acting as if everything were normal. Both girls stopped talking and looked at each other. A moment of awkward silence followed.

Elizabeth cleared her throat. "Jess," she said in a heartfelt tone, "I'm so sorry about my date with Ken. Or, that is, your date." A crimson blush stained her cheeks. She took a deep breath and plunged ahead. "I had no intention of stealing your boyfriend. I was desperate to see how I really felt about him."

Elizabeth stole a look at her sister. Jessica was listening patiently. "I'm not trying to justify my actions," Elizabeth continued. "I know I was wrong to pull a twin switch, and I'm sorry." Elizabeth's lip trembled. "I found out that I didn't have feelings for Ken after all, but the price was too high." Elizabeth bit her lip and tears sprang to her eyes. "You're my soul mate, Jess, and I'm lost without you."

Elizabeth broke out in sobs, and Jessica grabbed her in a bear hug. "You're my soul mate too, Liz," she said. She grinned and looked up at her sister. "And after blackmailing you I deserved to be tricked."

Elizabeth sniffed and smiled between her tears. "That's true," she said, wiping away her tears with the back of her hand. "You deserved that and more!" Then her expression became serious again. "You know, the worst of it all wasn't that I lost my boyfriend, but that I lost my sister."

"Of course you didn't lose me, silly," said Jessica. "You could never lose me." She slung an arm around her sister's waist. "And from the looks of Todd, it seems like you haven't lost him either."

"What do you mean?" Elizabeth asked.

"Well, he's obviously here to win you back," said Jessica.

Elizabeth shook her head sadly. "No, he's not. Jess, he won't have anything to do with me. I tried to talk to him before we left, but he wouldn't even listen to me. He's just here to keep Ken company."

"Elizabeth Wakefield," said Jessica, "sometimes you can be even more stubborn than me. Do you really think Todd would come all the way to Yosemite just for the ride?"

Elizabeth looked hopeful. "I—I guess not," she said.

"Liz, really," Jessica went on. "How many boyfriends would get dressed up as pom-pom girls just to keep their friends company?"

"Not too many," said Elizabeth with a laugh. "I guess you're right. Maybe he does want to make up after all."

"So are we going to put them out of their misery?" Jessica asked.

Elizabeth thought a moment. Then a mischievous look came into her eyes. "Yeees . . . but maybe not right away."

Jessica nodded as if reading her sister's thoughts.

"We should probably make their misery a little more acute first," she said.

"Hmm, let's see," said Elizabeth. "The guys have said that they're from Saskatchewan, Canada."

"And that they're just here to observe," added Jessica.

"Well, I think it's time the girls from Saskatchewan showed us their stuff," said Elizabeth, a wicked glint in her eye.

Chapter 13

"Wow, they look great," breathed Lila on Monday morning in the auditorium as they watched the Riverdale squad perform a fifties number set to the tune of "At the Hop."

"Neat costumes," said Jade Wu admiringly. "They look like they're at a sock hop." The girls were decked out in full fifties attire, wearing bobby socks and saddle shoes and letter sweaters with big *R*'s on them. They all had flippy ponytails tied high up on their heads.

It was the grand finale, the event that could change the competition. The ACA had gone all out for the affair. The band was sitting in the orchestra pit, breaking out into lively tunes between performances. Helium balloons were tied to the chairs and flapped gaily in the air. Colorful streamers adorned the walls.

Counting for one third of the total score, the

grand finale was the most important event of the competition, and the Sweet Valley High squad was prepared. They'd been on the lookout for foul play all day, and their fancy lace-trimmed uniforms were in perfect condition. They had locked them up in Lila's footlocker, where nobody could touch them.

"They're the best squad so far," whispered Amy to Lila as the Riverdale squad moved into position for the final segment of their program. "Rockin' and reelin', Riverdale's a-stealin'," sang the girls, twisting and whirling in pairs. "At the hop—bop bop. At the hop—bop bop."

"I can't believe how good they are," said Lila, suddenly overcome with doubt about their ability to win. She felt butterflies dancing around in her stomach, and her tongue went dry. They'd been sitting in the auditorium for hours, watching as one squad after another performed. The teams were pulling out all the stops for the grand finale, and each squad seemed better than the last.

"Don't worry," said Jessica reassuringly, twisting around to face them. "Their routine is fun and bouncy, but it lacks technical skill."

Jessica had a point. The girls were dancing and shaking more than they were jumping. "You're right," Lila agreed. "They're all show and no substance."

Lila was glad to see Jessica and Elizabeth back together again. The twins were sitting close together one rung below them, squeezing their hands together for support.

"It looks like our little scheme worked," whispered Lila to Amy, referring to their plan to force the girls together the day before. The entire squad had run off immediately following the final competition, leaving only Jessica and Elizabeth in their section of the bleachers. Lila and Amy had figured the twins would have to talk to each other if they were alone together. "It's good to see them back together again," agreed Amy with a satisfied smile. "Oh, look, the Reno squad is starting," she said nervously, turning her attention back to the floor. "And then it's our turn."

The Reno squad lined up on the floor, looking sharp and polished in crisp green-and-white uniforms. Lead by Marissa James, they began with an upbeat number that got the whole crowd moving.

Lila bit her lip as the Reno squad moved into position for the athletic part of their program. In pairs the girls stepped forward and executed impressive jump combinations. The crowd yelled as the last pair hopped back into line. One by one the girls shot up and landed in side-by-side splits, thrusting their green-and-white pom-poms up in the air. The crowd applauded heartily.

"You know, it really burns me up that they're doing so well," said Amy, gritting her teeth.

"I know," said Lila with venom in her voice. "It just doesn't seem right." Lila's jaw set in determination. "Well, we're going to knock them right out of the competition. And we're going to put

Marissa James and her scheming squad in their place."

Lila was surprised at the depth of her emotion. She had never realized cheerleading could be such a sophisticated activity. She had always found it to be a little gauche—a bunch of girls in tacky uniforms yelling out school-spirit cheers. When Lila had quit the squad ages ago, she had vowed never to cheer again. She had agreed to join Jessica's squad only in order to give her support. But with their chic uniforms and jazzy dance moves, the Sweet Valley squad had brought a whole new dimension to cheerleading.

"Check out the timing on that double wave!" said Amy, watching in awe as the Reno squad performed a double sequence of back crunches in perfect succession. "Now I know why it's called a wave."

Lila turned her attention back to the squad. They finished their routine with a splash, landing in a circle in Chinese splits and sweeping the floor from side to side with their pom-poms. "Wow, that's a really cool move," said Lila.

"It's neat, but kind of bizarre," put in Jessica. "I mean, it doesn't take much skill to wipe the floor."

"This is it," said Amy, putting a hand to her stomach as she noticed the Reno squad trotting off the stage. "We're up next."

The announcer's voice boomed over the loudspeaker. "And for the final squad in the final competition of the Tenth Annual ACA National Competition—Sweet Valley High!"

All the girls moved to jump up, but Jessica motioned for them to remain sitting. "Don't go on yet," Jessica said to the girls. "We've got a little surprise for you."

"Looks like the Wakefields are back in action," said Lila, grinning as Jessica and Elizabeth ran down the steps.

"What do you think they're going to do?" wondered Amy. "A special twin routine?"

"Maybe they're auditioning for a Doublemint commercial," joked Annie.

"What is this?" Heather snarled. "The Bobbsey twins make up, and they decide to steal the show?"

Lila watched with interest as Jessica and Elizabeth ran across the floor. The crowd applauded enthusiastically at the sight of the popular twins. With their beautiful matching red-and-white uniforms and shining golden-blond hair, they made a stunning pair.

Jessica leaned into the microphone, waiting for the crowd to quiet down. "We'd like to announce that we have a special treat for you today," said Jessica, grinning broadly.

Elizabeth spoke into the mike. "I think we've all been a little curious about the girls from Saskatchewan." The crowd stomped their feet in agreement, hooting and whistling.

"And we thought it was a shame for them to come all the way here from Canada without taking part in the festivities," added Jessica, leaning into the mike.

"So we're happy to announce that the Saskatchewan three have agreed to introduce our act with a little number of their own!" finished Elizabeth. She waved a tape in the air. "Please give them a warm welcome!"

Jessica and Elizabeth bounced off the stage, running up to the sound booth in the back of the auditorium to drop off the tape.

"Oh-mi-god," said Maria, clapping a hand over her mouth.

"They didn't!" said Amy.

"They did!" said Lila.

The audience went wild, hooting and screaming.

"Bring on the big girls!" somebody yelled.

"Let's see the Canadians move!" somebody else shouted.

"That's us!" said Ken, a horrified look on his face.

"But it can't be!" Todd said, scanning the crowds wildly for another Canadian squad.

"It is," Winston moaned, holding his head between his hands.

Ken stood up and gestured wildly to the crowd, signaling "no" by waving his arms across his face.

Todd stood up with him. "Sorry!" he mouthed to the crowd, waving like a movie star and blowing kisses. They both sat down.

"Sas-katch-ewan! Sas-katch-ewan!" clapped the audience in a cheer led by the Sweet Valley cheerleaders. "We want you on! We want you on!"

The crowd around them hustled them up, chanting and clapping the whole time.

"How could Maria betray me like this?" whimpered Winston as he was pulled to his feet with Todd and Ken.

As they stood up, they were greeted by thunderous applause and virtually pushed down the aisle.

"Well, girls," said Ken, linking arms with the two of them as they made their way to the stage, "looks like it's time for a little cheering."

"This is pushing the limits of friendship too far," said Winston, mortified.

"Don't worry, Winston," Todd said, trying to calm him. "Just follow me."

The boys trotted across the floor, smiling and waving at the audience. Todd racked his brains as they made their way to the stage, desperately trying to come up with a cheer.

"Start with the 'Be Aggressive' cheer," he hissed to the others as they reached the center of the stage. They'd heard the cheer enough, thought Todd. They ought to be able to remember the words.

The boys lined up with Todd in the middle and faced the audience. Todd gulped as he took in the masses in front of him. The auditorium was bursting with cheerleaders and fans. The judges sat in a row in front, staring up at them ominously. Bulbs flashed as members of the press took pictures.

"Oh, jeez, we're going to make the front page," groaned Winston.

Suddenly rock music began blaring through the loudspeaker. Todd took a deep breath. "Be aggressive! Be, be aggressive!" he shouted in time with the music, raising his voice an octave. He clapped his hands together and waved his hips from side to side.

"Be aggressive! Be, be aggressive!" joined in Ken and Winston in high voices, shaking their hips along with Todd and bumping them together. The crowd laughed with delight.

Todd rolled his wrists around each other in front of his body, lifting his right arm into the air and then his left. Winston and Ken watched him out of the corners of their eyes, following along with the motion. "C-A-N-A-D-A, we're gonna blow you a-way!" shouted Todd.

"C-A-N-A-D-A, we're gonna blow you a-way!" chorused Ken and Winston, imitating Todd's arm movements.

Todd put his arms above his head like a ballerina and began to whirl around in circles, Ken and Winston a step behind. The crowd laughed as they got a glimpse of the "girls'" muscular thighs.

"They love us!" Ken said as he began to execute his turn. "We're really pulling this off!"

"Whoa, it's slippery out here," muttered Todd under his breath as he suddenly twirled out of control, sliding to the ground. It seemed as if the surface of the floor was coated in some kind of oily substance.

"Yowee!" exclaimed Ken in the middle of a spin, his arms flailing out. Soon the three of them were on the ground together.

"OK, just act normal," whispered Todd. He jumped up quickly, balancing himself carefully on the slippery surface. Ken and Winston followed. Winston swayed dangerously from side to side, and Todd and Ken steadied him.

"Can-a-da! Can-a-da!" chanted Ken, taking over. He jumped into the air with one arm up and one leg out in an imitation of a herky. "Sis-boom-bah!" shouted Todd, jumping into the air after him. "Rah rah rah!" yelled Winston, flinging his arms and legs out wildly and hurtling into the air. Their legs went out from underneath them as they landed on the slimy surface, and the three of them went sliding wildly across the oily ground.

"Looks like the crowd's enjoying the show, huh?" said Elizabeth, her eyes glittering.

"Definitely," Jessica agreed. "Particularly our squad." The girls from the Sweet Valley squad seemed more amused than anyone else at the hysterical display of ineptitude on the stage. Maria was holding on to her stomach as if in pain, choking with laughter as she watched Winston dance awkwardly around the stage; Sandy and Jean were laughing so hard that tears were streaming down their faces; Lila and Amy were holding on to each other for support; Jade, Patty, and Sara were stomping their feet on the bleachers, chanting along with the boys.

Jessica, however, was eyeing the stage suspiciously. She had expected the boys to be clumsy, but she hadn't expected them to be flying all over the place. She squinted and peered at the stage. From the way the boys were slipping and sliding, it seemed as if there was some kind of oily slime covering the floor. Oily slime that had obviously been meant for the Sweet Valley team—compliments of Marissa and her crew.

Jessica turned and whispered into her sister's ear, "Have you noticed that the boys seem to be sliding around a lot?"

"Yeah," Elizabeth whispered back. "It looks like the stage is slippery." Suddenly she caught on to Jessica's line of thinking. She looked at her sister quickly. "You think—?"

Jessica nodded. "Marissa," she said.

"C'mon!" Elizabeth said. "Let's go find the referee."

"Be aggressive!" yelled Todd, scrambling up again. He loosened the heels of his sneakers and flung off his Keds, hoping to grip the floor better without his shoes on. "Be, be aggressive!" shouted Ken and Winston, flipping their shoes off as well.

"Take it off! Take it off!" yelled the crowds, clapping in time with the music. "Follow me," Todd said, out of breath. Barefoot, he put his arms out in front of him and flipped across the stage in a series of crooked cartwheels. Ken followed right behind.

Winston just watched, a stunned expression on his face. "C'mon, Winston," Todd hissed.

"Oh, boy," Winston said, steadying his gangly frame for the move. He sprang into the air, his long arms and legs flying in all directions as he attempted a cartwheel. He landed in a somersault and careened across the stage. His wig flew off in the opposite direction. The crowd roared with delight, thinking it was a gag.

"Oh, no!" Winston exclaimed, scrambling across the floor after it. He picked it up and frantically placed it back on his head. The wig was backward, and a sheath of red hair covered Winston's face. Winston coughed and quickly turned it around.

The crowd was in hysterics at this point, laughing and stamping their feet.

"Can-a-da!" yelled Todd, putting his hands on his hips and shaking his hips from side to side with each syllable. He held the position, his left hip stuck out dramatically.

"Sis-boom-bah!" shouted Winston, pumping his arms out in front of him like a monkey and holding the pose.

"Rah-rah-rah!" yelled Ken, turning around and wiggling his rear.

"Oh, no!" hissed Todd to the others. "Here comes Ms. Balsam."

"And an army of directors," said Ken, turning around. Ms. Balsam was marching down the aisle with a fierce look on her face, a bevy of directors close behind. They were clearly distraught to have discovered an invasion of boys in their midst.

"Let's get out of here!" said Winston.

"Thank you, thank you!" yelled the boys in falsetto voices. They curtsied and ran off the stage.

"It's that squad over there," said Jessica to the referee, "the girls in the green-and-white uniforms." Jessica and Elizabeth were walking with the referee toward the Reno squad. He was a burly man dressed in a black-and-white uniform. They had found him sitting by the judges' boxes and had notified him of their suspicions. He had seemed a bit dubious but had agreed to check out the situation.

"What if we made a mistake?" chattered Elizabeth nervously as they approached the Nevada section of the audience. "What if they didn't do it? What if there's nothing on the court after all?"

"Liz, don't worry," Jessica said. Jessica didn't have a doubt in her mind that Marissa's squad was responsible for the oil on the floor. And when they reached the Reno section, she was sure of it. The Reno squad was the only group in the entire auditorium that wasn't laughing. The girls were staring at the stage in consternation, their mouths hanging open. Marissa James sat in the middle of the group. She was wound up like a top and wore a fierce expression on her face.

"Excuse me," said the guard, taking a seat with the group. "Who's the captain of this squad?" Jessica and Elizabeth stood back a few feet.

"I am," asserted Marissa, sitting up straight. "I'm Marissa James."

"If you don't mind, I'd like to have a look at your equipment," the referee said, indicating the large black duffel bag sitting at her feet.

"But whatever for?" asked Marissa, the picture of innocence. Suddenly she caught sight of Jessica and Elizabeth. She locked gazes with Jessica and her eyes narrowed.

"It looks like there's been some foul play on the stage, and we'd like to find out who's responsible," said the guard.

"Well, we don't know what you're talking about, do we, girls?" said Marissa defensively. The girls all shook their heads.

"Open the bag, please," said the referee calmly.

"But—but this is an outrage!" sputtered Marissa. "How dare you accuse our squad of—"

"Look, Miss James," interrupted the referee, "nobody's accusing you of anything. This is a routine process. We're going to check everybody's equipment until we find the guilty party."

"Well, we refuse," said Marissa hotly. "This bag is our private property, and you have no right to inspect it." Marissa folded her arms over her chest stubbornly.

"Yeah, we're not going to reveal the contents of our equipment bag to anybody without a search warrant," chimed in one of the squad members.

"Sorry, but it doesn't work that way," said the referee. "The ACA has conferred on me full privileges to search the equipment of any team when I deem it necessary." His tone turned menacing. "And I do indeed deem it necessary." He looked at Marissa for consent, but she just stared back at him defiantly.

"It looks like I'm going to have to confiscate the bag," said the referee with a sigh, grabbing the bag from the floor and hauling it onto the bench. Marissa's face burned scarlet as the referee unzipped the bag and rifled through it.

Jessica and Elizabeth gasped as he pulled out a case of baby oil. There were twenty-four bottles in all, and they were all empty. Jessica noticed that each bottle had a small elastic band attached to it—a band that would attach easily to the handle of a pom-pom.

Jessica leaned over to her sister and whispered into her ear. "So that's why the Reno squad swept the floor with their pom-poms at the end of their routine!" she said. "I thought that was a strange move!"

"Looks a little suspicious," said the referee, turning the case around as he examined the bottles. He put his finger along the rim of one of the bottles, then rubbed the oil between his fingers.

"We were suntanning earlier," said Marissa quickly. "And we used up all the oil."

"You don't look like you've got a lot of color," said the referee.

"Well, is it our fault if we don't tan well?" asked Marissa huffily.

"And may I ask what these little elastic straps

are for?" asked the referee, inspecting the bands.

"They're easier to carry that way," said Marissa smoothly.

"Oh, Marissa, what's the use?" said another girl on the team. "They're just going to check the stage. We might as well admit it."

"Look, he's holding a conference," said Jessica to Elizabeth as they made their way back to their seats. She pointed to the front of the room. It looked as if the referee was conferring with the directors of the ACA. Ms. Balsam looked agitated. She was standing up, waving her arms about. The crowd was murmuring restlessly, wondering what was causing the delay.

"What's going on?" asked Lila. "What were you doing over at Marissa's squad?"

"And why did you get the ref?" asked Maria eagerly.

Jessica and Elizabeth quickly filled the girls in on the latest events. "And so they covered the floor with baby oil at the end of their routine," finished Jessica.

"Oil that was meant for us," added Elizabeth.

"I can't believe it!" Annie said, outraged. "Of all the low-down stunts!"

"It doesn't surprise me in the slightest," said Heather. "I wouldn't put anything past Marissa James and her squad."

"Well, it looks like they're going to get their comeuppance now," said Maria in satisfaction.

"Hey, what happened to the boys?" asked

Jessica, looking up at the stage. The floor was empty, and the curtains were closed.

"They were officially escorted off the grounds by some of the directors," said Lila.

"You should have seen poor Winston's face!" said Maria with a giggle. "He looked like he thought he was going to be put away for life!"

Just then Zoe Balsam and the referee climbed the steps to the stage and disappeared behind the curtain.

"They must be checking the floor!" said Sara.

"And hopefully cleaning it!" added Jeanie.

Minutes later the curtains opened and Ms. Balsam took the mike.

"This is it," whispered Jessica excitedly. "Say good-bye to the Reno squad."

"I'd like to apologize for the delay," said Ms. Balsam. "We've had a few, er, technical difficulties. But everything's in order now, and we're ready to continue with the final performance of the competition. So please give a warm round of applause to the squad from Sweet Valley, California!"

The girls jumped up as the crowd cheered. Elizabeth leaned over to Jessica, concern in her eyes. "She didn't mention the Reno squad!" she said. "What do you think that means?"

"I don't know," said Jessica worriedly, "but it doesn't look good."

With Jessica at the lead the Sweet Valley High squad bounced onto the stage and took their positions for their final routine. The girls stood readied in a V formation, with one side dressed in all red and the other in all white. The floor had been cleaned up, and the audience was eager for the final performance to begin. The crowd murmured appreciatively as they took in the fancy outfits of the squad.

"Let's blow 'em out of their seats, guys!" said Jessica, smiling at her team. As the music started, the girls launched into their final and most difficult routine. "We got the fever, we're hot, we can't be stopped!" they sang out, performing an intricate medley of dance steps, athletic jumps, and fancy footwork. The girls had never performed better, thought Jessica with satisfaction. They looked tight and professional, as if they had been working together for years.

As the last beat of the music sounded, the girls jumped into position for their final pyramid. They quickly hoisted each other onto their shoulders, forming an impressive four-tiered standing pyramid. Sitting at the top, Jade raised her pom-poms victoriously into the air. The crowd gasped audibly as they observed the unprecedented feat.

While the girls held their positions, Jessica and Heather launched into a spectacular jump combination. Standing opposite one another, they broke into a series of front and back flips, finishing off with triple herkies and a trojan-jump combination. Not a step was out of place as the girls moved in unison through the difficult combination. Jessica and Heather leaped into the air and came down in side-by-side splits in front of the pyramid, raising their pom-poms in the air and smiling triumphantly.

The din of the audience was deafening. "Bravo! Bravo!" called the crowd, throwing streamers and confetti. A tissue-wrapped bouquet of roses landed on the stage.

A few minutes later the girls were back in their seats, breathing heavily and waiting anxiously for the results of the grand finale to be revealed. The entire audience was abuzz, chattering nervously among themselves as the final scores were tabulated. The announcer appeared on the stage and tapped on the mike, signaling for the crowd to quiet down.

Clutching the flowers in her arms, Jessica turned to Elizabeth anxiously. "Tell me when it's over!" she said, covering her ears with her hands and burying her head in her arms. At the sound of clapping she didn't look up, afraid that her team had been mentioned.

"Jess," said Elizabeth, nudging her on the shoulder. "You've got to listen! They're about to announce the second-place winners for this round!"

Jessica warily lifted her hands and grabbed on to Elizabeth for support. "What if they didn't disqualify the Reno squad?" she said. "What if they win instead of us?"

"That's impossible," Elizabeth reassured her.

"And now for our second-place grand-finale winners," boomed the announcer from the stage.

"Please give a hand to the girls from Sweet Valley, California!"

Jessica's face fell. "We didn't win," she said in an unbelieving tone. "We didn't win." She looked over at Patty. "Do we still have a chance?"

Patty shook her head sadly. "I don't think so. It looks like we're out of the running for good."

Jessica stared dejectedly at the bleachers, hugging her knees to her chest. They had come so close. So close. And now it was all over.

"And the first-place prize for the grand finale goes to the squad from Reno, Nevada!" boomed the announcer's voice.

The Reno squad let out an enthusiastic shout. Jessica looked over at the girls on the Reno squad. They were all crowded around Marissa, hugging and yelling. Jessica felt like pulling her hair out. Not only had they lost out on first place, but they had lost to the Reno squad. "I can't believe it!" she exclaimed in disgust. "They didn't penalize them at all."

"I guess they figured we got to compete fairly after all," Elizabeth said. She shook her head. "It just doesn't seem right."

"I think . . . I am going . . . to scream," muttered Heather through clenched teeth from the row behind them.

Just then Zoe Balsam walked across the stage and took the mike. "If you'll please settle down, I have an important announcement to make."

Jessica grabbed on to Elizabeth. "Do you think—?" she asked.

"Let's hope so," Elizabeth said, holding up crossed fingers.

The audience quieted down, and Ms. Balsam cleared her throat. "I have some very unfortunate news. Before the final performance we discovered that somebody had tampered with the stage in an attempt to sabotage the competition," she said. "It appears that the squad from Reno, Nevada, is responsible for the damage."

A murmur rose from the crowd. Ms. Balsam held up a hand for silence. "I have discussed the situation with the other directors of the American Cheerleading Association. The Reno squad is hereby officially disqualified from the competition and from the ACA. Thank you," she said. The crowd chattered noisily as Ms. Balsam walked off the court.

The announcer took the mike again. "So congratulations to Sweet Valley High for winning the grand finale!"

Jessica fell back in her seat, weak with relief. She looked around at her team, her eyes shining with pride. The girls seemed moved. Some of them were laughing, and some of them were crying. They had really done it. They had taken first place for four competitions in a row.

The band struck up a chord while the officials prepared for the awards ceremony. The girls whispered excitedly among themselves while they waited.

"Patty, what does this mean?" asked Amy excitedly.

Patty was busy doing calculations. "I'm not really sure," she said, looking in confusion at the rows of numbers covering the page, "but I think it looks good."

"Ladies and gentlemen, please take your seats," boomed Zoe Balsam from the podium. "I am happy to welcome you to the awards ceremony of the Tenth Annual National Competition."

Elizabeth squeezed Jessica's hand as Ms. Balsam began. Jessica looked over at her with a happy smile, confident that they would place.

"The third-place prize goes to a squad whose jumps, stunts, and combinations have entertained and impressed us all this weekend. Please give a round of applause to the Texas Tigers from San Antonio, Texas!" The crowd clapped enthusiastically as the captain of the San Antonio squad ran onto the court to accept the bronze trophy. She made a short speech at the podium and ran off with her trophy, waving it in the air happily.

Jessica held her breath as Ms. Balsam continued. "And our second-place prize marks a landmark event," she said, smiling at the crowd. "For the first time in the history of the competition, we have witnessed a team move from last place to second. So, for the squad that has made an amazing comeback and has stunned us all with their originality, energy, and skill, I'm thrilled to award the second-place prize to Sweet Valley High from Sweet Valley, California!"

The squad erupted with joy, jumping up and

down and hugging each other. Lightbulbs flashed in their faces as Heather and Jessica ran down to the stage together to accept the big silver trophy Ms. Balsam was holding out.

Heather took the mike. "I'd just like to say that I've competed in nationals before, but I've never encountered a more talented group of teams. So on behalf of our squad, we'd like to thank all the teams that have competed this weekend for making this such an exciting competition." All the squads cheered. "Thanks to the Braselton Bulldogs for being such terrific cabin-mates!" The Alabama squad let out a shout. "And to the Reno squad as well—for making this such an, er, memorable experience!" The audience laughed. "And finally we'd like to express our appreciation to the ACA for making it all happen."

Jessica leaned into the mike. "And most of all, we'd like to thank the Sweet Valley High *boys'* cheerleading squad for their valiant attempt at cheerleading. I think they've made us all realize just what a difficult sport it is." The crowd went wild, whistling and yelling catcalls. "Todd, Ken, and Winston, we couldn't have done it without you!" She and Heather raised the trophy in the air, both holding on to one side.

"We did it!" said Jessica gleefully as she and Heather walked across the stage.

"See, Jessica," Heather said, holding the trophy to the light and admiring it. "Aren't you happy I came to Sweet Valley? Aren't you glad I agreed to stay on the squad? You never would have won without me."

I can't believe I let her back in, thought Jessica, rolling her eyes heavenward and smiling to herself. It looked as if Heather would always be Heather.

Chapter 14

"I think that was the most exciting weekend of my entire life!" exclaimed Maria, walking arm in arm with Elizabeth toward the parking lot of the cheerleading compound on Monday.

"Definitely," agreed Elizabeth. *A little* too *exciting,* she thought. She had enjoyed herself more than she had expected to, but she was glad that the weekend's festivities were finally over. The girls had packed up their gear and said good-bye to the girls from Alabama. The Alabama squad had done extremely well, placing fifth overall. "We'll see y'all next year!" Wilhemina had said. "You better watch out, though!" added Peggy May. "We're gonna be tough competition next year!"

The rest of the girls followed behind them, walking in groups and chattering happily. Still wearing their grand-finale cheerleading outfits, they were carrying duffel bags stuffed with clothing and equipment.

Heather brought up the rear, carrying nothing but the silver trophy, which she was treating like a prized possession.

Elizabeth pushed open the gate and walked into the lot. Suddenly she stopped in her tracks as she caught sight of Todd, looking clean and handsome in the sparkling sunlight. Todd and Winston were waiting for the girls outside the gates, dressed in normal clothing again.

"Winston!" Maria exclaimed, running up to the boys. "I almost didn't recognize you!" Elizabeth followed slowly behind, her heart pounding loudly in her chest. Jessica had convinced her that Todd was ready to forgive her, but now she was filled with doubts again. What if he still wouldn't talk to her?

Winston leaned against Todd's black BMW, folding his arms across his chest. "Girls, I will never forgive you," he said in mock anger. "How could you do that to us?"

"That was cruel and unusual punishment," Todd agreed.

"Winston, we just couldn't resist it," Elizabeth said, making a sorry face.

"You couldn't resist it!" Winston yelped.

"Well, you have to admit it was a once-in-a-lifetime opportunity," said Maria. "It's not often that you guys dress up in purple-and-yellow cheerleading uniforms. A performance was definitely in order." Maria looked up at Winston, her warm brown eyes laughing.

"Hmmph," Winston pouted, looking away.

Maria reached out a hand. "C'mon, Win, you guys looked great out there! You were the highlight of the competition," she said.

"We certainly were!" said Winston. "I never realized what kind of cheerleading talents I had." He pulled Maria toward him in a hug. Then he held her back at arm's length. "But don't you dare ever do anything like that again!" he warned. Maria laughed and snuggled up to him.

Todd and Elizabeth stood by their side, shuffling their feet uncomfortably and looking at the ground. Elizabeth glanced up at Todd shyly, and he gestured for her to step away. They walked a few moments in silence, sitting down in a grassy spot by the parking lot.

"Cruel and unusual punishment?" asked Elizabeth, picking at a piece of grass.

"Well, unusual, but maybe not cruel," said Todd. "I guess I deserved it."

"Does that mean you forgive me?" asked Elizabeth, a hopeful look on her face.

"Liz, I *do* forgive you," Todd said in an earnest voice. He took her hand. "I forgave you right away. I guess I just didn't want you to know it. I was so hurt, and—"

"Oh, Todd!" Elizabeth interrupted, tears springing to her eyes. "I'm so sorry! You're the last person in the world I wanted to hurt."

Todd gently wiped away a tear as it trickled down Elizabeth's cheek.

"Are those tears of sorrow or happiness?" he asked.

"I think both," said Elizabeth, starting to cry for real. Todd grabbed her in his arms and held her in a bear hug.

Elizabeth leaned into his arms, feeling the heat of his body envelop her. Her whole body relaxed. "Oh, Todd, I missed you so much," she said. "And I thought I'd lost you for good."

"You could never lose me, Liz," said Todd, his voice low and husky. "I'm with you now, and forever."

Elizabeth's heart skipped a beat, and she lifted her face to his. Todd leaned down and hungrily caught her lips, kissing her fervently.

Elizabeth smiled up at Todd when they pulled away. "You know what I missed most?" she said.

"What?" Todd asked, wrapping an arm around her.

"The little things," Elizabeth said. "Like talking on the phone and walking down the hall together and going to the Dairi Burger—"

"Well, we're going to have to get home so we can start making up for lost time," said Todd. "And I think the Dairi Burger is our first priority."

"Hey, y'all!" yelled a girl's voice. Elizabeth looked up to see Wilhemina and Peggy May bounding toward them.

"Sorry, are we interruptin' somethin'?" asked Peggy May with a twinkle in her eye as they approached the two sitting on the grass.

"No, no," said Elizabeth, laughing. She quickly introduced Todd to the girls.

"I thought you two had already left!" said Elizabeth with surprise.

"The bus is just getting ready to go," said Peggy May.

"Hey, you're the guy in the picture!" said Wilhemina. "I knew you two looked like you belonged together."

Peggy May looked at him strangely. "Haven't I seen you somewhere before?" she asked, looking Todd over carefully.

Todd's face turned beet-red. "Uh, I don't think so," he said.

"It must have been the picture," said Elizabeth, her eyes dancing merrily.

"Well, we've gotta go now," said Wilhemina. "You take good care of yourself, Liz. We're gonna miss you."

"I'm going to miss you too," said Elizabeth, leaning in to give both girls a hug.

"See y'all next year!" said Peggy May, waving as they walked away.

"Did you hear what Wilhemina said?" asked Elizabeth, taking Todd's hand. "We look like we belong together."

"That's because we *do* belong together," said Todd with a smile, kissing her gently on the cheek. They walked hand in hand back to the parking lot, smiling happily. They found Maria waiting by Todd's car. Winston had settled into the driver's seat. His eyes were closed and he was snoring lightly. He was clearly exhausted from his weekend spent dressing and acting like a cheerleader.

"Hey, Winston, you driving?" said Todd, opening the front door of his BMW. "Rah, rah, rah!"

Winston said, opening his eyes with a start. Laughing, Elizabeth jumped into the passenger seat and Maria hopped in back.

"I said, are you driving?" Todd repeated.

"No way, man, you're the chauffeur," said Winston, now fully awake. He clambered over the front seat and tumbled awkwardly into the back of the car, a pile of gangly legs and arms.

"Winston, it looks like you could still use a few cheerleading lessons," teased Maria as Winston scampered into an upright position, breathing hard.

"No way," said Winston, sitting back in the seat. "My cheerleading days are over!"

"Hey, Liz, is that you?" asked Ken as Jessica headed for the bus.

Jessica wheeled around, her eyes flaming as she recognized Ken's voice. Again! He had mistaken her again! And she was dressed in regular clothes with her hair down.

"I can't believe you—" began Jessica hotly; then she stopped as she looked into Ken's crinkly bright-blue eyes. He was only teasing her, she realized.

"Jessica, I promise I'll never confuse you with your twin sister again," Ken said in an imploring tone. He looked up at her with an incredibly sweet expression on his handsome face. Jessica could feel her heart melt.

"And I promise I'll never make you cheer in public again," answered Jessica with a smile. "But I kind of like you in a skirt."

"I like you in a skirt, too," said Ken, pulling her toward him. He wrapped his arms around her and hugged her to him. "Oh, Jess, I missed you," Ken whispered in her ear, nibbling on her earlobe. He dropped feather-light kisses on her ear, traveling along her neck until he reached her lips. He kissed her softly, tenderly, then more and more urgently until they were wrapped in a passionate embrace.

Just then a car passed, honking loudly.

Jessica pulled away from Ken, feeling a little dazed. She blinked and looked up. Todd and Elizabeth were driving by in Todd's BMW, with Winston and Maria in back.

"It looks like we're going to have to save this for a later date," said Ken with a grin.

"A lot of them," said Jessica happily, linking her arm through his.

"Bye-bye, Kendall!" Todd and Winston yelled, hanging out the windows and waving.

"Ta-ta, Tilda!" said Ken in a falsetto voice. "See you later, Winnie!" He blew them all a kiss. Todd honked his horn a few times and headed out of the parking lot, his purple-and-gold pom-poms floating off the back of the car.

"I guess it's the bus for us," said Ken, turning back to Jessica with a wry smile. "But first—" He pulled her toward him again and brought his lips to hers.

"Here's to our cocaptains!" shouted Maria, standing in the aisle as the bus pulled out of the parking lot. She raised a pom-pom in the air.

"To Jessica and Heather!" yelled Patty and Jade, waving their pom-poms wildly in the air.

"For bringing us to vic-tory!" added Sandy. All the girls let out a whoop and cheered. Jessica laughed in delight. She was seated in the middle of the bus with Ken, thrilled to be the center of attention with an adoring boy by her side. Ken wrapped an arm around her proudly and leaned in to kiss her on the cheek.

"Hey, hey, none of that," said Lila with a grin, sitting across from them with Amy.

"Yeah, keep it clean," said Amy. "This is a family show."

"Hey, Ken, what happened to your cheerleading outfit?" asked Annie, twisting around in her seat.

"Oh, I put it away for next year," Ken said good-naturedly.

"Are you going to join the squad?" asked Lila. "Tryouts are in the fall."

Ken looked as if he were considering the option, then shook his head. "I think I'm going to stick to football," he said. "It's less stressful."

"This *was* quite a nerve-racking competition!" exclaimed Jeanie.

"Yeah, I think the greatest challenge of all was dealing with Marissa James and her squad's tricks," said Heather.

"But we pulled it off," said Sara happily. "We went to nationals for the first time and we placed!"

"And next year we're going to win!" said Jessica. The bus driver honked the horn twice in agreement, and all the girls cheered.

• • •

Late that afternoon Todd deposited Elizabeth on her doorstep. She bounced up the walk cheerfully, breathing in the fresh, balmy air. Everything was back to normal again. She and Jessica were speaking once more, and she and Todd were back together again.

"Hey, Liz!" Jessica greeted her as she walked into the sunny Wakefield kitchen. Jessica was sitting at the butcher-block table with a lemonade, flipping through the latest version of Cheer Ahead. "I thought you would beat us back."

"We stopped at the Dairi Burger on the way home," said Elizabeth happily, opening the refrigerator and taking out a carton of orange juice. She was thrilled to have normalcy again—a conversation with Jessica, a kiss with Todd, a bite to eat at the Dairi Burger with friends. Elizabeth poured herself a glass and leaned against the counter, her legs crossed at the ankles.

Suddenly Jessica sucked in her breath as she turned the page. "Wow!" she breathed. "Hey, Liz, come look at this totally cool new uniform they've got in the catalog. It's like a jumpsuit, with suspenders."

"Uh, hold on a sec," said Elizabeth, looking down at the uniform she was still wearing and realizing that things weren't *quite* back to normal. Elizabeth downed her juice and ran upstairs.

Once in her room, Elizabeth ripped off her uniform and pulled on a pair of khaki shorts and a peach T-shirt. "That's more like it," she said out loud, happy to be back in regular clothes. Flinging her gym bag over her shoulder, she grabbed her journal and left the room.

Feeling like herself again, Elizabeth skipped down the steps and returned to the kitchen.

Dropping her journal onto the counter, Elizabeth reached into the gym bag and pulled out her folded uniform, holding it in her outstretched palms like a platter. "Here, Jess," Elizabeth said, ceremoniously presenting the outfit to her.

"But what's this?" Jessica said, her blue eyes wide.

"It was fun while it lasted," said Elizabeth, dropping the uniform onto the table, "but I officially resign." She pulled out her pom-poms and tossed them, one by one, on top of the pile.

"You mean I didn't convert you?" asked Jessica.

"Not by a long shot," Elizabeth said with a smile. She picked up her journal and sat down in a chair, chewing the edge of her pen thoughtfully. "But I sure did get lots of material to write about!"

If you enjoyed this collection of Sweet Valley High Books, why not try another super collection?

Three books in one!

Francine Pascal's

SWEET VALLEY HIGH™

Romance

THE BOYFRIEND WAR

Jessica Wakefield and her best friend, Lila Fowler, are at Club Paradise, a fabulous island resort owned by Lila's uncle – and they're at war with each other!

ALMOST MARRIED

Elizabeth Wakefield unearths an amazing secret from the past – that her mother was once married to Bruce Patman's father! Could history repeat itself? For now Bruce and Elizabeth are feeling an attraction too – to each other!

OPERATION LOVE MATCH

Jessica Wakefield's horoscope says that everything in her life is about to go wrong! But Bruce Patman's parents will get divorced – unless she can make them fall madly in love again! What chance have Jessica's plans if all the planets are lined up against her?